The Serena Wilcox Dystopian Trilogy

NATALIE BUSKE THOMAS

Disclaimer:

This book is a work of fiction. All events and dialog are for entertainment purposes only and do not necessarily represent the author's views.

RESEARCH CREDITS

http://www.dailymail.co.uk/sciencetech
http://www.ucsusa.org/food_and_agriculture
The Righteous Mind: Why Good People are Divided by Politics and Religion by Jonathon Haidt
Democracy in America Vol. 1 by Aexis de Tocqueville

Copyright © 2013 Natalie Buske Thomas
Edition 1; Print run 1
Independent Spirit Publishing
All rights reserved.
ISBN: 978-0-9666919-5-5

DEDICATION

To Brent, Cassandra, Nicholas & Savannah
my family, my heart

Special Thanks to Celebrity Guest Characters
Bob Krejcarek
Eric Dittelman

Congratulations Serena Wilcox Pet Contest Winners
1st place winner Finn (entered by Christine)
2nd place winner Toby (entered by the Sharot family)
3rd place winner Roxy (entered by Marie)

I especially want to thank everyone who is a part of "Team Nat". You make a difference in my life.

Author's Works:

The Serena Wilcox Mysteries: Books 1, 2 & 3
Gene Play 1998, *Virtual Memories* 1999,
Camp Conviction 2000

The Serena Wilcox Dystopian Thriller Trilogy
Angels Mark 2011, *Covert Coffee* 2012,
Bluebird Flown 2013

The Miracle Dulcimer
The Magic Camera
Fred Born Gifted

Free to enjoy online:
The *Dramatic Mom* comic stories
The Serena Wilcox Choose Your Own Mystery Game

For a complete list of Natalie Buske Thomas' works, including her oil paintings, please visit her website.
www.NatalieBuskeThomas.com

BOOK ONE

ANGELS MARK

1

She made X's in her mashed potatoes with her fork, staring at her plate without really seeing the food. All around her was the clatter and the chatter of people dining in groups large and small, huddled under the stained glass domed lights that adorned the ceiling above each cozy table. She was conspicuously alone in a large mid-priced chain restaurant in a suburb just outside of Minneapolis.

Parents donned bibs on hungry toddlers. Some fawned all over Baby, some were embarrassed by Baby's noisy demands, and the rest ignored Baby, despite glaring looks from nearby tables. Friends shared deep-fried appetizer platters, each group with an obvious identity: co-workers blowing off steam, girls' night out, birthday party. Couples clicked sparkling wine glasses; most pretended to share intimacy while distracted by other things. A few couples shared a real moment, with some moments more fleeting than others. Children bounced through the aisles on their way to and from the restrooms, occasionally led by a parent.

Tables with booth seating, running along every wall and tucked into every corner, were fully occupied by smiling people. The remaining tables, with traditional seating, were scattered throughout the middle of the restaurant and wedged in wall spaces too small for the booths. That was where she was sitting, the third table from the kitchen doors, hugging the wall.

"May I get you something?" said Bryce, a local college student who had recently taken this job waiting tables three nights a week. His tuition was paid for by his parents, books were covered by paternal grandparents, and clothes were gifted by his maternal grandparents. Aunts and uncles pitched in dorm and food costs. He worked solely to sustain his partying habits, which were substantial.

Seemingly never hung-over, over-stressed, or fatigued, his ever-present smile showed a history of good orthodontics and tooth whitening. Bryce's fresh good looks, topped with thick sandy locks, often netted him big tips from female diners -- but not from this one. This one didn't even look at him.

"Oh, no thanks," she said. "Wait, actually, yes. I'd like the hot fudge sundae cake. With whipped cream, but no nuts, please." She raised the glossy dessert menu and tapped her finger on the picture of the "Chocolate Lover's Deluxe Fudge Sundae Cake" special, complete with red cherry on top. The price was not special, but she wasn't thinking about cost.

"Sure," he said, his smile cranked up to full wattage. He turned away from her table quickly and merged into the swarm of patrons coming down the long carpeted aisle, his checkerboard-patterned shirt still visible until he reached the swinging kitchen doors. He should have collided with a female server, but somehow gracefully skated around her at the last possible second. The trays full of Buffalo wings she was balancing survived in defiance of all the laws of physics.

I probably made him feel uncomfortable, a woman sitting alone at a table large enough for six people. What on earth am I doing here? She sipped her soft drink slowly. How long could she make this evening stretch out? Eventually she would run out of room in her stomach. Then she would have to leave the warm restaurant with its pizzeria-like scent of garlic, and its competing craving-inducing smell of frying oil, its too-early Christmas music soundtrack competing cheerfully with the din, and its staff of people paid to be friendly. She would have to go home, except there wasn't a home to go to.

She had taken care of that late last night when she lit a red glitter taper candle and then deliberately tipped it onto a stack of piano sheet music – a gentle tap of the candlestick holder and down it went, candle and all. The paper caught fire within seconds and she watched the edges of each page from the recital version of "Let it Be" curl, blacken, and smolder before crumpling and disappearing into the fire. Soon everything else on the coffee table was ablaze.

She stood there watching the flames for what felt like hours. After the fire consumed the sheet music, an L.L.Bean catalog, an old electric bill and most of a Grisham novel, it licked at the wood of the coffee table. She worried that the fire would exhaust itself before catching on to the table, but the flames eventually took root in its mahogany frame. From then on, the fire progressed slowly.

As hard as it was to be patient, she couldn't hurry it along. She could only stand by helplessly, hoping that it would pick up power and speed, spreading itself until the whole room was engulfed. She waited; her feet hurting from standing so long, her bladder full, and her throat dry.

When the room finally began to fill with smoke, she went downstairs where her bags were packed and ready for her on her favorite chair. She slung the oversized backpack over her right shoulder, grabbed one bag with her left hand, and wheeled the third bag with her right hand. She waited a few more minutes, making sure the fire was spreading throughout the house.

She heard the thud of something falling in the kitchen and felt certain that the rest of the house would be gone within the next hour or so. She took one last look around, at the picture frames on the mantel: her daughters, her son, her husband. She set her bags down and opened one of the glass walk-out patio doors. She put a coat on, but didn't take the time to zip the front. Then she grabbed her bags and left the house for the last time.

"Would you like a refill?" Bryce set the dessert in front of her and reached for her glass. The trapped body heat in the restaurant had already melted the leftover ice cubes in her nearly empty beverage.

"Yes, please," she said. Why not? She had nowhere to go. She was amazed that she could have any appetite at all, but she *had* gone for almost 48 hours without much to eat or drink. She craved comfort foods and sugar.

"I'll be right back," he said, disappearing again into the steady stream of Friday night diners, many of whom were now waiting in line to be seated. Dirty slush had been tracked in from their feet, puddling into a gray sludge on the carpet. The crowd was thickening now, and the empty chairs around her table had been added to adjoining tables after the perfunctory polite inquiry, "Is this seat taken?" She shook her head no after each request. Five requests later, she was sitting in the only chair left at the table.

She ate her dessert methodically. She removed the cherry and ate that first, returning the stem to her plate. Then she moved on to the sides and bottom. When the cake was nearly gone, she saved the biggest dollop of whipped cream to go down with the last bite of chocolate. She spent the next two minutes people-watching while draining the rest of her second soda.

When Bryce returned, she asked for coffee. He didn't express any surprise, but surely by now he was starting to wonder when she would ever leave the restaurant, especially with tables in high demand. His restraint was motivated by pity, great customer service, or apathy – she didn't know, but she felt blessed that he didn't try to hurry her along on this starry Minnesota night.

She altered her coffee with two creams and five sugar packets, stirring the sweet slurry until it became the caramel color she was looking for. She held the orange cup with both of her cool hands wrapped around it and lifted the coffee to her face, letting the aromatic steam warm her. Nursing the coffee confection for ten minutes, she breathed in the comforting smell and allowed herself to remember a cup of coffee she had five years ago.

Tom had been grinding coffee beans. The shrill whine from the high-decibel grinder masked all other sounds. After he shut the grinder off both of them were startled by the new sound breaking the silence: the phone was ringing, and was probably on its third or fourth ring. He glanced at the caller-ID screen and said, "Ball State."

"Again?" she shrugged. Every weekend Ball State had been calling their alumni, presumably to raise funds for the university. She was relieved that the call was not one they needed to answer. She considered turning the phone's ringer off, but focused her sleepy mind back on to coffee. Normally she didn't have a cup of coffee so late in the day, but life was changing fast and a lot of things were going to be different.

Tom pushed the powdered creamer in her direction. She reached beyond him to open the silverware drawer and pulled out a spoon. She scooped sugar out of the counter canister, spilling some granules on the counter, adding more sugar to the crystallized ring around the canister. A few seconds later, she was sipping coffee that was brewed too strong for her. She added a spray of canned whipped cream. Tom took the whipped cream and added some to his coffee too.

Both stood in the kitchen, leaning into the cluttered and crumb-littered island counter, silently sipping coffee. The quiet was unnerving. Each of them expected the silence to be shattered at any moment, but the phone did not ring again.

The frigid air outside froze sound itself. Nothing was stirring. They looked at each other at the same time, and laughed softly, a laugh devoid of mirth. Laughter was nothing more to them at that moment than a nervous tic.

Tom drained the rest of his coffee and added his "Real Men Do Diapers" mug, a leftover from when they'd had babies in the house, to the dirty dishes in the dishwasher. He walked behind her and put his arms around her. She rested the back of her head on his shoulder. Her dark hair, naturally a "nutmeg" shade according to color charts, looked even darker next to Tom's short blonde locks.

They were physical opposites in other ways too. He was long in the torso, short on legs. Serena was short in the torso, long on legs. Both were on the short end of the height scale though, and fit together as a cute couple, friendly and wholesome. Nice. Sexy and powerful were not adjectives assigned to the pair of them, but they felt that way when they were alone together, especially when life had them feeling on edge, either because little things were not going their way, or, like now, because things were completely unsettled.

Serena drank in Tom's cologne and tried to quiet her energy, but she quickly grew restless with the embrace. Her back hurt from the slight pressure of Tom leaning on her. The feeling was mutual: Tom was antsy to pull away so that he could pace the kitchen. Each waited a polite moment before pulling away from each other simultaneously. This was how they were; married long enough to finish each other's thoughts and move in synchronized steps without any words at all.

"They're saying something," said Tom. He ran into the living room, grabbed the remote and turned up the volume. They planted their stance a few feet away from the large TV. They were too keyed up to sit or move, their bodies trembling and their stomachs in knots. Blinking their eyes felt foreign, swallowing saliva was difficult over their thick dry throats, and their every breath felt labored.

They felt united with all of America, and with people from all over the world, as they all watched the events unfold on live television together – the shared passive observance of tragedy that would bind them all together forever, and would alter future generations with every passing second. This was that moment in time that they had all dreaded, that time in history that populations had feared for decades. It had arrived, and it was every bit as monumental as every clichéd movie Serena had ever seen, and it was punctuated by live reporting on television.

The news anchors' faces would be etched in their collective brains as the faces everyone turned to for reassurance and information. New stars were born, as lesser-known reporters stepped up in stations outside of New York. The current face on the screen belonged to Brandon Swenson of Minneapolis.

We are hearing reports of a single blast from what we now know is a nuclear bomb that was a direct hit to New York City and we are just now, we are just now hearing, we are hearing that Washington D.C. has also been hit. The President is in an undisclosed location. The President has been confirmed to be safe. I repeat that, at this time, there has been no threat to the President.

We are now learning of another blast. There is another blast on Philadelphia. Yes, we are just now learning of another hit. The affected cities are now L.A., New York, Washington, D.C., and this just in, Philadelphia. We have yet to learn who is taking responsibility for these attacks. Where will it all end, America?

We are reporting live from our sister stations in Minneapolis and Chicago. I regret that many of our colleagues were in the affected cities at the time of the blast. This is a dark day for America, a very dark day.

Tom turned the closed captioning on and muted the sound. The reporters, and guest experts, were saying the same information in a desperate loop of nothing-new-to-report during the climax of the world's worst crisis.

He turned the sound back on when the footage cut back to Brandon Swenson. Brandon looked way too young and inexperienced to handle this moment in history. The baby-faced reporter read frantically from the teleprompter, not bothering to conceal the emotion from his voice.

We are now expecting to hear from the President. He will be speaking from the James R. Thompson center in Chicago within the hour, where people are already gathering in the streets in unprecedented numbers. A strong police presence and secret service detail is already in place, and the Army National Guard has also been called in.

The President is requesting that Americans not panic. He is asking that people stay by their televisions and radios and wait for information. He is expected to announce a national registry to locate missing persons, and to reassure the American people that the United States of America is containing this crisis and will make our country safe again.

The President is likely to address the United States' response to the attacks. It is unclear if the President will be taking questions at this time.

The two of them sat there, sunk into their respective lounge chairs, saying nothing for several long minutes. Tom muted the TV, but they continued to read the closed-captioning as it parroted the same information.

When Serena finally broke the silence, she and Tom entered a calm discussion as if nothing unusual was happening. They began rambling and musing, spinning conspiracy theories, as if retelling the plot of a favorite suspense movie. There was nothing about their conversation or demeanor to suggest that the nation was on the brink of World War III, Armageddon, or the end of the world as they knew it.

Each of them had an awareness of their behavior being completely off rhythm with the shocking events devastating the planet with each passing second, but neither could shake off their state of denial. So there they sat; the two of them as placid as if they were talking about the weather.

A sudden shriek from a toddler at a neighboring table snapped Serena back to the present moment. She realized that she could not linger at the restaurant table a minute more. She couldn't eat another bite, couldn't drink another beverage. Besides, if she stayed any longer, her stalling would turn into loitering, drawing attention to her. It was time to leave this warm safe haven, with its comforting babble of people noise, and her personal server whose job it was to make small talk with her, and hit the road again.

She left a generous tip on the table- in cash, of course- donned her winter coat, and made her way toward the lobby, which was empty. Everyone was snuggled inside while she was headed outside.

Cheery pine swags and artificial holly bade her farewell, a basket of candy canes invited her to take a parting gift, and in the relative quiet of the lobby, Christmas music filled her ears. *The thrill of hope, the weary world rejoices, from yonder breaks a new and glorious morn...*

2

Near the exit door she stepped around the puddles of slush the best she could, but the cold and slippery tile had few clean patches left to step on. Opening the heavy door, the outside chill did not hit her right away. The time spent in the cozy restaurant had heated her body like a charcoal brick – each human body connecting and keeping each other warm. Her body retained this heat as she walked down the cleared sidewalk, admiring the twinkling lights of the holiday decorations.

When she reached the end of the walk and stepped into the shadows of the parking lot, she felt no comfort from the street lights. The charcoal glow that kept her warm as she walked down the sidewalk was already gone. She felt the frigid air settle deep into her winter coat, covering her with a blanket of cold. She regretted wearing the pants she had on, some type of nylon blend. The cold was easily passing through the fabric, chilling her legs to the point of numbness.

After unlocking the minivan's doors with her electronic key, she paused to look up. Glorious stars sparkled brightly in the cold, cold, blue-black night sky. The moon shimmered. This, the way the sky looked, was the beauty that she associated with the frightening sensation of deep dense air in her lungs, making her every breath a struggle against the heavy cold air. *Beauty and fear; hope and despair.*

The van started up on the second attempt. She was lucky the thing still ran at all. It wasn't much to look at: a 1997 white-with-rust Plymouth minivan with both rear hubcaps missing. There was a deepening crack in the windshield from when a rock had hit the glass.

Inside the minivan was not any better. The van had a malfunctioning electrical panel and every warning light on the dash blinked incessantly until after the engine had been running for about two minutes. After that, the dash lights magically went out. Tom had a mechanic look at it, but he couldn't find anything wrong, so they learned to ignore the problem with the lights, forgetting all about it.

In addition to the panel malfunction, the passenger's side window no longer went up or down. If Tom or Serena forgot to warn friends and family not to use the window, they would be forced to drive with the window open until they could safely stop. One person would then hold the close button while another person stood on the other side of the door, pressing firmly down on the window until the window started moving upward. This procedure often took several minutes.

These quirks she had learned to deal with, as long as the van still ran. But now she was worried. Why hadn't they kept up with the maintenance issues, or pressed harder to get the electrical panel fixed? She would have a hard time buying another vehicle if this one failed, and she couldn't risk interacting with a mechanic to fix the minivan if it failed, *if* it was even possible to resurrect it. All she could do was hope that the minivan would hold up for as long as she needed to use it.

Serena adjusted her seat as far forward as she could. She had forgotten to adjust the seat after Tom had driven the van, which made the twenty mile trip to the restaurant like driving a go-cart, her leg extended its full length to reach the gas pedal. Long gone was the little red car she had when she and Tom were first married. Now she shared the mini-van, or at least she did when life was normal.

She sat for a second or two and noticed that her breath formed a perfect cloud in the ice-box interior of the van. The heater was chugging away but she didn't feel any comfort from it yet. She continued to obsess about the mini-van, and how the crack on the windshield looked slightly longer than it was the last time she studied it; scarcely feeling the cold steering wheel with her bare hands, until she remembered the fleece-lined driving gloves she had in her coat pocket.

She put her gloves on, slowly, concentrating on each finger as it went inside the gloves. *Enough already! Pull yourself together and get out of here!* She gripped the wheel with determination, put her foot on the pedal, now within a comfortable leg-reach from her body, and drove the van out of the restaurant parking lot.

There was no turning back. Farther and farther she drove, past suburban housing developments with their hundreds of tasteful white Christmas lights lining identical roofs on identical houses, past vacant department stores bearing illuminated icy parking lots, past gas stations with a surplus of frozen cut pine trees leaning against quick-stop stores, and past banks displaying the current outside temperature of -17, not including "wind chill factor".

After a long stretch on the freeway the steady blur of traffic lights, holiday lights, street lights, and headlights tapered off. Serena slowed to the 30mph speed limit to meet up with the wreath-lined streets of the small town of Cannon Falls, Minnesota, which was a frequent pit-stop for truckers driving between the Twin Cities and Rochester. The town, with a population of around 4,000, had benefited from media attention after former United States President Obama selected Cannon Falls for a town hall meeting stop on his tour of the Midwest states. The presidential stop helped The Old Market Deli become a tourist attraction, due to its framed photographs of the former president ordering a "Tom Turkey" sandwich. To this day, the chair he sat in was marked with duct tape.

As she reached the only traffic light in the town, she stopped in front of a multicolored canopy of Christmas lights draped across the intersection. She studied the lights as she waited for the light to change. She could almost hear the crackling of ice crystals as the lights swayed. She tracked the rocking motion of the lights with her eyes, eyes dry and bloodshot from fatigue and the hot air from the minivan's heater. She willed her eyes to stay open. She looked in the rearview mirror. Her green eyes had so much red around them that Serena thought, *I have Christmas eyes. Oh no, I'm getting slap-happy. I need to snap out of it. I still have twenty miles left to go.*

One second, two seconds, three seconds. There were no other vehicles around. It was tempting to ignore the red light, but she couldn't risk a traffic violation, or the unlikely event that a car would come out of nowhere and zip through the intersection, colliding with her, so she waited for what felt like a long time but probably wasn't. She surveyed the downtown area, noticing lights on behind one of the storefront windows: chiropractor Fletcher was tending to an emergency after-care patient who had been rear-ended in an auto accident an hour earlier. All other buildings were dark. Finally the light changed and she was on her way.

She drove past Cannon Falls' post office and grocery store, which shared a common parking lot, and past its only public school complex; all grades K-12 were taught among the two brick buildings located at the edge of town, just inside city limits.

Earlier in the day the area was a hub of activity with teen drivers leaving school, parents picking up students, and orange-yellow buses lined up along the full length of the sidewalk. Now the area was deserted, lit only by security lights.

As the school faded away from view, she passed St. Ansgar's Lutheran Church, a church that held both traditional and contemporary worship services, and served as an emergency shelter for the neighboring school district for emergencies that, post 9/11, included terrorist attacks and bomb threats. Serena idly wondered if the church had been full of school children on that horrible day that was the catalyst for everything else that happened.

St. Ansgar's was the last sight of Cannon Falls -- and the last sign of civilization. After she drove by the outlying residential areas, and a few rural properties, nothing greeted her as she maneuvered the windy roads and icy bridges between Cannon Falls and Red Wing.

Tangled leaf-less trees, *Halloween trees*, filled the bluffs on both sides of the desolate road, not a home in sight -- nothing but the moonlight that bounced off the snow and provided an eerie violet-white glow that illuminated the darkness. Other than the moonlight, which was partially obscured by cloud cover coming in, it was pitch black, the kind of blackness that only the most rural areas are steeped in.

There were no other vehicles, except for one abandoned car in a ditch. The minivan's headlights were the only artificial light source. Serena struggled to keep her eyelids from closing.

Exhaustion washed over her in waves of dizziness and her vision took on an altered-state quality. With no visible traffic lines on the road, she wasn't sure if she was weaving all over the center line or if she was precariously hugging the edge. In some places, if she ran off the road, it would be a sharp dive off an elevated area and into a ravine. It was hard to tell what type of landscape lurked around each bend, over each hill, in the low-lying valleys in between.

She had been driving about ten miles and she was now way outside any easily known physical address. Some of the farm residents in this area had a Minneapolis area code, a Goodhue zip code, and belonged to the Cannon Falls school district. In other words, it was fairly easy for them to fall off the grid -- even the GPS found their existence difficult to locate -- which was why Serena was almost home.

A few more rotations of the minivan's tires over the snow and ice covered gravel road, and she would be there. The driveway was long, and uphill, so she fretted that she would never get the van up the hill. She applied pressure to the accelerator pedal and heard nothing but the tell-tale squeal of tires that were spinning without traction. She blinked instant tears away. She was home now. No reason to break down.

A light went on in the house on top of the hill. She saw silhouettes moving in the windows: one, two, three, and a small fourth. Then a switch was turned on and dozens of evergreens, tall and short, lit up in red, green, gold, and white. The wintery hill was a Christmas wonderland welcoming her home.

That was when she lost it. Tears, nearly freezing upon impact, streamed down her cheeks. She sat there in the minivan at the bottom of the driveway, sobbing, her driving gloves still clutching the steering wheel, for what felt like ages. She'd lost all sense of the passage of time; she didn't know if she sat there for two minutes, five, or ten.

After her meltdown subsided, she pulled herself together and backed into the road to give the minivan a running start to make it up the hill. Gravity got her past the slick spots – fast. Going down was easy.

It took her three attempts, but she finally made it up the driveway, and into the garage, where the door had already been opened for her. After she parked the minivan and switched off the engine, Serena dug for a tissue in her purse and hurriedly blew her nose while looking at herself in the pull-down visor mirror. She wasn't going to win any pageants tonight, but it was hard to tell that she had been crying. Her face was already red from the cold, and her eyes were bloodshot from fatigue. Her meltdown was hardly noticeable – she was ready to reunite herself with her family.

After Tom and the kids tackled her in a group hug, Tom said, "I was about to go look for you. Why didn't you call? It's a disposable phone, and no one is looking for us anyway."

"I misplaced the phone."

Tom laughed. He knew how often she misplaced things. "I'm glad you're home." He gave her a kiss on the forehead and pried Rebecca from her death grip around Serena's waist. "Let Mommy take her coat off."

Serena draped her slightly damp coat over a kitchen chair and all of them sat around the table. Carrie had made sugar cookies earlier that afternoon and Rebecca had decorated one especially for her, a heart shaped cookie with French vanilla frosting and red candy sprinkles. Tom had both wine and coffee on hand, not knowing which one she would want. Samuel had learned a new song on his guitar to play for her homecoming. Cookies, beverages and music were offered to her all at once. After the flurry of excitement died down, the kids went to bed while the adults lingered in the kitchen for a few minutes longer.

There they sat, knowing their actions were irreversible. Two days ago Tom had finished up his last day of work – not that his boss, or any of his co-workers, *knew* it was his last day. He made sure that he worked a regular full day, with nothing in his attitude showing what he was up to. Meanwhile, he had been making preparations for weeks. He sold personal items using anonymous online auctions, stockpiling all the cash he could. He thought it was very unlikely that anyone would look for them, or that anyone would look into their "deaths" very deeply. Still, he was careful.

He was fairly confident that the house fire would be ruled an accident without a second thought. He had made sure that the gasoline container was staged to look as if he had been working on repairing a broken snow blower and made the tragic mistake of using the mud room as a workshop. The mud room was attached to the living space of the house. If the fire spread as they imagined it would, it was only a matter of time before the house fire created by the fallen candle in the living room would spread to the mud room, igniting the open drum of gasoline. Their only concern was that the fire needed to reach the gas before someone noticed the fire and called 911. Some of their plans were entirely out of their control, but they had a good feeling it would all work out.

From the beginning of their adventure, when Serena had been up all night looking things up on the Internet, things had fallen neatly into place. It only took a single phrase typed into a search engine ("Help me disappear") for Serena to find an underground society, known as the off-the-grid network. Next, she looked up the term "off-the-grid", and found a reference for people who wanted to live independently of public utilities, go green, and have less dependency on government. But extremists going off-the-grid, or just "off-grid", wanted to hide from the government; most likely for paranoid reasons, or to breed a militia clan. While the latter sounded scary, off-grid groups helped their members fall off the radar.

Serena posted a message to the off-grid forum, and within ten minutes heard back from a spokesperson from Off-grid-ghost, a grassroots organization which sounded like a human smuggling ring. Tom joined the group too, and by the end of the week, they'd both told their story. Off-grid-ghost immediately offered them a house where they could hide, an old farm house on a leftover slice of Minnesota farm land, completely obscured from the road. All they wanted in return was $10,000 cash and an agreement to keep their organization secret. Rent was to be paid through Off-grid-ghost: landlord and tenant were forbidden to know each other, although both were required to be members of the network.

The house was selected because records of the dwelling and property were from so long ago that no one would find them without knowing exactly what to look for, and maybe not even then. Archived paper records were often lost or destroyed from the perils of long term storage, and no one had bothered to go back far enough to digitize the records. Chances were good that there was no trace of this house existing, which qualified the location for endorsement by Off-grid-ghost, said their spokesman.

So far, everything was going according to plan, but Tom and Serena were both nervous about falling in with a radical organization like Off-grid-ghost. Yet what choice did they have if they didn't know how to disappear on their own?

It was only because they were computer savvy that they were able to learn about the underground off-the-grid network; and that was where their escape-plotting skills ended. They had no current passports and there wasn't enough time to obtain them. They didn't know what else to do, so they turned to what was, in their minds, a whack-job fringe group to help them hide. Tom and Serena considered themselves to be normal people, who just happened to find themselves in extraordinary circumstances. How could they explain their actions in a way that would not make them look crazy?

The off-grid plan was the only plan they had, so they had to trust that it would work. They weren't even sure what to wish for: was it better if nothing bad happened, and they messed up their lives for no reason? Or was it better to be "right", and not crazy? How could it be that two college educated people from suburbia would be so paranoid as to stage their deaths so that they could hide from their own government, dragging their three children with them?

They could analyze this over and over, but in the end they had only two choices: ignore the warning they believed to be true, or comply with what the government wanted. Always people of action when they believed in something, they felt they had no other option. So even though they knew very little about Minnesota, they committed to the plan right away. It was a place to hide. Hide and wait to see what would happen.

3

Paul greeted General Gustavo Marino with a hearty handshake. Gustavo accepted the gesture, but kept his eyes focused on the back of President John William's gray head, which was fast slipping away to the end of Gustavo's imaginary leash. Gustavo ended the handshake quickly, and then moved forward in the procession, without ever really looking at Paul. Paul mentally shrugged his shoulders – it wasn't important to his plan to be seen.

As Paul fell back from the entourage and let the media pass him by, he watched the President's well-tailored pin-stripe suit disappear into the crowd on the tarmac. He kept up as best he could from a distance, but he hoped he could close the gap before the President got on the plane. He wanted a closer look at the man who was the President of the Liberty Union, which was comprised of the East Coast states (the ones still inhabitable anyway), the Southern states, and much of the eastern Midwest, a union otherwise known as "The Free States".

Paul caught a break when President John Williams agreed to answer questions from a handful of reporters. Everyone knew that what this really meant was that Williams had a speech prepared, probably a long-winded one. Paul settled into a comfortable standing posture. While his view was mostly obstructed by the crowd and the mob of security detail around Williams, Paul would have plenty of time to study the man, while he himself went completely unnoticed. He turned on his cell phone to start recording. He planned to show the footage to Clyde later that night.

A surfer-boy aide with a perfect smile set up a portable podium right there on the tarmac and donned it with a fabric covering depicting the Liberty Union seal. Before the aide had given the final straightening tug on the fabric, President Williams placed himself in a rehearsed photogenic position behind the podium. He catered to the crowd for a few minutes before rattling off a speech that would make the speech writer, unknown to anyone until now, an instant celebrity.

Throughout history, our Constitution, the Constitution of the United States of America, has been rewritten. But if you're like me, you never thought that the Constitution would ever really change again. But we should have paid better attention in our history classes because, if we had, then we'd have known that the Constitution was built to be fluid.

Anyone hear of a little thing called the Bill of Rights, which added 10 amendments? You might not remember that the Bill of Rights was added eighteen months after the Constitution was drafted. From 1789 to 1992, the Constitution was amended 27 times!

And, through judicial review, the meaning of parts of the Constitution has been changed many times. But I bet you didn't know this: There's a magical Article that could change the Constitution completely, Article 5, which notes the concept of the Amendment Convention.

What's that, you say? Well, no one really knows. It's not been used. The power or limits of such a convention are unknown because there has never been a time in history, except for now of course, in which this article was utilized. Scholars tell me, though, that a Convention would be able to propose any change to the Constitution it decided to, including full replacement. Did you hear that? FULL REPLACEMENT! I bet you never knew that. I sure didn't.

So obviously, that's where we are today. That's how the former United States radically changed the Constitution and our government. That's how we ended up with President Kinji on the West and yours truly as President of the East, and states in between naturally. Some say that our great nation has been hacked, sawed in two, and destroyed. If you believe the late night talk show hosts, we've become like Oz, with witches of the East and West, and everyone waiting for Dorothy to deliver the broomstick.

But we've got to stop thinking that way! We are the same great nation under God. We are! We are merely exercising our right to tap into Article 5. We did this within the Constitution, as laid out to us by our forefathers. We are not divided! We are united in our history. We are united in our memories of an early America.

You don't believe that America has ever wanted change? We have precedent, you know. There have been many proposals for substantial change to the Constitution throughout history. Thomas Jefferson himself was wary of the power of the dead over the living, something that would happen if we had an unchanging Constitution. Without giving you too much of a history lesson, let me say this: To guarantee that each generation has a say in the framework of the government, Jefferson proposed that the Constitution, and each one following it, would expire after 19 or 20 years. Expire!

Jefferson advised that we retool, we update, we re-evaluate, we re-organize. Jefferson knew that life is about changing. America would change; and the government needed to change along with it. The people needed to have the freedom to change our government. Jefferson said this! Long before the Big War!

Let's stay in early American history for a while. In 1932, William Kay Wallace, a U.S. diplomat, proposed not only changing the Constitution, but replacing it! He would replace the states with nine geographically-based entities, each with an equal representation in a national Board of Directors. A President would be chosen from the Board; the new states would have similar systems. Sound familiar?

Back in 1932 we were talking about changing things up, governing ourselves differently; even dividing the states up into groups. What's so new about what's going on today? What's so new about the concept of two Presidents? Nothing! Turns out, it's not such a new idea after all. Someone thought of it way back in 1932.

Let's move ahead to the World War 11 era, specifically 1942. Henry Hazlitt, a conservative journalist, wrote that the time of the War was a perfect time to contemplate changing the Constitution; and that the War was pointing out several of the Constitution's weaknesses. Alexander Hehmeyer, who wrote a book in 1943, also thought that the war period was a perfect time to institute change, when people were in crisis mode. War time? Crisis mode? Sound familiar?

History repeats itself. We aren't doing anything new here! We are the <u>*same*</u> *America! We are responding to the times, just like we've always done.*

Which brings us to Thomas Finletter, a special assistant to the Secretary of State, who authored a book published in 1945: He proposed to allow the President to dissolve Congress and the Presidency. You see where I'm going with this?

We Americans have thought about shaking things up way before now. We are the creators here, the innovators, the movers and shakers. We are the Super Power. We did not crumble, we were not 'divided and conquered' as some have said. We simply pioneered a new trail; a trail that many of us have thought was a long time in coming. A trail that Jefferson envisioned from the very beginning!

Think this is all ancient history? Let's move ahead now to 1974. Rexford Tugwell, an economist who worked with FDR, suggested we have two Vice-Presidents instead of just one. Hey, we did that! We have two Vice-Presidents. Sure, we threw in an extra President too, but you see what I'm saying. We Americans have been mulling over making changes for years! Big ones! From our forefathers up until contemporary times!

This is not new, people. We are not brought to reform against our will. We walk willingly forward, boldly! The terrorists did not do this to us. We have the power here. We have the voice. We have the freedom to choose.

Let's move forward again in time. After Watergate, there were many calls for changes in the Constitution. That should surprise no one.

But let's skip ahead to even more contemporary times. Arthur Miller, law professor at George Washington University, wrote a book published in 1987, that called for, among other things, the redrawing of state lines. Redrawing of state lines! Re-structuring! See? We have done nothing new here. We have had these ideas in early history, and we've had them as recently as 1987.

Now we're getting close to present day, and we can't really talk about voices of reform without focusing on the Internet. Wow, do we ever have the freedom to voice who we are as Americans, and what we want. So what were people saying, in the years, months, weeks, and yes, even days before the Big War?

'The U.S. Constitution for 21st Century' web site had posted this quote: 'Unique, innovative, venerable in its time, our more than 200-year old Constitution now has become antiquated and obsolete — even detrimental and dangerous — for the nation.' Now does that sound like an America that doesn't want change? This is but a tiny sample of what the American people were saying about our Constitution right up

to the day we forever changed as a nation. The day we became 'divided' as some have called it – is that the right way to look at it?

Are we 'divided'? No! If you've paid attention, and I thank you for your patience, then you know I'm leading up to this: We are still the United States of America, one nation, under God. We are. We are whole. We are together. We are one. We have restructured. We have listened to the call for change. That's all. We are still America. And to that end: God Bless America!

John Williams gave a flourishing salute to presumably all Americans, and waited for the predictable cheers. William, who was last year a little-known but long-time senator, was now one of the most famous faces in the world, as the first President the New Conservative Party, which some had characterized as nothing more than a revamped version of the disbanded Republican Party. Conversely, the Democratic Union was often characterized as old guard Dems, even though President Kinji described herself as an Independent.

President Ann Kinji held the honor of being both the first female president, and the first Japanese-American president, of the Democratic Union. Kinji, who had been a Presidential cabinet appointee during the years leading up to World War III, was, not surprisingly, a well-known force in the then Democratic Party. The party system had been abolished post WWIII, but nonetheless, Kinji's cabinet, and all of her supporters, had been dubbed "The New Liberals". Many Americans, Paul included, believed that the two party system had never died, but lived on under new labels.

The split of the United States of America was the result of six months of emotional deliberation without a single recess, and was, in the end, swiftly agreed to with very little opposition, with no one but the media allowed in. Every American could watch history play out on their televisions, computers, phones, hand-held gadgets, and even large screens on metro buildings. But watching from afar was not good enough for Paul. Whenever he could be there in person, he was.

He was in the crowd in Chicago when the last President of the United States, the *real* President, shocked the world with words that still rang in Paul's head. That famous speech, the transcript, and excerpts, now re-printed on everything from posters to blankets, was in sharp contrast to the political rhetoric he'd just heard Williams spew. No, the most famous speech in the world was full of real heartbreak, real grief, real tears. It was worthy to be listed alongside any speech of Abraham Lincoln's. It was a speech in which no one took a breath, straining to hear every incredible syllable. For generations to come, people would recall where their ancestors were when they heard this speech:

> *Emergency times call for emergency measures. The needs of the East and the West are diverse. We have eight U.S. governors in a perpetual state of emergency, while five states are unsafe to reside in, and three states are completely gone. This is not the time for politics or party lines. We need to remove all obstacles. This must be a working government,*

running not on principles and ideas, but we must instead be as foremen leading re-construction.

For the good of the country, I will step down as President of the United States, after appointing not one, but two, Presidents to govern over this beloved nation. It will take all of us working together to rewrite our Constitutional laws, and to pass all the necessary bills to make this happen, but I know we can do it. We must do it. We must come together to create a new, more efficient, way to govern. Our nation has changed.

We are a nation in crisis, unparalleled to anything the world has seen. We need an emergency response, a response that will streamline government. We will face difficulties beyond what our forefathers ever imagined. We must find a way to get closer to the people, to get smaller, to delegate the workload of rebuilding our nation.

I believe in this plan. I believe that our nation is best served by two Presidents, and by both parties, in a shared system of government that divides the nation into two equal parts. With your blessing, I will appoint two people to serve for a period of 18 months. But I assure you, elections will be held swiftly, to replace my appointees with the choice of the people.

The two Presidents shall work together, but will govern separately, much the way our individual states have always been served by Governors. This is not the death of America, but an emergency response to emergency conditions. We shall forever in our hearts be one nation under God, and though divided by governing bodies, still indivisible in spirit. With liberty and justice for all, may we one day soon be a prosperous nation once again, whose citizens live without fear, and whose children know peace. God bless America.

Paul would never forget that speech, and he felt that President John Williams missed the mark entirely with his own attempt at making a speech for the history books. Williams could never match the passion or talent for oration that the former president had, even though Williams was pompous enough to try, and obviously thought of himself as an equal or, Paul sneered, even the better man. No, Williams was the inferior man in Paul's eyes, in polish, strength, and cleverness.

But when it came to honest conviction, Paul suspected that John might actually believe a little more of what he was saying, a little more. Williams was a dangerous hothead though, and Paul knew that he was better off working a different angle to get himself onto Capitol Hill, the new Capitol Hill. No matter, the doors were flung wide open for Paul, most unexpectedly. He had been waiting all his life for such an opportunity to come knocking, and here it was, an opportunity he created for himself.

From this moment on, the gap between himself and the heels of all the government insiders was shrinking. Paul, with his pretty-boy good looks, was an easy fit for the political scene. He was already well on his way to being an insider. All he needed was the right door to open, and he had found one. What he never expected was for his chosen doorkeeper to be tapped to be one of the first Presidents of the newly divided, formerly known as, United States of America.

4

President Ann Kinji tucked her smooth shiny locks behind her ears. Her beautiful hair, cut in a bob, was the envy of middle class American women. Salons received many requests for what became known as "The Kinji": a smart sleek bob, which often included coloring the hair to match Kinji's onyx shade. The woman who was now an international icon was little-known prior to the Big War. It was crazy to go from obscurity to having a hair style named after her.

Beyond lack of celebrity status, Kinji's work for the previous administration, the last administration of what was once The United States of America, had done little to prepare her. Of course, how could anyone prepare to be one of the first Presidents of the nation now referred to as "The States of America"? *Everything's pretty much the same – just add a second president -- and life moves on. And if you believe that, I have some nuclear wasteland to sell you.*

Kinji snapped herself out of her brooding and studied her desk. It was tidy, that was for sure. She had so many assistants fussing over it that there wasn't a thing out of place. There were no personal items on it yet, not a single framed picture or even a coffee mug. Kinji couldn't bring herself to move in. It didn't feel real, and she wasn't sure if she was living a dream or a nightmare. She was insane if she wanted this responsibility, this crushing burden of being a pioneer in a newly divided nation. And the first female President besides? *And* Japanese? Well, the days ahead were going to be interesting.

"President Kinji?" Breyana Robertson, a strawberry blonde 20-something in a purple pants suit, rapped gently at her open door.

"Yes?" Kinji locked eyes with Breyana. It was trademark Kinji: unflinching directness that intimidated most people, but Breyana was a confident young woman and returned Kinji's gaze unwaveringly. Breyana had nothing but open admiration, respect, and hopeful aspiration to friendship.

"Paul Tracy is here to see you."

"Oh yes, send him in, please."

Paul waltzed into the room as if his steps had been choreographed, and as often as he'd played this moment in his head, they were. "President Kinji, you look so natural in this office, in front of that seal."

The Democratic Union seal depicted an eagle with an olive branch in its beak. The eagle was tinted a pale blue. The Liberty Union seal, behind President John William's desk, was identical in design, with the only difference being the color tint of the eagle, a reddish pink hue.

"Thank you, Paul. We've both put on a lot of mileage since the Warsaw days, good old Warren Academy. I hear you are going places yourself."

"It's been awhile since I've seen you. You've heard right: I've been hitting the pavement to get those bills signed. I'm proud to claim my contribution to the New Liberals."

"Democratic Union. Let's drop the polarizing label."

"Democratic Union, then."

"Is there something you want, Paul? I am due for a press conference in five minutes."

"I would like a position in your cabinet."

Kinji laughed. "Finally, somebody around here who lays it on the table."

"You know me, Ann." Paul stared into her dark eyes, leaning forward with both of his palms on her desk.

"President Kinji. Sorry, Paul, I don't do casual. No friends, no favors. If I consider this, it will be based on what you can do for my administration, period."

Paul backed away, holding his hands up. "Fair enough, Madam President. I left a package with Miss Robertson that I think will interest you. When you see what I have to offer, I'm sure I'll be hearing from you."

Clyde was rugged without the handsome: oily reddish-grey hair that was sparse on top of his head, but long and stringy everywhere else; eyes set too far apart, giving him a wall-eyed look; a pitted face with a nose that snorted a long draw of mucus every few minutes.

"Morning!" he bellowed, in a deep voice that begged to be cleared of phlegm.

The sanctuary returned the greeting with a deadpan chant-like chorus of "Morning."

"You don't get Internet, and you get limited TV – just what the old rabbit ears pick up. You rely on us to keep you informed. That's why it's so important that all of you be here. Now I'll turn it over to Paul Tracy."

Paul was a man of frat-boy good looks. He was tall and lean, with thick wavy brown hair and perfect teeth – a refreshing contrast from Clyde. People were always surprised when they learned that the two men were brothers.

"Thank you for your faithfulness, and a warm welcome to the newcomers. Consider this your welcome wagon. You got your packet, and should have your new names." Paul paused while the tell-tale rustle of papers indicated that people were opening their envelopes to look.

Serena turned to Tom, "Only our last names, right? We figured that we would have to. We don't have to change our first names too, do we?"

Tom opened the packet. "They strongly suggested we change our names completely, but agreed to let us do only our last names."

"Good! What is our new last name?

"Meadows."

"Meadows?"

"You like it?"

"I guess so. Did you pick it, or did he?"

"He had a list. I thought it was the best one."

"Okay, I don't care. We'll get used to it."

"Right, that's what I thought."

"What else did he say?"

"We can't communicate with people who knew us when we were the Bridge family. I said okay, but I know we're not going to let our family and friends think we're dead forever."

"What does it matter, now that Mom is gone?"

Tom looked at her with his most sincere expression of sympathy and squeezed her hand. "She's not the only person who cared about you."

Serena didn't answer. The grief was only six months old. She was still struggling to hold herself together. Being her mother's caretaker had given her too many intimate moments with her. It would take time to heal, which was what she told herself whenever she felt like the rain would fall forever.

"As soon as things happen, we'll contact everybody, but in the meantime, I think we should do whatever the off-grid people want us to do."

"Exactly, I agree. What if we did all this and there was no reason to do it, and we're stuck in hiding because we burnt down our own house? How many laws have we broken now? I feel like such a criminal."

"I don't think anything else was illegal, just the arson."

Tom and Serena stared at each other and laughed at the absurdity, and the shock from a word like "arson" being owned by either of them.

"You should be used to it. You had to have straddled some legal lines when I met you," said Tom.

"Serena Wilcox, private detective? It's been so long since I've been that person. I'm Serena Bridges now. No, I take that back. Serena Meadows." Serena looked like she had tasted something sour.

"Maybe it's time you found her again."

"My 'mom' and 'wife' self doesn't measure up?"

"I just mean we could use a detective. We didn't learn much about this Paul guy, except that he's operating out of Minneapolis." He studied his wife's face and added, "Getting your old spunk back wouldn't hurt."

The crowd settled down and they directed their eyes obediently toward the pulpit, where Paul was gearing up for a sermon. His voice was smooth and steady, hypnotic in delivery. His eyes locked personally into each and every pair of eyes staring back at him. His audience was as captive as a warren of rabbits listening to a coyote sounding off in the distance.

> *They say we need the Identity Chip. What is this chip but a high-tech horror? It was the first thing I thought of when there was talk about inserting tracking chips under babies' skin so that we can solve our missing children problems. Everyone would be assigned a unique computer code – a number. You get it on the forehead or the hand. It assigns you a number, a number! Doesn't that sound familiar? Isn't that just like the Bible foretold would happen? Is this not the number of The Beast?*
>
> *The chip is like a bar code. Everyone's ID will be on it, including bank routing info. No more credit cards, cash, etc. All is instant transfer. Everything digital, no need for hardcopy IDs, no more checkbooks or credit cards – just scan*

the forehead or back of hand. They are already doing it. Remember that story about the rich people who were too lazy to bother getting out a credit card at their favorite club, so they got a chip in their hand that the bartender scans while they sit there enjoying their drinks? Buying and selling will be through this number. Anyone read the book of Revelations? It's all right there. This is prophesy, people!

Hard to believe anyone would get the number? Think that even people who aren't religious would be a little spooked by this? Well it's also hard to believe that the government would be focusing on this chip when we've just been bombed by nuclear warheads! No one's going to want to have a tracking device inside them, but they'll do it. People will rush to do anything if they think they'll be safe. And people believe in their government.

These are like pet locator chips, but for people, so the government can track us like animals. Or, as they put it, anyone on the terrorist watch list. And missing people or criminals. They give it a good sell. How to identify bodies and missing persons is always one of the first things a government does when there is a disaster. Think of earthquakes. Special interest groups who want that chip bill passed can slide it under the radar during this emergency.

Think it sounds far-fetched? Think that the President wouldn't be getting some obscure bill passed after we just go bombed? Think again. It's happening people. You know it is. And that's why you're all here.

Senator Birmingham has urged the President to immediately sign the Identity Chip bill as an emergency measure to handle the overwhelming task of identifying missing persons. Says our senator, "While the measure will not aid in the recovery efforts now underway, the measure could benefit any future national crises."

Think, people. The 'Beast' from the Bible is a computer, not a person. The chip, the number, will soon be the only way to pay for things, and it tracks every purchase you make. That's how they can keep track of people buying things that are a red flag for terrorism and other criminal intentions, and it's how they can track you! Us!

Economists say there will be no more problems with insufficient funds – important when the economy falls out. It all sounds logical, logical enough that a lot of people will line up voluntarily to get the chip. I am thinking that after today, it will be like the McCarthy era, and everyone will be paranoid about who everyone is. Our citizenship and other basic info, arrest record, anything, can be added to that chip. People will want this. They will think that they are protecting themselves.

And I mention 'the President' so casually. We are under the regime of not one, but two presidents, who want this chip. If you disagree with President John Williams and hope to jump a couple states over to the West to live under President Kinji, whatever farce her liberal administration is, well, you've got a rude awakening. They both want the chip. In fact, she wants it more than Williams does. This chip is the beginning of communism.

The weight of hearing Paul's right-winged speech of paranoid delusion was starting to press down upon them and both were suddenly very tired, so very tired. What was the most fatiguing of all was the fact that Tom and Serena shared this man's delusion. For it was the fear of getting this Identity Chip, this fear most of all of allowing such a chip to be inserted into their precious children, was the catalyst for their fiery exodus from life as normal upstanding citizens and into this land of crazy people. But these were crazy times.

During the next break between speeches, Serena said to Tom, "Five years since the bombings. And it's been two since the restructuring. I still can't get used to Chicago being the nation's capital. And with Minneapolis the new 'wall street', it's like the whole country has moved over to the left."

"The left?"

"To the left of the map, like if you were looking at it."

"You mean 'West'?"

"Okay, then, West."

"And East – we are moved in on both sides."

"With California gone, we have Denver as the 'new Hollywood'. It's hard to believe all of this has happened. Just a few years ago, life was normal, despite recessionary times."

"It's surprising so few actors died. Not too many were in California when they got hit."

"Makes you wonder if the rich and famous got a heads-up that the rest of the population didn't."

"It's possible."

"Our government knew. Politicians were out of D.C. and government buildings and military installations were evacuated."

"Nothing's been proven about that," Tom cautioned. He feared that they were becoming as crazy as the off-grid people.

"No, but it's not like we can't figure it out. How else did so many people get out in time? We didn't lose any senators, and no Generals."

"True."

"It's hard to accept that a senator's life is worth more than an ordinary American citizen's. How can that be right? Millions died, while the political people and the celebrities got a heads-up and lived."

"*We* lived," Tom reminded her.

Serena was quiet for a few seconds. "But we were lucky -- blessed. Why couldn't the government warn people? They would have had hard intelligence from satellites or something. Were they afraid of mass panic and then no one could get out?"

"Maybe. I saw a new map at the library. It was sad seeing the United States smaller, and divided. California, Virginia, Pennsylvania and part of New York were grayed out. Oregon, New Jersey and part of Michigan were filled in with a dot pattern for 'uninhabitable'."

"And now we are split in two, with two presidents. Nothing feels real anymore."

The break was over and Paul had returned to the pulpit. He took a sip of bottled water and revved himself up into his closing rant.

> *People, listen. It's coming fast. They are putting chips in all new babies born on or after January 1. In three weeks. And by April 1, every citizen is required to have the chip. They are already putting the chips in prisoners and anyone who comes in to renew a driver's license.*

Cameras they have now can scan license plates and alert the police if there's anything going on with your vehicle – unpaid parking tickets, crime committed, or stolen vehicle. We've had this awhile. But now they'll be using it to catch those who don't have the chip.

We at OGG, off-grid-ghost, we are officially urging people to get the chips.

Paul waited for his words to register with the crowd. He was not disappointed by their reaction of gasps, followed by shocked silence.

Seriously, we do. It's the only way to protect ourselves. We get the chip, and then come in to OGG. We'll set you up with a code that we'll add to the chip that blocks the data. It is like a virus blocker, like a firewall for when you're on the Internet and someone's trying to steal your identity. When anyone scans the chip, it will give them limited data: whatever the off-grid programmers put in. It won't track your real transactions. But it will protect you. It will satisfy the government that you have the chip.

And we control the number, so that no one here ends up with 666 embedded under their skin.

Paul laughed, and the audience responded in kind. Tom and Serena exchanged looks of horror, not mirth.

Paul continued.

I'm not sure that the Beast is a computer, or that the numbers are about the Identity Chip. But do we want to take a chance? Of course we don't! The Identity Chip is required to get a driver's license, and banks will use it for all transactions. Stores will use it for all transactions. What will we do for money? How will we get around? If you don't have the chip, you can be arrested.

Let us help you. What we are offering you is software to add to the chip, our mark. The software is called "Angels Mark", and we strongly suggest you get the chip, come directly to OGG, and get Angels Mark installed. Do this by April 1. It gives you three months. We want all of our members protected by then. And from that point onward, only those with the Angels Mark will be able to scan to get into the OGG campus. We are doing this for all of us. Outsiders will find us eventually, but we don't want to make it easy for them to get in. So get the chip. Then come to us. We'll help you hide. We'll protect you.

Paul ended his final speech with a confident nod to the crowd. They responded with strong applause and a few scattered Amens. Everyone quickly dispersed, with many making a beeline toward Paul and his staff. Tom and Serena dodged the beaten path and bolted for the nearest exit.

Serena barely waited until the van door was shut behind her before saying, "They won't know we don't have the Angels Mark unless we try to get on the off-grid campus. If we use these three months to stock up on food and supplies, we could stay here for a lot longer than three months without anyone knowing we don't have it."

"We stock up. After April 1, we stop going to the off-grid campus."

"How long can we live without going to the store? We won't be able to go shopping anywhere."

"We can get chickens."

"We'd need a chicken coop."

"I can build one."

"We can grow our own food. This is going to be an adventure."

"It will be fun, besides, what choice do we have?"

5

Paul Tracy left the seminar feeling as if he'd just sold his last vacuum cleaner of the day, in other words: victorious and vindicated. Funny how those old feelings resurfaced after so many years. It seemed like another lifetime ago that Paul had been a vacuum cleaner salesman, a job for which he had a natural gift. He outsold everyone, despite never getting a good client list. Most of his sales went to people who couldn't afford them, and virtually all of his sales went to people who had no intention of buying a vacuum cleaner that day, not until Paul showed up on their door step.

He was initially motivated to hard-sell to impress his boss, to prove that he was not too young to hold down a job, but Paul was quickly bitten by the bug; he craved the gambler's high that selling gave him. The rush, lasting for a few glorious moments, sometimes hours, was what drove him toward making the next sale. He became a master at conning homeowners and renters alike with his slick tricks to demonstrate how dirty their floors were from using their current sweeper, and then dazzling them with how clean the new sweeper got their floors.

Paul polished off his act until he had a fail-proof, show-stopping, demonstration and a one-in-three sales track record. Not bad for a kid fresh out of high school. Eventually, the job he viewed as a perfectly-legal con game was effortless. Paul was Salesman of the Month every month without fail, for the entire four years he worked for Morris Handley.

Morris was a weasel of a man. He even looked like a weasel: He had a slight build that couldn't accommodate his extra pounds, giving him a small-animal-with-a-pouchy-belly physique. Add his oval head with wide-set eyes and pointy ears, and it wasn't hard to imagine him as anthropomorphic vermin.

Paul, who enjoyed his own reflection in the mirror, noticed all of Morris' shortcomings, especially the receding hairline that was poorly, and absurdly, masked by a cosmetic spray that looked suspiciously like black spray paint. And if the physical appearance wasn't eye candy enough, Morris gave something special to the ears as well. He had a voice that defied explanation. It was both nasal and a low baritone; it was both gritty and strong. The rise in pitch went up two octaves when he was yelling at his salesmen, but would fall sharply and unexpectedly into the throaty bear growl of a mobster.

Saving the best attribute for last, Morris had an overbearing wife who called the office incessantly with her constant carping. When Morris was especially beleaguered by the steady barrage of nagging and barbs from his wife, he would vent his pent-up frustrations at Paul and the other young salesmen. All of the young men, and one unfortunate young lady who was perpetually the victim of sexual harassment by pretty much everyone (she only lasted two months at Handley Sweep & Repair), were reduced to putty when Morris bellowed, all but Paul.

Paul always took the abuse cheerfully and then set out to out-sell everyone else. Before long, he was the apple of Morris' eye. Day after day, Paul set out with his vacuum kit until that fateful day that he landed at the front door of Miss Donna. Miss Donna was known in the area, and avoided. But Paul had never heard of her, or her conquests, of which there had been many.

Miss Donna, home all day without a job, was leery of a stranger showing up unannounced, but after looking Paul over, she ushered him inside. She was lonely with the kids all grown up all off to their fancy schools. Why they needed college, she'd never understand. Her kids would be in debt for the rest of the lives and for what? Did they think they were too good for a real job? Didn't her daughter get it by now, that husbands leave or die? Why bother with more school when it won't pay the rent? Don't get her started on her son, he was a closed subject. And if the subject was opened, well, Donna had a lot to say.

Then along came Paul, who was the same age as Miss Donna's own son. Paul was good looking, better looking than her son. Paul looked like he played sports and his skin was tan from sun – not like her son, who was pasty white and couldn't catch a ball. Her son would rather stay inside and read a book all summer than join the team. Paul had a real job. She admired Paul's full head of hair. He looked so young and virile. Before she was fully aware of what she was doing, Miss Donna had reached out to touch Paul's hair.

Paul flinched, but he didn't pull away. He only stood there, blinking his eyes in surprise. He let his box of supplies slip to the floor, making a soft thump on the carpet. Miss Donna's cool blue eyes sized him up in an instant and she lunged at him, clutching both sides of his face with her dry thin hands and long stained fingernails. She pressed her lips onto his, so hard that Paul felt pain. She wriggled her tiny body like a hairless cat while working with her lips to open Paul's unresponsive mouth.

Paul was slow to react, but his brain finally spoke to his hands. He pushed Miss Donna away with more force than he intended. She looked at him with wide eyes and an open mouth: horror. Then her eyes and mouth relaxed into a mask of tragedy: humiliation. Last, her eyes narrowed into catlike slits and fixed on him with a vengeance: hatred. Paul knew those three H's well: horror, humiliation, and hatred. He'd seen them before, and he knew he was in trouble.

By the time he reached Handley Sweep & Repair, he had rehearsed his story dozens of times. It would be her word against his, and he guessed, correctly, that she had picked up the phone the moment he walked out the door. She would make a complaint about Paul before he could make a complaint about her, of that he was certain. The question was, who did she call? Did she ring Morris, or had she gone straight to the police?

Much to Paul's relief, the complaint had been made to Morris only, no police. But Morris was irate. All of the repressed anger he felt day after day in his shabby little life with his carpy wife boiled over. He let loose like a short fat bull throwing a tantrum. Paul was reminded of a cartoon character, the Disney-fied Danny DeVito in Hercules. He almost started laughing, almost.

"What did you think you were doing!"

"Sir, I didn't do anything wrong."

"I know you didn't!"

"I don't know what she told you, but I didn't do anything."

"I should fire you right now."

"But you won't." Paul said calmly. *Cool as a cucumber*, he coached himself. He knew he was the best that Morris had, and Morris wouldn't let him go based on one complaint from Miss Donna. He tried to push the image of the animated Danny DeVito character out of his head.

"You are my best salesman, but don't think I won't fire you if you don't make this right."

"I'll be on guard in the future."

"What? No you won't. You'll go right back to Donna's and make sure she's a satisfied customer."

Paul blinked hard, finally catching on to what Morris was saying. "What do you mean, sir? She didn't order anything."

"You know what I mean. Donna only complains when she doesn't get what she wants. You're young, you're her type. Don't think I don't know what happened."

"Nothing happened."

"Yeah. Make sure that something does."

"You can't be serious."

Morris came out from behind his metal desk, a desk littered with children's school pictures, office supplies and paperwork that Morris should have completed weeks ago. A pizza box with one piece left in it topped the stack. His body brushed the pile, causing the tower to slide off the desk. Morris seemed not to notice.

He walked toward Paul until he was standing only a few inches from his face. Morris, several inches shorter than Paul, had somehow made himself tall enough to look him eye to eye. He reached out and gripped Paul's shoulders with his hairy stubby fingers.

"Look kid, it's a tough world. I'm doing you a favor. You have something that women want." His halitosis expelled over Paul's face like an exterminator's fogger. He growled, "A pretty boy like you. Use it."

Paul left Handley Sweep & Repair and went directly home, to the empty house that had once been occupied a happy family. Well, to be fair, the family was never all that happy, but at least they were together, all of them alive. Imperfect parents were nearly always better than dead parents. They'd been gone a long time now and Paul had trouble remembering what it was like to have had parents; his brother Clyde had been his legal guardian since Paul was thirteen years old.

The empty house seemed to echo his every step, mocking him. Paul was aching for his parents even though he knew deep down that he probably wouldn't have shared any of this Miss Donna situation with them. It was a relief when a clatter from the kitchen caught Paul's ears: Clyde was home.

"Why are you home?" Paul asked.

Clyde didn't pause in his dish-washing routine. "I could ask the same of you, little brother."

"I'm in trouble, Clyde."

"Oh?" Clyde dried his hands on the faded green-checked dish towel hanging from the front pocket of his jeans. He turned away from the sink.

"This nasty old bat came on to me and I got out of there. Morris wants me to go back to her and do what she wants."

"Mole-man? He's pulling your leg."

"No, he's serious. And it's a gopher. He looks like a gopher."

"Mole, gopher – a rodent is a rodent. How do you know he's not messing with your head?"

"He wants the sale. He's not joking."

"You're telling me that the scumbag would pimp out my little brother to sell a vacuum cleaner?"

"If you don't believe me, listen to this." Paul fished his cell phone out of his pocket.

"You recorded him?"

"Audio. There's no video, I kept it in my pocket."

"I'm impressed."

Clyde listened to Morris' tirade, and could hear for himself the unmistakable meaning of what Morris told Paul to do. Clyde felt the blood rushing to his head, his hands clenched into fists. He willed his body to relax. He tensed his face and then released the tension. He took a couple deep breaths. When he had stabled himself he said, "I'll take care of it. You go on to the rest of your route. Say nothing about Donna."

"How did you know it was her?"

Clyde held up the clipboard Paul had set on the kitchen table. "You checked off all the names before hers. Besides, she has a reputation. Figured she was the one."

"You got it right. It's her." Paul shuddered at the memory of her moist hot lips on his mouth.

"Don't worry, kid. I've got your back. You check off her name. Mark it as 'not home'. Go to the next person on your list. Business as usual. Say nothing to Morris, or anyone. Got it?"

Paul opened his mouth to ask what Clyde was going to do, but something in his brother's face stopped him cold. Paul left the kitchen, went upstairs to his room, and spent the rest of his Friday afternoon listening to music. By Sunday, Paul had two nights of hard partying with his friends behind him and had almost forgotten about Miss Donna.

The following Monday morning, when Paul arrived early, without a trace of a hangover, Morris pulled Paul into his office for a chat. "Paulie, I got something to tell you."

What was that expression on Morris' face? Compassion? Pity? Were rodents capable of emotion? Paul waited, said nothing.

"It's about Donna. Drop her from your list. She's dead. Her son found her body on Saturday. It was a freak accident. Somehow she fell into her bathtub full of water – her clothes still on and everything. Her blow dryer was plugged in nearby, it was in the tub – switch was on. They think she might have grabbed at the cord as she was falling, or was stupid enough to dry her hair while in the tub. I don't know if she died from hitting her head on the tub, from zapping herself, or from drowning. Whatever. She's dead. Take her off your roster."

Paul blinked. He said nothing. His mind fleetingly went to Clyde. Could Clyde have had something to do with Donna's death? No, of course not! "Are the police investigating?"

Morris snorted. "I doubt it. What's one less skank in this town?"

Paul continued selling vacuum cleaners for another six long months, until he had enough money in his bank account to make a down payment on a small business loan. After that, Paul would never have to sell another vacuum. Because, according to Clyde, there was a little something that Morris was completely clueless about: who owned the building, the hole-in-the-wall hovel in a God-forsaken town, where Handley Sweep & Repair had been in business for three generations. Clyde knew, and he filled Paul's head with a plan to get out from under Morris Handley with his middle finger held high.

The history on the Handley building involved the late Mr. Ferro, a dear friend of Morris' grandfather, who helped the Handley family in the early days when Mr. Handley was supporting an ill wife and a young family with eleven children. Ferro set a lower-than-market-price rental agreement, something Mr. Handley could afford to pay – and yet maintain his pride in supporting his family.

In over forty years, Ferro had never raised the rent, even when Handley Sweep & Repair was passed down through two generations. When Ferro's daughter Martha inherited the Handley Sweep & Repair building from her father, she had no interest in the building and made no changes to the original rental agreement that her father had with Morris. She had never visited the building, probably never read the rental agreement, and Clyde suspected that she would rather get rid of it than continue the relationship with the Handleys; who, two generations removed from the original Ferro-Handley friendship, were strangers to each other, and not in the same league as Martha and her circle.

Paul made Martha an offer for the building. She didn't hesitate to sell it to the promising young man, so enterprising and energetic. Making something new out of something neglected? Her father would have appreciated such idealism and work ethic. How wonderful to be out from under the Handley building with a sale she could feel good about. Secretly, Martha was, above everything else, pleased that she no longer had any association with the Handleys, which was precisely what Clyde expected.

What Clyde also knew was that Morris was in debt, a deep dark abyss of debt that Morris would never be able to repay, even if he worked hard for the rest of his life. His shrew of a wife had overextended their credit cards, again, and the Handleys were in serious danger of losing their house. The poor chump couldn't even declare personal bankruptcy because he had already done that all too recently. There was no more recourse for Morris and Clyde knew that Morris would not be able to hold on to Handley Sweep & Repair if the rent was, say, triple what he was currently paying.

As per Clyde's instruction, Paul promptly changed the rental agreement. The original contract had long expired and had no legal standing, so there was no barrier in the way of immediately raising the rent to what the current market would bear. Eventually Morris would fall so far behind in payments that eviction would be the next step.

During the planning stage, Paul had asked, "But why bother with any of this? I can just quit Handley's and get a different job."

Clyde scowled, "Paul, you can't let him run you off. You have to take back your power."

"You've been watching too much daytime TV," Paul scoffed.

Clyde didn't crack a smile. "This isn't something to play around with. You let this rodent squeeze you out, and you'll be under someone's feet the rest of your life. There will be another Morris right behind this one."

"Why don't I just kick him out right away? Why wait months?"

"Patience, little brother. Watch him squirm. Revenge is sweeter when it takes time to unfold. And when it does, you can throw away your cheap polyester suit."

After three years of selling vacuums, Paul was done with that forever. And Clyde was right; it was a sweet victory to watch Morris beg for extensions when the rent came due each month. Paul stretched out the enjoyment by allowing extensions, with interest, for over six months. Then Paul sent Morris' account to collections. Finally, nine months after Paul had purchased the Handley Sweep & Repair building, he evicted Morris.

Paul, at twenty-one years of age, knew that his revenge marked the last time he would ever answer to anyone. But after his revenge on Morris was complete, he was stuck with Morris' old haunt. What to do with it? Lease it, sell it or use it? He turned the matter over to Clyde.

Clyde needed no arm twisting. He was waiting for Paul to finally realize that something would need to be done about the building now that it was vacant. He offered, helpfully, to partner with Paul, and he was quick to spin the situation until his younger brother believed that Clyde would respect Paul as an equal, or even, laughably, as a senior. It amused Clyde that Paul was so easily manipulated that Paul was actually seeking him out for help, without a clue that Clyde had been "helping" him all along. Clyde cursed the fact that Paul was not a twin, and was not even a full brother, but Paul was as close as Clyde would get to an alter ego.

Messing with Paul's head was child's play; he was a soft lump of clay that was no challenge for a skilled potter. After all, the conditions were ideal: Paul was a vain conventionally-handsome boy who had been flattered from birth. He would never believe that anyone could hate him or want to do him harm.

Yes, Clyde would go into business with Paul. He would be a silent *senior* partner: secretly spinning webs and twisting Paul's thoughts until Paul himself believed that Clyde's ideas were his own. That's how it had always been, and how it would always be. As for this latest development, Paul didn't come up with the Handley takeover. Of course it was Clyde who had filled his head with ideas, so naturally Clyde thought of the building as his own from the start. If Paul hadn't come to Clyde with the partnership idea on his own accord, Clyde would have spun a web to draw him to what he wanted, but Paul made things easy for Clyde, as he always did.

The two brothers agreed to hold their first business meeting at their parents' kitchen table. Catsup, two plates, two mugs, two forks, and two paper napkins were already on the table before Paul came downstairs. The smell of cooking oil greeted Paul when he entered the kitchen, reminding him that he was hungry. Without a word, Paul sat in his regular chair while Clyde fried the sliced baby red potatoes he had boiled the day before. A few moments later Clyde served up the potatoes and the coffee. Then he sat down opposite Paul.

"The old Handley building has real potential," Clyde began.

"I handled that slick, didn't I? I have to make money fast though. I burned through all my savings on the down payment."

Paul drizzled catsup over his potatoes. Fried potatoes like Mom used to make, Paul's favorite.

"You don't have much time to find a new job." Clyde's eyes were full of concern. Clyde had practiced that particular expression in the mirror until he could do it on command. He could have been an actor in another life, a character actor though – he was not good looking enough to be a leading man. Paul would be the man for that job. Clyde broke free of his own musings and realized that Paul was talking. How amusing, little brother was defensive.

"I don't want a new job. I want to be my own boss," Paul bristled. Paul was amazed sometimes at how little Clyde understood him.

"You don't have time to grow a business." Clyde took a bite of potato and slowly moved his eyes in thoughtful contemplation.

"What are you saying? Go into business or not? I need money now, but I want to do this. What should I do, Clyde?"

"Too bad people wouldn't just give you money, tossing dollars into an offering plate just to see you talk."

"I could be a preacher," Paul snorted.

"Now that's an idea worth considering! The old Handley building is in an excellent location for a church. The people will pack the pews. Magnificent!" Clyde jumped up from his chair and began clearing the dishes. Every movement he made was with great gusto: Stack the plates with a clatter, clatter. Scrape, scrape the scraps into the bin. Slip it all into the sink with a satisfying plunk into the soapy water.

"I turn it into a church? You're not serious." Paul twisted his body in his chair to follow Clyde's movements as he whirled about the kitchen.

Clyde sat back down. “Sure! Start up a new church. People will pay just to hear you speak.”

“I don’t know, you think so?” asked Paul.

He leaned forward on the table and hid a snide grin behind pious folded hands. Paul was warming up to the idea, his ego responding to the idea of people hanging on his every word. Soft clay was never a challenge for a skilled potter like Clyde.

6

President Ann Kinji typed the word “Cologne” into the online shopping search engine textbox. She was relieved to find only a dozen choices. She ignored Old Spice, which conjured up a fond memory of her grandfather, and anything that sounded like a teenage boy’s scent. That left her with only two options. Of the two, she chose the best looking bottle, the one with the best reviews. *There, done!*

She knew it wasn’t the most personal way to shop, but she was proud that at least she was doing her own shopping for her husband instead of delegating the task to one of her assistants. Ann had a perfect record of never missing their special occasions, regardless of how busy she was. It didn’t matter if she was an overloaded college student or one of the first two Presidents of the formally-known-as United States, she had always found the time for her best friend. However, with Ted’s birthday not quite two weeks away, it was too close for comfort. At least that was how it felt to Ann, who was always light years ahead of schedule. It was a telling sign that she was dangerously close to being sucked into the office; her former life a shadow.

Ann was determined to hold on to the person that she was, but that noble intention was proving more difficult than she could have imagined. The presidency had blindsided her and she was feeling unsure of herself for the first time in her life. How does one go from normal person to President? Never in her wildest dreams had she held such extreme ambition, or even the slightest expectation that a woman would become President in her lifetime, let alone an Asian woman, let alone herself!

Ann wasn't ungrateful. Her awareness of her unique place in history, her extraordinary influence in this unprecedented time of turbulence, and her power to alter fate for a nation, no, the *world*, was acute. And yet, she didn't ask for this unquantifiable responsibility. In her spirit, Ann was still that little girl sitting in the front of the class; assigned to the power seat by one teacher after another, never seeking attention for herself, but attracting it anyway. The only thing that Ann set her sights on was the pursuit of excellence in everything she did. The awards, the accolades, the acclaim – all of these were the cherry on top. Intrinsic rewards were always enough to keep her going.

Naturally, she was a teacher's dream: smart as a whip, creative, and talented, without a hint of arrogance. She was a model citizen, popular with her peers without ever joining the "in" crowd, or wasting much energy on worrying about what other people thought of her. She just did the right thing in every situation, and she worked very, very hard – joyfully; she was a ball of light. She moved as if she had the energy of the sun fueling her on, her steps as light and effortless as a flower fairy dancing in the morning light.

It was that way for Ann from birth. She was blessed to always be at the right place, at the right time, for each golden opportunity. So it was without effort that she found herself wearing a virtual crown, despite never playing political games and never compromising her moral code, not once in her twenty years of public service, not ever.

Ann was a living example of "work meets opportunity", an anomaly in politics; someone who had no connections, no family money, and not a devious bone in her body. No, she was just a very smart girl who worked her way up, up, up, -- up and out of her hometown of Warsaw, Indiana -- until one day important people tapped her to solve the world's worst problems in modern day history.

Her run-in with Paul had conjured up memories of Warsaw; walking after school to the library, waiting for her father to pick her up after work; going to Pizza King after a basketball game and giving her best friend a kick under the table to signal it was time to get away from her annoying date; buying a new dress to wear to the Snowball; feeling left out when kids told stories of cow-tipping and barn parties, even though she didn't really want to be the kind of girl who got invited to the secret parties where alcohol, and other things, flowed freely; riding with her boyfriend through the corn fields; swimming at Winona Lake and getting stuck in the seaweed.

Her mind rested on the Winona Lake story for a few minutes. When she had shouted for help, her father told her to relax, don't panic, relax. She did, and the seaweed fell away, drifting around her in a swirl of harmless green gunk. She easily swam back to the pier. *Life is like swimming in seaweed,* she mused.

She was a long way from Warsaw, where basketball was not a mere game or sport, but something as revered as a church service. She had never quite understood the love of basketball, nor did she ever really become a Hoosier – her family moved to Warsaw the summer before she entered fourth grade – but she grew up well there. Watching "brat pack" movies with her friends, attending both proms, tying for first place in the high school talent show, making the honor roll, even taking special classes for "gifted and talented".

Yes, she was still that girl, the charmed fairy princess, but her ball of light was fast dimming. She couldn't remember the last time she had really looked at her face in the mirror, beyond the face to the spirit within. She saw only what she needed to see to pull herself together each day; the blemishes to conceal, the curve of her lips to paint, the uneven complexion to smooth, the new lines on her face to mask.

In her reflection, her dark eyes stared back at her, awaiting the insertion of contact lenses and the framing of her lids with makeup, but there was no gleam, no spark of life, no glimpse of her soul. She was being eclipsed by the office she held. At what point would she disappear altogether?

Ann sensed that her husband could feel her slipping away. She hoped that her thoughtfulness on his birthday would reassure him, and she was confident that it would, for now. Ted was an easy man to please. He appreciated the simple things in life. He was also a patient man. Yet Ann knew that no marriage was immune from strain, growing apart, and ultimately ending. How long could Ted wait for intimacy to return? What was his breaking point?

Ann's moments of brooding were fleeting, but in recent days had become much more frequent, and more regretful and wistful in nature. A reoccurring theme was her longing to be a mother, which always resolved itself with the reluctant thought that her inability to conceive a child was a blessing in disguise. If she was struggling to hold on to her own identity, could she have nurtured a child?

No, she answered herself, the office consumed her; she could not have put a child first. Not only did she not have time for a theoretical child, she knew that if she didn't figure out how to get a grip on herself, she could lose her marriage by the time this was all over. But of course, maybe her destiny included making such personal sacrifices for the greater good. When put into that framework, how could she not rise to the occasion, regardless of the toll?

"President Kinji?"

"Yes?"

Breyana Robertson, in a magenta pants suit today, rapped gently at her open door, as was her ritual. "Paul Tracy is back."

"You've got to be kidding me." Ann's shiny bob waggled, giving away the angry shaking of her head.

"Sorry. I could tell him you're not available?" Breyana suggested, all the while knowing that Kinji would never back down from a challenge.

"No, send him in please."

Paul strolled in front of the Democratic Union seal, looking smug and mysterious. "How are you and the New Liberals getting on?"

"Democratic Union. Get to your point."

"Harsh, especially after what I offered you."

"I don't know anything about an offer, and I don't see any reason to talk to you. I allowed you in here for the sole purpose of telling you face to face that I don't want you to contact me again."

"You didn't get my package?"

"I disposed of it without opening it. I do not appease bullies."

"That's how you see me? A bully? Why, Ann, I'm offended."

"Look, Paul, I am not a game player. I do not have any skeletons. There is nothing to blackmail me with. You have no bargaining tools. I'm asking, no, *telling*, you to leave."

"You should have opened the package, but that's okay. I have copies. You'll want to see what I have to offer."

Ann picked up the phone, but Paul flipped the stack of papers around before she could punch anything in. And the face she saw gave her pause: It was Ted. *Her* Ted. With a little girl. Walking hand-in-hand. Clearly, obviously, this child had a bond with Ted. Clearly, obviously, Ted was likely her father. Clearly, obviously, Ann did not know this child existed, nor did the rest of the world.

"I'm offering you my silence, in exchange for a job."

"I don't give in to terrorists. Not even when my personal life is at stake."

"Oh I know you don't. But you won't stand on principle at the expense of a little girl's life – think of how that child will be exploited if you let my people go public with this. I know you'll think this through, and then you'll call me. And when you do, you'll accept my offer."

He set the stack of photos on Ann's desk. As he turned around to leave, he said, "Looking forward to working with you, Ann."

"Get out."

"You'll call me. I'll give you 24 hours." And on that note, Paul spun sharply on the heels of his $700 shoes and left the office of the President of the Democratic Union, with Ann's dark eyes burning holes into his suited back.

Paul worked his way through the maze of the building, leaving the marbled-floor hallways far behind him. Fifteen minutes later, he was finally in the parking garage and searching for his beloved Porsche Carrera GT, a supercar with a top speed of 205 mph+; and, as he'd tested the claim for himself, he told anyone who would listen that it could reach 0-60 in 3.9 seconds. He'd spent $428,000 on the car, a bargain.

The economic downturn brought about opportunity for the newly rich like Paul. He loved his silver baby, and hated leaving it unprotected in a common parking garage. That was why he parked it as far away from the entrance as possible, where he was the most likely to be able to take two parking spaces for himself, a move that he regretted today.

He was all alone, on the far opposite of the highest parking ramp exit, where no one could hear him if he screamed – a thought that occurred to him when a large beefy hand grabbed his mouth shut from behind his head.

Paul tried to twist his head to see the man who held him captive, but he felt such strong resistance that he feared his neck would break if he dared try that move again. He advised himself not to resist his captor, and to wait for his chance to run.

He spied his Porsche just yards away. The sight of his car gave birth to anger, more anger than fear. Paul bit the beefy hand.

"Sonnofa..." bellowed the six foot six man, who released Paul instantly.

"Grab him," yelled another.

"Where do you think you're going?" said a third.

For the first time, Paul understood that he was grabbed by official thugs, not a mugger. Secret Service it looked like. So Ann had made good on her threat then? She was really going to toss her husband's illegitimate love child to the wolves? Heartless shrew! Paul had underestimated Kinji. And yet Clyde had been so sure that Ann would crumble.

"Sweet ride. I'll drive," said the possessor of the beefy hand.

Startled, Paul gulped, "No you won't!"

"You bit me. I drive." The giant stepped into the car and glared at Paul. "Keys."

"Get in," the second man growled as he pushed Paul closer to the passenger's door.

Beefy Hand drove Paul in the Porsche while the other two men followed in a black sedan with government plates. They traveled through heavy commuter traffic, sometimes at a stop-and-go pace, without exchanging a word. Paul tried to initiate conversation, but his attempts were answered with a silent glare. Not that he could see the man's eyes behind the dark glasses, but he could feel them. An hour and forty-five minutes later, they arrived at a private airport where a small jet awaited them.

Beefy Hand snatched Paul's coat jacket and yanked him around like he was a marionette. He propelled Paul up the narrow metal steps to the jet's open door. Once Paul was inside the plane, Beefy

Hand released him and turned outward to face the tarmac. He stood guard. Against what?

Paul blinked his eyes to adjust to the difference in lighting, and walked slowly down the small aisle of, what he now recognized to be, a luxury jet. And there, two feet in front of him, sitting in a leather chair, sipping coffee, was none other than President John Williams. Paul stopped in his tracks. He feared his mouth had fallen open.

"Take a seat, Paul."

The leather chairs were positioned to face each other. There were two chairs on each side. Paul sat directly opposite the President, as that was the chair that President Williams was gesturing toward. Paul's mind was racing. Had he done anything to flag himself as a potential terrorist? What could the President want with him?

"Nice work today."

"Sir?"

"That's Mr. President."

"Sorry. Mr. President, I don't know what you are referring to. How do you know me?"

"We have ears in Kinji's office."

"You're bugging the President's office?"

"Oh don't look so surprised. You've been getting your hands dirty your own self."

"You know about that?"

"The pictures of her husband with the child. How did you do it?"

"What do you mean?"

President Williams arched an eyebrow. “Don’t play stupid with me. That kid isn’t his. She doesn’t even exist. How did you manage to airbrush a kid who looks the spitting image of him? I want the name of your guy.”

“Okay, you got me.” Paul shrugged. “I don’t know who did it. I have a team that works for me. They took a photo and morphed it, changed her features to look more like his. I hear it wasn’t that hard to do. He has an easy face to copy.”

“It’s good work. I want to use it.”

“Excuse me?”

“There’s nothing wrong with your hearing. I want to use it, you. You’re going to work for me now.”

“No one owns me.”

“Think again. I’ve caught you in this pathetic scheme of yours. What is it you were planning to do, anyway? Did you really think she would hire you if you blackmailed her? That was never going to happen.”

“I know her better than you think.”

“Oh, old school chums. Yes, I heard. Although I’m curious, why did you call it an Academy? My people tell me that your only childhood connection to Kinji is a babysitter in common. A Mrs. Mason, who we’d have talked to, but she’s deceased. Died from a freak accident in the home.”

Paul’s eyes registered the shock he felt.

“You didn’t know she was dead? What’s it to you? Answer me about the Academy bit.”

“We ran into each other when we were about sixteen or so. We made a joke about the old Academy days, Mrs. Mason headmaster. It was sarcasm. Warren Academy is a mobile home with nicotine-stained walls and mildewed furniture. We hated that place, and the nasty slug who ruled it; watching soaps all day, giving us nothing but animal crackers to eat and Kool-Aid to drink, telling us to shut up while puffing away on one cigarette after another."

A familiar face appeared at that moment. It was the blonde aide from the tarmac. Paul always remembered another good-looking man. The aide produced coffee for the President; no offer was extended to Paul. The aide sat next to John and remained there for the duration of the conversation, which Paul found curious and off-putting. Now he had two sets of eyes starting him down.

"And that's your only connection to Kinji?"

"Yes."

"She came from humble beginnings, so did you."

"What's your point?"

"No point. Forming a picture. Tell me why you wanted her to hire you."

"I can't tell you that."

"Son, I have no time for this. I have to meet Kinji myself in less than two hours. My staff can dig around and figure this out. If you make me wait for that I won't be in a generous mood anymore."

"Generous?"

"I want to hire you, Paul."

"I don't understand."

"Tell me what I need to know. Then I'll tell you what you need to know."

"I wanted to work for her so that I could influence that Identity Chip bill. I want it to pass."

"Ah, now I get it. You want fear mongering to bring more money into your church, your pocket in other words. You and your homely brother Cliff."

"Clyde."

John Williams waved his hand to indicate that Clyde's name was irrelevant to him. "Your plan was, and is, ridiculous. But your blackmail photo is quite good. I hope you are paying those kids you've got running your computer lab. It's not child slavery is it? You got them working in your cult for food and water?"

Paul's eyes again registered surprise.

"Oh you didn't think I knew all about your operation? Paul, my guys briefed me about your whole life in about fifteen minutes. It's all right here." He tapped the brown folder he held on his lap. "They said I could read it on one of them gadgets, but I like paper."

Paul knew he was beaten, in way over his head. He was nothing but a two-bit con man compared to the President of the Liberty Union. "What do you want with me?"

"I want you to take that photo of yours to the media."

"You want to embarrass her?"

"You don't need to know my reasons. But yes. Making trouble for her keeps her off balance."

"I can't believe we're having this conversation."

John snorted. "You ain't no Boy Scout, Paul. You know politics can be messy."

"Why didn't you send one of your people to talk to me? Why is the President himself doing this?"

"You're an oily little snake, Paul. You wouldn't be loyal to a staffer. But you'll be loyal to me, won't you?" The President leaned forward and locked his steely blue-gray eyes with Paul's. Satisfied, he relaxed his posture. "See? We understand each other."

"That's all you want me to do, leak the photo?"

"No. That's not all."

"Then what? And what about hiring me?"

John chuckled. "Someone will pay you. You'll find money in your account. Untraceable to this office, of course."

"And what do I have to do?"

"Leak the photo. My people will pick you up when I want you again."

Paul tried to think of something more to ask, but couldn't come up with anything.

"Paul, we'll be watching you. Your church? It's infested. Your home? It's infested. My people say you have a bug problem. Feel like you're being followed? You are."

7

"All the leaves are brown…" Serena crooned into the microphone, aiming for a bluesy groove with her vocals.

"All the leaves are brown," her daughters echoed.

"And the sky is gray," she sang, feeling the lyrics heavily in her heart. Minnesota winters were harsh and long, so very long.

The girls echoed dispiritedly. Tom, their son, and their youngest daughter plucked away on their acoustic guitars. Serena tapped out a beat on the cowbell attachment on her snazzy red drum set, her Christmas present from Tom. Their eldest daughter played a pink electric guitar, which didn't really fit the sound of this particular song, but no one cared. With no audience to worry about, their standards were relaxed.

Last year, while acclimating to their new life in a rural area, and avoiding popular family activities where they would be seen by too many people, they joined a bluegrass group composed almost exclusively of friendly and warm senior citizens. The group welcomed their young son into the fold, teaching him how to play both the harmonica and the guitar. The rest of the family sat watching, week after week. Eventually the girls in the family felt comfortable singing along. Tom decided to take up an instrument, and was advised that the mandolin was an easy one to start with. After mandolin, he took up guitar.

One thing led to another, and before long the formerly-known-as Bridge family had evolved into their own family band. Now they stayed home and rehearsed their own line-up of songs. Sometimes they posted their sessions on the Internet to share with the world. By now, they didn't seriously fear that anyone would recognize them.

America, just one year after the bombing, had already changed so much that no one would care who they were, or what had happened back then when the world fell apart. No, the Bridges would be left alone, and could probably shed their Meadows persona whenever they wanted. And they could leave Minnesota, where they were light and sun deprived and craving color.

But until Tom found a new job, here they were, suffering through another long frigid winter, with no warmth in sight. Jobs were hard to come by, and it would take a miracle to be on their way to a new life anytime soon. So, for now, they stayed in their roles as the Meadows family. To make themselves feel better they turned every light in the house on, lit their faux wood stove, and played music.

"I'd be safe and warm if I was in L.A."

"If I was in L.A.," the girls droned.

"California Dreamin' on such a winter's day…" Serena felt the tragedy of the song. There was no California post-bombing. Would life ever feel good again? How could the world recover from this evil? Would they ever recover?

She was shaken from her thoughts when the music came to an abrupt halt. She watched Tom bolt from the room. "Phone!" the kids yelled in unison.

Ah! Maybe a job offer! Serena prayed silently. Unbeknownst to her, their three kids were doing the same thing.

Tom was back in a flash. "Telemarketer."

Everyone groaned, wallowed in self-pity for a moment, and then started back up again, "All the leaves are brown…" Their session went on for four more songs before they wrapped up their evening.

They always ended with the song "I'll Fly Away", and since snacks followed their music session, everyone moved fast after hitting the final note, all leaving the room at the same time. By the time they hit the last verse, "Just a few more weary days and then, I'll fly away. To a land where joys shall never end. I'll fly away…" they were hungry.

They scrambled up the stairs and into the kitchen, but Serena had fallen short with the grocery shopping and hadn't prepared anything special for after-music snacks. Tom suggested that they go out, which was met with a round of cheers, a flurry of clothes-layering activity, and a mad dash to the mini-van, which was still drive-able, but barely. Once behind the wheel, he turned to Serena, "Where to? We could just go to Red Wing, or if you want to go someplace bigger we could go to the Cities."

The kids immediately voted for the Cities, and Serena had no objection. They set off down their long gravel driveway. The kids plugged in their iPods while Tom and Serena chatted. The forty-five mile road trip was comfortable, even though the skies weren't any cheerier than they'd been earlier in the day.

About half an hour into the trip, Tom interrupted Serena's passenger-side conversation with him mid-sentence. "I think we're being followed."

"What? What do you mean?"

"I know you haven't been Serena Wilcox, private detective, for over a decade, but haven't you noticed?" Tom glanced at the rearview mirror.

"No? You really think someone is following us?"

"Yeah. He was on our road. I figured he'd be turning off eventually, but he's still with us and we're already in Apple Valley."

"What are the odds someone would be on our road and still behind us? You must be right. Maybe someone saw us on those YouTube videos and recognized us. I knew we shouldn't have put those up there." Serena looked in the side-view mirror, wondering which car was tailing them.

"Why would anyone care about us?"

"I don't know. Following up on the arson? Which car is following us? The SUV right behind us?"

"No, he's three cars back now. I don't think it's about the arson. Could be someone we know?"

"Here in Minnesota? I don't think so. Everyone we've met here knows us as the Meadows. Besides, why would they follow us all the way to Apple Valley without signaling to us in some way?"

"What do you want me to do?"

The kids by now had taken interest in what their parents were talking about and all three were eavesdropping. Serena turned around in her seat to face them. "It'll be okay, don't worry." She looked at Tom and said, "Pull over in the next populated parking lot you see, pick a restaurant."

Tom came up on a restaurant quickly, as they were in the heart of Apple Valley. He parked the van in the first parking spot available. "What now?"

"Just wait. He'll come to the van."

A "gecko green" metallic VW beetle pulled into the parking lot and parked one space over.

"Is that him?"

"Yes."

"How could I have missed *that*?" Serena laughed.

"Because you're you."

The driver of the VW unfolded himself from the tiny car quickly and easily, with the agility of a teenager. He strode purposely over to the mini-van.

"But I never forget a face. I know that guy," Serena said quietly.

The young man approached the driver's side of the van and stood patiently waiting for Tom to open the window. Tom glanced at Serena.

"I'll explain later, go ahead and open the window," she said.

Tom pressed the button to let down the driver's side window, the only window control that was still operational on the mini-van. He looked expectantly at the blonde twenty-something man who was smiling at him.

"Hey, Tom, isn't it?" he began.

"I'm sorry, you are?"

"Otto. You probably noticed me following you back there."

"Yes. Your car stands out."

Otto grinned wider, looking like he'd been crowned Homecoming King. "Can we talk? Want to go in?" He nodded toward the Broadway Pizza entrance.

Tom looked at Serena, who nodded. "Sure," he said.

Otto didn't wait, but headed straight for the door. Tom closed the window and said, "How do you know him? Who is he?"

"Well, he's not Otto. He's Bryce. Or maybe he was lying the first time around. Or maybe he's not Bryce *or* Otto."

"You're sure you've seen this guy before?"

"Yes, sure. He was my server at the restaurant the night I was driving back from the fire. So maybe this *is* about the arson. Should we just go? Keep on driving and not come back?"

"No, let's hear what he has to say. He can find us again if we run."

"He doesn't look like somebody to be afraid of. We better go in, he'll wonder what's taking us so long."

The Bridge-Meadows family joined Bryce-Otto in the empty reception area of Broadway Pizza. After a few pleasantries were exchanged with the hostess, the group was seated. Serena initiated conversation as soon as the hostess left them alone.

"I recognize you, from about a year ago. You were at a Perkins, not too far from here. It was near Christmas. You were wearing a name tag that said Bryce, you were my server." Serena said this calmly, as smoothly as if she was talking about the weather.

Bryce-Otto looked surprised, but quickly recovered. "I didn't expect you to remember me. Yes, I was waiting tables there."

Tom said, "Why were you following us?"

"I was watching you before you torched your own house. Why did you do that, by the way?"

Tom and Serena didn't bother to disguise their horror. They didn't know what to say. What could they say?

Bryce-Otto laughed and clapped Tom on the shoulder. "Don't worry, man. I'm not after you or anything."

"What is this about?" Serena asked. She looked at her three kids- all three were noticeably frightened. None of them had spoken a word since they overheard that someone was following them.

"How did you know something was about to happen? We assume you faked your death because you thought someone would come after you? Why did you think that? What did you know, and how did you know it?" Otto-Bryce was suddenly serious now; his Homecoming King vibe had disappeared. In its place was an expression that transformed his features into a person who seemed both cunning and powerful.

"Who are you, really?" Serena asked.

"I work for someone important, let's leave it at that. Now, you obviously feel nervous right about now. You know- that I know- that you lit your house on fire and skipped out, created a new identity for yourselves and are hiding under Paul's mega-church, which is a fraud, by the way. He's a con man."

"We thought so," Tom said.

"They helped us hide. We haven't been to any of their meetings since that first month," Serena said defensively.

"We want you to go back."

"To the meetings?" asked Tom.

"Yes. We're watching Paul and his fugly brother Clyde. We need eyes and ears on him." Bryce-Otto halted his interrogation while their server took down their order. Serena ordered a deep dish Chicago style pizza, planning to eat very little of it. The last thing her stomach needed right now was pizza.

After the server had left, Bryce-Otto continued, “Let’s go back to what you were doing when you torched your house. I was watching you then, you’d triggered off a few alarm bells in my organization.”

“What organization is that?” asked Tom, knowing he was unlikely to get an honest answer.

“I’m not at liberty to say. But we were watching, looking for anyone showing signs of prior knowledge of the bombings. And you obviously knew something.”

“And so did you. You couldn’t do anything to stop it?” Serena countered.

“You didn’t report anything. You lit your house on fire and ran.” Bryce-Otto squinted up his eyes and fixed them into a stare that was intended to intimidate Serena, but failed to do so.

“What could I say that anyone would believe? I was watching the news; I had a really bad feeling. I had a vivid nightmare that I felt was prophetic, but I’m no psychic, at least not proven to be. I had a couple dreams that relatives died, and then they did, but, they were sick at the time so it was kind of a logical conclusion. I dreamed that the United States was going to be hit with nuclear bombs, and I believed the dream was real. We took a leap of faith that my dream was a real warning, and we did what we could to keep our family safe.”

“And your husband went along with this? You burned down your own house based on a dream? And safe from what? You were already in a safe area of the country. Why move? Why hide?”

Bryce-Otto shook his head. "I don't believe you. You knew something. What did you know, and how did you know it?"

"Safe from the government," said Tom.

"I had a bad feeling that the government was going to fall apart after the nuclear bombings, and that we'd be better off if we were not in the system. I can't explain why, just a bad feeling," Serena insisted.

Bryce-Otto looked from Tom to Serena; and back again. "I can't tell if you people are crazy and delusional, or if you're lying. If you're crazy, you got it right – bombs happened. WWIII, everything hit the fan. So you're not crazy. Which means you must be lying, because I don't believe in that psychic dream crap you're giving me."

"My mom isn't lying. She had a dream. And we left because something bad was going to happen," Carrie spoke up, causing everyone at the table to look at her. She stared back at all the faces. "Well, it's true. My parents are not crazy, and they are not lying."

Bryce-Otto leaned across the table and said in a raspy whisper, "Tell me about your mother's friend. The one she e-mails in Iran. Her friend have a dream too?"

Serena froze for half a second, and then she began to sing, "Just a few more weary days and then, I'll fly away…"

Her singing caught Bryce-Otto off guard and he sat stunned, as the girls' voices joined in.

"To a land where joys shall never end, I'll fly away…"

And on that note, the family did what they always did after singing that song. They left the room with great haste. The surprise factor gave them only a few seconds lead, but it was enough time to get into the van and lock the doors before Bryce-Otto reached them. He put his face two inches from Tom's window and yelled, "I know where you live!"

"Just go, go!" urged Serena.

Tom drove, and drove. They looked over their shoulders every few minutes. No VW beetle, of any color. "Where do we go? Our safe house is not safe anymore."

"Let's take Karyn up on her offer to visit."

"You have her address?"

"She lives up North, a cabin in Deer River, near Bowstring Lake."

"We won't get there until after midnight. Will she be okay with that?"

"She'll have to be."

8

After driving for about five hours, the Bridge-Meadows family arrived at the lakeside cabin where Karyn lived with her husband Dan and four children. "Cabin" was a misleading description. Their home was impressive – large and rambling with many levels. There was a family room, living room, sitting area, large open kitchen, and enough space to sleep about a dozen people. Serena thought the cabin looked like a bed and breakfast hotel, generously roomy for a single family home.

"Wow, this is really nice," said Carrie. She squinted at the fully lit front entrance. Even the landscaping was illuminated, with soft solar lighting along the pathway to the door.

Serena glanced at her three children, who all looked a little rough around the edges after their harrowing exit from the restaurant the day before, traveling into the wee hours of the night, and sleeping on and off with their heads mashed against whatever they could find to lean on. Well, this wasn't a reunion, and besides, Karyn was not a pretentious person, or at least not the Karyn she remembered.

Serena reached out to ring the doorbell, but before she could press the button, Karyn flung the door open wide. “Serena! You made it!” She ushered the family in.

“Is that coffee I smell?” asked Tom.

“Karyn, you do realize we’ve imposed upon you at 2:30 in the morning?” Serena laughed. She couldn’t believe the feast she saw for them on the table. Artfully arranged on a country checked tablecloth was a bowl of fruit containing perfectly ripened bananas, deep purple grapes, and red apples worthy of Snow White’s temptation, a basket of assorted breads with a side dish of butter pats and jellies, a tier of three different varieties of breakfast muffins, a pitcher of what appeared to be fresh-squeezed orange juice in a bucket of ice, serving dishes, cloth napkins, and elegant long stemmed glassware – all waiting for Serena and her family to consume it.

“I’ll take you any time, day or night. It’s been too long, dear friend!” Karyn threw her arms around Serena for a quick power hug, a tight squeeze that projected puppy-like affection. “Sit, sit,” she said to the rag-tag group. “Dig in, whatever you want. Tom, you wanted coffee? I did make some. How about you, Serena?”

“Yes, I’ll take a coffee, thanks,” she said. Tom and Serena chose to remain standing, after having been cramped in the car for too many hours. The three kids sat and shyly helped themselves to the buffet. The adults stood quietly for several minutes, content to bask in the relief of having reached their destination.

“Hey, you made it!” Dan’s booming voice preceded his appearance in the kitchen. “So, what’s going on? Why are you here at two-something in the middle of the night?”

"Dan!" Karyn admonished him as she returned from getting the coffee, but she waited expectantly for an answer.

"Well, it's about you, actually," said Serena, as she received a mug of hot coffee from Karyn.

"About me? But it's been forever since I was your partner, and your cases weren't anything that would come back to haunt me."

"No, it's not about our private detective work."

"Then what is it about?" asked Dan, without waiting for an answer. "I made a fire in the living room. We can talk in there." He looked at the three kids sitting at his table, as if it was the first he noticed their presence. "Kids, there's a TV if you want to find something to watch. We have a game system too. Whatever you want."

"Dan, it's the middle of the night. I made up beds for them. They probably want to sleep," said Karyn.

"Thank you. They'll be fine, we can talk in the other room," said Serena. "But we can't stay long, they'll be looking for us."

"What?" Dan was startled. "Who's looking for you?"

The four adults left the kids to their buffet and sank their bodies into the pair of matching overstuffed suede sofas facing the fire. "We don't know for sure that they'll come here," said Tom.

"Yes we do. They know who you are," said Serena. She stirred her coffee to mix the sugar and cream, and took a few sips.

"Start at the beginning, how is this about me?" asked Karyn.

"It's about your adventure in Kish," Serena said.

"Oh no, why?" said Karyn. She avoided looking at Dan.

"Kish, the gorgeous island in Iran, where the snorkeling is the best in the world? And you went there because Kish doesn't require a visa, right?" asked Serena.

"We didn't have time for visas, it was a spur of the moment thing," said Karyn. "If I'd known how dangerous it was to go there, I wouldn't have done it."

"And if I'd known that Karyn wasn't going to be allowed at the beach, I wouldn't have gone snorkeling. I had no idea she was going to be shuttled off to the 'women's beach'. I shouldn't have gone off without her, especially after they gave her a scarf to cover her head. I should have known better than to leave her there." said Dan.

"I was the one who wanted to linger in the shops. It wasn't your fault," said Karyn. "The women's beach was lovely. There was nothing about it that sounded off any alarm bells."

"I'm not blaming either of you for what happened," said Serena. "I'm just giving a recap: Karyn ended up taken to Tehran, to a safe house. How she got there is not your fault. Kish is a hotbed of smuggling and terrorist activity. You didn't expect her to be taken, but she was."

"Nothing was ever done about it. They released her, brought her back to Kish, dropped her off at the hotel we were registered with, and we never knew why they took her, or who they were. Our government made some empty promises to look into it, and that was it," said Dan.

"But I was safe, and that's all that really matters. Why is this coming up?" asked Karyn, still avoiding looking directly at her husband.

"Yes, I know, not your fault. But, you might remember that when Karyn got back to the island, she went to the Kish Cyber Café at Shayan Hotel, where she sent me several e-mails," Serena continued. "These e-mails were apparently read by more people than just me."

"They probably read everything in that Café," said Tom.

"Who's 'they'?" asked Dan.

"I don't know. Our government is involved, either directly or indirectly," said Serena.

"Which one? The Williams camp or the Kinji camp?" asked Dan.

"My guess would be the Williams camp, but I don't know," said Serena.

"I don't understand any of this. The only person I e-mailed was you. I don't remember my exact words, do you?" asked Karyn. "Why are they interested in this now? That was over ten years ago."

"They think I knew something about Iran before the bombings," said Serena. She locked into Karyn's eyes and held steady eye contact for a few long seconds until Karyn squirmed and looked away.

"Oh." Karyn's voice was barely above a whisper.

"Honey? What is this about?" asked Dan. "Karyn? Is there something you want to tell me?"

"Should we leave the room while you two talk about this?" asked Serena, hoping to escape the awkwardness that was sure to follow.

"No, no, you can stay," said Karyn. "Dan, I didn't want to say anything because you felt bad enough about me being abducted."

"What happened?" asked Dan.

"The head scarf they gave me at the island was slipping and getting in my face, so while I was at the safe house I took it off," said Karyn. "That made the guards mad. One of them yanked my head back by grabbing the hair on the back of my head, and the other one spit in my face. That's all that –"

"He spit in your face! When were you going to tell me this?" Dan yelled. He was up now, pacing the room.

"Uh, never. I didn't think you ever needed to know," said Karyn.

"Tell me the rest of it," said Dan in a normal tone of voice, sitting back down.

"The guards must have been feeling cocky because they started running off at the mouth. One of them said, 'Americans will not be so bold when so many die.' And the other said, 'We bomb them their Holy Day and they will cover heads.' And then they laughed," said Karyn. "It was all in English, so they wanted me to hear them."

"And you wrote this in an e-mail?" asked Dan. "And this was nothing important? Don't you think 'bomb' and 'Americans die" could be the keywords that triggered you as a terrorist? Come on, Karyn!" Dan jumped off the couch again to pace the floor space between the sofas and the fireplace, which had dwindled down to ashes but no one noticed or cared.

"Wait, wait! I don't think Karyn is on a terrorist watch list. They'd have come to her before now if she was," said Serena.

"Then what's going on? What else don't I know?" Dan asked.

"I'm going to go check on the kids," mumbled Tom. He made a hasty retreat out of the uncomfortable room.

Serena looked at the two of them. "I'll go see if Tom needs any help with the kids." She hadn't made it out of the room yet before she heard Dan bellow, "You did WHAT?"

Shortly afterward, the house was awake. Dan and Karyn's children seemed to pour in from all corners of the house, scrambling toward their parents. Tom and Serena stayed out of the fray, tucking their own kids in for the night and quickly joining them. They lay in the guest bed, trying to shut out the noise from the other room, but it was impossible. First there was a flurry of parental duty as Dan and Karyn divided the children and escorted them back to their rooms, next came the conversation that Serena and Tom were hoping to miss.

"Okay, back up. So you are saying that not only did you hear that the Iranians were going to bomb us, but you've been talking to them for all these years?" asked Dan, forgetting to keep his voice down.

"I've not been talking to *them*! I said I met a nice lady there. I gave her my e-mail address. She started writing to me," said Karyn.

"While you were in the safe house, being tortured, you made a friend."

"I was not tortured. The hair pulling and spitting was the only thing that ever happened. I would have told you if anything really bad happened."

"Really? You would have?" scoffed Dan.

"Look, I know you're mad. I should have told you, but you already felt so responsible that I was taken in the first place. I thought it would make things worse if you knew about the spitting."

"And the bombing, you couldn't mention that?"

"Not without telling you about the spitting."

"And your Iranian mole friend? You couldn't work that in either?"

"Not without the spitting. I'm sorry, Dan. I should have told you. And she's not a mole. She's an ordinary citizen."

"Everything makes sense now. That's how Serena knew that something bad was going to happen, why she burned her house down and went into hiding. I knew she wasn't psychic! I've been such an idiot."

"I forwarded the e-mails Farideh sent me to Serena. And you're right, that's why she went into hiding. She encouraged me to do the same, which is why I wanted to stay here, and pull back from society. I figured we were pretty safe in such a remote location by the lake."

"And you never filled me in, all because you lied about being manhandled in Iran? Or as you call it, the spitting."

"Yes. One lie led to another, and then I didn't know how to tell you. I knew you'd be mad."

"You're right. I'm mad."

The two sat in silence for so long that Tom fell asleep. Serena stayed alert, even though she was resting. Time was of the essence. She was giving the couple a few more moments alone only because she felt guilty for her part in keeping secrets. She had advised Karyn to tell Dan at the very start, but when Karyn was too insecure to do it, Serena had played along. She regretted that, but it was all in the past now.

Just when she thought she would need to help things along, the couple resumed talking. "How long will you stay mad at me?" Karyn asked, her voice choked up with tears.

"Come here," Dan pulled Karyn closer to him. "I can't stay mad at you, you know that. That's why you should have told me. What did your friend say that convinced you that the Iranians were going to do this?"

"Farideh said that everyone was talking about it. There was a date – the right one, by the way. Everyone knew, and there was no doubt it was true, that these bombings were going to happen. They were saying 'Death to America' in the streets," said Karyn.

"But they've always said things like that, how did you know it was the real deal?"

"I'll show you the e-mail that Farideh sent me, the one that I forwarded to Serena. It is long, and it is convincing."

"You saved it? And you didn't send it to the FBI or at least the police?"

"Dan, I did send it to the FBI! I got a confirmation e-mail back. They said they sent the information to Homeland Security."

"You have that e-mail saved too?" asked Serena. Her presence startled both of them and they jumped.

"Yes, I still have the e-mail. I save everything."

"That's exactly what they're afraid of – they wonder what you have. They'll be here soon. Back up your computer files, now."

"Who's they?" asked Dan for the second time.

"I don't know. Really, Dan, there are no more secrets. You are all caught up to where we are. Well, you will be after you read

Farideh's e-mail. But no time for that now. Grab a flash drive and get your files. I have my own flash drive in my purse. I need a copy of the files too. Then – wipe your computer clean."

"I don't know how to do that," said Karyn.

"Don't look at me," said Dan.

"For that, I'll wake up my son. He can do it. The main thing is that we get those files. Now."

9

>>My Karyn,

I write you heavy heart. You must know for it is my hope you can go safe.

Iran make fools of everyone. For years they lie about nuclear missiles. Nuclear Nonproliferation Treaty is nothing, they spit upon it as easily as they spit on you, dear Karyn.

They threaten who wants make peace with Israel. Pro-West Arab Saudi Arabia and Egypt see Iran success nuclear, but have no fight. Iran pressure Lebanon, Syria, the Palestinians, and the Iraqis. Many thousands, hundred thousands, join radical Islamist. "Death to America!" on Iranian street for too many year. No one stop Iran. Now they make nuclear weapons in short period. They make stockpiles uranium for nuclear device in few months—make nuclear weapons in short period. They make centrifuges to pipe work. They learn technology when they talk to UN, many lies. Now they can do bomb. They will do this. It will be soon. I hear it from husband. You trust me to know truth. I tell you day and time. I tell you where missiles strike. You go safe.

Your Farideh <<

Paul read the forwarded e-mail over and over again, but still didn't understand why someone had sent it to him. His head was swimming with theories that fell apart. What had begun as a simple blackmail plot to get himself onto Kinji's staff had evolved into playing serious dirty politics with the big boys.

When Paul had scoffed at President William's speech that day on the tarmac, he had no idea that he was being watched, and followed, the entire time. Of *course* William's people tracked every onlooker, how could he have thought otherwise? It had been foolish for Paul to show up there, expecting to go unnoticed. It was probably that very move that got him discovered, although the jig would have been up anyway, since William's team had Kinji's office bugged.

The wind out of his sails, he didn't trust himself to pinpoint the exact moment of his downfall. He sat with slumped shoulders, waiting to be told what to do next, like the minion he was destined to be.

The phone rang. He answered with trepidation, having a strong feeling that the sender of the e-mail would be on the other end of the line. He was not mistaken.

"You opened the e-mail."

"Yes? What is that?"

"It's a big problem for the President."

"For Williams?"

"Yes, for Williams."

"What does this have to do with me?"

"You're going to be the one to fix it."

"How do I do that?"

"Go outside. I'm standing in your yard, in the back of your house."

Paul was only a few feet away from his back door. He peered out the window and didn't see anyone. He slowly opened the door and saw a young blonde man sitting on one of Paul's own lawn chairs that he'd placed amongst the landscaped shrubbery, well concealed from the road. He studied the man's face until recognition washed over him. "I know you. You're the intern I saw that day on the tarmac. You got the podium ready for William's speech."

"I'm more than an intern," Bryce scoffed.

"Obviously. So what's your deal?" Paul picked up a second chair, walked to where Bryce was, sat upon it, and leaned in close, conspiringly, "We're both players. We even look alike enough to pass for brothers. So why are you sitting in the power seat when I'm sitting in a puddle of drool?"

"Why should I tell you anything? You work for me."

Paul shrugged to feign indifference, not even fooling himself. "I was just curious."

"How did I succeed where you have failed? What have I got that you don't?" Bryce smiled with the same full wattage he'd flashed months ago in the restaurant, when showing Serena his frat-boy good teeth, but this time his smile was sinister; a gleam shone on his canines, accentuating his wolf-like grin.

"Ouch, I wouldn't have put that fine of a point on it," said Paul.

Bryce backed his chair away from Paul's invasion of his personal space and said, "I'm here, and you're there," pointing his right index finger like a gloved Dr. Seuss character, first at Paul and then back to himself, "because I am John's nephew. You are nothing more than a pretender."

The light dawned. Blue blood, nothing Paul could do about that. He could curse his lot in life, but where would it get him? Scratching and clawing and conning his way up had at least gotten him this far, sitting with President John William's right hand man, his own kin no less. It wasn't over for Paul yet.

So the Kinji plan failed, who cares? He'd gotten away with it, no harm done. And now he was in William's camp. Did it matter to him which President he was barnacling himself to? Tuh-may-toe, tuh-mah-toe. He reassessed his situation in milliseconds and said, with a condescending tone, "I see things clearly now."

Bryce reddened and his jaw clenched with unmistakable anger. "He doesn't partner with me because I'm family. I'm good for it."

Paul smiled, patronizing him now. My, how this felt good. Bryce was easily played. For all of his bravado, Bryce was nothing more than a punk kid with ego issues. This would be easier than he thought to extract information. "Oh really? You don't really know anything, do you? You told me that's all I need to know because you don't know it yourself." Paul folded his arms across his chest, sat there grinning like the Cheshire Cat, and waited for Bryce to take the bait.

Bryce leaned forward, his eyes narrowed into angry slits. "The e-mail was sent before the Big War, and was forwarded to FBI. We knew, we knew about the attacks before they happened."

Paul struggled to maintain a strong poker face. He was blown away by this, it was much bigger than what he expected to hear; although he had no clue what to expect, he didn't expect this. Wow. Mind blowing. So we knew. Why didn't we stop it? We *couldn't* stop it? Or we *wouldn't* stop it? Aloud he said, "You've got me. That's big stuff. Okay, you're a bona fide insider, not just the nephew."

Bryce relaxed his posture and smiled easily, baring no teeth. "No more questions. Now I tell you what to do, and you do it."

"Got it. What do you want me to do? Find out who sent this e-mail? Or who it was sent to?"

"No, we already know both. The sender is an Iranian woman, the receiver is her American friend. The American friend has another friend we've been watching. She could be a problem."

"You want me to follow her? Keep an eye on her?"

Bryce grinned with his lips curled back, his wolf smile back in full wattage. "No, we want you to kill her."

"What? Seriously? I'm not a hit man." Paul was too stunned to think of a way out of this slippery hole he was falling into, but he knew he couldn't kill someone, especially a woman!

"We need her taken out."

"Come on, she's talked to people. I can't kill everyone who knows about the e-mail," Paul protested.

"Don't worry about that. I will threaten everyone she's told. When she's dead, they'll know I mean business."

"How do you know who she's told? And why not kill her yourself?"

"I've been following her for a while, and have her place bugged. She keeps to herself. She's told her husband, that's it. Other than him, there's the friend who forwarded the email, and her husband. Three people left after she's gone. And if they act squirrely, we'll kill them too before they can talk to anyone else."

"Why trust them at all? Kill them now. Or is the body count of innocent people getting too high?"

"Get off your high horse -- you're scum. If you weren't, we wouldn't have tapped you for this."

"And if I don't do it?"

"I'll find someone else who will. You'll go to prison for the Kinji blackmail. And while in prison…"

"I'll have an accident?"

"You catch on fast. So we have a deal?"

"What choice do I have?" asked Paul weakly. Again he was bested… and this time he couldn't con his way back into the power seat.

10

"Clyde, I'm in trouble," Paul began. The brothers were in their parents' kitchen again. Clyde was frying bacon and making coffee while Paul leaned heavily on the table, standing over it with both arms locked at the elbows, hands planted on the tablecloth with fingers outstretched. His head was hanging low, his boyish locks falling forward. Clyde thought he looked about twelve. Bailing him out of trouble had been as routine then as it was now. "Did you hear me, Clyde?"

"I heard you. I knew you were in trouble the moment you walked in the door. I told you not to do that Kinji thing. She's smart and a woman, two reasons why she's not worth it."

"No, it's not her. John Williams is blackmailing me. He found out what I was doing."

"What? How did he know?" Paul had Clyde's full attention now.

"He has a bug in Kinji's office. He knew everything, and he had me in his cross hairs."

"What does he want with you?" Clyde felt a familiar stirring within him. It was the same force that had led him to despicable acts in the past; all to protect his little brother… or, maybe, it was beyond that. It was a hunger, a craving, and his protective nature was an excuse? Possibly, but why then did he not act on these urges unless Paul was in trouble? No, this was about protecting family. Clyde was not a psycho, of that he was sure.

"He wants me to kill somebody."

"He what?" Clyde laughed, thinking Paul was making a clever joke. He had him going, what a corker that brother of his. Clyde laughed until his belly shook. Only when he stopped to take a breath did he notice that Paul wasn't laughing with him. Paul was still frozen in his stance over the table, arms holding his body up, head bent; a beaten man, a scared man, a fugitive. Clyde sank into a kitchen chair, the bacon left to grow cold on the counter.

"He sent his nephew to give me the message. If I don't kill Serena Wilcox, he'll have me put in prison and then they'll have me killed in there, in prison."

"Serena who?"

"She's a former private detective. She's one of ours, Clyde."

"What do you mean, one of ours? Our Off Grid people?"

"Yes. She has three kids, husband. We set them up in Goodhue. We gave them the new name of Meadows. Before that they were the Browns, no, the Bridges."

"Okay, yeah, I think I know who you're talking about. Why do they want her dead? What does she know?"

"She knows something big, Clyde. I can't believe it. The government knew about the attacks before they happened. She has proof, e-mail proof sent from an Iranian woman."

"Our government?"

"Yes, our own. We knew and didn't do anything."

Clyde sucked air between his teeth and then exhaled slowly with a prolonged wispy whistle. "Paul, they were never after you. They were following *her*. We made it easy for them. They've been watching us all along. They know me too, don't they?"

"Yes, they know you. They know about your computer lab, and they're calling Off Grid a cult."

"It is a cult. Sort of, anyway. Just a big sham, and I suppose they know that too, don't they?"

"They know all about us, they think we're buffoons. When I showed up at the tarmac, they had to be laughing their asses off."

"We know nothing about them. That will change."

Paul finally freed himself from his vigil at the table and sat in the chair across from his brother. He stared at his empty plate, and as if Clyde could read his thoughts, bacon suddenly appeared on it. He ate three strips, one after the other, and then spoke, "Clyde, this is bigger than my problems in the past. We're talking about killing a person."

Clyde raised his eyebrows and snorted. "And what makes you think I haven't done that for you before?"

Paul stared at Clyde. He knew it was no joke. The repressed memory of what John Williams said to him came back. *My people tell me that your only childhood connection to Kinji is a babysitter in common. A Mrs. Mason, who we'd have talked to, but she's deceased. Died from a freak accident in the home.*

Clyde cleared the plates and loaded the dishwasher. He let the information settle, knowing that Paul would accept the situation and would move on if given enough time to digest it, process it. He was Clyde, the big protective brother. He only did what needed to be done. If Paul didn't see that now, he would come around to it eventually, of that Clyde was certain.

"Mrs. Mason?" Paul croaked. He tried to don his poker face, but he couldn't con a con, especially the better of the two of them.

"Don't look so shocked, Paul. The old bat had it coming. She did it to herself. No one messes with my brother."

"Is she the only one?" *Please, please let her be the only one*, thought Paul.

Clyde smiled gently, placating a child. "If that's what you need to hear, we'll leave it at that. Let's move on. We have a serious situation on our hands."

Paul's self-preservation instincts kicked in and this time he was successful at putting on his best poker face. Never show your true feelings to a sociopath, especially if he is also your brother. As Paul's life was crashing down on him, he still felt that Clyde was his best, and only, option. "What do we do?"

"Well, we don't kill her."

"We don't?" Paul was careful not to let relief creep into his voice.

"No, we let *him* do it."

"Him?"

"John Williams. We'll bring the girl to the President himself."

"What? Why would we do this? Wouldn't he have us all killed? And how would we even get close enough to him? I only got close because he nabbed me. And before that, they must have let me get close, because they knew who I was, and they were following me. They won't let me near them if they don't want me there."

"We go through his nephew. We get the nephew, then he'll want to see us. He gets the nephew and the girl. Lets us go. That's the deal. We won't kill her, that's what they want us to do."

"Yes, I know that's what they want. I don't get what you are saying. Even if we manage to get both of them, and get them to the President, and go as far as making the deal, wouldn't they kill us after they got what they wanted?"

"Paul, they want to frame you for the murder. They get rid of both of you that way. They'll kill you, you know. But if you refuse to kill her, and they have to go another way, you have leverage."

"They'll just kill me anyway, remember? If not on the spot, they'll get me for the blackmail attempt and kill me in prison."

"No, they won't. You will have too much information on them, with the proof uploaded to our computer lab. Our kid hackers are very good, Paul. They can get them at their own game. They'll have everything recorded in the cloud, so to speak, including the e-mail they sent you – you still have it right? Why did they get sloppy about that, did they think we wouldn't forward it, save it, copy it?"

"I don't know, maybe they made a mistake. The nephew is cocky. He might be going off the rule book."

"They won't be able to get their fingers on all the recordings, they'll be digitally floating everywhere and anywhere, all timed to be released should something happen to you."

"Recordings? All I have is the e-mail."

"I'm talking about what we will have, what the kids will get for us. They'll love this project. I'll tell them they'll get college credit for it."

"So they get the girl, we get left alone. Why should we give them the girl at all? I don't like getting a woman killed, a mother with three kids."

"It's the fastest way out of this. They want you because of her. Sever that connection."

"Then we leave the country?"

"They can find us anywhere, even in the remotest of African villages. But it's unnecessary to hide. What will keep us safe is our insurance policy. We blackmail them, we stay safe."

"Blackmail didn't work out so well for me, remember?"

"That's because you didn't have me running the show. Don't worry, little brother, I've got your back. This will work. I'll talk to my pimply faced hackers and get them on it. They'll have you all suited up to record everything."

"What if they check for bugs?"

Clyde winked. "You haven't met Nicholas, my best – he's the new kid. That boy is a magician. He'll put a bug in play that not even you will know is there."

"They'll scan."

"Not an issue. He has a remote controlled bug; that looks like an actual bug. He can fly it remotely, very remotely. He programs the thing and it can transmit from wherever it is, from long range too. We can bring it with us; release it before meeting their people. It's so small it's nearly invisible to the naked eye, and it's fast."

"I don't know, it's the President's security detail, they probably have ways."

"The bug is fast, it'll zip right by them. You'll see, it will work." Clyde rubbed his hands together gleefully. At heart, he was a computer nerd too, but he was born too late to take to computers as naturally as the younger generation. He lived vicariously through his dream team of young geniuses.

Paul shook his head in amazement. "Where did you get these kids anyway? How do you get them to do what you want? They aren't on payroll."

"Funny how building a state of the art lab can reel them in. Free lab time is enough, and I do pay them a little something out of my pocket. If I bring in pizza, they're happy to stay all night long."

"I never knew how you got them there. I never knew a lot of things," said Paul.

"You aren't still hung up on old Mrs. Mason, are you? I only do what's necessary. You trust me, don't you Paulie?"

"Yes, I trust you Clyde."

"Then we'll get the kids to set us up with everything we need, and find the nephew and the girl for us. I'll get the nephew. You get Serena-whatsherface. I'm sure you can talk her into coming to our place. She knows you."

11

Serena belted herself into the passenger's seat. "Where are we going?"

"I was hoping you'd tell me," said Tom.

"We can't go home if Bryce, or Otto – let's call him Bryce – knows where we live."

"He seems able to find us anywhere. Let's go home. We can secure the house."

"What do you mean by 'secure the house'?"

"What do you think I use to shoot at coyotes and raccoons?"

"You wouldn't really shoot Bryce, would you?"

"Sure I would, if it's him or you."

"You're going to walk around all the time holding a gun?"

"I can booby-trap the house."

"How?"

"I can do it."

"Home does sound good. Our own bed, our coffee, our food."

"I want to go home," chimed in all three kids from the back. Ipod and tablet earbuds were temporarily removed. Unplugging happened when their parents said something they wanted to hear.

Home was agreed upon and they drove the six hours back from Deer River, making a stop at the McDonald's in Cannon Falls. After a trip to the restrooms, the Meadows family wandered back to the parking lot, carrying drinks and bags of food. They stopped short when approached by a familiar figure.

"Hey, Meadows-es!" Paul rang out cheerfully. "Long time no see. Haven't seen you around seminar lately." He didn't wait for a reply, but clapped his hand on Tom's shoulder. "How's the place in Goodhue working out?"

"It was great, until people found us," said Tom.

Paul didn't need to feign surprise, because he *was* surprised to hear that they were already aware of discovery. *Who was after them? Was Paul their second choice? Or had Bryce laid down the foundation for Paul to close the deal on?* It was infuriating to be out of the loop. However, he bounced back quickly, and feeling a grin not unlike the Grinch's spreading over his face, he came up with a plan. It was too, too easy. "Wow, we can't have you in a dangerous situation. Follow me back to my place. We can talk there and figure out a plan to relocate you." Whatever possessed him to strike up a spontaneous conversation in a "chance meeting" location had produced brilliant results. This was most unexpected, especially since he hadn't really thought this through ahead of time. He hadn't worked up how to get Serena. He'd simply gotten lucky.

"Oh, that would be perfect," said Serena. "Thank you."

As Paul headed back to his own vehicle he reflected on his good fortune and dug into his pocket for his phone. He had only one number programmed, Clyde's. He dialed it now. Clyde picked up after the first bar of the "Everybody Wants to Rule the World" ringtone he'd assigned to Paul's number.

"You rang?"

"I got them. The Meadows family will be at our place in about fifteen minutes."

"The whole clan, not just the girl?"

"Serena."

"Doesn't matter, I'll deal with the collateral damage."

"Collateral damage? What?"

"Put them in the kitchen, give them some coffee, milk for the kids. There's a bag of chips in the pantry. Keep them happy and talking. Stall. I'm thirty miles out."

"Did you get your job done?"

"Where do you think I've been?"

"So you've got Bryce with you?"

"He's in the trunk."

"In the trunk!"

"He's not dead, you moron! I shoved him in there to put the fear of God in him."

"I don't think you know anything about God."

"And you do?"

"You threw me with the trunk thing. Sorry."

"He's cramped in there, not much air to breathe. He'll be humble by the time I get him home. Humble and ready to chat."

"I should have known that you knew what you were doing, sorry I doubted you," Paul said, his voice dripping with contrition. *Hold on, Paul, don't let him know you're unnerved*, he scolded himself.

"Apology accepted. See you in a few minutes. Show time!" Clyde tossed his phone onto the empty passenger's seat beside him, forgetting to disconnect the call.

Paul began to disconnect from his end, but hesitated when he heard noise. *He forgot to end the call.* Paul could hear clicking sounds and then dialogue:

> An unknown female voice: "Why didn't you write me? Why? It wasn't over for me, I waited for you for seven years. But now it's too late."
>
> An unknown male voice, with Clyde's voice saying the same words along with him: "I wrote you 365 letters. I wrote you every day for a year."
>
> The same female voice again: "You wrote me?"
>
> Male, again with Clyde: "Yes... it wasn't over, it still isn't over."

What IS this? I recognize this. Paul scratched his brain trying to come up with it. *I've got it! This is from "The Notebook". My deranged brother is playing audio tracks from "The Notebook" and is quoting it from memory as it plays.* Paul disconnected the call before he could hear any more.

The Meadows following behind Paul noticed that he was on the phone. "I wonder who he's talking to, maybe he's setting something new up for us already," said Serena.

"Maybe. Good thing we ran into him, huh?"

"That was strange though, don't you think? We've never run into him randomly before. What are the odds of a chance meeting, really?"

"Providence?"

"Or?"

"Not? You think he was following us? Why would he do that? Are you sure you aren't paranoid?"

"I don't know, seems like a big coincidence to me. We know for sure that Bryce was following us, and then Paul just happens to show up where we are. What if they are working together?"

"It would explain why our safe house isn't safe."

"I think we should assume we can't trust anybody at this point."

"Better safe than sorry?"

"So what do we do?"

Tom slowed down, letting a car slip between him and Paul. "I don't know."

"There's not much traffic on these roads, it's not like you can get lost in the crowd. You won't even have another traffic light between here and there."

"I have a gun with me."

"You *what*?"

"I was in the Army, I'm not Barney Fife."

"So it's loaded then?"

"That's how it works."

"What if the kids had gotten it out?"

"Our kids wouldn't touch a gun."

"We wouldn't," came from the backseat.

"Don't ever, ever touch a gun," said Serena, turning around in her seat to address the kids. "Maybe we should have them stay in the car."

"Good idea. You guys stay in the car."

"One problem, how are you going to bring that in there? It's a hunting rifle, not like you can hide it."

"Not the rifle. I bought a handgun." He lifted up his shirt to expose the handle.

Serena's jaw dropped and she gasped in a dramatic how-dare-you exclamation. "A handgun!"

"We're here. Kids, stay in the car. Serena, stay in the car." Tom stopped the vehicle and quickly stepped out.

"No, I'm going in too. Kids, stay in the car. Don't open the door for anybody but us." Serena got out of the car and followed her husband onto the front walk where Paul was standing, waiting.

"The kids are welcome to come in, too," said Paul, smiling like a good host.

"They're doing their own thing, they'll be fine while we talk," Serena said, while walking toward the front door. Both she and Tom looked expectantly at Paul to open the door.

Paul looked back at their vehicle and could see the kids' heads bent over books and handheld gadgets. Satisfied that there was no reason to bring the kids into this, and hoping that Clyde would see it the same way, he let Serena and Tom into the house. He ushered the pair into the kitchen and offered them coffee.

"No thank you," said Serena. Even though coffee did sound good, she didn't want anything from this man.

"I'll take a cup," said Tom.

Serena glared at him. Tom met that glare and raised one eyebrow that said, "Why not?"

Paul studied the coffee maker, not sure how to proceed. Clyde always made the coffee. This wasn't rocket science, he told himself. He found the filter basket, put a fresh filter in, and took a guess on how much coffee to put in. He filled the back with water and turned the switch. *That was easy, why did I wait for Clyde all those times I wanted coffee?*

As the coffee machine gargled and spit its brew Paul gathered up the sugar bowl and two mugs. He set them on the table, glancing briefly at his captives. He considered himself to be pretty good at reading people, and these two were completely clueless. He would have no problem keeping them here until Clyde returned.

Serena studied Paul as he bustled about the kitchen. She considered herself to be pretty good at reading people, and she could tell that he was definitely involved. What his involvement was, she didn't know, but he was not to be trusted. She made eye contact with Tom, using their been-married-for-a-long-time silent language to say, "You might need that gun." Then she made the most of Paul having his back turned to them by examining everything around her.

She noticed a roster of Off Grid Ghost members. If Paul left the room she planned to snoop through it. Maybe Bryce, or Otto, was in the roster. Of course, someone going by two different names could easily invent a third name. The roster was probably useless. She looked around the room for another clue. Something, anything, to give her an idea of what Paul was up to.

She wondered whose taste was reflected in the kitchen. A collection of country roosters including a rooster salt and pepper shaker, a rooster cookie jar, and a rooster planter? Really? Whose kitchen was this? Did Paul have a significant other? She didn't think so. Her eyes rested on the framed photos on the wall. Ah-ha! Pictures of three little boys, all in plaid suits too large for them. Family picture taken later, with two of the boys, now older, one whose face was clearly Paul's. So this was his parents' house.

Finding nothing else of interest in the kitchen, Serena asked where the bathroom was.

Paul, suspecting her motives not at all, directed her down the hall and to the right. Serena went promptly down the hall and to the left, where the door to the office was open. A netbook was on a small table with the lid open. Serena looked over her shoulder – she couldn't see the kitchen from where she was. She ventured in. What she saw on the screen caused her to temporarily stop breathing:

>>My Karyn,

I write you heavy heart. You must know for it is my hope you can go safe.

Iran make fools of everyone. For years they lie about nuclear missiles. Nuclear Nonproliferation Treaty is nothing, they spit upon it as easily as they spit on you, dear Karyn.

They threaten who wants make peace with Israel. Pro-West Arab Saudi Arabia and Egypt see Iran success nuclear, but have no fight. Iran pressure Lebanon, Syria, the Palestinians, and the Iraqis. Many thousands, hundred thousands, join radical Islamist. "Death to America!" on Iranian street for too many year. No one stop Iran. Now they make nuclear weapons in short period. They make stockpiles uranium for nuclear device in few months—make nuclear weapons in short period. They make centrifuges to pipe work. They learn technology when they talk to UN, many lies. Now they can do bomb. They will do this. It will be soon. I hear it from husband. You trust me to know truth. I tell you day and time. I tell you where missiles strike. You go safe.

Your Farideh>>

12

President Ann Kinji didn't feel presidential at the moment. She hadn't felt presidential since she'd seen the picture of her best friend and husband with a little girl who was most certainly his daughter. She had been wrestling with indecision about how to respond for three sleepless days and nights. Between the anxiety and the sleep deprivation, her briefings with staff, ambassadors, governors, military heads, and the UN were impossible: her mind was drifting away, consumed with thoughts of a child she didn't know about, a child she wished was her own, but nonetheless was living proof that her marriage was over, and apparently had been for years.

She had to nip this thing in the bud before she put the divided nation at risk. Worst of all, she could not hold her own in the shared space with John Williams. That man chilled her to the bone as it was, and if she was off her game she would never be able to stand up against his rhetoric, conspiracies, and bigotry. He was not just a harmless blowhard. He was an ignoramus with power. And if Ann didn't get her act together, she'd be giving him free reign over the entire nation as a whole. So, it was with that attitude that she decided to confront her husband with the truth, all the while knowing it would end her marriage.

But her marriage was already over, she scolded herself. How could she stay with a man who not only cheated, but kept a separate life that involved a child? Maybe even an entire family! *Enough! Go to him, talk. Get this over with. Pull yourself together. You gave up a right to drama in your personal life: You are the President!* Having steeled herself up for the devastation to follow, she entered the great room where Ted was lounging, playing Angry Birds on his iPad. She had gotten him hooked on that silly game and now it felt absurd to end her marriage while talking over the noise of cartoon birds exploding. She stood two feet in front of him, silently waiting. He turned off the iPad.

"Ann, something wrong?" Ted examined her face. Ann said nothing, stayed with her feet rooted into the carpeting. He set down the iPad and stood up, annoying the couple's beloved long-haired cat Greta who had been sleeping with her head on his lap. He walked over to give her a hug but she pushed him away. Greta left the room in a hurry. Startled, he said, "Did *I* do something wrong?"

"Someone is trying to blackmail me with a picture of you with your daughter."

"My *what*?" Ted blinked.

His look of surprise looked genuine. Could it be possible this was a mistake? "Your daughter. The little girl in the picture looks too much like you for me to dismiss the claim as not credible."

"Ann, I'm so sorry you are going through this, but honey, I do not have a daughter. I'm afraid you've been fooled by a Photoshop expert. They probably found a picture of a little girl bearing a resemblance to me and Photoshopped her in, to look like we are in the same shot together."

"I didn't think of that. I want to believe you."

"We can find an expert of our own who can tell us if the picture has been altered, and who can even find the little girl in the picture, find out who she is."

"I need to clear this up, Ted. It's one time I can't take you on your word alone. I'm sorry, but I have to know factually, beyond a shadow of a doubt. You are my world, my best friend. I need to know that I'm not a fool, that I'm not blinded by what I want to believe." Ann's eyes welled up and she forced herself not to lose control.

"I understand, but you'll see. I have never cheated on you, and never will. Tell me more about the picture."

"There was a time stamp on it. It was taken five years ago, so the girl is probably around ten years old now."

"Five years ago? And I had hair, the way it looks now? Ann, that was before I had chemotherapy. You have your proof right there!"

Ann's eyes widened as the light dawned. How could she have missed that? Ted's cancer scare had brought them a year of chemo treatments and fear like no other. At the end of that year Ted was cancer free, but watching his blood count closely for the rest of his life; and he'd also lost all of his hair, which only sparsely grew back. His current sporty "news-anchor-man" do had been created with expensive plugs and faux hair artistry. Prior to his cancer treatments Ted had thicker hair, with a noticeable cowlick. Anyone who knew Ted would instantly recognize his "old" hair. That picture definitely showed off his new hair. She had missed it. She felt wretched.

Ted opened his arms wide. "Come on, bring yourself in." He embraced his wife with all the warmth and strength he could deliver. "I'd never betray you, Ann. We need to find the people responsible for hurting you."

"I'm sorry I ever doubted you." Ann sobbed tears of relief, dampening her husband's shirt with her tears. Much more of this and her nose would be dripping on him too. "How could I have missed the hair?"

Ted gently pushed her away. "Hey, look at me! You are the President! You have the toughest job in the world. I don't think there's room left in that big brain of yours to deal with this. Don't beat yourself up. I'm over it already. You over it? Because I am. Don't let them hurt you or take your power for a second longer. Fight, honey, don't let them win." He drew her back into his chest for another hug.

"I love you," Ann bawled. She let it all hang out this time, her body racked with all-out crying, her nose and eyes running together into one messy puddle. All the stress of the Office was unloading like a rain shower, soaking the First Gentleman's shirt.

Ted held her for several long minutes before he abruptly released her. "Ann, you have to pull yourself together. Go clean up. You have a Vid Red." He jerked his head in the direction of the large flat screen on the wall. A red indicator light was flashing and an electronic warning tone was emitting, easily heard now that Ann had stopped wailing.

Ann was instantly composed, but looked a sight with her red splotchy puffy face and obvious need for a Kleenex. "Turn off the return video feed. Audio only from my end." She dashed to the bathroom to blow her nose and splash water on her face. By the time she returned to the room, the Vid was live.

"I'm here, Breyana. Why are you contacting me with a Vid Red? I expected to see a General's face, not yours."

"Your security detail talked to me. They thought I should do a Vid Red."

"They are there with you?"

"Yes, Madam President," called a voice in the background.

"Step up where I can see you. Tell me what's going on."

"Madam President, we have information about the man you asked us to track."

"Gentlemen, this feed is for national security risks only. Paul is a personal security risk, I made that clear."

"With all due respect, Madam President, we understand the definition of a Vid Red."

"Are you telling me that this man is a national security risk? Even so, a Vid Red means it requires my immediate attention."

"Yes, Madam President. Understood."

Ann exchanged a baffled look with Ted. What on Earth? "You have my attention."

"We have been monitoring his Internet activity. He got an e-mail you need to see."

"Send it through the feed, all windows are open."

Seconds later, this text filled the screen:

>>My Karyn,

I write you heavy heart. You must know for it is my hope you can go safe.

Iran make fools of everyone. For years they lie about nuclear missiles. Nuclear Nonproliferation Treaty is nothing, they spit upon it as easily as they spit on you, dear Karyn.

They threaten who wants make peace with Israel. Pro-West Arab Saudi Arabia and Egypt see Iran success nuclear, but have no fight. Iran pressure Lebanon, Syria, the Palestinians, and the Iraqis. Many thousands, hundred thousands, join radical Islamist. "Death to America!" on Iranian street for too many year. No one stop Iran. Now they make nuclear weapons in short period. They make stockpiles uranium for nuclear device in few months—make nuclear weapons in short period. They make centrifuges to pipe work. They learn technology when they talk to UN, many lies. Now they can do bomb. They will do this. It will be soon. I hear it from husband. You trust me to know truth. I tell you day and time. I tell you where missiles strike. You go safe.

Your Farideh <<

Ann pointed her finger in the air, swiping the text window off to the right. She stared at the young security officer's face that filled the screen. "What am I looking at? Who forwarded that to him, when, why?"

"The date of the original transmission is the concern."

"I'm sorry, I am not getting any of this. What does Paul have to do with Iran? I am not following this email content."

"The e-mail was originally sent before the Big War, Madam President."

Ann held her hand to her mouth. She remained speechless for several seconds. Ted came up behind her and wrapped his arms around her waist. He whispered in her ear, "You can do this." Then he let his arm slide down to her hand, squeezed her hand, and left her alone to concentrate. She waved at his disappearing back. She turned her attention to the feed. "Who sent this to Paul?"

"Bryce."

"*The* Bryce? John William's Bryce? Be careful now."

"Yes, Madam President."

"I assume you tracked the origin of this e-mail all the way back to the source?"

"Yes, we have. Correct."

"And what did you find?"

"The e-mail has been transmitted many times, Madam President."

"Did it ever reach John Williams' office."

"Yes, Madam President."

"Did it ever reach the President of the United States while he was still in office, prior to the Big War?"

"Yes, Madam President."

13

Bryce was terribly uncomfortable crunched up in the trunk of Clyde's car. His long lean frame was contorted over a now-full bladder. His mind raced until he hit upon something a former girlfriend once babbled about. What was it she'd said? She saw it on Oprah, or got it in a forwarded e-mail, something like that. It was about if you are ever stuffed into a trunk of a car, what to do. Ah! He remembered. Kick out the taillight. Someone would notice. Hopefully the police.

Bryce kicked and kicked. He had no idea if he was anywhere close to the taillight area, but his foot was hitting on something. He struck out again and again until his heel popped some kind of latch. What was that? Had he popped open the trunk? Yes, the road noise and the rush of air confirmed it. He was free!

He was not bound, gagged, or restrained in any way. Clyde had simply pushed him into the trunk, held him down, and slammed the lid over him. Nothing hurt really, except for his pride. All he needed to do now was climb up and jump out, and hope he could get far enough away before Clyde noticed the trunk lid was open. His opportunity for escape came right away, when Clyde slowed for a four-way stop.

Bryce didn't wait for the car to stop. He hoisted himself up onto his knees, then, as quickly as he could, he climbed out of the trunk and jumped onto the road. He didn't look behind him, but ran on nearly-numb legs, hoping the adrenaline would give him the strength and speed he needed to slip away before Clyde could get to him.

Clyde, confident that Bryce wouldn't be able to get out of the trunk, was unaware of his escape. Not a big fan of defensive driving, Clyde didn't make much use of mirrors or overall attentiveness. His driving time was his down time for personal recreation. He was currently snacking from a new bag of Peanut Butter Bugles while quoting along with "The Notebook". He didn't notice the trunk was open until he parked the car in the garage.

"What's that?" asked Tom.

Paul froze. He could hear Clyde slamming around in the garage, cursing, throwing things. "That would be my brother in a foul mood. I better go see what's going on." As he headed out to the garage, using the door located in the back of the kitchen, Serena returned to the kitchen.

With Paul gone, she could speak freely, but she whispered to be safe: "Tom, he has the e-mail, the one from Karen's friend in Iran."

"The kids are in the car."

"I know, we have to get them out of here."

Tom rose to leave just as Paul and Clyde came in. Clyde snarled, "Where do you think *you're* going?"

"Clyde, calm down, he just finished his coffee. I haven't talked with him yet…" Paul placed himself between Tom and his brother.

Clyde pushed Paul out of the way and grabbed Tom's arm. He pulled him back into the chair. "Toss me some duct tape. It's in the junk drawer."

"I don't think this is—"

"Necessary? Necessary Paul? That's what you were going to say? Well I didn't restrain that idiot Bryce and now he's gone. Won't make that mistake twice. Give me the tape!"

Paul rooted around in the drawer, found the tape, and handed it to Clyde. "There's not much left."

Clyde secured Tom to the chair by wrapping the tape around Tom's middle and the back of the chair, over and over again until the tape was almost gone. He gave Paul the rest of the roll. "Tape his ankles to the chair legs. I'm getting more tape."

As soon as Clyde left the room and Paul was bent over, working on the ankle taping, Serena leaned close to Tom. "Hang in there honey, it will be ok," she said. She tried to give him a meaningful glance but his eyes reflected puzzlement. What was his wife up to? Whatever the secret code was, he didn't get it.

Paul looked up. "Sit down, Serena. You're going to be next."

"I guessed as much. I want to put my chair next to Tom's." She slid her chair near him.

"No, put it back. I don't want you to try to get him out." Paul bent over to work on the second ankle.

"Okay, I'll put it back," she said, and made sliding noises with her chair while slipping her hand under Tom's waistband. Fortunately Clyde's duct tape was above his belly button, nowhere near the handle of the gun. The gun slid out easily. and before she knew it, she was holding a gun, a real loaded gun. If she had time to digest that information she would have been intimidated, but she was reacting on auto-pilot now, feeling nothing, just doing what she needed to do.

Serena held the gun to Paul's head. He looked up at her from his kneeling position near Tom's legs. His eyes registered surprise, but surprise was quickly replaced by mirth. He snickered. "You wouldn't shoot me."

Serena cocked the gun. "I'm Momma Bear and my babies are threatened. You have no idea."

Clyde entered the kitchen from behind Serena, sized up the situation and grabbed a large cast iron skillet. Tom saw him and yelled "Look out!"

Serena whirled around, firing the gun without thinking twice. The bullet hit Clyde's arm. He dropped the skillet. Serena dropped the gun.

Then they both started screaming. Clyde sounded like a wounded animal, Serena hit an octave she normally reserved for when she saw a mouse. The two screamed and screamed, the guttural strangled scream conjoined with the shrill siren scream. The combination shook up the kids in the car.

Carrie called 911. So did a couple of the neighbors. No one knew what was going on, but whatever it was, it sounded like a bloodbath, and then suddenly it was quiet. They thought they heard a gunshot, but weren't sure. The kids were terrified but did not get out of the car. The neighbors locked their doors and stayed away from the windows. Everyone waited for the police to arrive. As they waited, the foursome inside the house took stock of the situation.

Serena broke the silence. She also picked the gun up from the floor and waved it at Paul. "Go stand next to your brother."

Paul didn't move. He looked at her, stunned.

"Now! Go, go! Or I'll shoot you too."

Paul did as she wanted. He moved close to Clyde and stared at his brother's arm. The wound did not look life threatening, but it did look ugly, and painful. Clyde examined it scornfully.

"What's your plan, lady? I bet you don't know what to do now that you've shot me," said Clyde. He spat into the sink from his position a couple feet away. "Do you even know why we have you? We weren't the ones who were going to kill you. They won't care if you've shot me or not. They want me dead too."

Serena looked at Tom. "Paul, I want you to let my husband out. And then he is going to drive our kids somewhere safe."

"I'm not leaving you here, Serena!" said Tom.

"Then let's make this fast so I can go too. Paul, get that tape off of him. Start talking. What did you want with us? Why do you have that e-mail from Iran? How do you know Bryce?" Serena held the gun with both hands. She was struggling to hold her arms steady. She also realized that Paul was not in her line of fire anymore. "Clyde, go stand next to Paul. Go!"

Clyde moved a few steps in that direction.

"Okay, good enough, stay there, don't move." Serena adjusted her stance so that both men were covered by the gun.

Paul took his time cutting the duct tape, stalling. The sooner he freed Tom, the sooner Tom could take over. If there was a reason to shoot, he didn't think Tom would stop at a flesh wound. "I have the e-mail because Bryce sent it to me. He works for President Williams. Williams knew about everything before the Big War.

There's a cover up. They want to get rid of anyone who knows about it. You're the target. So am I, and Clyde. We were planning to help you. You shot the wrong guy."

"I don't trust you. What aren't you telling me?" Serena asked, looking from one man to the another.

"What he's not saying is that we planned to give you to Williams to save our own skin. You'd have done the same," said Clyde.

"What about Bryce?" asked Tom. He flexed his ankles, the first part of him that Paul had freed. Paul worked on the duct tape girdle next.

"Bryce escaped. I had him in the trunk. He got out. It's just down to you now," said Clyde.

Paul added, "Now we have nothing. With him gone and you with the gun, we have no leverage. You might as well shoot us -- it would be better than whatever they'll do to me after they put me in prison."

"Would they have killed you anyway, even if you had me and Bryce?" asked Serena.

"We have that e-mail. I've sent it to several safe places," said Clyde. "And we had a plan to record our meeting with them. We'd have enough incriminating evidence to keep us alive. It would have worked. It still can if you play along."

"No thanks. I don't need your plan. You have enough proof with the e-mail. All I have to do is tell the FBI," said Serena.

"That didn't help your friend much, did it?" said Paul. "What protection do you expect from them? William's team found you even when you joined Off Ghost. We're better than witness protection. If we couldn't hide you, they can't."

"I'll go to the top," said Serena.

"He *is* the top," said Clyde.

"You're forgetting about President Kinji. She has just as much power as Williams," said Serena.

"Theoretically," said Clyde with contempt.

"The police are here," said Tom.

"What are you going to do? Press charges? You'll kill us all. William's people will find us," said Paul.

"The police are already at the door," said Serena.

14

Bryce chuckled to himself. What an idiot Clyde was. He was as stupid as he was ugly. Not only did he not restrain Bryce, but he also didn't think to strip him of his cell phone, which had been on the entire time. Bryce used it now to call his security detail. They could pick him up, no problem. There was a GPS tracker on the phone, which was a good thing since Bryce had no idea where he was, just some country road in the boonies, they all looked the same after a while. He swatted at a deer fly. The sooner he got back to the Windy City the better.

The sound of multiple cars speeding down a nearby gravel road caught his attention. Wow, that was fast. How did they find him already? They must have sent local law enforcement to pick him up. No matter, just as well. He needed a restroom and after that some water, and some food. A good night's sleep sounded good too.

The cars reached him, three government-issue sedans total. It sure looked like secret service detail. But how did they reach him so fast? It had only been about five minutes. Four car doors opened simultaneously: one hulk of a man each from two of the vehicles, and two bureaucratic looking individuals, one male and one female, from the third vehicle.

"Hey guys, how did you get here so fast?" Bryce smiled full wattage, his social smile, not a trace of wolf. He was taken aback when no one responded. One of the beefy men yanked his right arm, another grabbed his left. They steered him toward the nearest sedan. "Hey! What's going on?" Bryce protested. No one answered. "You're taking me to the President? You are, right?"

"Yes, she's waiting for you," said the female bureaucrat.

"She?" Bryce hoped he had heard wrong.

"President Kinji. She's waiting for you. Get in the car."

The convoy, with Bryce pouting in the backseat of one of the sedans, made its way to its next pick-up, about four miles away. Their tires crunched on a long gravel road and then rolled to a stop. Doors opened and shut. The driver of the sedan carrying Bryce did not get out.

"Where are we?" asked Bryce.

The driver looked at Bryce through the mirror but said nothing.

"What is this place?" he tried again.

Still no answer.

"Hey! I know them! What is going on?" Bryce tapped on his window. "Open this up!"

The driver ignored Bryce. Bryce was forced to watch silently from his backseat point of view as four familiar figures were escorted to the other two vehicles. Clyde, his flesh wound bandaged and his arm in a sling, and Paul were led to the sedan behind the vehicle holding Bryce. Serena and Tom, stripped of his gun, which was bagged and tagged, were led to the sedan in front of him. Bryce couldn't hear what they were saying. Completely baffled, he tried to puzzle out what was happening.

Serena spoke to the female bureaucrat, Nancy. "Our kids are still in the car."

"No, they are already with us. They're fine," said Nancy.

"Where are they?" asked Tom.

"We're right here," called Carrie, leaning out the open door of the sleek government vehicle.

"Please get in," said Nancy, gesturing to the generous seating space that her children occupied. Nonetheless, five people made the backseat uncomfortable. No one dared to complain though. After the Meadows were settled in, Nancy shut the door to the backseat, walked to the front passenger's side door, and got in.

"You aren't the police. FBI?" asked Tom.

"No. We are President Kinji's detail," said Nancy.

Her partner Rick started the vehicle and pulled away, leading the convoy of three. "Where are we going?" asked Serena.

Nancy exchanged a look with Rick, who returned her question with a shrug. Nancy hesitated, but then answered Serena's question, "Chicago."

"Chicago!" Serena exclaimed.

"Isn't that a whole day's drive? I need to go to the restroom," said Carrie.

"Do you need to make a rest stop now?" asked Nancy.

"YES!" said the kids and Tom in unison.

"Why are we going to Chicago?" asked Serena.

"President Kinji wants to see you."

"We get to meet the President!" Carrie said. More quietly, addressed to her family, she said, "Had I known, I would have worn something else today."

"Why does she want to see us?" asked Samuel, who had been quiet during all of the excitement. All three kids had kept themselves nearly invisible, but they heard everything that happened within their earshot, and hung on every word. Earbuds or no, when something exciting was happening, they managed to listen.

Nancy shut down the conversation with a firm, "You'll have to ask her that. I am not authorized to brief you. We'll be stopping shortly for a quick restroom break." With that, she pressed the divider button. The Meadows were alone in the backseat, where they quickly took up chatting. The past few harrowing days had renewed their appreciation for each other and suddenly they all had so much to say.

It was far from happy family chatter in the sedan carrying the two brothers. Clyde was seething. "We need a plan," he hissed.

Paul recoiled from Clyde's breath. He couldn't quite define the stench. It was a revolting mix of garlic, coffee, and long-trapped odors from years of plaque build-up, Clyde's own special blend. "I don't know what we can do, Clyde. We might as well hope for the best. At least they aren't taking us to John. Kinji might have a heart and put us in witness relocation."

"Where they will find us and kill us, you know that. At their level, they can ferret out witnesses, protected or not."

"I don't see any solution. I also doubt we're having a private conversation right now."

Clyde snickered. "Of course we aren't, they're listening to everything we say."

"Then I don't know what you expect to plan."

"You're right, we might as well admit defeat," said Clyde. Then he slyly winked at Paul and said, "Just like when we were kids and we were losing at kickball against the Keller kids."

Paul nodded, aware of where Clyde was going with this, and hoping he remembered their secret language. "Yes, who could forget Groin Or Toe Injuries Too?"

Clyde smiled approvingly. Paul did remember: invent a sentence that, when taking the first letter of each word, spells a phrase. Paul had said, "Got it." Just like when they were kids. The code was easier to speak and comprehend with practice, and being brothers, they could practically read each other's minds anyway, so it was easier for them to follow than it would be for most people.

Clyde said, "How Are Children Kickball Enthusiasts? Really Stupid." He felt in his pocket for his cell phone. Yes, there it was, all charged up and everything. Yes, they would know he had used the phone, but it would take them awhile to puzzle out what he used it for. He sent a quick text to one of the kids on his team, the new kid, who wasn't listed on the roster yet. "Activate Clyde. Urgent." Clyde put his hand behind his back, feigning to massage a painful lower back, while discretely slipping his thumb under the waistband of his jeans until he could feel the elastic band of his briefs. Yes, it was still there: a tiny microphone. Obviously this could be problematic if Clyde had intestinal problems, but it was a good solution to the problem of: what if they forced him to strip down? He figured they were unlikely to make him take off his underwear. He knew Nick would have it up and running before they reached Kinji's office.

"Wacky Happy Youth," said Paul.

Clyde, struggling to come up with a word for each letter, stumbled through the next few sentences at an agonizingly slow pace: “People Let All Youth, Alone. Now Nobody, Just Opens Homes. Neighbors, All Get Annoyed -- Is Never Safe To, Ever Allow Children Home, Outside Their Homes. Everyone’s Reality.”

Paul traced the beginning letters on his hand until he could piece together what Clyde was saying: *Play Ann, John against each other.* He nodded, ending their tedious conversation. He stared at the divider wall between their seats and the ones occupied by the Muscle. Were they listening? Probably. Paul’s mind raced. Clyde’s plan was idealistic: he assumed they would be released, free to put the plan in motion. Bring the recordings to both political camps, work a deal.

But Paul had his doubts that either of them would ever be free men. He didn’t expect to be alive much longer either. But what was reality to Clyde? Paul’s heart sank the more he realized that Clyde had always been crazy, he simply hadn’t seen it. He had been caught up in Clyde’s plans and schemes for his entire life – could Paul have lived a normal upstanding life had it not been for being raised by an insane brother? Sadly, he would never know the answer. Nor would he have an opportunity to live his life differently.

While Clyde plotted and planned his next move, and Paul sulked, Kinji’s surveillance team back in Chicago was cracking up, having figured out the brother’s secret code in a matter of seconds. One man laughed so hard that he shot water out of his nose. “We can’t make this stuff up,” he said, after he recovered.

“I thought they’d break into Klingon,” said another.

“Should we send this to Morey in Encrypton?”

“Only if you want your head snapped off.”

"Seriously though," said a third, "What do you think they meant by 'play Ann and John against each other'? What are they up to?"

"Doesn't matter," said the first. "They won't be going anywhere."

"It's not like President Kinji is going to waterboard them. There's nothing to hide."

"John has reason to fear a bug."

"Doesn't matter, they won't see him."

"Yes, they will. He'll be there."

"Seriously? What's going down?"

"I don't know. We share the building, it's not that surprising."

"I hope he rots."

"Think these two idiots have something on him?"

"Maybe. If they do, we'll be the first to hear it."

The team continued to monitor the activity in the three sedans, analyzing the feed the mobile team was uploading to them; there wasn't anything else that caught their attention. The Meadow's family was still chatting, but none of what they were saying was of interest to the team. Bryce was silent, as were Tweedle Dee and Tweedle Dum, who the team had dubbed "The Double D's", for Dee and Dum, or "Dumb and Dumber". The rest of the journey went by uneventfully for both the team and the eight passengers they were keeping an ear to.

When the sedans slowed to circle the post-Big-War White House, in the queue to enter the three-mile descent to the underground secured parking area, Serena thought to ask about the third sedan. She had seen Clyde and Paul enter the second vehicle, but what about the third? She knocked on the divider window.

Nancy responded right away with an open window and an invitation, "Yes?"

"Who is in that third car?" asked Serena.

"Not sure you'd know him, but you can see for yourself, he's getting out," said Nancy.

As their own vehicle came to a stop, the other two sedans pulled up alongside them, flanking their car. Paul and Clyde were in the car on their right, so Serena and Tom kept their attention focused on their left, waiting to see who would emerge. They saw the top of his head first, a familiar blond wave, that ridiculous surfer-Prince Charming-frat boy look. Could it be? No, surely not. But it was.

"Why is Bryce here?" asked Serena, panic in her voice.

Nancy's tone revealed nothing. "That's Bryce Otto, one of President William's staff. I don't know why he's here."

"Otto is his last name," muttered Tom.

"Please get out of the car," said the driver of their sedan.

The other two sedans were now empty. The Meadows were slow to get out of the vehicle. "Where are we going?" asked Tom. He and Serena did not move. The three kids looked at their parents for guidance. Rick held the door open for them, but the family didn't budge, unsure of what to do.

"You are not in any trouble, Ma'am, the President just wants to speak with you," said Rick.

"Please come with us now, " said Nancy.

Tom and Serena exited the backseat, taking hold of their children's hands, even though Carrie was a young adult. The five of them looked ready to break into a musical number as they walked hand-in-hand into the White House. It was only after they had been walking down one corridor after another for several minutes that they relaxed enough to release their grip.

The unlikely procession was headed up by Nancy and the Meadows family, followed by Rick escorting Paul, Clyde, and Bryce. The massive drivers of the other two vehicles brought up the rear, sporting ear pieces and ready to tackle anyone who looked at them wrong. They trudged along silently, all of them brooding over what would happen next.

15

President Ann Kinji waited in her office for the unlikely cast of characters to arrive. She was briefed on each individual and was intrigued by them all. Sensing that at least one of them was certifiably nuts, she requested that a team of psychiatric experts be on hand in the conference room. Each of her guests would have a private meeting in that room before seeing Ann. Those evaluations were now finished and the indicator light on her screen flashed.

Dr. Malik's face appeared in the primary frame. "Madam President, I examined each individual as requested. I found tendencies toward narcissism in both Bryce Otto and Paul Tracy. Both are also prone to delusional, grandiose visions of themselves."

"Are they dangerous?" Ann asked.

"Not usually, not alone. They are easily manipulated and can be dangerous when paired with someone else who is."

"Is that what we are dealing with here?"

"Yes, quite likely so. Clyde Tracy pulls Paul's puppet strings. Clyde, as we already knew from background investigation reports, has sociopathic behavior. He gave us confirmation, tentative of course without further testing, that he is indeed a sociopath."

"He is dangerous?"

"Yes, probably so."

"And Bryce? Who is his puppeteer?"

"President John Williams, Madam President." There was a long silence that Dr. Malik broke by clearing his throat and adding, "I make no political statement. I am merely reporting my findings."

"I understand."

"Tom and Serena Wilcox and the children are all cleared. We found no reason to suspect mental health issues in any of the five."

"The children? Why are children here?" Ann was alarmed. She'd had no idea that children might be caught up in all of this.

"I don't know the answer to that."

"I want the children moved to a secure location, set them up with pizza and movies, anything they want. Get Breyana on that. Send the others in after President Williams arrives. You can babysit them until then?"

"Yes, of course, Madam President."

"Dr. Malik, thank you and your team for your service. It should go without saying, but this is confidential."

"Of course, Madam President."

"Of course," whispered John from the Listening Room his secret staffers had set up for him. He sounded the alarm. Within minutes he had five covert professionals staring back at him. He didn't know where they came from, or who they were – he didn't need to know. His people handled all of that. Whoever these men were, they operated completely off any records. He wasn't sure they were even fully human.

John's phone lit up. "Yes? No, I'm unavailable. I don't care what you tell her. I was available, and now I'm not."

Breyana brought that message to her boss. “He says he’s not available. He’s not coming.”

Ann felt shivers running down her spine. Something seemed off about this, what could it be? Could he know what was going on? If so, how did he know? She gasped. He was listening. She was sure of it. The more that horrible thought sank in, the more she realized that she never felt alone in her office, even when she was alone. That had to be it. Bugs.

“Madam President?” Breyana looked worried.

Ann scrambled for a pen and paper, hard to find these days, since she seldom wrote anything with real paper. She managed to find a notepad with her Presidential seal on it. She scribbled: “Be careful what you say. Bugs in here.”

Breyana’s eyes flew open wide. She nodded. “Do you need for me to reschedule your appointments now that President Williams can no longer make it?”

Aloud Ann said, “Yes, please postpone the meetings until the President can make it.” Silently, she wrote: “Get them out NOW. Undisclosed location, secret service.”

Breyana nodded. Aloud she said, “I’ll move those appointments around after I check in with President William’s staff.” Then she grabbed Ann’s notepad and wrote: “You too?”

Ann nodded. “Thank you, Breyana,” And because she couldn’t resist, and knew he was listening, she added, “I hope that John isn’t ill. I don’t know how we’d do without him.”

Breyana paused at the door, but Ann waved her to go. It took only ten minutes for Breyana to get the message to the secret service detail, and another ten minutes for the group to be loaded back up in the three sedans.

All passengers were seated comfortably, all but Bryce, who was instructed to lie down in the backseat, even though the windows were tinted, should he be seen through special ops glasses. Hiding Bryce from prying eyes was successful, but the twenty minutes it took to move the group was too long. Deep in the pit of the White House parking catacombs lurked five hulking men.

16

The five men watched the three vehicles. Everyone was accounted for, and orders were to kill them all. They were ready, and were waiting for the vehicles to start moving. At that moment a fourth sedan pulled up.

"Who is this? You know about this?" grunted one of the hulks.

"Williams said three."

"I don't like surprises."

"What the? There's kids in there. I don't do kids."

As they watched, scopes to their eyes, the Meadows children exited the fourth sedan and climbed into the first sedan in the row, reuniting with their parents. The fourth sedan pulled away, leaving the original three vehicles, but not for long. Two more unexpected sedans pulled up.

"The President is in there!"

"Why is he here?"

"No, not him. The other one."

"Abort. Call John."

The hulks confirmed that John wanted the mission called off. He agreed that it was too complicated now that Ann was involved. He could have sacrificed the kids, but covering up Ann's death would have caused him too many headaches. The investigation into that would have led straight back to him, sooner rather than later.

He'd have to go about this a different way. How? He didn't know. But getting rid of them before they talked to Ann wasn't going to work – his window of eliminating them without a connection to himself had closed.

What did they know anyway? Nothing they could prove, nothing they could tie back to him, and, best of all, their credibility as witnesses was shaky: two con artists, one or both of them mentally unstable, and a family who had been on the run. *Did they have any hard evidence?* He thought not.

John would keep a tail on them and send the team to take them out if necessary – it might not be necessary. If they didn't know anything important, he was trigger happy on this one. He'd find out soon enough when Ann talked about what happened, whether in her office, on her computer, or on her phone – all had John's ears.

The five hulks became phantoms as soon as they confirmed that the mission was aborted; the convoy proceeded unhindered. No one from John's team was following them yet; for the time being they would track them through their phones. With so many cell phones in play, it would be easy to pick up their trail. Meanwhile, they'd let them go for now. The White House underground exits were too vulnerable – a tail would be spotted by many trained eyes.

The convoy reached the last bend of the White House catacombs and then stopped. Nancy and Rick got out of the first sedan. They went to each vehicle and asked for all cell phones, even

President Kinji's phone, surprising her with the request. Ann quickly understood and relinquished it.

The last sedan in line carried no passengers. The driver loaded all seven cell phones, including the President's special line, into the trunk of the vehicle. When the convoy reached the end of the catacombs, the last sedan drove in the opposite direction from the other four sedans, carrying their cell phones to an undisclosed location separate, and far away from, President Kinji's undisclosed location destination.

The convoy didn't drive for long- the undisclosed location was Air Force One Plus, Kinji's plane (William's was Air Force One). Air Force One Plus did not share a tarmac with William's plane, and security was tight. Kinji knew that Williams did not have access to her plane, but nonetheless, she had the plane swept for bugs before they boarded. Nothing turned up.

Nor were cameras easy to hijack, but she had her team check and double-check just to be sure. She trusted her people, and after a short security briefing, she felt secure in her choice.

Everyone boarded the plane and waited for something to happen. Two secret service agents guarded the cockpit, others were at the exits. President Ann Kinji remained standing, facing her captive audience. Seated in the front row was the Meadows family. Seated in the second row were Paul, Clyde, Nancy, Rick and Bryce. The remaining rows were used by the rest of the secret service detail.

President Kinji began, "Thank you for putting up with this cloak and dagger routine. Together we'll get to the bottom of this. To start, I'd like to say that I know about the e-mail from the Iranian woman. I also know that the former President and President John

Williams knew about the attacks before they happened. What I want from all of you is anything you can add to that."

Serena raised her hand.

"No formalities here, go ahead," Ann said.

"President Kinji, I'm sorry, but I think you know everything that we do. We have only that e-mail." said Serena. She was impressed with herself, how she was able to talk with the President, a woman she greatly admired, as if it were a normal everyday occurrence.

In person, President Ann Kinji was even more amazing. She was beautiful with her shiny black locks and intelligent dark eyes, coupled with a commanding presence and a strong speaking voice. Charisma, confidence and charm were only part of the package; there was a hard-to-define quality that made President Ann Kinji genuine, someone to trust. She was intimidating, and Serena was pleased that she held her own without stammering all over herself.

"But we could get you more," said Paul. "Our plan was to meet with John and record our conversation."

Ann laughed. "Don't you think he'd see that coming?" Her eyes turned up in a smile.

How could she be so jovial and social in such a pressure cooker situation? Serena's respect for Ann went up another notch.

Clyde, however, took offense to the President's amusement. His face flushed crimson and he stood up, causing six secret service officers to also rise. He looked behind him, hesitated for a few tense seconds, and sat back down. He said, "We have high tech ways of recording that can't be detected by bug sweeping."

"Even so, I don't think anything can be gained from that. John wouldn't talk to you, not the truth anyway," said Ann.

"He talked to me!" Paul protested.

Ann's attention was riveted on Paul. "When did he talk to you? Where? What did he say exactly? Leave nothing out." Ann gestured toward two of her staffers who had been standing near the secret service detail in the cockpit. She wanted everything noted, recorded, witnessed. A flurry of activity resulted, followed by silence as all waited for Paul to speak.

Paul glanced around him, suddenly aware that he had the floor. He relaxed, feeling his social grin transforming his face. He might not be doomed after all: *what if Kinji was starting to see him as an asset? Would she toss him aside then?* This was where he was born to be: in the spotlight, important people hanging on his every word.

"Paul, please," said Ann.

"They took me onto his jet, like you've done. He said they 'have ears in Kinj's office'."

Ann blanched at that confirmation of what she already suspected. She had not had her team sweep her office, not wanting Williams to get wind that she knew. "Go on," she prodded.

"He asked how I made that picture, the photo, um, you know the one. I'm sorry about that…"

"I don't care about that right now, keep going."

"He said 'It's good work. I want to use it.' I told him that nobody owns me, but he threatened me."

"Threatened you how?"

"He was going to bug me, follow me, make sure I did what he wanted."

"He likes his bugs. What exactly did he want?"

"He wanted me to bring that photo to the media. He agreed that he wanted to embarrass you and that making trouble for you keeps you off balance."

President Ann Kinji drew up her full height and took a deep steadying breath. All of her martial arts training came back to her. She felt her body go into "ready position" even while appearing outwardly to not move a muscle. "So far this is nothing more than dirty politics, smear campaigns, intimidation. Same-o, same-o. I need proof that John knew something about the Big War."

Clyde said, "He broke the law, you could get him for that. And then interrogate him."

"I don't think I could get anywhere with nothing but the word of a known con man," said Ann.

"Don't take my word for it, get his records. He has a folder with everything in it, even references to the Academy and good old Mrs. Mason, may she rest in peace," said Clyde.

Ann took notice. "What records?"

"He, um, wanted to talk about my, as he put it, 'fear mongering' about the Identity Chip bill, the reason why I wanted to work for you, why I brought that doctored photo to you for leverage," said Paul.

"You would have never been able to leverage me, but go on," said Ann.

"I wanted to work for you so that I could influence that Identity Chip bill. I wanted it to pass so that people would buy Clyde's Angels Mark technology," said Paul.

"You're losing me, what does anything of this have to do with records?" asked Ann.

"I'm getting to that. He said, 'you didn't think I knew all about your operation?' And told me 'my guys briefed me about your whole life in fifteen minutes. It's all right here.' He had a brown folder."

Ann laughed, "No! He wouldn't have anything on paper. You expect me to believe he had a brown folder!"

Paul protested, "He did! He even said, 'I could read it on one of those gadgets, but I like paper.' He said he *likes* paper. He has a paper trail. We can find it."

Ann's hopes were raised, but she didn't want to get too excited. "Hmm, I'm not convinced."

Paul said, "He said that someone would pay me, and the money in my account would be, and I quote, 'Untraceable to this office'. But I know that Clyde's lab could crack whatever code they have."

"Clyde's lab of child hackers? This isn't going anywhere," said Ann. She sighed.

"Wait, wait!" Paul said. "*He* was there!" He pointed at Bryce. "He heard everything, and he works for John."

"Bryce was there?" Ann smiled. "Interesting. We'll be getting to Bryce, but have you told me everything you know? Everything John told you? Everything you saw?"

Paul shook his head slowly from side to side, like a small boy interacting with his kindergarten teacher. "I can't think of anything else."

"Okay then, what we've got so far is the possibility that President Williams has paper records that may or may not incriminate him. I hope Bryce can offer us something more substantial than that," said Ann.

All eyes were on Bryce. He said, "What makes you think I would tell you anything? He's not only my uncle, he's my President."

President Kinji glared at him and took a few steps toward where he was sitting. She said, "One word: *treason.*"

Bryce made a dramatic *ppft* sound and said, "How can it be treason to protect my President? That's the epitome of loyalty, not grounds for treason."

"Your loyalty is to your country, and your people, not to any one President. You knew about this e-mail—you are the very person who shared it. You knew that President Williams was involved in acts against our country, and you said nothing. You even perpetuated this massive cover-up, and whatever it is that John is trying to do," said Ann in a quiet, controlled, voice. Slow, steady, and smooth, like talking to a rabid dog.

Bryce tried a new tactic, "How do you know that the e-mail isn't a fabrication?"

Serena interjected, "I know it isn't. My friend Karyn is the original recipient of that e-mail. I saw it on her computer, and I even have the flash drive with the entire history of her correspondence with Farideh on it." She waved her flash drive, jingling the crowded key ring that the flash drive keychain was attached to.

Ann said, "I was going to get to you next, Serena, but I'm going to go straight to you right now." She clucked her tongue, her eyes turning up at the corners to match her grin. "Amazing, you have something we can actually use. Oh most definitely!" She clapped her hands together and said, "Nance, take that flash drive from her, would you please? Get everything off of it. *Now* we're getting somewhere!"

"Uh oh, I'm afraid that's really all I have," said Serena. "Although I did have a thought. We knew back in 2011, when the Iranians shot down our spy plane, that Iran was getting close to having the technology to make weapon-grade uranium for nuclear weapons."

"Yes, Tehran's nuclear program, the Fordo uranium enrichment site. What's the connection to John?" Ann said.

"Well, obviously some of their actions since then led to the Big War, and there would be records of those actions. I am thinking that John may have been deeply involved in those talks. Maybe you can follow that all the way up to the days leading up to the bombings," Serena offered.

Ann frowned. "I don't think those records would be revealing. Anything sinister would have taken place outside of recorded meetings. I need John's personal files, and I want you to get them, Bryce."

"Even if I wanted to help you," said Bryce, "I can't get to his files without being seen. I mean, if people saw me, they wouldn't think twice, but I'd leave an identity mark that would sound off an alarm. No one but Uncle John, uh, President Williams, can authorize or access his office or computer. They'd have those files from me before any of you ever saw them."

"Are you sure about that? I have an idea," said Serena.

"Yes? Listening," said Ann.

Tom looked at his wife. *What idea did she have?* After all these years, he still couldn't tap into her head.

No one else on the plane could guess either, and all strained their ears to hear what she had to say.

"I thought of it when Paul mentioned the Identity Chip. President Williams uses it already doesn't he? I remembered that I saw on the news that his entire wing of the White House switched over to that system, sort of a demo, showing how the IC works," said Serena.

"Yes, they've been using it for months now, garnering support for the IC bill by showing off its success," said Ann. "Where are you going with this?"

Serena turned around in her seat to look directly into Clyde's rheumy eyes. "Is your Angels Mark technology for real, or is that part a scam too?"

Clyde made a show of being offended, but he was gearing up for a grand-standing moment. "Yes, it's for real! We would have made millions off of it."

Paul chimed in, "Did you think our grand plan was to minister a mega church forever? I had those people wanting the Angels Mark technology even before its release."

Clyde, getting revved up, said, "It's all in the marketing. You know your market, you feed into their fears, their paranoia, their delusions, then give them what they want: something to make the evil go away."

"I can't believe people are so easily led, " Ann argued.

"We'd have gotten the entire flock of sheep, we'd have cornered the Christian-right market!" Clyde snarled, spittle frothing in the corners of his mouth. "You don't know what you are talking about."

Paul added, calmly, "It's moved out of beta. It works. We were ready to roll it out whenever the IC bill passed."

Ann said, "You've lost me. What is Angels Mark?"

Serena, Paul and Clyde all started talking at once, and it was only when young Samuel spoke up that everyone stopped the race to be the spokesperson for defining the Angels Mark.

President Kinji gave the nod to Samuel. "If you can explain it to me, I'd appreciate it," she smiled.

Samuel's passion for computers bubbled over and his words tumbled out of his mouth quickly, his conversation difficult to follow. "Angels Mark is software that can override the system of the Identity Chip. They can program whatever they want in it and the system of the IC will think it's the right code when it's really any code that they want. They call it Angels Mark because they say that the IC is the mark of the beast, from Revelations, but I don't believe that, I think they made that part up, not that Revelations is what they made up, they made up the part about the chip being from that. They say the beast is a computer, not a person, and his mark is the IC, which I don't believe at all, they can't fool me. But if you get the chip and get the Angels Mark it's like not taking the number of the beast because they can change the number to anything they want and the IC is overridden…"

"Wow, thank you, young man, whew!" Ann cut him off, realizing that the child would keep going for as long as she allowed him to ramble. "So, if I'm getting this right, we can use this Angels Mark software to erase Bryce's security breach? Use his well-known face to get him into the office with no problems; then erase what he's doing in there? Correct?"

"Yes," said Serena.

"Technically, I'm not sure they can erase the fingerprint, they might need to substitute John's code for Bryce's. I'll have to leave that up to the crew to determine," said Clyde.

Ann waved that off. "Doesn't matter. We can get the files, can we not? It can be done?"

Paul and Clyde said in unison, "Yes."

Everyone looked at Bryce.

"What happens to me? Do I get a deal?" he asked.

"So much for loyalty to Uncle John," said Ann.

"When you guys get through with him he won't be able to help me. I'm not going down with him when he tanks, he'd do the same if he were me, do you think he wouldn't bail on me? But before I switch teams I want a guarantee: Lawyer, papers, signed by a judge. I want it in writing, I repeat, signed by a judge," said Bryce.

"You've got it," said Ann, her voice dripping with disgust. She stood for a few seconds, lost in thought. "Oh, I do have one more issue to bring up. Serena, your friends Karyn and Dan have been moved to a safe house. She asked me to be sure to tell you."

Serena felt a twinge of discomfort upon her conscience, realizing that she hadn't stopped to think about what had happened to her good friend Karyn. She was relieved to hear that she was okay. "Thank you for letting me know," she said.

And with that, the meeting was adjourned. President Kinji's staff flew into action, and the pilots were brought on board. Everyone was instructed to buckle up to prepare for their flight to Minneapolis, a city they'd seen more of lately than usual. As a result, the media was starting to make some noise, speculating about why President Kinji had stepped up the frequency of her trips there. Even though her trips were not made public, the world always knew of her whereabouts eventually.

Once in the air, and after the plane leveled out to a smooth steady plateau in the sky, Serena and Tom held a private conversation that was only partially overheard by their children, and went no further.

"Tom, I feel so humiliated by this Angels Mark nonsense," said Serena.

"What do you mean?"

"To be caught up with those deranged brothers, it's awkward. Their scam is so icky, preying on religious people. They are twisting things that people really do believe passionately in."

"We weren't taken in by it."

"I know, but we are not as gullible as some. Even so, it's embarrassing to be connected to this. I really admire President Kinji," Serena said, barely above a whisper. "All that stuff about the Beast, she probably thinks we're crazy by association."

"No, I'm sure she doesn't. Besides, Angels Mark is a real technology they invented, if it works."

"I think it will. I don't trust the Tracy brothers, but I do trust those kids in the computer lab," said Serena.

The two continued to talk in hushed tones, and when they had finally exhausted all topics relating to anything important, their conversation drifted to what their plans might be for dinner.

Meanwhile, President William's covert detail was following the decoy sedan, with its decoy convoy, all the way to Newton, Kansas. The lead driver, relieved of his Chicago duty, was hurrying home to his wife, a petite brunette named Kelly who was cooking his favorite farm-raised beef in her often-used crock pot.

It would be a long night for the covert team, smelling a supper they couldn't have, hearing the sounds of TV and laughter, and eventually blinking in the darkness; finally admitting to themselves and to each other that they had been had.

No one wanted to report their failure to Chicago, but one unlucky member of the team drew the short straw. President Williams needed to know: they'd been had. And none of them had the slightest idea where Madam President or her odd cast of cohorts were. The unlucky short-straw bearer held his earpiece away from his ear as Williams bellowed, ranted, and cursed until he ended the call.

17

As William's five men watched the three vehicles, one of them reported back that everyone was accounted for. The response: Orders are to leave no witnesses. All eyes were trained on the targets; two of the less fortunate assassins were assigned to keep their scopes on the most volatile and least physically attractive witness Clyde Tracy.

Clyde hugged himself tightly, as close as he would ever get to being embraced by another person. This was the highlight of his entire life: the fate of the world was up to Clyde. He had always known that this was his destiny. Everything he had ever done in his life was worth it, for this very moment, one of few moments he had left here on this earth. He would have done it all over again.

Clyde was with President Kinji's new covert A Team, to oversee the install of Angels Mark and the re-insertion of the modified Identity Chip under Bryce's skin. He watched the testing of the chip, and gave it his approval. He nodded authoritatively toward President Kinji's secret service agents. The procedure was complete. He looked with satisfaction at his lab, newly staffed with government suits, buddied up with his teenage hackers: how else could they be brought up to speed on everything so quickly? These kids were having the time of their lives, just as Clyde was. The mood in the lab was buoyant to say the least.

Nancy and Rick were taking lead on the Angels Mark project. Rick said, "We'll be bringing Bryce back to Chicago now."

"What about me, about us?" said Paul.

"No, we won't be needing you," said Rick.

"Yes you will," fumed Clyde. "You need someone to analyze the data."

"We have people who will analyze it. You're staying here," said Nancy.

"You can't take my technology and leave me behind," said Clyde.

"Someone will be in touch," said Nancy curtly. She spun on her heels and took Bryce by the arm. Rick took up his other arm. They half-dragged him out of the building even though Bryce was leaving willingly.

"Wait, wait!" called Bryce. The two agents ignored him, so Bryce kept talking, shouting over his shoulder, while Clyde and Paul followed him out the door to catch his every word. "Gustavo, the general, he's sympathetic to your cause. Talk to him!"

Bryce was pushed into yet another government vehicle and rushed to a secret runway where a small jet was waiting to return him to the White House.

The two brothers went back into the computer lab; Bryce's parting comments weighing on their minds. Clyde asked Paul, "Where's that detective lady?"

"Who?"

"Serena what's-her-name."

"She's a detective?"

"She used to be."

"What do you want her for?"

"My lab is tied up, my hackers are tied up, and besides, they're watching us."

"You want her to find the general?"

"They said they don't need us. We'll see," said Clyde defiantly.

"She went home with the rest of her clan. But there's security on them."

"We aren't going to scare her. No reason for security to have their panties in a bunch. Let's pay her a visit."

The farmhouse the Meadows family was resting comfortably in was only a few miles from the lab. In less than ten minutes Paul and Clyde were at her doorstep, where they were greeted with suspicion by two secret service agents.

"What are you doing here?" asked the one with carroty red hair, hair that was impressively fluorescent even while diminished somewhat by his crew cut.

"We just want to talk with Serena," said Paul.

The second agent, a black male who stood an impressive six feet nine inches at his full height, was stooped over to fit under the standard-sized door frame. "You can talk to her from here."

Serena heard the conversation and came closer. "What do you want?"

"We got a tip that General Gustavo is willing to work with us, but we need help in finding where he is. President Kinji's team is using the lab," said Paul.

"Gustavo…Wasn't he interviewed a few years ago, before the Big War, back when the national debt ceiling crashed?" Serena shut the screen door before unidentified biting bugs made their way into the house.

"I don't know, maybe," said Clyde, who hadn't flinched when the door was shut almost in his face.

"Yes, I remember," said Paul. "He was part of a press conference, about our readiness to go to war. It was right after the markets seized up and the U.S. caused the world economy to crash."

"The default had a catastrophic effect on financial markets. We made a lot of enemies. I can remember a little of Gustavo's speech now," said Serena.

"What difference does this make?" asked Clyde.

"Maybe none. Why are you here?" asked Serena.

"We told you that already. We got a tip."

"From who?" asked Serena.

"Bryce. From Bryce. Look, we need your help in finding the General. The lab is all tied up with Kinji's people. You're supposed to be a detective, or at least you were. Can you find where he is?" asked Paul.

"Does President Kinji know about this?" asked Serena.

"She's the one who wants us to talk to him," Paul lied.

"She didn't contact me," said Serena.

"She went back to the White House, when they brought Bryce back," said Paul, which was the truth.

Clyde, sensing she needed more verification of Kinji's involvement, appealed to her ego, "President Kinji said that you'd be able to find him, no problem. Was she wrong?"

Serena blushed at the idea of President Kinji recommending her specifically. "I don't know if I can find him, but I can try. Come in."

Clyde flashed a leering grin at the two agents as he walked past them. *The puppet master hasn't lost his touch!* He and Paul joined Serena and Tom at their kitchen table, where they sat for a good hour before Serena found what she was looking for.

"I had to pay one of those services to dig a little deeper than what I could find for free, but I finally found a home address for him. You didn't tell me he had a residence in Minnetonka. That's what, less than two hours' drive?"

Paul and Clyde registered genuine surprise on their faces. "We didn't know he was so close," said Paul.

"You're going to go talk to him?" asked Tom.

"Yes," said Paul.

"Did she want us to come with you?" asked Serena.

The brothers hesitated, working through the pros and cons quickly. On one hand, they wanted all the glory of the mission. On the other hand, they could use some help. Serena might be the better conversationalist, especially if the general wasn't home, and only his wife was available. "Yes, she assumed you'd be coming with us," said Paul, looking at Clyde for validation, and receiving it with a slight nod, that he made the right decision.

"We need to go right away," said Clyde. He looked back through the kitchen into the living room at where the kids were working on various projects. "This time, leave the kids at home."

"Good point. You'll be fine, won't you? The agents will be here," said Serena.

"Yes," the three kids said, nearly in unison. By now they were unflappable.

The red-headed agent stopped them as they headed out. "We're supposed to stay with you."

"We'll be right back, please keep an eye on the kids," said Serena.

"We are not babysitters, ma'am."

"Isn't the detail assigned to the house?" asked Tom.

The red-head answered, "I'll go with you. Special Agent Thompson will stay here."

Clyde and Paul went together in Clyde's vehicle. Tom and Serena rode with the red-head who introduced himself as Special Agent Salisbury. With the team of Thompson and Salisbury split up, neither man had backup, but given the egos of both agents, neither one thought twice about breaking protocol.

The journey to General Gustavo's home felt long. It had been a draining twenty-four hours. And now it was getting dark. It was hard for Tom and Serena to keep their eyes open. Fortunately neither of them was driving.

The two vehicles, Clyde's jeep and Salisbury's government issue, pulled up alongside the front entry of the house, a modest home in a nice suburban neighborhood. The four of them lagged behind while Salisbury led the way, as he insisted upon doing.

Before Salisbury could ring the bell, the door was opened by General Gustavo himself. "Identify yourself, Agent."

"Special Agent Salisbury, Sir."

"Where's your partner?"

"He stayed back on detail."

"Come in." General Gustavo ushered them all inside. "We can talk in the den." He led them down to the finished basement level, to the farthest room from the stairs, a room with no windows. "Please secure the room, Agent."

"Sir? Secure the room?" Salisbury was confused. Why would the general need his home office swept? Wouldn't he know if there was someone lurking in there? But his legs carried him into the room as ordered.

Gustavo promptly shot him in the back. It made little sound. The thud of Salisbury's body as it fell to the floor seemed louder. Blood pooled around him as the four visitors stared at his prone body, his trademark red hair now made a dark crimson. It seemed like blood was everywhere.

Salisbury must have hit his head on something on the way down to account for all that blood, thought Serena. *We're all going to die*. She began to pray.

"Bryce!" yelled Clyde.

General Gustavo grinned. "It was a nicely set trap. The President wants you out of the way. But not until you tell me what Kinji knows."

"If you're going to kill us anyway, why should we tell you anything?" asked Serena.

Tom did not have his gun with him; the secret service had not returned it. He looked around him for a means of escape. He could find none. He kept looking.

Paul looked at Clyde with despair; Clyde's arm was still in a sling and neither of them had a weapon. He said, "Make us a deal and we'll tell you want you want."

"I don't make deals. I'll pick you off one by one until you talk." Gustavo snorted like a bull. "Starting with *you*."

Gustavo pointed the gun directly at Paul's head. Seeing his brother in danger triggered something primal in Clyde. Unhindered by the sling, and feeling no emotion, no pain, Clyde charged at Gustavo, screaming a most unholy shriek as he lunged.

The attack was so quick, so unexpected, and accompanied by such a surprisingly hideous sound, that Gustavo was caught off guard. Clyde was at this throat, with both of his hands, the arm sling twisting under pressure, as he grasped hold of Gustavo's neck, strangling him with his bare hands.

Gustavo's eyes bulged and he managed to squeeze off a round, but he was no match for Clyde's insanity. He was limp and lifeless without ever uttering another syllable.

Gustavo dropped to the floor, immediately followed by Clyde himself. That one round, that the general had fired off while in the throes of death, had hit Clyde at extremely close range, a fatal wound, which was now obvious to the remaining three witnesses to the past few seconds. No one moved at first, and then Paul rushed to Clyde's side.

"Nooooo! Nooooo!" Paul wailed. He held his brother's head in his lap, staring down in horror as blood frothed from Clyde's mouth. "Quick, Serena! You believe for real, right? My brother deserves last rites."

Serena stammered, "I'm not a clergy. I'm not sure what you want—"

"Pray! He's dying! My brother is dying!" Paul sobbed.

Serena didn't know how to pray for the soul of a man like Clyde, so she recited the Lord's Prayer from memory:

"Our Father, who art in Heaven, hallowed be thy name, thy Kingdom come, thy will be done, on Earth as it is in Heaven…"

The mention of Heaven caused a great outburst from Paul, who was now soaked in his brother's blood. He clutched at Clyde's shirt, grabbing him into a floppy, unresponsive embrace.

Serena let her words trail off and tried to look away from the macabre sight, but a mixture of horror and fascination kept her eyes rooted to the two brothers. Seeing the blood pooling on the floor, and all over Paul, and the blood spatter from Gustavo all over the walls, furniture, and floor, she studied her new green trench coat with its trendy styling and chic belt for signs of crimson: *whew, no blood stains*. She glanced at Tom, who was turning quite pale and looked ready to faint.

Paul began rocking from side to side, holding his brother's body and wailing. While Paul was consumed and distracted, Serena and Tom took the opportunity to slip out of the room. They called 911; then President Kinji at the special number she gave them.

18

While Bryce's trap was ensnaring Clyde, and General Gustavo as collateral damage, Bryce was dutifully playing for the other side. He slipped into President John Williams' private office areas without raising any suspicion whatsoever, which was as he expected. The tricky part would be to access and copy his uncle's files without his fingerprints setting off any alarms. He hoped the Angels Mark worked. He couldn't care less about helping Ann; he did care immensely about being caught helping her. He had every reason to have a healthy fear of how far John would go if he knew that Bryce was selling him out. He feared John much more than he feared prison, but he preferred to avoid both. If this Angels Mark technology worked, he would extract the files with no one the wiser.

He held his breath as the download indicator bar filled. The transfer speed was the best there was, and Bryce was soon out of his misery. No alarms. Nothing. He had done it! He worked his way through every folder, including those that were hidden. He himself had organized most of these, so he knew where the secret files were. At this point, he was all in and wanted as much incriminating evidence as possible to get protection for himself from John. He figured the only chance he had was if they branded John as not only a traitor, but the world's most wanted terrorist. If they got all of John's people too, Bryce had a fighting chance of hiding away somewhere and starting a new life. He copied everything he could find, even files he didn't think were important.

Just as he finished copying the files, Bryce's heart stopped beating. President John Williams, his revered and feared uncle, was standing in the entrance to his private office area. "Hey, Brycer! What are you doing in here?"

A practiced liar after years of picking up girls and lying to his parents about his whereabouts, it was natural for Bryce to concoct a plausible story on the spot. "I was hoping to check my e-mail. The battery on my phone is dead."

"What's wrong with your office?" John asked. Not suspicious, not judging, just a simple question an uncle might ask his nephew.

"I'm avoiding Caroline," he said, which was partially true, actually. He had slept with Caroline a few times, and now she expected a ring. That was never going to happen, especially now.

John chuckled. "Understood."

Bryce smiled full wattage, a ladies' man just like his uncle, the good old boys' club, partners, on the same team. "You have a full plate today. How are you going to fix this thing with Kinji?"

"Oh don't worry about that, I have my people on it. By this time tomorrow, she won't be a problem," said John ominously.

Bryce shuddered inwardly. *Better her than me*, he thought. Relieved that he had gotten away with betraying his uncle in plain sight, Bryce slipped down the corridor and left the White House for a restaurant well known as a spot for politicians to gather. No one would think twice about Bryce being there, or seeing him meet up casually with someone from Kinji's staff, placing his flash drive into the palm of Breyana's pretty little hand.

Back at the White House, President Ann Kinji waited anxiously for Breyana to return. She had no fewer than seven secret service agents with her, so surely Breyana would be safe. However, after hearing the disturbing news about General Gustavo and Clyde, she had every reason to worry. She feared that Bryce was laying down another trap, but then again, she banked on Bryce wanting to save himself.

She wondered if John even knew yet that things had gone wrong. Was Gustavo instructed to merely hold them, not kill them? Obviously John wouldn't have thought that the general would get killed. When Ann had spoken to Bryce, Bryce had the attitude of someone who had finished a mission, cocky, relaxed. She didn't think that he knew that Gustavo was dead. And if not, how could that be? Wouldn't John be expecting Gustavo to report in regularly? Either John didn't know what happened, or he didn't trust Bryce anymore. The first scenario worked well in their favor, the second one was chilling.

"Bird is in the cage," said Special Agent Smith in her ear.

"Thank you, Special Agent Smith. No problems?"

"No, Madam President. She'll be with you shortly."

"Thank you, thank you!" Ann breathed a sigh of relief. Breyana was young, with her whole life ahead of her. Putting her in danger was wrong. But Breyana had volunteered, and in the end, Ann couldn't think of anyone else she trusted to make the exchange. With great reluctance, and a whole swat team of agents, Ann had let her go. And here she was!

“I got it,” sang Breyana. She extended her arm, opened the fingers that had been gripping the flash drive tightly for the past fifteen minutes, and showed her boss the smoking gun: a small shiny gadget that held who knew what.

“Oh, thank you, Breyana, I sure could use a cup of coffee,” said Ann.

Breyana froze, a puzzled expression on her face, until Ann put her index finger to her lips, then pointed to the general direction of President William’s office and cupped her ear. Breyana nodded. “No problem.”

“I think I’ll take my coffee on the way out the door. I have a meeting with the governor of Indiana this afternoon.”

“Should I let them know you’re ready to go?” asked Breyana.

“Yes, please do,” said Ann.

Within the hour Ann was seated once again on Air Force One Plus. The computers were safe here on the plane, transmitting on channels that were tracked by more agencies than John would have been able to corrupt. Her hunch was that if her phones were tapped, her office bugged, well, naturally John had his dirty fingers all over her computer. She didn’t dare open those files until she was on a secure connection. But here she was, in a safe place, on a safe connection, with people who would keep her, and the information she held, safe. As much as she dreaded seeing the truth laid out in black and white, it was time for the big reveal.

The first thing Ann did was copy all of the files and send them to multiple places. Next, she asked one of her IT agents to put what she was seeing up on multiple screens. “Thank you, Agent Lehman. I’m ready now; please tell them to come in.”

Serena and Tom entered the plane, still traumatized by the day's events, but in enough shock that nothing felt real. After Serena had phoned President Kinji, right after Clyde's horrific and revolting demise, a team of agents was quickly on the scene at the house in Minnetonka, where Gustavo had never actually lived – funny how fabricated records can appear instantly in the right places when powerful people want them there.

The agents had whisked them out of the house, some staying behind to clean up the mess, and taken them to yet another secret airstrip. This one appeared to be in use by hobbyists, but it was available at that moment for a government jet – off record.

Once again, Serena and Tom were flown into Chicago, but this time they left their children in the safe keeping of Special Agent Thompson- who was beginning to think of himself as an over-muscled nanny- and two more agents who had been assigned to replace the ill-fated Special Agent Salisbury.

"I'm so sorry for what you've been through," Ann began. "I want you to know that your country, that I, appreciate all you've done."

"Thank you, President Kinji," said Serena.

"No problem," said Tom, which elicited a look of disbelief from both Ann and Serena.

"I hate to ask more of you, and I'll be sure that you are both generously compensated, but I trust the two of you as witnesses, and well, you are already involved. I want you to read this material along with me. I have sent the material to several sources, but it will go unread until I give the word. I have also asked my husband, Ted, to sit in with us," Ann gestured toward the seats behind them.

Ted stood up and shook their hands. No one spoke. The three stood for a few awkward seconds. Ann broke the tension, "Sit, we are ready. Look at the screen nearest you." She took a deep breath. "Here we go."

Ann clicked through twenty five folders, each containing over a hundred individual files. She skimmed through the first folder, with everyone watching on the various screens, and then realized that it was going to take a lot more time than she expected to wade through all the trivial saved documents to find the incriminating evidence.

She instructed Special Agent Lehman to set up shop for Ted, Tom and Serena to work through files on three more stations. Her request was quickly granted. For the next four hours, the four of them pored methodically through every folder and file, each person with their own section, so as not to miss a single document. Finally, it was Ted who signaled he found something by whistling softly through his teeth.

"I think you better put this up to share on all screens," he said. Special Agent Lehman scurried to comply. And there is was; one of several guns that were smoking big black billows of toxic, toxic air.

<<I do not recommend reliance upon the MDS /Missile Defense System/ as a means to protect the nation from the imminent nuclear attack /CLOSED DOCUMENT: 2 authorized>>

<</PAGE 2/You continue to rely upon the MDS against my recommendation. Insubordination not withstanding, what the hell is going on?>>

"What are we looking at? Who is this, and is it the same person in both messages?" asked Ann.

"Yes, same source," said Special Agent Lehman.

"If I were to guess, the general?" said Tom.

"Makes sense," said Ann. "Move on."

Ted clicked on the next message:

<<Think of a nation without debt, without reliance upon foreign oil. Think of starting over, closed borders. Think of our economy – restored /CLOSED DOCUMENT: 3 authorized>>

<<You are saying that we let them bomb us? Who did you CC, I have you and the Pres only/CLOSED DOCUMENT: 2 authorized>>

<<You, me, the President – that's 3. How did you do your math/CLOSED DOCUMENT: 3 authorized>>

<<Sorry, Big W, I forgot to CC myself/CLOSED DOCUMENT: 3 authorized>>

Serena said, "President John Williams is well known as 'Big W'. This should work toward proof of his involvement."

"I think we can get more solid proof by tracing these messages back to their digital fingerprint, am I right?" asked Ann.

"Yes, Madam President, exactly," said Special Agent Lehman.

"There's more in the next folder," said Ted. He opened the next series of messages:

<<Before I agree to recommend the MDS plan, I need it from you President. No offense, John, but I need a reason before I agree to let them drop nukes on our own people/CLOSED DOCUMENT: 3 authorized>>

<<Bipartisan government, deadlocked, economy in the sewer, lobbyist in all of our pockets, oil so high we can't pay it, borders so open we can't keep them out. Bigger and bigger we get,

resources smaller and smaller. No plague to shrink us, no war to eradicate us. Can't stop this mutating nation from self-destructing. This is our plague: we can start over. I will step down, give the nation a rebirth./CLOSED DOCUMENT: 3 authorized>>

<<This doesn't sound like a Democrat/CLOSED DOCUMENT: 3 authorized>>

<<John, why would we want this chaos? We will never agree to the Republican view, but we've come together on this: we must destroy ourselves to fix what's broken. Satisfied, General?/CLOSED DOCUMENT: 3 authorized>>

<<I want you to confirm in person with your own two lips that this is what you want, and if it is, I will do what you ask/CLOSED DOCUMENT: 3 authorized>>

"Wow, this is hard to believe," said Serena.

"Is there more, Ted?" asked Ann.

"Do we really need more?" asked Ted. "Let the law take it from here. You don't need to be personally investigating this."

"I have to agree with the First Gentleman, Madam President, let us get all the agencies on this," said Special Agent Lehman.

"May I suggest that you stay out of the White House for a while? Whatever happens next shouldn't touch you or your Presidency," Serena volunteered. She patted herself on the back for how much she sounded like an official advisor to Madam President.

"Back to Minneapolis? Reunite you with your family?" Ted suggested.

"I can't get used to Minneapolis being the place to be," said Tom.

"The new Wall Street, the Pentagon, the split Capital building. Brings us in," said Ted.

"But why Minneapolis? Why are they rebuilding the Pentagon in Minneapolis and not Chicago near the White House? And why have two Capital buildings?" asked Tom.

"After 9-11, some questioned the wisdom of us having all of our governmental buildings in one basket. Spreading ourselves out, with the full capacity to govern out of two separate cities seemed wise, given that we'll never fully be rid of the threat of terrorist attacks," said Ann.

"And look at us now, needing to leave Chicago. It's good to have a secondary location," said Ted.

"I know of a farmhouse where you could wait for the green light to go back to Chicago," said Serena.

Would it be too much to ask to have the President to her house for coffee and a girlfriend chat? No matter how wretched the day's events were, it was hard not to feel a thrill at the thought of entertaining President Ann Kinji in her home.

"I haven't been in a real house in years. I'll take you up on that offer," Ann said.

Serena resisted the urge to squeal with glee.

19

Paul obediently followed the agents out of the house in Minnetonka. He struggled through that first hour in a daze, not knowing how to formulate a single thought. How could he exist without Clyde? He stumbled down the sidewalk and allowed himself to be tucked into a government vehicle.

As he sank into the leather seat his heart welled up with fury and grief. The longer he sat, the more his grief was channeled into fury. President John Williams, and the previous President, pre-Big War, pre-apocalypse, had killed his brother. Paul was no sociopath, but Clyde had killed for him, and had ultimately died for him. It was the least Paul could do to avenge his brother's death.

He knew that John would be taken care of; he'd be tried as a traitor, a terrorist. The divided nation would turn on him and curse him to the end of his days. But the former Prez? What of him? Had Kinji even put two and two together yet? Paul wasn't so sure. And how deep was the cover-up? Would John take the Prez's involvement with him to his grave?

The thought of him getting away with it, with Clyde's blood on his hands, made Paul's blood boil. The only thing on his mind was finding the former president of what was once the United States of America.

The agents dropped him off at home. They informed him that he would be contacted shortly, to be interviewed for a criminal investigation into President John Williams' conduct before and after the Big War. Then they left him alone, re-assigned elsewhere. Apparently no one considered broken down wanna-be Paul to be a threat.

Paul locked the door and latched the dead-bolt. He went into the laundry room and took off his blood-drenched clothes. He hesitated, not knowing what to do. He had never done a load of laundry in his life. Where did the detergent go? Did he put it in now or after the clothes were in? Should he even bother – would the blood stains come out? He lifted the lid of the washer and, much to his surprise, saw directions for how to use the machines right there on the lid. He followed the instructions on the chart and started the washer.

Then he shuffled his way to the bathroom to take a shower. He did a double-take at his reflection in the mirror: was that Clyde's face staring back at him? He closed his eyes; then opened them again. No, he saw his own face. He couldn't tell if he was relieved or disappointed. He would never see his brother's face again: he didn't have a single picture of Clyde, unless he counted the ones his mother had insisted their father put on the kitchen wall. He and Clyde had taken them down shortly after their parents died, but when they saw permanent silhouettes from years of nicotine stains coating the walls around the frames, they put the pictures right back up and left them there.

There were two photos on the wall: the first was from when there were three brothers, and the other was when it was down to just him and Clyde, like it remained until now. But Clyde's death didn't feel anything like it did when Bradley died, he told himself. Bradley had drowned, and was only a little boy, a baby really. Paul tried to recall his last memory of Bradley. Could he recall the day he died?

He remembered playing in the kiddie pool. They had toys in there, pool toys. Bradley toddled inside the house to get more toys. Paul could see it now as vividly as if it had happened yesterday. Bradley had Paul's new electronic car he got for his birthday. It had been expensive, the best present Paul had ever gotten. Bradley was about to throw it into the pool. No! Paul grabbed the car and tried to wrestle it out of Bradley's tight grip. Bradley clung on, working himself up into a powerful tantrum.

"Help, Clyde!" Paul yelled.

Clyde reached over the knee-high inflatable pool wall and pushed Bradley's head under the water. He held him down until he released his grip on the car. Paul took the car, got out of the pool, and went inside to put the car on a higher shelf in his bedroom. On his way back outside, he got distracted by cartoons on TV and sat down to watch. A while later he heard their mother screaming like there was no end to the sound her lungs could make. She screamed over and over and over. Little Bradley was dead.

Paul shivered. It was the first time he fully remembered that day. Always before, he could recall that he was playing in the pool, went to watch cartoons, and then their mother was screaming because Bradley had drowned. He had completely blocked out the part about the toy car, and Clyde holding Bradley's head under the water.

Maybe that was what had turned Clyde into a killer? Surely he hadn't intended to drown their little brother; he was only trying to help Paul get his car back. *Poor dear baby Bradley, poor big brother Clyde.* It was down to Paul now to do right by both brothers' memories.

After he showered and put on clean clothes Paul went directly to the computer lab. He recalled Clyde saying that the kids spent a lot of time in the lab. He hoped one of them was in there now. Sure enough, he saw the top of a boy's head behind the rows of computer monitors.

Newbie child genius Nicholas was hard at work on a private project, oblivious to Paul's appearance until Paul said something. "Nicholas, can you find somebody for me?"

"Sure, who do you want me to find?" Nicholas pushed away from the computer station he was working on and fired up a new station.

"The President of the old United States," said Paul.

"What? Seriously?" Nicholas evaluated Paul, but Paul always seemed a little daft to him, how was this any different?

"Yes. Can you do it?"

"Can Linux outperform Windows?"

Paul stared blankly. "Just tell me if you can do it."

"Yes! I can do it."

"I'll pay you," said Paul. Then he remembered what Clyde said. "And order a pizza."

Nicholas' face lit up at the mention of food. "Veggie? Extra toppings?"

What kind of kid was this? Veggie. What ever happened to pepperoni and sausage? "Whatever you want. You phone it in, here's some cash. Keep the change." He threw a substantial wad of bills, mostly hundreds, on the table in front of him.

"Hey, Paul, that's a lot of money. You don't have to do that." Nicholas studied his face. "Are you okay?"

"My brother died," he said simply. He sat heavily into a computer chair on wheels, causing it to roll backwards. He didn't seem to notice.

"Clyde? No! I liked that old guy," said Nicholas. "What happened to him, heart attack?"

"He wasn't old. He had lots of years left," mourned Paul.

"What happened to him then?"

"He got shot while saving my life."

"Whoa! He's a good big brother," said Nicholas. "You should be proud."

"I *am* proud. Find the president."

Nicholas clacked at the keyboard for several minutes and then said, "I shouldn't take your money for this."

"Take it. I want you to find him, no matter how long it takes."

"Done."

"You found him already?"

"Yes, that's why I said I shouldn't take your money. It was too easy."

"How did you do it?"

"I didn't have to do anything; someone is blogging about the pre-Big-War days. She posted all of the former president's addresses. This one says ‘until present’, so if she’s correct, he’s still there.”

“Keep the money. Buy yourself that pizza.”

“What are you going to do? You going to go see him?”

“Yes.”

“You think he’ll let you in? He won’t call the police?”

“He won’t be calling the police.” On that note, Paul left the lab, leaving young Nicholas to wonder if *he* should call the police.

20

President John Williams seethed. How could he have been bested by Ann Kinji? He stormed the halls, special agents scurrying to keep up with him. He spun around and glared at everyone in his path. "Stay away from me!" he snarled. He ducked into the restricted area that led to the underground maze of secret parking.

"But Mr. President!" protested Special Agent Billings, because it was his duty to do so, not because he particularly cared about the president's well-being. In fact, he had applied for a new detail assignment and was biding his time until he could move on.

John ignored him and quickened his long angry strides. Billings kept up with him easily, being half the President's age, and in much better physical shape. Billings signaled the team to keep up, and they too had no difficulty. The party of nine ended their manic flight only when they reached the presidential limo station. There they all stood, glancing questioningly at each other.

Billings made the decision for them: let John go alone, they'd do a convoy. He assigned his eight agents to William's impromptu road trip and returned to the White House. There was one perk to not having a bond with the Prez: Billings felt no twinge of guilt when he opted out of these unplanned ventures.

The limo driver opened the door for the president, and returned to his seat behind the wheel. "Just you today, Mr. President?" he asked.

"Yes, Jason."

"Your security detail driving separately then?" he confirmed.

John grunted. He knew he couldn't shake his own detail, but he could at least be alone in the limo. He pressed the divider button. Jason and his partner Penny were not offended, John was often prickly. Seldom was he interested in conversation. They didn't take it personally.

In contrast, President Kinji knew all about Jason's dreams of becoming a personal chef, or opening a café in Italy one day, or both. She knew about Penny's dreams to become a lawyer, and that her paycheck went straight to the Dean's office where she was attending law school, living on the cheap as she paid cash for her tuition. Yes, President Ann Kinji cared enough to listen, and she made them feel special. It is for this reason that Jason and Penny felt loyalty to her over John – it wasn't politics; they simply liked Ann more.

So when President John Williams requested that they drive him to the home of the former President of what-used-to-be the United States of America, they placed a call to President Kinji on her special line; the line she gave each of them if they ever got into any serious trouble. What was happening now was something they thought she should know about. Ann agreed, and thanked the pair of them for their courage.

Penny had made the call while still on the road, taking advantage of the privacy barrier that John himself had established. With a hushed voice, she got the message across, while John sat not two feet behind her head, completely oblivious that his nemesis had been tipped off about his upcoming meeting.

After quick deliberation with her team of experts, Ann instructed them to leave the phone line open, so that her team could record everything. They would easily clarify the sound, removing ambient noise, enhancing the sounds of the voices; all of it was fairly routine work for the team, no problem: if they were close enough to hear the conversation with their own ears – the phone would pick it up too. Both Jason and Penny agreed to get as close to President Williams as possible, two open lines were better than one.

Upon arrival, President Williams' security detail stayed outside of the former president's house, as John requested, giving him a false sense of privacy which liberated his tongue. Unbeknownst to John, the upper window of the cathedral-ceilinged home was ajar. With the acoustics of the home creating an amplifying effect, eavesdropping on the conversation between the two men was hard to avoid, and the hearing was made easier because every one of them was actively listening.

William's security detail could hear every word that was said, and Jason and Penny were in an excellent position to record everything. Best of all, ten credible witnesses were even more valuable than the recordings; recordings that could be doctored, as surely the other side would suggest. Ten witnesses? All of them with good clean impressive records? Much harder to dismiss.

"John, long time."

"Not long enough." The former president stared into John William's blue-gray eyes; eyes that should have been deep dark pits by now, haunting him like the eyes of Scrooge's business partner Jacob Marley. But he found no sign of remorse or regret, or even awareness. Williams was no ghost of America Past come to make him repent, he was just another old man with used-up power, same as himself.

Neither man offered his hand to the other. They squared off, sizing each other up. Both thought the other was showing his age. The years had brought each of them hairlines baring more of their foreheads, more grays in the hair that was left, and more creases weathering their faces. Both men were on a variety of medications to control high blood pressure, high cholesterol, and accelerating heart disease.

The stand-off over, John walked inside the house and shut the door. "We have to talk," he said.

"Are we alone?"

"My detail is outside," said John. "What, you think this is entrapment? I'm as vulnerable in this as you are – more so, as sitting president."

The former president led the way down a marbled hallway: the house was only modest from the outside. The interior of the home was tricked out with the most expensive materials and the gaudiest displays of lighting, art, furniture, draperies, fixtures, and collectibles.

He entered the library, a room that held over two million dollars' worth of rare books and artifacts. The library was two stories high, with the top row of books nearly aligned with the cathedral ceiling. In this room, not one, but *two* windows were ajar.

The conversation between the two presidents was even easier to listen in on. The agents quietly celebrated.

"John, what do you want?" he said.

"To the point, you're a man after my own heart."

"Then get to it." He settled into a chair, lit a cigar, and took a long draw. His deep red shirt, sharp, beak-like nose, and the unfortunate placement of ornamental horn-like fixtures on the back of his chair directly above his head added to the overall image of the devil himself on his throne. The rings of smoke drifted toward John like a graveside fog.

"They know about the e-mail." John did not wait for an invitation, that he knew would not come, to sit down. He selected the chair directly across from the devil, feeling no trepidation, as he was largely unaware that he was staring into soulless eyes.

"I know."

"You know?"

"I have people." The former president stroked the goatee he had grown since he'd left office. It was remarkably dark, with no gray hair at all. The contrast between the nearly-white hair on his head and the jet black hair on his sallow face was startling. The grays on his head had made his hair coarse and wild – giving him the look of a madman.

"It's all going to come crashing down. I tried to cut it off, but Kinji is running with this thing."

"It doesn't matter."

"Doesn't matter?" John threw up his hands in disbelief. He stood up to pace the room.

"It doesn't matter to *me*. I'm sure it matters a great deal to *you*, John." He folded his hands across his narrow chest. He was a tall man, of an enormous stature due to having Marfan's syndrome, a condition similar to, or possibly the same as, the disorder that Abraham Lincoln had. His arms were unusually and disproportionately long, and his overall frame was imposingly lanky. He towered above most other men. Marfan's syndrome had also given him a weak heart, which had been rumored but never confirmed while he was in office.

"You'll be arrested right alongside me. Your legacy will be that of a traitor."

"I'd do it all again. We had endless deadlock, bi-partisan bickering, lobbyists in everyone's pocket. While we were buying up weapons, kids in our own country went hungry, went homeless. Our food supply was toxic but we kept right on selling more of the poison -- while Europe banned the same stuff we served our kids for breakfast."

John groaned. "I thought I heard enough of this rhetoric while you were on the campaign trail. You don't really believe your own spin doctors, do you?"

"Yes, John, I do. I could see our America headed for ruin. There was no end in sight, what with our open borders and our out-of-control spending. We couldn't make it stop. No one could agree on anything. The old boys club got bigger and bigger. We'd been reduced to distracting people with gay marriage debates so that no one would notice that our country was dying."

"I look at you and see someone who doesn't fit in the old boys club."

"Because I represent the gay community? Is that what galls at you, John? But flaming liberal that I am, I couldn't change a thing, not even with democrats taking the majority."

“Then how can you blame my party? You had the majority.”

“The Republicans wouldn’t ever see reason, or they didn’t care, I’m not sure which. They’d never stop throwing money on defense, getting us further and further into debt – while lining the pockets of contractors and manufacturers, over the blood of our young men and women.”

“What do you care about them? I seem to recall that you cut their pay.”

“Everyone has to make sacrifices. You’d stand behind the Republican agenda? Shelter the richest Americans in the world while letting the poor and the middle class wither and die, sometimes literally. Our health care went from bad to worse.”

“Hey now, don’t lay all that on Republicans.”

“We are going to debate now, John? Not your strong suit, never was.”

“Big government is not the answer. How far did liberals get with all those bailouts? And don’t get me started with Obamacare,” said John. “Whatever happened to *that* disaster?”

“Exactly. Nothing worked. Nothing. We were never going to agree. The Republicans manipulated the ‘Christian Right’ to believe that they were their party. To keep the masses loyal, the Republicans gave them what they wanted. What did they care either way if women’s health care services were cut? Tax breaks to the wealthiest Americans? Why not, that’s who finances the party. And I have three words for you: oil, oil, oil.”

“You hated Republicans so much that you’d nuke our own country to get rid of us?”

“You feel the same about Democrats.”

"Touché," said John.

"We both got what we wanted. And the country is the better for it. We were headed for complete economic ruin. There was no way out, and you know that. It wasn't a recession; it was a depression that kept on depressing. There was no way out of all of that debt. We were bankrupt. Our money wasn't worth the paper it was printed on."

"We were headed for Communism. We were already halfway there," said John.

"That's where you and I disagree, but that's water under the bridge. The country is functioning much better as a split nation, well on its way to recovery. It was time for the two ideologies to go their separate ways."

"I knew Democrats hated us, but I must say that your malice toward Republicans is impressive," said John.

"And you loathed us also. Nothing like common hatred as the tie that binds."

"You are delusional if you think we're doing better. We are *not* doing better. We are doing worse. The cost of the Big War sank us. We're still cleaning up. People are still dying or getting sick from the nuclear fallout, the waste, the contaminated water in places we didn't expect it to be. Talk about toxic food? We have much bigger problems than that now. You mentioned homeless kids, starving kids? What do you think happened when the Big War ended? You think the land repaired itself? You think it was a clean kill, and those who survived are just peachy? Haven't you seen a single podcast?" John ranted.

"The way is open for strong leadership. America can heal herself."

"With a liberal agenda of big government? Restricting freedoms until children are property of the state from birth, parental rights stripped to nothing – that is if the babies even make it to life, given that abortions are now legal even at the late stages. What's next, killing them *after* they're born?"

"That's ridiculous and you know it!"

"I see we've made no progress, and here we are with a torn, battled country littered with nuclear fallout and death."

"You should step aside, John."

"What? How dare you! You think Kinji can fix this nightmare? This apocalypse? If anything, *she* should step aside. I could repair this country much faster without her interference. But why are you going down this road? Weren't you making the point that America functions better as a split nation? Or has the truth come out: your hidden agenda was to rid the nation of Republicans!"

"Now, John, simmer down. I know you won't ever die off. You are like cockroaches. And so are your issues. Take pro-life for example. Neither of us give two figs about what happens to these women, or if a baby is a baby in the womb. Hell, I don't care if a baby is a baby when he's two. Raise them, kill them, I don't care. But don't tell me that God has tied my hands – at least we have statistics and results to back up our stand – your only argument is 'God'. But we are the same at the core. We both cater to our parties: we tell them what they want to hear. You say you care about the sanctity of life. I say I care about a woman's right to choose. The irony, or hypocrisy, is that we are both misogynistic prigs who'd sooner deny our own seed than claim it."

"I was on board with everything. I have a vigilante spirit. I actually believed that a split America would do as you said: break us to heal us. But it didn't work. And hearing you talk right now – you're crazy."

"John, you were walking right alongside me in those days. May I jog your memory – how we alone conspired to stall the debt ceiling negotiations? Deliberately letting the nation default, sabotaging nation and world markets, crippling our own government? You have amnesia?"

"The idea came after coming close to default in 2011, I wasn't the only one involved. It wasn't you and I like you allude to. We had support from both sides of the aisle."

"But John, it was the two of us who kept a cool head and had the balls to go through with the plan. The others would have caved, would have signed off at the last hour. The two of us made the play to switch sides, stalling the bill, running the clock. We had no tea-partiers in our way this time around, and after cleaning house of most of those zealots, we were home free for the big crash and burn – phase one of the plan for America to go its separate ways – a covert civil war, if you will."

"I lay awake at night wondering if we needed to take it a step further – wasn't financial ruin enough to split the union? Did we really need to let the bombs fly? We knew that the Iranians had moved their weapons within range – we could have taken them out."

"Regrets, John? I don't believe you. You and I are cut from the same cloth. I appeal to common sense and you appeal to the rest."

"You've got some serious hate going on for Christians."

"No, those poor people are only sheep to the slaughter."

"So your hatred is only toward Republicans then?"

"I wouldn't say that I don't have contempt for the Christians, of course they're a thorn in my side. They cloud simple issues with their morality, blocking my path. Not a one of them can think for himself, yet they manage to bring the machine to a grinding halt, over and over again. No, I hold no love for Christians. But I have no more contempt for them than *you* do: you manipulate them for your own political gain, pretending to be one of them, catering to their religious zeal. You don't know the first thing about their God, do you, John?"

"I see myself through your eyes and I have a strong feeling I'm going to hell," said John.

The two men looked at each other and then broke into laughter. "I missed you, John."

"No you didn't."

"You got that right."

Their banter was disrupted when they heard gun shots outside the house.

21

Serena admired the photos of herself with President Ann Kinji – standing in her very own kitchen! She copied the entire 120 pictures of her family with the President onto her laptop. Then she synced it with her iPad. She made desktop pictures for each. How she wished she could post them to Facebook, but she was officially still in hiding. She wondered if her connection to the President could help her get her family's identity back without penalty – it would be so liberating to shed the Meadows persona. Then she could freely share her prized pictures of herself with the first female president!

The photos had taken only a few minutes to take, her rapid-fire digital camera beep, beep, beeping, taking dozens of pictures of nearly identical poses. Samuel raced for his own camera, and the session began anew. Ten minutes later, the cameras were off. Serena didn't want President Kinji to regret accepting her invitation to come to her home. Enough already, it was time to serve the president coffee and a snack; and, she anticipated, talk like old girlfriends! Oh, how she'd love to pick the president's brain. This would be the best coffee chat ever!

Unfortunately, that was when Ann received a call on her special line. She made her goodbyes quickly, after having spent less than fifteen minutes on the Meadow's property, and was out the door before the coffee could even finish brewing. The Meadows, clinging to their fifteen minutes of fame, stood on their lawn; watching the convoy, and waving until the president's entourage was completely out of view. Then they all trudged back into the house.

"At least I got pictures," said Serena. When she got back inside that was the first thing she did: download the pictures, and she couldn't resist sending a few to Karyn and Dan via e-mail. When she was finished gawking at and preserving her photos, she joined Tom at the kitchen table, where he was not letting the fresh coffee go to waste.

"I keep thinking about poor Clyde," she said.

"Yeah, me too," said Tom.

"I wonder how Paul is doing," said Serena.

"The secret service is probably still watching him, he's probably fine," said Tom, without conviction.

"No, they left. President Kinji said that all of her team was heading back," said Serena.

"If it would make you feel better, we can check on him," said Tom.

"I think we should do that, yes," said Serena. "I feel kind of responsible for him since we went along with his plan without double-checking to see if President Kinji really did authorize it."

"It wasn't our fault."

"I had a nagging feeling that they were lying, but I ignored my gut feeling," said Serena.

"You didn't kill Clyde. But we'll find Paul."

Serena suggested that they leave the kids at home, not wanting a repeat of the disastrous occasions of the past few days. Then they were out the door to find a person who, as recently as just a couple days ago, they had been trying to avoid. They first tried the house Paul had shared with his brother Clyde, but finding no one at home, they went to the computer lab. Serena had a hunch that he might go there to feel close to Clyde.

At the lab, they found only a young boy, around fourteen years old. They knocked on the glass window of the entrance door. He stared at them for a few seconds, dismissed them as non-threatening, and opened the door for them. He didn't say a word, but looked at them expectantly, a non-verbal invitation to speak.

"I'm Serena Wil—mmm, Meadows," she said. "This is my husband Tom. I used to be a private detective, but I've lost my knack for finding people. I'm looking for Clyde's brother, a man named Paul."

Nicholas' face lit up. "He was just here!"

"Do you know where he was going?" asked Tom.

"Yes! He freaked me out."

They waited for him to continue, and when he didn't, Serena said, "Where did he say he was going?"

"He gave me a lot of money, more money than I've ever had in my whole life! Look at this pile of money! He threw it down on the table and told me to keep it. I tried to say no, I really did. He told me to keep all of it," Nicholas' energy was that of a puppy fetching a ball.

"Why would he do that?" asked Serena. Getting information from this kid was tedious, but she had a feeling that a little patience would be well worth the effort, and boy was it effort.

Nicholas stammered and spoke at an octave that was barely audible. Serena and Tom strained their ears to hear him. "He asked me to find somebody, somebody really famous. I mean, *really* famous."

"Who?" Serena struggled against the urge to hurry the boy along, as she suspected it would only make communication even more tedious.

He lowered his voice to barely above a whisper, "The former president, before the Big War."

"And did you find him?" asked Serena.

"Yes, it was easy. I did a search and found the blog, where a fan page was and she had written about a list of the homes of all the places where he, the former president, before the Big War, had ever lived before, all of the places, and she had the one he lives in now, his current residence, and I told Paul that it was too easy and not to give me money, that I couldn't take his money, but he insisted and I still have the money. Do you think I can keep the money?" Nicholas asked shyly, hopefully.

"It's yours now, keep it."

Nicholas tried gallantly, and unsuccessfully, to suppress the big grin that took over his face.

"Did you give Paul the address?" asked Serena.

"Yes. I have it. I got it in the window behind this one, see?" Nicholas was using one of the touch screen monitors. He used his fingertip to select the hidden window. The former president's address came up, complete with a map marking the exact location.

Tom plugged the address into his handheld GPS. “Got it, thanks.”

“I better call President Kinji,” said Serena.

“Wow! You’re friends with the President?” said Nicholas.

Serena beamed. “Well, I’m not sure I can go that far, but yes, I know President Ann Kinji.”

She pressed the speed dial pre-set for Ann’s special line, avoiding typing in a long series of numbers. What she got was a recording. “That’s odd. It says that ‘this number is closed to all incoming calls’.”

“Try it again?” said Tom.

She did. “Nope, same thing, ‘this number is closed to all incoming calls’.”

“What do you want to do? I’m willing to go, it’s up by Burnsville.”

“Burnsville? I didn’t know he was in the Minneapolis area,” said Serena.

“Yeah, he was at the ribbon cutting ceremony at the new wing, where the stock exchange is, the financial center, where they buy and sell stocks, it was on the podcast, I saw it,” said Nicholas.

“Why do you think Paul wants to see the former President? Should we call the police? Or the FBI?” asked Serena.

“That’s what I was thinking!” said Nicholas.

“Then again, this isn’t really our case anymore, not that it ever really was. We have only a loose connection to this,” said Serena.

“Right, it’s not like you’re hired. It’s up to you. I’m willing to go if you want to,” said Tom.

"I think we should do it. Patriotic duty, right? Whatever Paul is up to, it can't be a good thing that he's gone to see the former president."

"Up to you," Tom repeated.

"They never gave you your gun back. What if Paul is uncooperative, or what if he has a gun?"

"We'll call the police."

"Good point. I'll keep trying President Kinji's phone, but… I don't feel right doing nothing at all while we wait. We might as well go up there and if we see anything alarming we can call the police."

Nicholas looked from Tom to Serena and back again. "Can I come?"

"No, but we can give you a ride home if you want," said Tom.

Nicholas shrugged. "I rode my bike. You guys better hurry, Paul is probably almost there by now." He stared wistfully beyond them through the lab door window at their car for a long second. Then he raced back to his computer station. "I'm going to watch the podcasts. I'll probably see you on the news!"

22

"Hey, man, you don't have to do this," said Special Agent Whikehart. He heard Paul coming around the back of the former president's house long before Paul could see them. Paul had parked near the back entrance, oblivious to the numerous government vehicles parked at the front entrance.

It was only after he entered the backyard that Paul saw the team of agents gathered to meet him. It was then that he broke into a cold sweat, suddenly chilled and shivering. He didn't stop moving though- he walked doggedly forward, putting one shaky foot in front of the other.

"Looks like suicide by police," said Special Agent Zech.

"We should call someone in on this," said Whikehart.

"We don't have time, this guy could pop off at any time," said Gasiorowski. He stared at the unsteady figure a few yards away. Nothing about this guy seemed right.

"Call it in," said Zech.

"Meanwhile, we deal with it," said Special Agent Wooding. Wooding signaled for four team members to move in.

Special Agents Gasiorowski, Bledsoe, Whikehart and Jorissen slowly circled around Paul while Special Agent Delk called it in.

"The FBI is sending a team, but we have to keep him talking until they get here," said Delk.

Zech initiated dialog with Paul. "Easy now, tell us what you want, we can help you."

Paul stood with his arms passively by his sides, his face emotionless. He said nothing.

Zech tried again, "Why are you at the house of the former president?"

The circling agents came a few steps closer.

Paul reached into his pocket.

Agents Gasiorowski, Bledsoe, Jorissen and Wooding all fired at once. None of the shots were aimed to kill, or even to maim. They were merely noisemakers. The desired effect was easily accomplished: Paul froze, dropping what he had in his hand. No further shots were necessary.

The gun fire got the attention of the two men inside the house, and the attention of the couple who was pulling up behind the line of government vehicles parked in front of the former president's residence.

"Oh no!" cried Serena. "It's too late! We should have called the police."

"That's a lot of rounds," said Tom. "Look around; there are government vehicles all over this place. They already know."

"What do we do, stay in the car?" asked Serena. "We should at least tell them what we know. Poor Paul, he's probably dead." She couldn't see much from her perspective, but she did notice an agent walking purposefully toward their car. She shook Tom's arm to get his fast attention.

Neither was startled when Special Agent Whikehart rapped on their window. "Identify yourself, please."

Serena leaned across Tom's lap to speak out his window, "We were helping President Kinji, and Paul is part of that. We were looking for Paul to check on him. It looks like we were too late. We tried to call President Kinji on her special line, but we couldn't get through."

Whikehart handed Tom a slim gadget through the open window. "Press 3."

Tom pressed 3 and heard a click.

"Yes?" said President Kinji.

Tom handed the tiny phone to Serena. She held it to her ear the best she could.

"Yes?" President Kinji repeated, louder.

Serena held the phone up to her mouth, as if holding a microphone. "President Kinji, it's me, Serena. I'm at the former president's house. I'm guessing you already know what's going on here?"

"Yes, my team is working on the situation. Why are you there?"

"We were checking up on Paul, and learned that he was coming here. I tried to reach you on your special line but couldn't get through."

"Don't worry; we got everything we needed before he showed up. No harm done. Give the phone back to Special Agent Whikehart please."

Serena passed the phone to Tom, who handed it back to Whikehart.

Whikehart listened to President Kinji's orders via his wireless earpiece. He nodded to no one in particular, then disconnected the call.

"She's cleared you. She says if we can't get Paul out of here quickly and quietly, then we are to let you have a try at him." His voice was toneless, but he conveyed with his facial expression and body language that he didn't agree with the president's decision, and he didn't lack confidence that he and his team could take care of the problem.

Whikehart returned to the chaos in the former president's backyard, not hearing, or possibly ignoring, Serena's plea to "Wait!"

Serena said to Tom, "Are we supposed to follow him?"

"They'll come get us if they need us," said Tom.

Serena got out of the car. "He said President Kinji cleared us. I think we should go."

Tom followed suit and the two of them were quickly through the front gate, around the side of the brick McMansion, and into the immaculate, professionally landscaped, backyard. There were no gnomes or plastic flamingos, no swing sets or trampolines, no BBQ grill, no pool. There was nothing to indicate that anyone actually used this yard. Today's circus was probably the most activity the property had ever had.

"Now what! Who are they?" barked President John Williams.

Serena tried to squelch her surprise, and disgust, at the sight of Williams standing on the lawn. She answered, with impressive confidence, “I’m Serena and this is my husband Tom. We know Paul and might be able to help talk him into leaving without any problems.”

Williams grunted and waved his hand dismissively. “Clean up this mess,” he said to everyone in general. He zeroed in on Special Agent Wooding in particular when he said, “Give me ten minutes; get the boys ready to roll. I want to be back at the White House before daybreak.”

Even though it meant another convoy, another flight, and a final convoy, the agents were relieved to hear that they’d be going home soon. They’d had enough of Minnesota. The temperatures were dropping much lower than they were used to during this time of year.

Serena waited until Williams was back inside before she walked over to where Paul was standing without moving, his arms still hanging limply at his sides, his eyes fixated on the small object he had dropped on the ground. “Paul, what are you doing here?” she said in a soft, gentle voice.

Paul snapped out of his trance then, and looked at her with clear sharp eyes. “I’m here to deliver this,” he said. He reached down to scoop up the object he had dropped.

A half dozen agents’ weapons made mechanical noises all at once.

Paul waved his arms over his head. “I’m not armed! I’m not armed! It’s not a weapon. It’s a bug. It’s a bug!”

Whikehart walked past Serena to pick up the object. “What’s this? It looks like a fly.” He pulled the high tech insect out of its case.

"Be careful with that! It was my brother's. Clyde had it made. I was going to set it to fly around during my little chat with the former Prez," said Paul. "Hey! Stop messing with it! It's very sensitive. It can record audio from yards away. It's very valuable. I want that back!" He watched woefully as the agents passed the bug around. "At least put it back in the case!"

"They can put it back in the case, right, Agents?" Serena negotiated.

Agent Wooding brought the bug to Special Agent "The Beav" Black, whose love for spy gadgets made him an expert on unusual tech situations in the field. Agent Black's turn examining the bug ended with putting it reverently back in the case. The agents were losing interest in Paul now that they knew he was unarmed. They relaxed their stance.

"Paul, I'll ask that they return the bug to you when they are done inspecting it. Why don't we talk in the car? We are parked at the front entrance, just around there." Serena pointed to the side yard. She took a few steps in that direction.

Tom and Paul followed her. The agents gave them a look of dismissal. Whikehart had confirmed that Paul was her charge. The agents returned their attention to the two men in the house. They were hopeful that the visit was winding down and soon they'd be on their way home. Several had dates that evening that they hoped to make it home in time for.

Paul settled into the backseat of the Meadow's car. He shut the door and waited for Tom and Serena to invite him to speak. "Well, what's going on?" asked Serena.

That was all the opening he needed. "I planned to confront the former president with everything we know, record it, and give it to the White House."

"President Kinji said that they already got everything they needed, so they must have been thinking the same thing you were," said Serena. "It sounds like you can probably go home now. I don't think anyone is going to bother you."

"I see FBI was turned away," Tom agreed. "They aren't going to bring you in. You better not come around anymore though."

"I'm not done yet," said Paul. His eyes glowed with intensity, and insanity.

Serena ignored his words and ramped up her persuasion, using Paul's grief to grab his attention. "Without you and Clyde, Bryce wouldn't have gotten those files. The Angels Mark's role in this will go down in history. Clyde will go down in history as a hero. That's gotta feel good, right Paul? I know he would have liked that."

Paul said nothing. His expression did not change.

"Paul? Clyde's memory will be honored, it will. I'm afraid if you won't let us talk you into going home, we'll need to let those agents take care of you. You can't stay here," said Serena.

She tried to gain the attention of one of the agents, but none of them were looking at her. Most of the team was focused on the house, listening intently to the conversation within the presidential walls. The only two agents who seemed to be assigned to them were watching the area surrounding the vehicle, protecting them from the dangers outside the car, not anticipating the dangers from within.

"You have no idea what Clyde was capable of. He got his team to invent incredible things, Clyde's own ideas brought to life by child geniuses," said Paul.

"I'm sure he wouldn't want you to go to prison, Paul. President Kinji seems ready to let your missteps slide, because of all you and Clyde did to get at the truth. I know you think you are doing this for him, but…" said Serena.

"I *am* doing this for him. You have no idea what he's done for me. He has killed for me, he has died for me," said Paul ominously.

"But President Kinji has all the evidence we need. Justice will be served," said Serena.

"She's right, Paul. There's nothing more you can do. You need to let it go," said Tom.

"I will never let it go!" screamed Paul. His face turned crimson while the veins in his forehead throbbed.

Tom looked around to see if Paul had been loud enough to attract attention. Apparently not. At that instant, out of the corner of his eye, he caught movement. He flinched; then he laughed at his fear. "One of your bugs got out."

A tiny mechanical flying object zipped around the interior of the car, bouncing off of surfaces and dropping down, then taking off again, repeatedly. Tom and Serena watched it, first amused and then annoyed. "How do I catch it?" asked Serena.

"Oh I wouldn't touch that if I were you," said Paul mysteriously. He was now sitting with his hands neatly folded; his body strangely still and calm.

"What do you mean? Will it zap us if we touch it?" asked Serena.

"Oh, far worse than that," Paul said slowly. He grinned as mysteriously as the Cheshire Cat from Alice in Wonderland.

The mechanical insect whirred madly around and around, bumping and falling, bumping and falling. It knocked into the passenger's side window, nearly hitting Serena. It bumbled along over the interior of the car door until it bounced far enough from the vinyl that it was able to take flight again.

"I'm going to get out, and that thing will get loose!" said Serena.

"I don't mind," said Paul, a tight-lipped grin plastered across his flushed face.

Serena was a people-reader, and she took note of what she saw on Paul's face, not only his odd coloring, but the look he got every time the bug bumped into something: he flinched. *Why? Is he afraid the flying gadget will break? Is it fragile?*

No, no, that isn't it. He was bracing himself as if he thought the mechanical insect might explode when it bumped the dashboard. Her heart filled with terror as her mind clicked, clicked, clicked along until it finally understood.

It felt like the seconds were suspended, as if time stood still when Serena turned to Tom and said, "It's a bomb." She and Tom fled from the car, unintentionally letting the mechanical fly out.

Paul cackled, a high-pitched witch-like cackle. He took something out of his pocket.

"Hey! Whoa! No! Don't do it!" Tom leaped out of the car and threw open Paul's door. He tried to grab Paul's arm, but it was too late. Paul had pressed the button on the gadget and had even managed, with lightning reflexes, to set a very small joystick lever to send the mechanical insect directly into the former president's house.

"It's a bomb, it's a bomb!" Tom ran full-out into the gaggle of secret service agents, his voice hoarse and ragged as he continued to yell as he ran, "It's a bomb, it's a bomb, it's a bomb!"

"You said you were unarmed!" gasped Serena. She backed away from the car, pausing only slightly to look at the man whose madness she had so greatly underestimated.

Paul smiled. "I lied."

And with that, the miracle created in Clyde's prized lab, with intuitive flight technology, flew into the open, screen-less, window of the former president's house. Before any of the agents could respond and orient themselves to the word "Bomb", there was a sharp whistling sound, like the sound a tea kettle makes just before it blows. And then, with no harm to anyone but the two men inside the house, the world's smallest bomb blew.

23

President Ann Kinji greeted Serena and Tom with a hug, which both accepted as easily as if the hug was from a neighbor, like it was an everyday occurrence to be hugged by the President.

"So happy to see the pair of you alive, well, and standing in front of me."

"Thank you," both of them murmured.

"With Paul in custody, Clyde dead, and Bryce out of the way, you won't have any more trouble. Which is why I think you should ditch the Meadows name," she said, with a sly wink.

Serena blushed.

"Of course I knew all about you. You couldn't have gotten so close to me otherwise. I know that you set your own house on fire, so that you'd be presumed dead. I know that Paul's Off-grid group gave you a new identity, and kept you successfully off the grid until William's camp came along."

"This is the part when the Scooby-doo gang tells the criminals who was wearing the monster mask," said Serena.

"Oh, I don't see you as a monster, not even of the Scooby-doo variety. You protected your family. I only wish that you and Karyn had shared that e-mail from Farideh with more than just the FBI, since our own government was not to be trusted, but of course you wouldn't have known that," said Ann, frowning, letting her words settle for a few seconds. "How could anyone have known such a thing? But now that we do, knowing that we could have taken a different course, one that would have saved many lives, or maybe even avoided the Big War altogether -- it's so hard to fathom. It was better when we didn't know. And yet, the truth shall set us free."

"It will feel good to be free," said Serena.

"Freedom is something we still have, yes. Thank God for that, agree?" said Ann.

"I'm sorry about the presidents," said Tom. "I didn't know it was a bomb until it was too late."

"I know, it wasn't your fault. Really, it was mine. I'm the one who suggested you could take Paul, going against my agents' wishes. I should have had him searched and cleared first, especially since I knew he was emotionally unstable. And he was a nut job before he was unstable. Extreme lapse in judgment on my part," said Ann.

"What's going to happen now?" asked Serena. "Will the records be buried?"

Ann's eyebrows shot up with surprise. "Of the most deadly, most massive cover-up in the history of the world? Why on Earth would we do that? Of course we respect the sanctity of human life – this is no doubt a great tragedy to be preparing for two presidential funerals, but we cannot hide from the truth. It's been buried for too long and it will not be buried with them. Their reputations and ours will have to suffer – the world needs to know what really happened."

"I admire that," said Serena.

"This opens the door to new dialog, dialog that I believe America has needed to hear for a long time. Whether or not people will be open to what I have to say, I don't know. I'm sure to find out come voting time, which is right around the corner."

"You have our vote," said Tom.

Ann smiled. "And you have mine. That's one reason I called you in here. First, I want to thank you for all of your help."

"We didn't do much," said Tom.

"It seemed like we stayed one step behind your team the whole time," said Serena.

"You were in the thick of it all, you just benefitted from resources in high places. You'd have been able to deduce things for yourself, maybe more slowly, but you'd have done it," said Ann.

"Good thing we don't have to find out – it's over now," said Serena.

"I have a strong feeling that I'll need your help in the near future," said Ann.

"What do you mean?" asked Serena.

"Well, I don't know exactly, but I liked that you and Tom had my special number. I liked knowing that someone outside of the White House, living as a normal person, had my back. I tell you, I've lost myself here in this office. I live in a bubble, with the pressure of the world pressing on the surface of that bubble at all times. You are outside of this bubble, free to roam around without secret service agents. And I trust you. How valuable is that? I have a feeling that I'll need someone I can trust," said Ann.

"You can call me anytime," said Serena.

"I know you were a private detective several years ago," said Ann.

"Yes, before the kids," said Serena.

"I'm asking if you're willing to be on call for me. I may never call you, but if I do – are you for hire?"

"Of course. What would I be doing? Investigating outside of official channels?

"Possibly. I might need a friend."

"You've got it," said Serena, grinning from ear to ear.

President Ann Kinji showed them the door, meeting adjourned. Then she went back to her desk and drafted the speech of a lifetime, a speech she delivered the very next day, without much advance notice to the media, to the secret service, to her press secretary, to anyone. But they all scrambled and were in their places before she began.

She stood boldly in front of the flag of the former United States of America, completely poised despite the awareness that cameras were delivering her voice and image live to millions of people all over the world. Slowly and methodically, she weighed each word before allowing it to spill from her lips. Years later, her grace would be remembered almost as much as her words.

> *My fellow Americans, my heart is heavy as I speak to you tonight. By now, the world has heard about the death of our two presidents, the death of two men who conspired to allow America to be destroyed, to destroy us in a misguided attempt to save us; an attempt that did not work; but served*

to sink us further into the pit of despair, hopelessness, lawlessness, and poverty.

But those men did not act alone. Their warring ideologies were bred by all of us, by the American people themselves. From the Oval office to the Senate, from the Congress to the Pentagon, from the corporations to the small businesses, from the universities to the schools, we have held contempt for each other. May God forgive us.

Ann paused. Then she began again.

Did that surprise you just now? That I uttered the name of God? We fight over whether God should stay in, or be cast out of, money, songs, literature, even art. Why are we wasting our life's breath on this? God is love, correct? Regardless of what you believe about God, God is not the problem. Respect everyone's beliefs. Do liberals hate Christians? Are Republicans judgmental, greedy and hypocritical? There's so much hate going around and not enough love. If we keep chasing our tails like this, separating ourselves into two opposing camps, we will never come together.

Maybe if we were all more tolerant of each other, we'd have fewer government shutdowns, we'd have more food on the American table, we'd have less division. We are now literally a divided nation, but we've been polarized and broken for many years. We will never heal until we stop hating our own people. It is for that reason that I am stepping down from my party. I no longer believe that a two party system has any real chance of healing America. It is what has destroyed America.

Therefore, I am running as an Independent candidate. I will make clear where I stand on the issues, and you'll see that I probably lean more liberally than conservatively on most issues, but I'm middle-of-the-road on some issues, and very far to the right on other issues. How can a party represent any one candidate? Don't we need to evaluate each issue as it comes? Few people are so rigid that they lean to the right or to the left all the time. We humans are capable of reason and balanced judgment. Let's agree to avoid extremes!

I challenge every candidate running against me to throw down their party lines – enter this race as an Independent. Let's shake up how we do this. No more lobbyists: we cannot be bought! Let's put a moratorium on campaigning. What's wrong with using the Internet to reach voters? It's free! I challenge my opponents to live-streaming debates. All of this reform will create a mess you say? Well, it just might. And it's a mess worth making!

For the good of our dying nation, we might need to dig back into our newly-revised Constitution and tweak it many, many more times until we get it right, to re-establish ourselves as a united nation. Whatever it takes to get us thinking like rational loving human beings again – we need to do that. And that, my fellow Americans, is what's going to save us. Abolishing parties that divide us – for real this time. And most of all, learning to love our own people.

It is my prayer that the United States of America be one day united, united in her physical self, but more importantly, in her spirit. May God give us the wisdom to know what to do to heal as a nation, to become prosperous once again, to become as one nation, under God. We can heal, we can rise again – I believe that. Seek into your heart to make the changes you need to make, right along with me. Be willing to make sacrifices, be willing to think of your neighbor; be willing to love your neighbor as yourself. May God bless America.

As soon as President Ann Kinji, first female president, first Asian American President, finished her last word, the buzzing of the bees began. She answered all of the questions, all of them. She stayed on her feet, responding to every media representative from the seasoned professional, to the celebrity on-air talent, to the junior reporter. She answered questions from foreign press. She stayed on and on; late into the night. Finally, when the room grew gradually, and then completely, silent, she said good-night.

She went home, home to her imposing bedroom in the White House where Ted was sprawled out on the massive four-poster bed, snoring. Ann looked at him longingly, and even nudged his arm, but he didn't stir except to clear his throat. She lay on the bed, but could not rest. She rang the kitchen and requested a snack.

Then she picked up the phone, even though it was by now almost midnight, and hoped that Serena was still awake, and would understand.

Serena answered on the second ring. She didn't sound sleepy, but she did sound worried, "Hello?"

"Hi, Serena, it's President Kinji."

"Is something wrong?"

"No, no. I feel silly calling you, but after a night like this, a girl needs to talk to a friend."

Serena smiled warmly enough to send the feel-good vibes through the phone line. "Are you worried about your speech? It was wonderful."

"Yes, anxious. Not many people will think my address is wonderful. And I might be needing you sooner rather than later if I've made new enemies."

"Well, you're probably right. We are still polarized, and it's impossible to please both sides. But 'a wise man avoids all extremes'."

"What's that quote from?" asked Ann.

"The Bible. Ecclesiastes."

"Oh! I certainly can't start quoting Scripture. That would make both sides take offense! I pushed things as far as I could by referring to America as 'one nation under God'."

"I'm sure many were unhappy with you putting God into your speech, saw it as a nod to the conservatives probably, even though I thought it was clearly heart-felt. Liberals say they respect all views, but don't really. Conservatives say they want God in country, but aren't happy unless it's on their terms. I don't see where you can please either extreme, so why worry about that?"

"Most of us are so jaded that we find it hard to believe that anything is heart-felt, but you are right, I meant every word I said."

"Well, if your critics can't see that you are speaking from the heart, there's not much you can do. Some are so closed minded that they only hear the same things in the same way, even when someone is saying something new. Their ears hear the same old blather, and they will never stop fighting the same old arguments," said Serena.

"It does feel hopeless sometimes. In a warped way, our two departed presidents had a demented logic."

"But it's not hopeless, and at least you are trying. How can anyone fault you for seeking a balanced view?"

Ann laughed. "Oh, they can and they will. My speech will be offensive to many, many people. I might not get re-elected."

"I admire you for speaking the truth. The Emperor really is naked," said Serena.

"I'm going to have a long day tomorrow."

"Yes, I'm sure you will, but we can't be the only two people who are tired of all the hate. I mean, enough already. Don't most people by now see both sides as equally destructive?"

"We'll find out. I essentially said that both parties are wicked, are responsible for the evils in the world, and should be destroyed. I keep going over it and over it in my mind, and I don't know how else I could have said it better. And yet, I know that the far right and the far left will hate my words, and *me*, with equal passion, even after all we've been through with two presidential funerals."

"Surely there is intelligent life left on planet Earth. They just might not be in government, well, except for you."

"What did you think of my address to the divided nation, honest opinion?"

Didn't we already cover this? thought Serena. *Wow, friendship with the president is going to be high maintenance.*

Aloud she said, "Besides wonderful? Well, I think someone should have said those things a long time ago. I'm glad *you* did. The only thing that surprises me is that you are second guessing yourself and seeking someone like me out for reassurance."

"I didn't use a speech writer. I feel insecure when I've gone forward without professionals crafting and editing my words."

"Maybe you should do more of your own writing. What do writers know? Educated as they may, it's still just one person's opinion."

"True. Being a rebel doesn't sit comfortably on me. I was the girl whose report card said, 'Ann is thoughtful of others. Ann is conscientious about her work and keeps a tidy desk.' I suppose I need to get used to taking risks if I want to be a pioneer in this post-Big War world we live in."

Serena said, "Again, I thought your address was wonderful, but you're preaching to the choir. Besides, my views are probably too idealistic."

"Better to be naive than jaded, like I mentioned before – most of us have given up on ever getting past our differences. I find your views refreshing."

"I think it's more like 'view', you've pretty much heard all of my thoughts."

Ann chuckled.

"Seriously, I'm not a very political person. I don't watch the news because I find it stressful and depressing. This is probably the most I've ever said in one sitting about anything political. I normally stay out of these conversations – I hate how anything about politics escalates into heated debate."

"You don't watch the news? Never?"

"Sometimes, not never. I know, I'm apathetic, but I don't have any faith that staying informed is possible; I don't believe what the media says about anything. And I don't believe politicians either.

Except for you. So, I'm sorry, but that's all I've got. I don't have anything else to say."

Ann laughed, "I knew there was a reason why I liked you."

24

President Ann Kinji waved her hand in front of the flat screen in front of her. Six hundred and seventy-nine Town Hall messages appeared. She prided herself on reading a sampling of these daily messages from American citizens every morning, after her fitness routine, and before breakfast, she skimmed through as many letters as she could in twenty minutes. She pointed at the screen to open the first message.

<<Dear Madam President,

Thank you for reversing the direction of the previous administration regarding government control of food, private farms, supplements, etc. I have a child who has food sensitivities and I need control over where our food comes from. As much as I'd like to grow all our own food, that's not realistic for me. The freedom to select natural foods that have not been restricted by government regulation is why I voted for you. I do have one issue though. You have taxed small farms and that higher cost is passed on to families like mine, but I'll take that. I do appreciate the lifting of regulations.>>

Ann smiled. The issue of food regulation had been the bane of her existence for several months of heated debate with Congress, farming representatives, and the Food and Health Administration, among others. It was good to see that her work was appreciated. So far so good, today's messages were positive. She opened another one.

<<Dear President Kinki,

I spell your name Kinki because you is Kinki.>>

Ann laughed. There were always a few trolls in the mix, and this one seemed harmless. She swiped her finger in the air to delete the message and move on to the next one.

<<President Kinji, you condemn past presidents because they rewrote the Constitution, and you are doing the same thing! Also, the idea of a Super Congress was brought up by debt ceiling negotiators back in 2011, and that is a change to the Constitution. I think you are a hypocrite. You did not have my vote, and WILL NOT have my vote!>>

Ann had heard similar rhetoric before, backlash over her recent remarks about the changes to the Constitution after the Big War. For every three Americans who wanted a reunited America, there was at least one American who wanted the union to stay divided. History had, on some level, repeated itself: even though the union was split in two between East and West, it was the North and the South that had a division. In general, the North wanted to reunite, while a growing number in the South wanted "less government", believing it was better to stay separate.

She shook off her fears about a civil war, should she be successful in reuniting America. She moved on:

<<President Kinji, When my dog Macie was lost, I got her back because of the pet locator chip. I think all people should have these chips. You said you'd never even look at a bill to put identity chips on everyone at the DMV, so everyone has to get a chip when getting a driver's license. Why not? It's a good idea. If everyone got the chip I could find my ex-boyfriend. He unfriended me and I can't find him. If you cared about the American people you would care about this. Sincerely, Belinda>>

Ann chuckled, and then felt a twinge of guilt. This letter had a genuine voice to it. She selected "reply" and ignored the Identity Chip argument, which wasn't Belinda's real issue.

<<Dear Belinda,

I'm sorry for the loss of your boyfriend. I know there is someone new in your future. Take good care of yourself, stay busy, volunteer to help others. You'll meet the right man when you are not looking.

Sincerely, President Kinji>>

Ann glanced at the clock. She had enough time to read a few more messages. She skimmed through a collection of similar letters: cranks, critics, fans, and the occasional off-topic, but sometimes extremely articulate, political rant. She kept going until she heard an alert: a new message had been sent from a code red mailbox – President's eyes only.

Ann blinked her eyes, daring the screen to show her the message. There it was, a code red. She opened the message.

<<President Kinji, this is Penny. You might remember me? I was the driver for you and President Williams, one of the team of drivers, the one who was going to law school. I have something to tell you that I can't say in front of any of your secret service. Can

you set me up with someone you trust outside of Chicago, someone who is totally unknown, with no agents. Then meet that person in some way without agents or anyone to listen. I don't know if you can do that, but I can't talk to you. They will know and they will kill me. I will send my friend to meet with whoever you want. I can't be seen with you, or anyone connected to you. Please, Madam President, there's not much time. They are watching me.>>

<<Penny, thank you for your bravery. Whatever you have to say, say it now, this is a secure line.>>

<<Not as secure as you think. They are tracking keywords. If I type anything with those keywords, they will see my message to you. Please, set me up with someone to talk to, in person. I have only a few minutes before they know I am gone. Please give me a name.>>

<<Serena Wilcox. You remember her? You'll have to travel. She's gone to Germany, of all places.>>

<<I will send my friend to her. And then Serena can meet with you.>>

There was a shrill beep: line closed.

Ann shook her head. *What could this possibly be about?* She sat and stewed about it for a few minutes, and then went to one committee meeting after another. At the end of a very long day, she picked up the phone to call Serena and give her a head's up.

Serena answered on the first ring.

"Serena? I know you're having a grand time abroad, and I hate to interrupt, but a friend of mine will be meeting with you soon to give you a message for me."

"Your friend has already found me, he's standing right here." Serena's voice sounded stilted. "But he's no friend, not unless you want me dead." And with that, the call was disconnected.

BOOK TWO

COVERT COFFEE

PROLOGUE

President Ann Kinji waved her hand in front of the flat screen in front of her. Six hundred and seventy-nine Town Hall messages appeared. She prided herself on reading a sampling of these daily messages from American citizens every morning. After her fitness routine, and before breakfast, she skimmed through as many letters as she could in twenty minutes.

She pointed at the screen now to select the first message, eager to see what was waiting for her. It wasn't so much that she enjoyed these messages, although she did to some degree, but it was the time spent alone in her office that was so magical about her Town Hall sessions. Yes, Secret Service agents were just outside the door, and their presence was felt, in the same way that a dog made himself known when he was waiting outside the door for his people to come back, but nonetheless she was currently alone in the room, and she treasured every moment. She opened the first message.

<<Dear Madam President, Thank you for reversing the direction of the previous administration regarding government control of food, private farms, supplements, etc. I have a child who has food sensitivities and I need control over where our food comes from. As much as I'd like to grow all our own food, that's not realistic for me. The freedom to select natural foods that have not been restricted by government regulation is why I voted for you. I do have one issue though. You have taxed small farms and that higher cost is passed on to families like mine, but I'll take that. I do appreciate the lifting of regulations. >>

Ann smiled. The issue of food regulation had been the bane of her existence for several months of heated debate with Congress, farming representatives, and the Food and Health Administration, among others. It was good to see that her work was appreciated. So far so good, today's messages were positive. She opened another one.

<<Dear President Kinki, I spell your name Kinki because you is Kinki.>>

Ann laughed. Again? This was a message frequently seen in her inbox. There were always a few trolls in the mix, and this one seemed harmless, simply following the trend of sending variations on "Kinji is Kinki" that were sometimes humorous and creative, sometimes not. Most of the time these messages didn't make it past the spam filter, but every now and then one slipped through. She swiped her finger in the air to delete the message and move on to the next one.

<<President Kinji, you condemn past presidents because they rewrote the Constitution, and you are doing the same thing! Also, the idea of a Super Congress was brought up by debt ceiling

negotiators back in 2011, and that is a change to the Constitution. I think you are a hypocrite. You did not have my vote, and WILL NOT have my vote! >>

Ann had heard similar rhetoric before, backlash over her recent remarks about the changes to the Constitution after the Big War. For every three Americans who wanted a reunited America, there was at least one American who wanted the union to stay divided. History had, on some level, repeated itself: even though the formerly-known-as-United States of America was split in two between East and West in a literal physical sense, it was the North and the South that were truly divided as a people. In general, the North wanted to reunite, while a growing number in the South wanted “less government”, believing it was better to stay separate.

Ann shook off her fears about a civil war, should she be successful in reuniting America. With all the strategists and Generals working on possible scenarios, and all the technology in their vault, surely a civil war could be averted, or at the very least nipped in the bud quickly. She moved on from the critical e-mail and her brooding thoughts about potential civil unrest by opening the next message:

<<President Kinji, When my dog Macie was lost, I got her back because of the pet locator chip. I think all people should have these chips. You said you’d never even look at a bill to put identity chips on everyone at the DMV, to make everyone get a chip when getting a driver’s license. Why not? It’s a good idea. If everyone got the chip I could find my ex-boyfriend. He unfriended me and I can’t find him. If you cared about the American people you would care about this. Sincerely, Belinda>>

Ann chuckled, and then felt a twinge of guilt. This letter had a genuine feel to it. She selected "reply" and ignored the Identity Chip argument, which wasn't Belinda's real issue.

<<Dear Belinda, I'm sorry for the loss of your boyfriend. I know there is someone new in your future. Take good care of yourself, stay busy, volunteer to help others. You'll meet the right man when you are not looking.

Sincerely, President Kinji>>

Ann glanced at the clock. She had enough time to read a few more messages. She skimmed through a collection of similar letters: cranks, critics, fans, and the occasional off-topic, but sometimes extremely articulate, political rant. She kept going until she heard an alert: a new message had been sent from a code red mailbox – President's eyes only.

Ann stared at the screen impatiently, even though she was kept waiting for only two seconds. There it was; a code red. She opened the message.

<<President Kinji, this is Penny. You might remember me? I was the driver for you and President Williams, one of the team of drivers, the one who was going to law school. I have something to tell you that I can't say in front of any of your secret service. Can you set me up with someone you trust outside of Chicago, someone who is totally unknown, with no agents? I'll meet that person in some way without agents or anyone listening. I don't know if you can do that, but I can't talk to you. They will know and they will kill me. I will send my friend to meet with whoever you want. I can't be seen with you, or anyone connected to you. Please, Madam President, there's not much time. They are watching me.>>

<<Penny, thank you for your bravery. Whatever you have to say, say it now, this is a secure line.>>

<<Not as secure as you think. They are tracking keywords. If I type anything with those keywords, they will see my message to you. Please, set me up with someone to talk to, in person. I have only a few minutes before they know I am gone. Please give me a name.>>

<<Serena Wilcox. You remember her? You'll have to travel. She's gone to Germany, of all places.>>

<<I will send my friend to her. And then Serena can meet with you.>>

There was a shrill beep: line closed.

Ann shook her head. What could this possibly be about? She sat and stewed about it for a few minutes, and then went to one committee meeting after another. At the end of a very long day, she picked up the phone to call Serena and give her a head's up.

Serena answered on the first ring.

"Serena? I know you're having a grand time abroad, and I hate to interrupt, but a friend of mine will be meeting with you soon to give you a message for me."

"Your friend has already found me, he's standing right here." Serena's voice sounded stilted. "But he's no friend, not unless you want me dead." And with that, the call was disconnected.

BOOK TWO

COVERT COFFEE

1

President Kinji tucked her hair behind her ears, a fruitless gesture since her signature bob was cut too short for hair to stay tucked over her ear lobes. She picked up a pencil and began chewing on the eraser, something she hadn't done since she was a child. Completely unaware of what she was doing, or the stunned looks on her staff's faces, she gnawed at the eraser until there was nothing left of it. Then she tossed the pencil back on the desk and formulated her thoughts. Finally, she spoke.

"So who's getting Serena out of there?" she asked. It was unclear who she was addressing, so no one answered. Ann made eye contact with each of the five young people in the room. "Get me someone."

No one moved.

Ann said, "Get me my husband."

Everyone moved.

Ann surveyed the now-empty Oval Office. Could it be called Oval? The room had been built like a giant ice cube. She hated it. Hated, hated, hated it. She hated everything inside the walls of the closed society known as the new White House: the walls of ivory, beige, cream, tan, sand, caramel and "linen"; the soaring modern-day-architectural cathedral ceilings that created a chill not unlike the dreary drafts felt by monks in centuries-old monasteries, but without the ethereal air; the gaudy display of wealth represented by insanely priced presidential pens and an office chair with hand-sewn upholstery worth $10,000; and most of all, the plastic people holding her sequestered in this prison.

What kept her sane were the regular coffee chats with her dear friend Serena Wilcox, someone who didn't have a political bone in her body. Half the time, she didn't even watch the news. She was outside of the fray, untainted by the dirty fingers of lobbyists and power-hungry star-climbers. She was a pure outsider to "The Cube". Best of all, she was delightfully funny, unconventional, witty, and genuine. Ann had pushed hard for the friendship with Serena, as if Serena were a pet she adopted; needy and odd behavior coming from Ann, not Presidential in the slightest.

And now Ann had potentially killed her new pet. Too much affection can do that.

"It's not your fault," said Ted.

Ann moved away from her desk, where she had been glowering at a stack of ridiculously overpriced notepads. She had requested notepads due to her love-hate relationship with computerized planners and her lack of trust in any staffer to record her thoughts for her. Nonetheless, she despised the notepads. She could be using scratch paper like her Mom used to keep in the kitchen drawer by the phone – no need for her scribbles to take on such formality. Waste. No wonder the country was in such a mess.

"You have to know that you had nothing to do with this," Ted tried again.

"You and I both know that if she was not a personal friend of the President, she wouldn't be in this situation."

Ted shrugged with the resignation that all long-time-married men know, and said something wise that few men would realize to be the best answer for this situation and many others: "What do you want me to say?"

Ann mirrored Ted's shrugging and said, "I don't know. But while we stand here talking, Serena could be dead."

"We know the threat is credible?" asked Ted.

"I spoke to her myself. It came from Serena's own lips. Yes, credible."

Ted whistled; a low steady tone he had rehearsed to perfection.

Ann cringed. His "whistle of drama" got under her skin. She cracked every knuckle on both of her hands. Then Ted promptly did the same. We've been married too long, she thought. She smiled.

"What? You have an idea?"

"No," said Ann, "Just thinking that I'm glad you are here."

"Me too. Is her husband with her?"

"I don't know. Tom and the kids were with her, but he was there for business. He could have been at work. The kids were probably with her though. I don't know anything, just guessing."

"What business does he have in Germany?"

"He works civil service now. He's there as support to a Guard unit that's over there on a routine two-week annual deployment."

"We're still doing that? Even with the bases over there closed?"

"Not all are closed. And yes, we are still doing that. Serena went with him to vacation, to show the kids all the famous hot spots in Europe."

"Any reason to suspect this is about what Tom is doing?"

"No, this is all me. Remember my driver Penny?"

"The one who wants to be a lawyer?"

"Yes. She sent me an e-mail right before this happened. She wanted to talk to someone I could trust, someone outside of The Cube."

"And you told her to talk to Serena?"

"Yes."

"Ah, I see."

"What is taking them so long?" Ann glanced at the mammoth screen on the wall: no new activity. She stared at it for a few seconds, willing it with her mind to change. And it did. She and Ted raced to the center of the sensor range. Ted gestured for the menu to appear.

They read the simple message from Agent Donnelly: <<Bluebird flown. Nothing there.>>

Ann raised two fingers in the air to signal the teleconferencing function. She raised her voice even though it was sufficient to speak in normal conversational tones; she just couldn't quite get used to not having a phone at her ear while speaking over a connection. "Agent Donnelly, you there?"

"Yes, Madam President."

"She's gone then? What about her husband? The kids?"

"He is with us now, and the kids."

"Where were they? They weren't with Serena?"

"They were at the library."

"On the base?"

"Yes."

"So Serena was alone then? They got her at home?"

"Yes and yes. No trace. Sorry, Madam President."

"Nothing at all?"

"They are sweeping the apartment now, but they aren't optimistic."

"I understand." Ann looked at Ted's face for any sign that he had an idea of what to do next. He didn't. After a long pause she resumed conversation. "Stay with Tom and the kids. Let me know if anything happens."

"Yes, Madam President."

"And Agent Donnelly?"

"Yes?"

"This is covert – me, you, Ted, and your team. That's it. Got it?"

"Yes, Madam President."

"Donnelly, your team is need-to-know."

"Understood."

"Follow protocol, but report to no one but me for now."

"We have a name for this operation?"

"Call it Covert Coffee."

2

Serena Wilcox Bridges, known professionally as Serena Wilcox, toyed with the idea of eating another slice of loaded and greasy pizza. "I don't eat pizza very often anymore."

"We could send Jeff out to get you something else. Taco? Burger?"

"No, it's okay, but no pizza again for me for a while." She had to admit it was fun to have American fast food again, but she would miss her favorite Gasthaus dishes, like Rahmschnitzel; veal served with a mushroom sauce made by sautéing garlic and onions, adding red wine and heavy cream (Rahm), and allowing the sauce to thicken. Yet she felt her stomach complaining at the very thought of more rich foods. No, Rahmschnitzel would not be good after the jet lag, pizza, and kidnapping trifecta.

Serena surveyed the hotel room. It was pleasant enough, with its bland art in tasteful frames, its neutral walls, and strong smell of cleaning chemicals, but she knew if she had a black light she would see the proof of thousands of revolting human secrets.

"When do you think my husband and kids will be told I'm okay? When can I talk to them?"

"I don't know."

"I want to help President Kinji in any way that I can, and I stand by that decision, but Penny told me that my family wouldn't be left worrying about me. I'm not willing to put them through that."

"Sorry, I don't know. I'm just the bodyguard, and the butler I guess," said Agent Estep as he cleared Serena's plate away from the mahogany desk she had taken up residence in front of, having found a bit of personal space from the three men who sat in the small lounging area that contained a couch, a chair, an end table with a lamp on it, and two floor lamps.

All of the lamps were turned on, but even though the window blinds were closed, the powerful street lights in the parking lot outside the window illuminated the room, rendering the need for three lamps unnecessary. She appreciated the extra lighting – all the easier to see who she was dealing with.

Estep was a man in his early twenties; tall, dark and handsome; good looking enough to look like an actor, but humble enough to be refreshingly likeable. The only son in a family with five girls, Estep knew, respected, and enjoyed women, while also solidly bearing all of his father's testosterone-grounded hopes for the future fully and happily on his broad shoulders.

A man who was sensitive, funny, smart, and masculine who was still single? Not for long, thought Serena. "Can you get me in touch with Penny please?"

Serena caught Estep sizing her up, and he apparently deemed her to be trustworthy. "Yeah, I can do that." He pressed a couple of numbers and gave Serena his phone.

"Penny? This is Serena. Yes, I'm fine. One thing though, you said that Tom and the kids wouldn't be left worried sick, wondering what happened to me. Yes, I understand, but that was my one condition when I agreed to do this. Yes, I can see that. Alright, if that's the best you can do. Thank you, Penny."

Estep took his phone back and raised his eyebrows. "Well?"

"She says they'll have to snatch Tom and the kids. It's the only way to protect them, and the only way to give them a message about me. She said it would have been easier if we'd been together when you took me, but now they'll have to do this separately."

"I see."

"They won't be brought here. Too risky that someone might follow them here. Best to bring them somewhere else."

"Those guys are good. Your family will be okay, don't worry."

"Thanks Estep."

"I doubt you'll be apart for long."

"I hope not. When can I get to work?"

"I can brief you now if you are ready."

"Yes, now is good." Serena's voice revealed her surprise.

"I know, briefings are usually not delivered by the butler, but I'm a little higher up on the chain than I've led you to believe." Estep winked at her, a move that would have made a younger woman blush. Serena simply felt old and tired.

What am I caught up in? I should be home with my family, she thought. She wondered if anyone had checked on the dog to see if he needed fresh water. They hadn't gotten him an ISO pet microchip, jumped through hoops for a USDA certified veterinary form to obtain a pet passport, and flown him all the way to Germany only to have him die of dehydration! Aloud she said, "Please fill me in."

Estep folded his long lanky frame into the only available chair and pulled data up on his phone. "Look at this face. Ring any bells?"

Serena glanced at the photo. "Is it supposed to?"

"No, didn't think you'd know him."

"Who is he?"

"He is the man behind a lobbyist group. He's not happy about new legislation on the table." Estep pulled out a slim silver stylus and selected another photo from the database. He placed the phone into her hand. "Do you know this face?"

Serena glanced at the photo, did a double-take, and studied the photo more closely. "I think I do. He's older now than when I last saw him, but I think this is the same boy. I met him in Minnesota. He was a child prodigy, a computer genius, nice kid. What does he have to do with this?" Serena's curiosity was now piqued enough that her fatigue was forgotten.

"Nothing, but we've been following him, and grooming him for a scenario like this. He can help you find the people involved, track them via satellite and the typical footprints, and hook you up with any other technology you might need."

"I understand. But I still have no idea why I'm pretending to be kidnapped. Why did I tell Ann – President Kinji – that someone would kill me? I thought you said that she specifically asked for my help, so why doesn't she know what's going on? And, by the way, I don't know what's going on either."

"The President was warned by one of her staff that security has been compromised." Estep stopped talking and stared at her face for a long moment. "Someone from the inside is involved."

"Yes, I understand what compromised means."

"That's why she asked for you."

"But why the kidnapping if she asked for me?"

"To protect the president. We know she trusts you, and we respect her judgment. So we got you. And it's in her best interest if she doesn't know what you are doing on her behalf."

"But aren't you drawing more attention to what we are doing? How is this helpful?" Serena raised her voice to be heard over the vacuuming din coming from the housekeeping service in the room next door.

Estep, with his deep baritone, did not need to raise his voice, but he did anyway. "Because the President has no idea that you are already working with us, she is protected from whatever happens."

"She's going to want to find me. I don't see how this is helpful. Am I not getting something?"

"She has assigned our team to an operation to recover you, and that is all she knows. We'll keep her briefed enough to occupy her, and anything you are doing meanwhile won't touch her."

"You do realize that I'm not an insider to anything, right? I solve mysteries, mainly over the computer. That's all I can offer. I still don't get all of this secrecy and drama."

"It's better that she think we're looking for you than for her to be briefed on what you are doing, which is what she would be ordering us to do if she knew you were working on this. If her office is compromised, and we are working on that assumption, we need to protect the President from even herself. We vetted you out, and you held up, but we can't do that with all certainty for everyone else that the President might think she can trust. So, if she doesn't know anything, she can't talk about it." This was the most Estep had said at one time, and he said it without seeming to breathe.

"I see. Smart plan. Did you come up with it?" Serena's antennae were raised. Who had the authority to make decisions in the name of security that went over Ann's head and without her knowledge?

"No it wasn't me. I don't go that far up the ladder, only a few rungs up from butler." Estep grinned, enjoying his butler joke beyond its expiration date. Seeing no reaction from Serena, he quickly switched gears, erasing his smirk and resuming the blank-faced expression of a solid Secret Service Agent. "I can't tell you who is in charge, you'll have to trust the process. I already spent way more time explaining why you are here than I expected to. From now on, ask fewer questions. Once we get you set up, you'll have to work fast. We can't stall her for more than a couple of days."

"What happens if I can't figure this out before then?"

"Operation Covert Coffee will need a resolution. We'll tell her we've found you, and go from there."

"Operation Covert Coffee? That's what she's calling my rescue?"

"Yes."

"I like it." Serena smiled, basking in the glow of having an operation dedicated to her. "How did all of this start? Don't leave anything out."

Estep's only response was to scowl at Serena. His handsome face was instantly transformed into that of an intimidating, flint-eyed thug – a side of him that his sisters and mother had never seen. He unfolded himself from the chair he had occupied for only a few minutes. "We have to move you."

"Already?" Serena looked around the room, startled at the sudden turn of events. "You don't think we are safe enough here?"

"My alert sounded." Estep pointed to his ear, where a microchip was hidden, communicating with him at all times.

Serena grabbed her purse and hurried out the door. Estep was quickly met by a team of equally athletic and capable agents that swallowed the petite detective so completely that she was invisible from outside of the swarm. It was with this entourage that she walked from one room to another, shuffling along at a steady but manic pace.

Once inside the room, Estep took up position in an identical chair to the one he'd been in just moments earlier. "We are secure now. Let's proceed."

"What? We only moved up a floor. How is that more secure?"

"We won't be staying in the same place for more than thirty minutes at a time. Keeping you moving is a precaution."

"How can I get anything done if I'm moving around all the time?"

"Only until we get you to the computer lab. You'll stay there as long as it takes."

"Is that why you brought me back to Minnesota? Are we talking about the same lab where I saw the boy in the photo? I remember his name is Nicholas."

"Yes, same lab. Nicholas will be there when you arrive."

"I didn't realize the lab was still in use. I guess I assumed it would be shut down."

"No, it was claimed by the agency."

"Which agency?"

Estep raised his eyebrows.

“Asking too many questions?”

Estep growled.

“I’d like to talk to my family. When would that be possible?”

Estep stared back at her, his face void of all expression. Several seconds passed. Serena studied the framed art on the wall – same bland factory prints as in the previous room, same color scheme, slightly different subject matter. The paintings struck her as funny for no real reason, and she looked away before she started laughing. She was feeling the weight of the jet lag, and fatigue from everything else too. She wondered when the agents would leave her alone so that she could sleep, if she could sleep.

“I’m here of my own free will, I don’t see why I should be denied talking to my family and making sure that they are okay.”

Estep’s expression remained unchanged. His eyes didn’t even seem to blink.

“I am here of my own free will, right?”

“Define ‘free will’”, said Estep.

3

Lora put her purse on the belt and allowed herself to be patted down. She didn't mind the "wanding" but the frisking got a little out of hand. She leered at the guard. "Enjoying yourself?"

The guard ignored her.

Oh, so that's it, then, I'm not good enough to talk to? Lora bristled. She knew his type. He probably had a plain wife sitting at home, chasing after his freckle-faced sticky-fingered rug-rats, cooking his dinners, and watching the clock for when he would be home. Well, Lora would never be that wife: she was good enough to touch, but not good enough to marry. Story of her life. She scooped her purse off the conveyor belt, opened it as she walked away from the security check-in, dug for her signature vial of Tic Tacs, flipped open the plastic lid, popped one in her mouth, and returned the Tic Tacs to her purse, all without missing a step.

"You can't go in there," said a female Special Agent named

Carla Keefer. Keefer's red hair bobbed upon her shoulders in coils of thick curls while unruly tendrils framed her face. So sweet and lovely was she that it was difficult for her to be taken seriously as an agent.

Lora scoffed at her now. "I'm just going to sit down." She darted for the row of chairs situated behind the ropes. Keefer snatched her by the arm and yanked her elbow behind her back, dragging her back within the confines of the holding area.

"Hey! You didn't have to do that!" Lora yelped.

"Stay behind the ropes," Keefer said simply. She locked eyes with Lora, but did not engage her. Her stare-down was firm, no-nonsense, and dismissive; a combination that asserted her authority over Lora in an instant. Of course the show of force had already paved the way for that.

Lora gave her no more trouble; she waited in compliance, standing, shifting her weight from one foot to the other, sighing every few seconds.

"Come with me," said Keefer. She led Lora down a long tiled corridor. Lora's high-heeled pleather fashion boots clicked with every step, announcing her arrival long before her slender frame reached the conference room. Keefer opened the door for her, gestured for her to go in, nodded to the agents inside, and left, leaving Lora behind. More than one agent stared out the windowed door at Keefer's curvy figure as she turned away. Lora rolled her eyes. Men are all the same, she thought.

"Sit down," said Agent Browning.

Lora slid her long manicured fingers along the top of the back of the only chair at the table. When her fingers reached the end, she eased her body into the seat of the chair, imagining her movements to be slinky and sexy. She then studied her fingers, admiring the fingernail art on each painted nail.

The agents were unimpressed. Browning pulled a second chair up to the table, directly across from where Lora was perched. "Do you know why you are here?" he began.

"The President wants to have me to dinner?"

"Is that your final answer?"

"This is about my e-mail? It was a joke."

"Before sending the message you consented to the contract between yourself and this office. When you added your virtual signature, your consent to our terms was recorded and verified."

"I didn't read it."

"Your signature indicates that you have waived your right to object to any inquiry we may make into the source, content, or intent behind your message."

"I didn't sign anything."

"You selected the option allowing this office to assign a virtual signature to your message. It was required before the message was allowed to be sent. Whether you remember doing it or not, we have records of you having done so. Would you like to see our records?"

"No," said Lora dejectedly.

"Do you understand that the purpose of this inquiry is to establish the intention behind your message? Do you also understand that you are here of your own accord and can leave at any time?"

"I guess so."

"Please describe your message and explain why you sent that message to the Town Hall forum, to President Ann Kinji, recipient."

"It was a joke – Kinji is Kinki – everyone does it. It's yesterday by now, not even funny anymore. Thought it was funny when I wrote it. Do I look like a terrorist?"

"Why did you write it?"

"I told you, it was a joke."

"What made you decide to send it?"

"Someone dared me. I can't remember who. It was at a bar. I sent it from my phone."

"Who told you to do it?"

"I said, I don't remember who."

"Does that happen often, that you don't remember who you are talking to?"

Lora threw her head back to give her hair a good toss. "What do you think? They know my name there."

"Are you saying you were intoxicated when you sent the message to the President?"

Lora snorted. "Yes! I'm saying I was wasted. Can I go now?"

"Yes, you can go now. Agent Keefer will escort you out. But Ma'am?"

"Ma'am!"

"Miss?"

"Better."

"No more drunk-dialing the President."

On that note, Lora left the heart of American government behind her as she clicked and clacked her way down the long corridors and back out into the outside world, where a cab was waiting for her. She got in without saying anything to the driver, ignored the seat belt, and flipped open her phone.

"Vic? Yeah, it's me. Yeah, I did it. No, they didn't see me. I attached it to the table, underside like you said. No, they didn't notice, too busy staring at my chest. Nobody's listening, Victor. Okay, okay, see you soon."

Lora looked down at her fingers. The nail art on her left ring finger was down to one layer, like all of her other fingernails. However, before she entered the interrogation room, that nail had had two layers. One was nail art, like now. The top layer had been a tiny film, containing a microchip, which was now recording everything said in the interrogation room.

Why Victor wanted her to do this, she didn't know. But he was paying her good money and that was all she cared about. He had paid her at the bar to send the message, and he had promised her more money today, at the hotel room where she was going.

What Lora was about to find out was that Victor had no intention of seeing Lora again, and when his people were done with her, no one else would ever see her again either. So it is unfortunate then that Lora didn't enjoy the view from her cab passenger window, because it was the last time she would ever see the great city that she loved, or anything else for that matter.

4

Serena was back in Minnesota and boy could she feel it! The air was so dense with cold that her lungs hurt when she breathed. Brisk, baby! Brr! She rubbed her hands together and felt herself grinning from ear to ear.

"This is freaking August," Agent Estep complained. He bent his head against the wind that was ripping across the tarmac on a private runway near the International airport in Minneapolis-Saint Paul.

Beyond the tarmac, early morning light was barely coming up over the low horizon, a horizon foreign to those who had never seen a Northern skyline before. Serena described the Minnesotan sky as a low ceiling, like the skyline of a snow globe when tilted at an angle. The sky-ceiling felt claustrophobic to her, especially when compared to the higher clouds found nearly everywhere else in the nation. Chicken Little would have really thought that the sky was falling if he lived here, she thought.

And yet, instead of feeling the old dread about Earth-hugging clouds, dense air, and Canadian chill, she felt nearly giddy to be back on Minnesotan soil. While Serena had lived in many places throughout her forty-plus years, she had spent most of her adult life in the Twin Cities area and she now thought of it as home. Home. So good to be back.

"Where is the lab? We aren't headed back to the Cannon Falls area," said Serena.

"No, it's been moved."

"To?"

"Wisconsin."

"Wisconsin!"

"Not far, thirty miles from here. Near Hudson. It's an old Girl Scout camp, no longer used for scouting, obviously."

"Obviously."

"The original building that housed the campers is still on site. You'll be staying there."

"I'm familiar with Hudson. I've been to the lakefront there with my family. Got some gyros, and sunburn because we forgot sunscreen. We went downtown later, very cute. It was all lit up and I couldn't believe how populated it was, really hopping. We wanted to go to that Pier 51 restaurant, could smell the food and saw the outdoor dining was packed, but we didn't make it there."

Estep didn't reply.

Serena gave up on conversation, and in the silence that followed, could hear a faint voice, a narration-sounding voice. She strained her eyes a little to study his ears. Ah, plugged in! It appeared Estep was listening to an audio book. Serena tried not to take it personally.

If she were a young guy in his 20s, she wouldn't find herself interesting either.

The rest of the trip passed by quickly. Serena was so tired that the silence was welcome. She allowed her thoughts to drift. What am I in for, and will I really be of any use to President Kinji? Will I even know what to do? And when will I see my family again?

She hadn't felt homesick in a long time, because ever since she'd become a mother, she was seldom alone, even if away from home. She had forgotten how miserable homesickness was. Whether one is a child at camp, a student at college, a soldier at war, or was a middle-aged mother-of-three sequestered off to a secret government computer lab, the heart felt the same – heavy, dark, empty. She wanted to cry, but she held herself together. Again, she questioned why she was the President's best option, a question Estep had been pondering from the first mention of Serena's involvement in Covert Coffee.

"Here we are," said Estep. Serena noticed that he had recaptured his good humor, probably from having had a break from entertaining her in the quiet car. He had also received a text from his girlfriend, a fact that Serena had correctly assumed based on the goofy grin plastered on Estep's face when he thought Serena wasn't looking. This in-a-new-relationship repartee renewed the spring in his step, for which Serena felt his girlfriend deserved a medal. "You should find everything you need here."

"I still don't know what it is that I'll be doing."

"You'll figure it out. Go on in." Estep unlocked three sections of a nearly invisible door via a pre-programmed code on his phone. The door slid open and closed immediately after sensing the two had entered. It snapped shut so quickly that Serena made a mental note never to reach back suddenly after passing through the entry – she could lose an arm!

"Hi, Mrs. Meadows," said Nicholas cheerfully.

"Meadows? Haven't heard that name in a long time," Serena said, looking as if she had tasted something sour. "It was an alias, Nicholas. I'm Serena Wilcox Bridges. You can call me Serena."

"Miss Serena?"

"Sure." Serena smiled. She liked polite children. He had won her over already. This would be an easy assignment, except for the obvious fact that she had no idea what they were doing.

"You can use that computer over there," said Nicholas. He pointed at the sleek blue model on his left.

"Wow, this lab is fantastic! How did you get this setup?" Serena gushed.

The lab was futuristic, and vibrant. The color scheme looked familiar, but she couldn't quite place it. Nicholas' next comment answered her unspoken question.

"I am a Superman fan."

Serena laughed. "That would explain the blue, red, and yellow machines." She glanced at the walls. "And the posters of course."

Nicholas pointed at the ceiling.

Serena laughed again. "Ah! And there's the man of steel himself!" A large mural of Superman, with fisted arm outstretched, red cape unfurled behind him, in classic flight pose, had been artfully painted on the domed ceiling.

"Goodness, they must think a lot of you, Nicholas."

Nicholas smiled modestly and nodded.

"Makes me wonder what it is that you do for them to get such royal treatment."

Nicholas didn't answer.

Estep came out of nowhere and clapped a gloved hand on Serena's shoulder. "No more questions."

Startled, Serena spun around to look Estep in the face. If she'd had any experience with bears clapping her on the shoulder, she would have described it as similar to being clapped on the shoulder by Agent Estep, minus the claws – those were only implied. "I wasn't seriously trying to press him for answers."

Estep didn't step back. Instead, he drew himself in closer and stayed inside Serena's personal space for the duration of the conversation. "His role here is not your business. Stay on task."

"I don't even know what my task is," Serena tried again, in vain, to get some direction.

"My shift with you is over," said Estep, without disappointment. "Behave yourself, or they'll call me back."

"And you wouldn't like to come back?" Serena smiled sweetly.

"You wouldn't like it if I have to come back." And on that note Estep left the lab without so much as a wave.

"He's crabby today," said Nicholas.

"I ask too many questions," said Serena simply.

Nicholas shrugged. "You better stop that then." He jerked his head toward the back of the room where the next agent-in-charge was already in place.

Serena slid her chair closer to Nicholas and whispered, "They aren't keeping you here against your will are they?"

Nicholas shook his head no.

Serena tried again, "Do you need any help?"

Nicholas turned his chair to look her in the eyes. "I like it here. There is nothing wrong. We should get to work."

Serena studied his face and saw that he was telling her the truth. "Okay then, tell me what to do."

Nicholas' long reach allowed him to tap Serena's monitor without leaving his chair. "Read these."

Serena blinked at the screen. She thought she knew what she was looking at, but she wasn't sure. "Is this what I think it is? Is this President Kinji's private e-mail account?"

"Kind of. It's the Town Hall e-mail."

"This is a more comprehensive list than the few samples published for the general public to see."

"Yeah, this is all of them."

"For? The week?"

"No, just one day."

"And I'm looking for?"

Nicholas shrugged. "I don't know. I just give you the data."

"And she doesn't know you have this?" Serena felt like she was catching on now. This really was work that she could do with her private investigator experience, and the best part was that she didn't have to collect the intelligence herself.

"When you are done with that, listen to this." Nicholas removed his dapper wool cap, an unusual accessory for a boy his age. He peeled a sliver of material off the underside brim of the cap and handed it to Serena.

"What is this? It looks like a fingernail."

"It is a fingernail."

"What?" Serena blanched. She could take blood, she could take gore, but she hated gross human stuff like hair, mucus, and fingernails.

"The nail is a bug."

"How do I play it?"

"Insert it under the audio scanner," said Nicholas, standing up and moving toward her machine. "Like this."

"I see. And it will upload to the computer?"

"Yep. And the audio file can play directly off the scanner too. You can use those ear buds." He gestured toward the plastic packet containing tiny Superman-colored wireless ear buds. They were so small that Serena feared she would lose them before she could attach them to her ears.

"Where is the bug from? Not President Kinji's office without her consent, I hope?"

"No. It's from the interrogation room, interviewing the Town Hall people."

"The ones who wrote those e-mails?"

"Yes."

"So they think that the person, or persons, we are looking for wrote one of those e-mails?"

"They don't think, they know."

"How do they know?"

"The lady who put that bug in the room is dead."

5

Agent Estep was back on Chicago soil. The sprawling city was home to the newly re-united States of America, as the D.C. area was still in recovery post Big War. The White House had been built quickly, with most of the rooms still unfinished, unfurnished, and uninspired. It seemed that no one embraced the idea of a White House in Chicago, and Estep suspected that the building would never be finished. As soon as D.C. was deemed inhabitable again, he was certain that they'd all be headed back home. But meanwhile, here he was, outside of the building where President Ann Kinji was serving a second term as President of the United States of a recently divided America, a war-torn and politics-shy nation. And while they continued to slug their way forward, it was obvious from present events that there were some who didn't want to let go of the past.

Estep wondered who those people were, and if he would ever find them. His role in Covert Coffee was to head the team protecting

Serena Wilcox, a task he felt was beneath his pay grade. He consoled himself with the fact that he wasn't restricted from following leads that would indirectly protect Ms. Wilcox; at least that was what he told the two junior agents he brought with him to Victor's door.

Victor didn't respond to the doorbell or the vigorous rapping on the door.

"Do we go in?" asked Agent Champlin.

"No warrant," said Agent Bonifield.

Estep pulled out a sophisticated set of lock picks. He opened the door in seconds. He drew his gun, entered the apartment, and immediately found Victor, alive and well, sitting on the couch watching TV.

Estep did not lower his gun. "Why didn't you answer the phone or the door, you hiding from us, Victor?"

"Not from you, from them."

"Who?"

Victor shut off the TV. "The ones who killed Lora. They'll be after me next."

"And why would they do that? We know you're the one who hired them to kill her." Estep was in all-out interrogation mode, using every ounce of his bulky physical presence to intimidate the defeated looking man on the couch. He had the deep voice of condemnation, the furrowed brow of the accuser, and the arms of an enforcer. But none of these were necessary.

Victor began to sob. At first it was a confusing sound, a mix between a snort and a hiccup. The agents exchanged glances, thinking that he might be getting sick. Then the sobbing grew louder, and it was clear that the man was crying with full abandon.

The three men subconsciously backed away from the couch, and tried not to look directly at the man's face.

Agent Bonifield left the room in search of a tissue box. He returned with a new box of tissues. Estep grabbed the box out of his hands, ripped off the perforated top, tossed the cardboard packaging on the floor, and threw the box at Victor, who did not catch it. Victor picked the box up and spent the next few minutes alternating between blowing his nose and crying.

Estep dragged a chair closer to the couch and sat in it. "Enough already! Start talking."

"They'll kill me."

"So will we."

Victor froze in mid-blow, his tissue at his nose. His eyes were as wide open as a clown's; his face just as pale, his nose just as red. With Victor's bald head and tufts of red hair on the sides, he could join a circus.

The junior agents nearly suffered from whiplash after whirling around to gawk at Estep. One of them dared speak up. "I won't be a part of this," he croaked, his voice barely above a whisper.

"Then go," said Estep. "Now!"

Agent Champlin fled out the door. Agent Bonifield stayed rooted in his place, but his facial expression revealed his desire for the floor to open up and swallow him whole.

"You too. Get!" Estep snarled.

Victor shrank into the couch, cowering and clutching his saturated tissue. "I'll tell you what I know," he said in a trembling falsetto.

Estep sighed. The ease of this interrogational breakdown was absurd; his agents and this sniveling idiot were cowards. Some days, the agency didn't pay him enough. He drew his chair even closer to Victor. He growled, "No, we'll start with what I know."

Victor gave up his slouch and cower routine, reassured that he was not facing imminent death. He peered into Estep's eyes to gauge the level of the threat. Estep was pleased to note that Victor saw nothing but unwavering canine focus on the target. Victor resumed his slouch. "I'm listening," he said.

"We contracted you to create the bug and outfit Lora with it. We vetted you before the hire. There was nothing in your background to suggest that you were anything but a patriot and upstanding citizen. So what happened, Victor? Did you lose money at the races? You aren't the traitor we were looking for, but you know who he is. He found you before we found him."

Victor blinked rapidly, saying nothing.

"Who bought you?" Estep hissed, his question more of a strangled exclamation.

Victor sat up straight, the flicker of recognition in his eyes. "Oh, that's what you think! No, no, you've got it all wrong. I'm the victim here – isn't that obvious? I don't have the stones to be a double agent; your words, not mine. I barely had the courage to work for the good guys. You can search the apartment. I have no weapons. I don't even have a dog. You saw for yourself how easy it was to walk right in and threaten me."

Estep nodded. "Agreed. So that's your story then? You were threatened?"

Victor began gesturing with his arms in big loopy circles, looking so much like Bozo that Estep had to suppress the urge to grin. "Yes, I was threatened! They wanted me to tell them everything, or else they would kill me, but not without torturing me first. They showed me they meant business too!"

"How so? Did they hurt you?"

"No, but they did take Henry."

"Your son?"

"No, I don't have any kids."

"Who's Henry?"

"My computer. I give all my computers names. Henry holds a lot of data, data that is encrypted and only someone of my caliber could hack it, but nonetheless, they stole my work."

"What are you mixed up in, Victor?"

"Oh no, it's nothing like that. Again, you jumped to the wrong conclusion. This information is research type stuff, statistics."

"So you sold out your country, and got Lora killed, over nothing – over the theft of your computer?"

"Lora's dead?" Victor gasped. His mouth formed a large O, his face a mask of horror and terror.

"You are trying my patience. You better start making sense." Estep leaned in close to Victor's face and let his hot angry breath unfurl onto Victor's forehead. "Tell me what I want to know. Now!" He slammed his hand on the coffee table, causing everything on the table to bounce, clatter, or tip over. Water spilled and trickled off the edge of the table, making a steady dripping sound onto the well-worn pea-green shag carpet.

"Okay, okay! I'll try to say it more clearly. Three men came into the apartment, just like you three did today. They said that they knew I was working for the government and that they needed to know what it was that I was doing."

"And you told them?" Estep let his disgust show on his face.

"The one like you, the big one? He held a gun at my head. So, yes, I told them."

"And when you finished telling them, they left?"

"Not without taking Henry, and flushing my turtle down the toilet." Tears began to flow at the thought of his turtle being flushed. "They told me they'd be back for me if I didn't tell them everything I knew, and they'd hack me up, and flush me down the toilet along with Jared."

"The turtle?"

"Yes, Jared is my turtle. Poor Jared." Victor was sobbing now, and nearing the bottom of what had been a full box of tissues. His used tissues were wadded up and laid on the cushion next to him, and had created quite a pile.

"Who are these men?"

Victor pulled the tissue away from his face, surprised. "How should I know?"

"These men knew a lot about you. They knew about your computer, and they knew you'd be upset if they flushed your turtle. I, for example, wouldn't have gone for your turtle. I would have shot your knee cap." Estep drew out his gun and held it against Victor's bended knee.

"You don't have to do that! Put the gun away, put it away, put it away!" Victor shrieked the same words over and over until Estep removed the gun from his knee.

"So who are they?" Estep scowled in the menacing manner that he had rehearsed in front of the mirror. He nailed that look, and was pleased to see the effect it had on Victor. Even better than the gun, he thought with satisfaction.

"Okay, okay. Yes, I know them." Victor dropped his head in defeat; staring dramatically at the floor, letting his arms fall limply at his sides. "Are you going to arrest me now?"

Estep gritted his teeth. Oh how he wanted to hit this clown. "Just tell me who they are."

"They are security for FYD."

"FYD?"

"Food Yield and Development."

Now it was Estep's turn to be surprised. "The lobbyist group?"

"Yes."

"Do you have that information on any other computer?"

Victor scoffed. "Of course I have back-up. I have back-up to the back-up. I always save my data in triplicate. At least. I know it's on Emily."

"Which one is Emily?"

Victor pointed to the iMac in the back of the room.

"Really? How can you encrypt on that thing? My dad used one of those when he was in college."

Victor rolled his eyes. "It's just a shell of an iMac, for kicks, vintage. The guts are state of the art technology, a dream system you wouldn't even know what to do with."

"Unplug it, get it ready. We're taking it with us."

"Us? By us you mean you and those two agents?"

"No, by us I mean me and you."

"Where are we going?"

"To Wisconsin.".

6

Serena could get used to working in the secret Superman computer lab. She had coffee, yogurt, and Chocolate Peanut Butter Bugles for breakfast; enjoyed a two-hour-long video chat with Tom and the kids after Nicholas got them connected (while Estep was away and unaware); and sank herself into a deep leather chair behind the luxury metallic-blue computer model of the future.

Serena laughed, a sound that Nicholas responded to by rotating his chair a few degrees via the wireless digital controls on his computer screen.

"Are these Town Hall messages always this nutty?" she asked.

"I don't know. I didn't read them," said Nicholas, disappointed that Serena's laugh wasn't a response from a joke, funny video, or anything else that might interest him. He rotated his chair back to its position in front of his own machine.

Serena was nearly finished reading through the hundreds of

Town Hall messages. While President Kinji only received a cross section of messages, Serena had been given every message that had been submitted during the 24 hour period in question. Highlighted were the messages that Kinji had seen, and Serena suspected that those were the ones she should be focusing on. Because, whatever was going on, wouldn't the person or persons involved have found a way to get their message through? After all, they had become a serious threat of some kind. If their message, or messages, had hit the slush pile, never seen by Ann or her core people, would Serena be here right now? She thought not. She puzzled it out now, talking to herself. Nicholas glanced her way a few times, frowned, and looked away. Apparently Serena was throwing off his mojo.

"Nicholas? How do I use this bug reader scanner thing again?" Serena smiled sweetly. She rummaged in her purse for a pack of watermelon flavored gum that she had been saving for an emergency Tooth Fairy present for Rosie. She found the gum and kept it hidden inside her hand, her hand still in her purse.

Nicholas demonstrated the scanner again. As he turned back to his own work Serena tapped him on the shoulder and presented him with the pack of gum. Nicholas grinned. "Thanks!"

Yes, Serena could get used to working in this lab. Kids were so much easier to work with than adults. Just think; she could come to work with her purse loaded for bear: yo-yos, harmonicas, candy, and gag toys. Co-worker problems solved instantly. Nicholas was in a mellow mood now, smacking away at his new bubble gum. He had an entire pack of gum to himself; big smile, sunny attitude, problem solved.

Serena wished a pack of gum would work on Estep and grinned at the thought. She didn't smile for long though, what she heard on the fingernail bug was disturbing. She knew this voice to be Lora's – the woman who had planted the bug and was then promptly murdered.

Listening to Lora's voice nagged at Serena's conscience. Isn't this a violation of privacy, a disrespect of the dead? And yet, if I can help find her killer the end justifies the means.

Serena prepared herself for a heavy session of investigation by visualizing her ears hard-wired to her brain so that she could have total recall of the information later. But since that memory trick didn't always work, she also took notes via computer keyboard. She increased the volume, pulled the file back to the starting position, and listened to the recording from the beginning:

First was the sound of a chair scraping across the floor and then a male voice said, "Do you know why you are here?"

A female voice that Serena knew belonged to Lora said, full of sarcasm: "The President wants to have me to dinner?"

The male voice, sounding flat and unemotional, said: "Is that your final answer?"

Serena stopped the recording. "Nicholas, who is the agent questioning Lora?"

Nicholas swiped his screen a few times until he found the data file he was looking for. "I see Agent Keefer listed, but she's a lady."

"Can you get me the name? If you can't, it might not be important anyway." Serena didn't want to send the kid on a wild goose chase.

"Give me a minute." Nicholas thumbed through the file for a few seconds. "Got it. His name is Gary William Browning."

"Agent Gary Browning?" Serena asked just to be clear.

"Yes."

“Thanks, Nicholas.” Serena noted that Nicholas was already back to work on whatever it was that he was doing. She resumed the play-back of the recording:

Lora said: “This is about my e-mail? It was a joke.” Serena picked up something in Lora’s pitch. Lora was not at all surprised that she was being questioned about the e-mail. Which begged the question “Why not?” Had she sent the e-mail to catch the attention of the White House?

Browning said in a reading-straight-off-the-paper voice: “Before sending the message you consented to the contract between yourself and this office. When you added your virtual signature, your consent to our terms was recorded and verified.”

“I didn’t read it.” Serena made note that Lora’s flippant response didn’t sound worried. The flippancy wasn’t defensive; it was -- something else. Bored.

So, why was Lora so blasé about the whole thing? She was confident she wasn’t going to be in any serious trouble. Why was she confident? Was she arrogant and ignorant, or did she know that someone powerful would protect her? Hmm. Serena clacked away at the keyword: Who did Lora know? What connections does she have?

Browning said, again revealing no insight into his emotional state; still sounding like he was reading from a script: “Your signature indicates that you have waived your right to object to any inquiry we may make into the source, content, or intent behind your message.”

Lora said, with the same flippant tone, “I didn’t sign anything.”

Browning continued, “You selected the option allowing this office to assign a virtual signature to your message. It was required before the message was allowed to be sent. Whether you remember doing it or not, we have records of you having done so. Would you like to see our records?"

Serena typed: I want to see those records! Her fingernails hit the keyboard with such clatter that Nicholas turned his head to see what she was doing.

Since she already had Nicholas' attention, she said aloud, "I want to see Browning's records. I assume he means the e-mail trail, her IP address or smart phone trace, iPad, iPod, Implant Chip, or whatever else she was using."

"On it," said Nicholas cheerfully. Serena was back in his good graces now that she was giving him work to do, and of course the watermelon bubble gum didn't hurt either.

"Another thing, was anyone else present? Anyone who isn't on the audio file or in the log?"

Nicholas shook his head. "No, I don't think so, not unless you count the vice president."

"Morgan Canon was there? Yes, I count the VP. Why was he there?"

"I don't know, all I see is that the security detail reported that he checked in."

"Okay, good to know." Serena turned her focus back to the audio file.

Lora said no to Browning's offer to see her records. Serena noted that Lora sounded genuinely disinterested – not playing a game. Lora was either very simple, very confident, or both.

Browning continued, "Do you understand that the purpose of this inquiry is to establish the intention behind your message? Do you also understand that you are here of your own accord and can leave at any time?"

"I guess so." Again, Lora sounded bored, impatient to leave. She did not sound at all intimidated, anxious, or angry. Just restless. Distracted? Already thinking about where she was headed next?

Browning's tone remained unchanged. "Please describe your message, and explain why you sent that message to the Town Hall forum, to President Ann Kinji, recipient."

Lora perked up at this point, seemingly enjoying her response. "It was a joke – Kinji is Kinki – everyone does it. It's yesterday by now, not even funny anymore. Thought it was funny when I wrote it. Do I look like a terrorist?"

Browning said, revealing nothing, "Why did you write it?"

Lora stated, not defensively that Serena could tell, but simply stating the facts, "I told you, it was a joke."

Browning followed up with, "What made you decide to send it?" Serena couldn't get a read on Browning at all. He seemed like a guy doing his job, nothing personal that she could detect.

"Someone dared me. I can't remember who. It was at a bar. I sent it from my phone." This sounds rehearsed, scripted. Hmm. Serena made note of that in her file, both her mental file and her typed one.

Browning finally sounded like he was interested in hearing Lora's response. "Who told you to do it?"

"I said, I don't remember who."

Serena heard the sound of Browning writing something on a notepad. Filing out a report, doing his job. "Does that happen often, that you don't remember who you are talking to?"

Lora's voice reverted back to the sarcasm she'd displayed at the beginning of the interrogation. "What do you think? They know my name there."

Browning followed up, his voice flat again, losing interest. "Are you saying you were intoxicated when you sent the message to the President?"

Lora snorted. "Yes! I'm saying I was wasted. Can I go now?" Serena's lie detector went off. Interesting. Why the storytelling?

Browning wrapped up, "Yes, you can go now. Agent Keefer will escort you out. But Ma'am?" After a pause, Browning said, louder, "Ma'am!" Another pause. Browning said, "Miss?"

Lora said, "Better."

Browning said, "No more drunk-dialing the President."

Serena didn't hear anything in Agent Browning's voice to make her doubt that he was doing his job, nothing more. She didn't think of Browning as a person of interest, not at all. In fact she made note not to bother looking into him. However, she did want to know what records he had, so she listened intently when Nicholas told her what he found.

"Agent Browning had Lora's e-mails, which I already sent you. He didn't have anything else. Well, except for her criminal record. She didn't do anything really bad, but this is weird."

"What did she do?" asked Serena.

"It says charge of public intoxication. That means drinking beer on the street, right?"

"Something like that, yes. What's weird?"

"She was arrested with that guy that Agent Estep is bringing in."

"Bringing in? What guy?"

As coincidence would have it, Agent Estep graced their presence at that very moment. He escorted an odd-looking clown-faced man into the building, a man who surveyed the lab with greedy anticipation.

Nicholas groaned. "Looks like he'll be working here too. That's the guy. Victor."

Estep stopped in his tracks. "Nick, what did you just say?"

"That's the guy. Serena asked me to look up Lora's background check. Victor was listed on her criminal record."

Estep leaped at Victor in a pounce like a cougar attacking his prey. Victor, slow on the take and not anticipating an ambush, gave up the fight immediately, letting his body go completely limp. Estep caught him before he fell on the floor, swept him up by his upper arms, and bent both arms behind the man's back. He cuffed them at the wrists and threw his body into the nearest chair, a chair that was, unfortunately for Victor, on wheels. This time Estep didn't catch him before he hit the floor.

Serena and Nicholas, both on their feet, peered down at the sprawled and cuffed form of a man on the floor.

Serena said, "Are you going to explain this?"

Estep said, "I was going to ask you the same thing."

7

Victor squirmed and rolled around on the floor slowly, like a slug in a salt shower. His bloated body even resembled a slug's. But it was his clown-like head that was the finishing touch to create a hideous blend of comedy and horror.

Estep looked like he was ready to spit on the man, Nicholas stared in fascination, and Serena averted her eyes, only to bring them back around to Victor again. She couldn't help herself. It was a train wreck situation.

"I didn't do anything, I didn't do anything!" Victor squealed.

Estep grunted and snorted like a bull. Serena expected him to follow through on what looked like an intention to spit on Victor's hideous moon face, but he showed restraint. When Victor's squealing died down, Estep said, "We vetted you. And yet, you had a criminal record. Someone messed with your files to make you look clean. Who are you working for, Victor?"

"Help me up! I'm not saying anything until I'm off the floor and these cuffs are off," said Victor.

Estep grabbed him by the arm and yanked him up, causing Victor to wince. He shoved him into the nearest chair and said, "Cuffs stay on. Talk!"

Nicholas said, "Agent Estep, I can find out who changed his files. It will only take me a short time."

Estep nodded at the child genius, and said, "Thanks, buddy, you do that. But this maggot is going to tell me right now." He growled at Victor, bending close to him until his face was an inch from Victor's pale sweaty head.

Serena glanced at Nicholas. "Agent Estep, we should bring Victor into another room, don't you think?" She jerked her head toward the boy who had already turned toward the computer. Maybe Nicholas was desensitized to violence, but that didn't make the situation any more appropriate. Thankfully Estep agreed.

Since Victor's chair was on wheels, it was easy for the two of them to roll him into the office. Estep shut the door and pulled up a chair directly facing Victor, their knees touching. Serena remained standing, in a position deep into the corner of the office – just in case things started to get a little rough. And things did, immediately.

Serena had shielded Nicholas' young eyes from seeing the madness, but hearing what was going on in that room was unavoidable. Estep barked and growled like a pit bull, while Victor squealed like a stuck pig. The mingling of the two sounded like a farmyard brawl.

Serena contemplated leaving the room. How much longer would this play out? She counted ceiling tiles, shuffled her feet, and read every poster on the wall. Just when she felt she could take it no longer, the noise ceased. After a momentary pause in the action, in which both men wiped spittle off their lips, the exchange finally settled down into a real interrogation.

"Are you ready to tell me what you know?" asked Estep. He was calm now, controlled. Serena wondered if Estep's drama was all an act from start to finish or if the man really was unstable. Either he was very good or very much in need of an anger management course.

"What you told me before is that the FYD is behind this, and sent thugs to scare you," Estep began.

Serena asked, "FYD is the Food and what?"

"Food Yield and Development. Something the previous administration had in the works, but nothing went forward with it. After war and hell broke loose, FYD disappeared – yet still technically exists as a matter of record. Lobbyists are keeping FYD alive, barely. Not a big newsmaker, and not on anyone's radar. If you ask me, staying informed is the responsibility of every citizen." While talking within his comfort zone Victor's body had completely relaxed, relaxed enough for his face to resume a pompous expression, his trademark look.

"Get off your soapbox before I kick you off it. One day soon you can play professor to inmates. You'll be real popular in prison, they love egghead freaks who murder young women," said Estep.

"I had nothing to do with Lora getting killed!" Victor protested.

"Then how is it that the two of you were arrested together? You kept that tidbit to yourself, so what else are you lying about?" asked Estep.

Serena interjected at that point. She had been leaning against the wall; thinking about what she might add, and finally came up with what she thought was a good question. “What kind of work do you do, Victor?”

Victor looked at Serena in surprise. He seemed to have forgotten she was in the room. “Finally, someone who knows what to ask. You got it, it’s Henry they wanted, and they got him. I don’t know why they went after Lora, but if they got her, they were coming after me next.”

“Who’s Henry?” asked Serena.

Estep made a guttural noise in his throat to indicate his disgust, and his abrupt re-appearance. “It’s his computer,” he said.

“Henry and I spent years together. I still can’t believe they took him. But I have Emily and that old gal will clear my good name,” said Victor, his eyes tearing up again.

“Emily is…?” asked Serena, already having guessed the answer.

“Another computer,” said Estep.

“That still doesn’t explain the arrest. Why did you lie to Agent Estep about that?” asked Serena.

“It had nothing to do with this. What happens behind closed doors should stay behind closed doors!” Victor’s face was flushed and sweaty.

“He was arrested for…?” asked Estep. He looked at Serena, not bothering to ask Victor directly.

“Lewd behavior in a public place,” said Serena.

“That doesn’t sound like closed doors to me,” said Estep.

“Movie theater. And we were alone,” said Victor.

“You were in a public place, which makes your right to privacy null and void,” said Estep. He came close to calling Victor a few of his favorite derogatory names, but reigned himself in; a struggle that was evident to both Victor and Serena. After a moment of frustrated silence he addressed Serena. "I'll have my team fact-check, but it rings true to me."

"Yeah, I'm good. I don't think he's lying." The last thing Serena wanted was more details about the lewd behavior. "Well, not about that anyway. I think he had something to do with Lora and that bug."

"Of course he did! Weren't you listening? Our team asked him to set up the technology and outfit Lora with it," said Estep.

"Why didn't you brief me on that? I wasted my time reviewing and analyzing the audio file when you already knew everything. Were you deliberately giving me bogus work to keep me busy?"

Estep walked closer to Serena, turning his back on Victor. He looked down upon her from his towering height and said, "Yes."

Serena struggled to maintain her composure as she felt the heat of humiliation sweep across her face. "I get that you don't respect me, but can you at least let me try to help? Doesn't President Kinji's endorsement of me mean anything to you?"

"Yes, I respect the President. Point taken. Look, we both want the same thing here."

"Agreed." After a bit of reflection she went on to say, "So our biggest lead is with him, then?" Serena looked at Victor, and then quickly averted her eyes.

"Yep, for now anyway."

Estep and Serena continued talking as if Victor was not in the room. "I hope it's obvious what the FYD wanted from his computer. Are we even sure it's really the FYD behind this?" asked Serena.

"No, we aren't sure. We haven't had time to dig into much of anything," said Estep.

"Of course it's the FYD. I met with them before!"

Estep and Serena whirled around to face Victor. Victor gasped and placed both of his pale hands over his grotesque mouth. "I said too much, didn't I?" he said.

Before Estep could lunge at Victor, Serena told Estep firmly, in her Mom voice, "I've got this – let me handle it."

She hated to pull rank, but a middle-aged woman with many years of experience in dealing with dramatic children trumped a young single male who had no experience with heading off melt-downs. No, Estep's specialty lay in the realm of hardened criminals and sophisticated spies. He was out of his league.

Serena swallowed her revulsion at having to get up close and personal with Victor, who, she quickly discovered, reeked of BO mixed with something else – Doritos? She tapped into her surgeon-like nerves of steel to propel herself forward until her face was mere inches away from Victor's pasty mask of comedy and tragedy. She stared into his cement-colored eyes with bird-like intensity: Victor was a piece of road kill and until the eagles and hawks took over, Serena would enjoy the first pickings.

"Tell me everything about your meeting with the FYD," said Serena.

Victor was taken aback: somewhere in his subconscious was the memory of his own mother's eerie green-sky warning before the tornado; the calm voice that was scarier than the punishment that would quickly follow if he didn't obey. He complied with Serena's order without hesitation.

Agent Estep looked both vexed and impressed. Serena squelched the urge to gloat as Victor began to spill what seemed to be the whole story, and beyond, if she was paying attention to Victor's embellishments.

"I was minding my own business, trying to break into the app market. You know, get a good game in there, start out free then charge as much as the market will bear after the gamers are hooked. I was messing with the new codes and stumbled upon a slicker, faster language. I thought, why sit on my thumbs and let some other guy make millions off of my idea? It's a gold mine in apps and I was going to be the first panhandler to dive in with this new language, this newer, more efficient, pan so to speak. I went to the big money bakers and showed them what I had. Most didn't let me through the front door, but two of them did."

"Victor, as much as I love a good nerd story, get to the point," said Estep.

Victor placed his hand over his heart in a wildly dramatic gesture of offense. "Am I boring you?"

Estep grunted. His handsome looks were masked by his perpetually dark moods. He looked particularly ugly at the moment.

Serena tried in vain to think of an excuse to get Estep out of the interrogation room before he blew. She was relieved when Victor had the same idea.

Victor said, "I'm not saying another word until he leaves. From now on I'm talking only to you, Miss…"

"Serena."

"Miss Serena." Victor smiled broadly. He looked almost charming.

Estep didn't put up a fight and he didn't waste any time heading out the door. And, as if his feelings about leaving Victor for Serena to deal with weren't clear enough already, he was finally smiling. Ah, there was that handsome face again, thought Serena.

Before leaving the room Estep said, "I want that when you're done." He tossed the recording device that he had been wearing all along, concealed, at Serena. She was not expecting something to be thrown at her. Fortunately her reflexes were sharp and she caught it before it hit her in the face. She puzzled over it a little while, and was about to ask Estep if she needed to turn it on or something, but he was already gone.

"Well, then, it's just you and me, Princess," said Victor.

"No more interruptions. I'm listening – take your time," coaxed Serena. She was aiming for the voice of an enchantress, slow and husky, halting, hypnotizing. Tell me everything, I won't hurt you, she imagined herself projecting.

"Is there something wrong with your eye?" asked Victor.

Serena dropped her attempt at bewitching Victor and said, in her normal voice, "No. Back to what you were saying about the FYD."

Victor asked for water, drank it all in one long gulping session, crossed his legs, folded his hands on one knee, then, after a bit more fidgeting and preening, he began his monologue:

"The FYD was created as a result of the increases in food prices which led to the decrease in gains, the reversal of gains, in poverty reduction. Take Africa. In 2008, food prices were getting alarmingly high. Food prices stabilized some, came back down – although not as big of a percentage of decrease in Africa – and then costs began to climb overall again. Of course after the big war, food prices were out of reach for the American poor, let alone the African poor. Anyway, rice, cereals, maize, wheat – all are imports out of reach for poor nations across the globe, not just Africa. But I mention Africa because they are a nation more vulnerable to unstable food prices. Am I losing you?"

"No, I think I've got it. Other nations can bounce back from fluctuations in food prices easier," said Serena, who was wondering where this was all going. How did they get onto Africa?

"Well…to work toward sustainable food security in Africa, the Bank established in 2008 the Africa Food Crisis Response initiative, AFCR."

"The Bank?"

"The African Development Bank Group is probably the correct reference, but basically the World Food Bank. The goal is to reduce food poverty and malnutrition, short term, and achieve sustainable food security, long term. The Bank provides low-interest loans, interest-free credits, and grants to developing countries. The list of what they finance is long. They invest in education, health, public administration, infrastructure, financial and private sector development, agriculture, and environmental and natural resource management. They don't foot the entire bill – they co-finance with the countries themselves, or with investors. It's complicated. But bottom line, we're talking millions, and billions, of dollars poured into these projects."

"Millions and billions of dollars. You have my attention. Where's there's big money…"

"There's corruption. The African Development Group had as its goal to increase rice production, so high-yield rice would be ideal, yes? So they involved the private sector for food security and promoted agricultural research. The African Crisis Response Facility was established. There were five countries directly benefiting from the AFCR initiative, and its success was a model for many more such initiatives involving many more countries."

"And these countries were not directly benefiting, I'm guessing?

They got off course, tainted by greed. The money didn't go to the impoverished nations, but instead lined the pockets of the private sector, or corrupt governments. Am I right?" asked Serena.

"Well, yes and no. The World Bank was still doing amazing things, and their goals were still admirable. But, yes, some of the growth of the WB led to a situation in which there were organizations without a watchdog. In those cases, there was a mixed bag of greedy government officials and greedy private individuals. Which leads me to my point: FYD, Food Yield and Development, was created to assist the Bank, but that never quite took off. The plan was for each nation to have their own FYD, so ours would be FYD-US, Food Yield and Development of the United States. And then the WFYD—"

"World?" Serena guessed. She was trying to hurry Victor along. She was also getting an acronym headache.

"Yes, the World Food Yield and Development would be a watchdog over all the others. To prevent corruption. And all would support the World Bank, and all its initiatives. It was thought that more government was needed, others disagreed. As usual, nothing was accomplished. We dropped the ball on this, if you ask me."

"So is this the part where you tell me what the FYD wants with you? And what do you have on your computer?" asked Serena.

"Henry," said Victor.

"Henry? Oh right, the computer. Go on," prodded Serena. She looked wistfully at the door.

"FYD would have, if they'd taken off, submitted statistics and pitches to the World Bank, to get funding. Like, for example, if research proved favorable on high yield corn, as I mentioned earlier in regards to poverty in Africa, well then, that could be a project selected for major funding," said Victor. He hesitated and looked around the room.

"What are you looking for?" asked Serena, even though she thought she knew the answer.

Victor didn't say anything. He gestured a writing motion. Serena gave him a pen and some paper. He wrote: "Walls have eyes."

Serena studied the sections of the room where she had seen Victor looking. Hmm, yes, there it is. A not-so-hidden camera. "While I get your concern, these are cameras. They can see you writing. So, how about you lower your voice and hope for the best? Besides, you're already detained. If you cooperate you'll get some leniency."

Victor whispered, "If I talk, we all die."

8

Ted was being watched. He could feel it. He felt it when he was awake; he felt it when he was trying to sleep. At night he tossed and turned so much that Ann had asked him on more than one occasion what his problem was. He wished he could tell her. He hated lying to his wife, who was also the President of his country. It was also hard, as the First Gentleman, to find time to be alone – how did he think he could get away with something like this? But he was going to give it his best shot.

Today was the day to go for it – everything was all set up and the green light to proceed had been given. It had taken him and his confidant over 48 hours to arrange. There was no way he wanted to jump through all these hoops again tomorrow; he vowed not to screw this up. Clandestine and absurd game-play was hard for a man who had enjoyed freedom for most of his life to accept as his new normal, but he would do what he had to do.

Ted went to McDonald's, which was not unusual. He stopped there for coffee occasionally. Sometimes he even had a Big Mac, which drew Clinton jokes from old timers from the D.C. days. Ted's secret service detail didn't think anything of it when his driver got into the drive-through line at a busy McDonald's on a Saturday afternoon. They followed him, of course, but Ted had anticipated that typical course of action.

Ted's driver ordered for Ted at the speaker – a small coffee only. They drove forward in the line. As Ted predicted would happen, the young agents in the car behind him had their mouths watered for burgers and fries. He waited until it was their turn at the speaker. When one of the agents was barking his order into the speaker Ted slipped out of his car, guessing that the agents would assume he had gone inside the restaurant to use the restroom.

Were they distracted enough by the busy drive through lane to let him go inside on his own? Ted resisted the urge to look over his shoulder. He kept moving, walking toward the restrooms. He didn't look behind him until a family with three kids filled the door frame. One of the kids was carrying a birthday gift bag, which came as no surprise to Ted, who had chosen this precise moment to come to McDonald's today -- the start time of a large children's party.

The party schedule for McDonald's was not difficult information to come by, and it was even easier than he had thought to hide himself in the chaos. The added bonus was that most of the kids and their parents were wearing paper hats that added more height and eye-clutter to the gaggle. His privacy barrier was even better than he expected!

By the time his agents drove around the other side of the building, he was already back out the same door he'd come in, where another driver was waiting for him – a driver of a non-government vehicle. Ted was confident that no one would have seen him walk back out, but he was not home free. His agents would be expecting him to come out the door near the drive through exit, where his regular driver was waiting for him, a driver who knew nothing of Ted's plans.

They'll go in there looking for me; I give them less than ten minutes. Probably closer to five. Ted hurried into the vehicle without drawing attention to him. He got in the back seat and reassured himself that the windows were tinted. Although it was unnecessary to do so, he couldn't resist saying, "Go!"

His new driver eased out of the McDonald's parking lot and into the congested street. Ted knew this area and had chosen it for its traffic patterns: fast moving, heavy flow, no traffic lights for a long stretch. As he had anticipated, the car Ted was riding in was quickly sucked into the flow, absorbed by Saturday shoppers and tourists. It was satisfying to look back and see nothing behind him that resembled a government vehicle. He was free!

And that was when his new driver pulled over, stopped, and turned around in her seat. Ted gasped. "It's you," he said.

"Yes, it's me. Did you really think that I wouldn't know that you were hiding something from me?"

"I hoped," Ted said.

President Ann Kinji, aka Ted's wife, laughed. "Your first mistake was recruiting one of my friends. Of course she went straight to me and told me what you were doing."

"My secret service detail? They knew all along?"

"No, you fooled them. No one knows about this but you, me, and our mutual friend Penny."

"How did you get away from your detail?"

"I put Penny on the detail today. They are following us discretely."

"We can trust Penny."

"Of course we can, she's the one who told us that something was rotten in the Cube."

"Then we can proceed with the plan?" asked Ted.

"I don't know your plan. All I know is that you asked Penny to help you evade your security detail. Are you going to tell me what you planned to do?"

Ah, that explains it, he thought. She didn't know.

"I can tell from your hesitation that you are wondering if you should tell me or not. Whatever it is, you know I'll find out eventually," said Ann.

"I know where Serena is," Ted said without fanfare.

Ann perked up. "Why didn't you say anything?"

"Because they are keeping it a secret from you, from us," said Ted.

"Who are they?"

"I don't know, but I'd like to find out. I don't think the President of the newly united States should be any part of this."

"And you should?"

"If not me, who? If something stinks in the Cube, I don't know where the smell is coming from. We have to trust someone though, and we do trust Penny. I assume we can trust her judgment in people too."

"Yes, my detail is sound," Ann confirmed. She felt no

reservation in asserting her confidence – her intuition had never failed her before and she had no reason to doubt her God-given gift now. "Your plan was what? Go to where Serena is and fight all the bad guys yourself?

"Of course not."

"Then what was the plan?"

"I was told to meet with someone in a Gasthaus, and he would tell me everything."

"A Gasthaus? She's still in Germany?"

"Apparently."

"Why the cloak and dagger routine?"

"He said he was worried about the others knowing that he was meeting with me. I'm supposed to be there two days from now."

"How did you expect to stay away that long without anyone noticing you were gone?"

"I was going to tell you before everything hit the fan, but not until I was already on the plane. Besides, no one really cares what I do with my time as long as it doesn't reflect badly on you."

"I see. Your plan is severely flawed. First of all, you aren't meeting with him yourself. We have trained people for that."

"He specifically said that no one could be trusted. He made it clear that he wanted me to be the one he talked to, and given the compromised situation we have I agree with him."

"You know we never negotiate in these situations. It's ridiculous that the First Gentleman would be acting like an agent, and that you'd do something like this behind my back."

"This is why I didn't tell you. I knew you'd try to talk me out of it. Besides, I wanted to protect you. What you didn't know wouldn't have hurt you, but here you are."

"Yes, here I am. What else did he say? And how did he contact you in the first place?"

"He somehow got directly through to my private line."

"What? Who would let that happen? Follow that security leak and we will have a lead on where the stink is coming from. Anything else I should know about?"

"He said something about too many people knowing about 'Covert Coffee'. That mean anything to you?"

"Covert Coffee is my operation."

"Now you're acting like an agent."

"Of course not! My team is on this."

Ted reached forward from his position in the backseat to touch Ann's shoulder. He gave her a gentle squeeze and said, "Madam President, are you sure you know who your team is?

9

Paul didn't mind his prison life. It was oddly liberating. No longer the puppet of his deranged older brother, Paul was free in a way that transcended prison bars. Besides, he had The Social Media Channel to keep him company: the voices of the masses, plus millions of published digital books. He could feed his mind and spirit with no limits – with no job and no house to maintain he had all the time in the world.

All the social networking, reading, meditating, praying, deep breathing, yoga, pottery, painting, and Zen gardening were clearly a big part of his therapy, but was only part of the transformative process. It was his spiritual awakening that was the most responsible for the man Paul was today. His life-changing epiphany: When one feels dead, there is nothing left to fear; how boundless life becomes!

Not content to keep such new-found wisdom to himself, Paul shared his secret to joyful living with anyone who visited him and in a series of self-help books that hit all of the important bestseller lists. His PR team had tweaked his now-famous quote to be more marketable: When one has no fear of dying; how boundless life becomes!

The book would have sold itself because naturally everyone was curious about what Paul, the man who blew up two American presidents, one former and one sitting, was thinking. Not that anyone mourned the loss of the two men who had perished under his hand: clearly the newly re-united nation was much better off without those misogynistic prigs. So, while Paul was a murderer and a terrorist, he was nonetheless an American hero according to The Social Media Channel polls, which Paul tuned into daily.

In fact, he never tuned out. The SM Channel was a television station devoted to a running stream of never-ending, seldom-slowing social media content. International, national, and state official tweets ran along the bottom of the screen like the old CNN tickertape. Opt-in and personal social media filled the main screen. Multiple users could view SM Channel together, a common situation in a household with a wide screen television, although most people hid their personal feeds when sharing a screen with others.

Paul, alone in his prison cell, had no such privacy concerns. He programmed his own name into his customized SM Channel settings so that he was always plugged into what people were saying about him. The SM Channel drew tweets, blogs, statuses, blurbs, messages, forums – all of it – everything out there, every and any social media, into one screen. Paul tracked several keywords, or tags, all at once. He even kept multiple screens open, like a picture-in-picture TV. Some of his screens were stacked in multiples. And yet he kept up with all of it.

Paul heard a ping on one of his tags. Interesting, he thought. Haven't seen that name pop up in a while. What's going on?

The ping signaled that Nicholas was active on the SM Channel. Nicholas was the young computer genius that his brother Clyde had recruited for the computer lab – the lab had been Clyde's baby, not Paul's, but regardless of ownership the lab was seized by the United States government even before cuffs were chafing Paul's hands. The news that Nicholas was apparently now working for Big Brother didn't surprise Paul in the slightest.

But what was surprising was that Nicholas was reaching out into Cyberspace to dig for information. Why would he do that when he had access to the best security technologically possible? The SM Channel had only consumer-level encryption. A hacker could crack that wide open in minutes. So why was Nicholas using it? Why, indeed.

Paul spoke into his SM Channel watch. Most households were given an SM Channel pen, gratis from the government. The argument for providing SM pens, known as "digi pens", to every household was the same as in the days of funding public television – every citizen should have access to information. All law-abiding Americans could access the SM Channel and cellular phone service via the digi pen, but inmates were not allowed to have such an instrument. They were issued watches instead.

Speaking into the watch was something Paul did every waking hour, a habit that grated on his fellow inmates' nerves. And yet, certain inmates listened to everything Paul said, hoping for a tidbit that would interest a reporter. After all, there might be a book deal to the hangers-on.

“Show me location,” he said.

A map spread across the screen with a virtual pin over Hudson, Wisconsin. The pin lowered and the map zoomed in tighter, tighter, tighter, until Paul was looking right into the computer lab windows. He could see Nicholas at the window, as clearly as if he was doing a teleconference. Paul looked the kid over. Yep, that was the same kid. He had grown a lot since he had seen him last, but yes, that was him. Paul was about to zoom back out, but it was too late. Nicholas had apparently seen Paul’s signal pop up on whatever security application he had been running. Ahah, so Nicholas was using secret and advanced stuff all along. This makes sense now.

Paul read the message on his screen a few times, letting it sink in: PAUL – I SEE YOU! KNEW YOU’D BE WATCHING. THANKS FOR MENTIONING ME IN YOUR BOOK. I THREW YOU A SIGNAL, WANTED TO GET YOUR ATTENTION. NEED YOUR HELP, YOU IN?

What could he possibly need Paul’s help with? Paul was intrigued, to say the least. He replied, speaking into his watch, “Count me in, what can I do?”

CAN’T KEEP THIS LINE SECURE FOR LONG. SM CHANNEL NOT THE BEST PLATFORM. SERENA ASKED FOR YOU. YOU CAN ASK HER WHEN YOU GET HERE. SORRY, HAVE TO DISCONNECT.

Serena? Serena Wilcox? She was the last person he would have expected to seek out his company. Last he knew Serena was personal friends with the president of the United States, President Ann Kinji. So this was big. Very big.

Paul did something he had not done for months: he turned off the SM Channel. Then he packed up the few belongings allowed in the cell, made his bed, and brushed his teeth. He was beginning to floss, with a tiny inmate-approved flossing tool, when he heard footsteps approaching his cell door.

10

President Ann Kinji absorbed her husband's words: "He somehow got directly through to my private line." She let her body sink into the plush seat cushion of one of three chair-and-a-half loungers in the presidential library, the incredible room custom built for her and completed just three weeks ago.

The room was rushed into production after Kinji was overheard referring to her new home as "The Cube". It was unacceptable that President Ann Kinji, a heroine seeing the nation through the worst chapter in American history, should be unhappy. President Ann, a president so loved that she was often affectionately referred to by her first name, should have the presidential room of her dreams.

Private citizens worth millions, some worth billions, gathered in emergency fund-raising sessions; large gala events complete with paparazzi to cover them. Within a few short days the money was in the bank and the best architects in the world were hired. The entire project was brought from conception to finish in less than 18 months, a feat so incredible that Americans were inspired to believe that the new America had rekindled innovation reminiscent of the days when Walt Disney was still living, Virginia believed in Santa Claus, and Jimmy Stewart's George Bailey learned that it's a wonderful life.

And the result was sensational! The library was designed to look like an old vaudeville theater. The bookcases had the appearance of audience seating – rows and rows of books, spiraling up and up, to the highest heights where balconies were nearly flush with the glass ceiling. The stage area held a platform reading space with burgundy stage curtains framing the seating area. From the stage Ann could look out over her audience of books, books, and more books.

For no matter how many digital books she had downloaded over the years, she never gave up her love of holding a real book in her hands. These days, real books were like pieces of art: collectables. Not many people read printed pages anymore, and certainly few contemporary works were inked on real paper, but books themselves had never lost their beauty, or the power to calm her. Ann's library was the only place in The Cube where she felt at home.

While she had only had the space for a little over twenty-one days, she had already developed a daily habit of spending at least an hour a day in the library and she was firm about the rules regarding the new space. She banned The Social Media Channel from her library – no screens of any kind were allowed in. No gadgets, no digi pens, nothing. The intercom system was the only way to reach

Ann when she was in her sanctuary, her resting place that literally did have a sanctuary, an incredible one.

The "audience" of books filled half of the library's sphere, and the stage/set (seating area) was across from the audience, as expected if imagining the room looking like a traditional theater house. The space where an orchestra pit would be was the space set aside for Ann's sanctuary. Ann's design team had worked with her to create a prayer and reflection space in the center of the library.

The sanctuary was an indoor garden, both ingenious and beautiful. The entire garden was no larger than the imagined orchestra pit space – it was compact and space efficient. Every inch of it was utilized: pavers with mosses and flowering ground-cover between stones served as flooring; flower beds were arranged organically around the trellis, pond, and butterfly garden; retaining walls held fruit trees, berry bushes and a small assortment of vegetables. There was a lattice arch with flowering vines that created a canopy of blooms; climbing roses, morning glories, sweet peas, and more exotic vines like the "Double Blue Butterfly Pea Vine" and the "Chocolate Vine", a beautiful climber with distinct chocolate colored flowers that give off a slight hint of chocolate fragrance.

The exotic vines were zoned for tropical climates. Therefore the garden was kept quite warm, with a high level of humidity created by a system of over a hundred misters discretely hidden amongst the plants. Ann relished the warmth and anticipated the freedom of wearing sleeveless summer dresses even in the dead of winter, which would creep up on her again sooner than she cared to think about.

Even the library bathroom was planned by a team of designers. It was generously sized and included a luxury dressing room where Ann kept all of her favorite cotton clothing, mostly beach dresses and oversized T-shirts. She also stored a collection of straw hats to protect herself from the surprisingly harsh rays that blasted through the library's enormous skylight dome.

The center of the dome was above the heart of the garden where flowering vines created a focal point for water fountains, bird baths, and bird feeders – an attractant for the many beautiful song birds that resided in the garden. Other garden residents were Koi in the pond, butterflies in the butterfly garden that surrounded the pond, and helpful-to-plants insects such as ladybugs, found in largest concentration in the plants near the masterpiece sculpture fountain.

At the base of the fountain was a 2-person wrought iron bistro set, perfect for enjoying a morning cup of coffee. But Ann's favorite place to relax was under the flowering vines in a futon swing, the final touch to complete the enchanted garden. Overlooking the entire glorious display was the stage seating, where Ann was currently still slumped in a lounger.

As she looked out over her flowers, past the natural beauty of the gardens to the balconies of man-made books, a flurry of movement caught her attention. She smiled. Ah, a hummingbird was at the trumpet vine. She allowed herself to relax again – she was safe within her domed library, her enchanted garden. This really was a beautiful world that her people had created for her, their queen.

But as she had said in her speech on ribbon-cutting day, this multi-million dollar project dedicated to her by some of the world's most successful people in business and the arts "is nothing but a vulgarity if not repeated. Take this example of what can be done when the best of American ingenuity unites, and apply it to a project worthy of the best and brightest."

She challenged the Kinji Library & Conservatory Foundation to adopt no fewer than ten of the neediest inner-city areas of the nation, ten of the neediest mid-sized towns, and ten of the neediest small towns. Reassemble the think tank. Generate funds. Bring back the galas, the red carpet, and the paparazzi. Make something beautiful. Use the triumphant library project, their new national treasure, as a shiny jewel to inspire something even more magical: something real, that would make a real difference.

Her speech was met with a standing ovation. The president of the Kinji Library and Conservatory Foundation stepped forward to say, "You make a real difference. You are worthy of something beautiful. I'm sure I speak for the entire foundation when I pledge to build upon what was started here today, and recreate America one community at a time." It took no convincing to get the team back together. They re-named themselves The New America Foundation and went to work planning a "re-building America's poorest" event that would make President Ann proud.

Yes, it seemed that the nation was headed into a wonderful era of healing and growth. And yet, here she was, worried about a rat in The Cube, an infestation that lingered from the previous administration and all the tragic events that preceded its hideous and shocking demise. Yes, there was leftover business to take care of.

And that was why Ann broke her own rules for the library, the sanctuary that she was now calling her enchanted garden: she brought in her digi pen. It was easy to smuggle in without notice. It was the size of a regular ink pen and no one would suspect that Ann, as vehement as she was about banning all technology from the Dome, would then herself bring in a gadget.

Before she used the digi, she took measures so that she would not be in view of the security cameras. She knew of one spot where the cameras could not focus on her. She sat on the swing under the floral cover, the plants having grown so lush that the view of her under the trellis was completely blotted out by blossoms, leaves, and vines. She breathed in the hint of chocolate from the Akebia quinata and steadied her nerves. What she was about to do was ridiculous. She was going rogue – no one in her cabinet, on her staff, not even the First Gentleman, would know what she was up to.

11

Former Special Agent Lehman felt the warmth of his digi pen through the fabric of his shirt pocket – he had set it to “heating mode”, as it was quieter than vibrating mode. Because he wasn’t expecting an urgent message, or any message for that matter, he took his sweet time reaching for the pen. Another bite to eat, another couple of sips of wine from a bottle of Barbera --his favorite Italian variety – then he’d look into who was trying to reach him. His time was his own! Why not enjoy the best benefit to being a private citizen?

His professional life after he left the civil service was quietly devoted to his lucrative career in the IT department of a well-known company, and while he was often on call, his assignments were hardly the emergency status or danger level of a covert mission. As for his personal life, what a change from lonely hurried weekends of his civil service days when he never had time to do much more than catch a movie – and when he did finally make it to the cinema he rarely got to stay to the final credits.

Now Lehman had plenty of time for leisurely pursuits. He scheduled week-long vacations on exotic beaches and regularly indulged in his new hobby: dining in new restaurants with his wife and later reviewing them for his blog. This was what he was doing right now – the dining part of his foodie lifestyle. Later he would re-live the experience by blogging it. Yes, life was good, and he didn't miss the fray of D.C. or the new digs in Chicago.

Nonetheless, when he saw the caller ID on the tiny digi screen, his pulse quickened. He slid his entrée, the Veal Osso Bucco, toward the middle of the table to use the table surface for writing. Flustered, he dropped the digi pen twice before finally grasping it firmly. He wrote, "Madam President, I'm here."

Lehman's wife leaned over the table and mouthed, "Who are you talking to?"

Lehman whispered, "President Kinji." He resumed talking at a normal level, "There's a delay in transmission, I'm on hold."

His wife gasped. "What does she want? Doesn't she know you aren't an agent anymore?"

"I think so, yes, of course she does. She gave me a nice card when I left, remember? You said I should frame it."

"Then what does she want?"

"I don't know, she hasn't answer— wait, she's saying something," said Lehman.

He pulled the rubbery tab on the end of the pen to extract the digi ear bud. He inserted it into his right ear and listened to the message.

"I need your help. In fact, I need a team outside of The Cube. Who can you find on short notice? People you trust, and no one active."

Lehman wrote with the pen, "You need me to create a team and head it up? What is the mission?"

"There's a, for lack of a better word, traitor in the Cube. I don't know who, or how many. Something left over from President William's days and probably earlier."

"Can I talk to my wife first?"

"Of course."

Lehman's wife nodded vigorously when he brought her up to speed. "I know you'll do the right thing. I'm behind you," she said.

Lehman wrote: "My wife's here, gave me the green light. I can get a team together, but some of them had their security clearances revoked."

"That won't be a problem," said Ann.

"You have a location?"

"You'll be working at the lab in Hudson."

"The Minnesota lab?"

"We moved it to Wisconsin."

"Got it. When do I go?"

"There's someone outside waiting for you, about a block away from GianMarco's – that's where you are, correct?"

"Yes. You tracked me through my digi pen?"

"I don't know how they did it, I told them I wanted you found and they found you."

"No offense, Madam President, but you are on your digi. Did you disable the tracking feature?"

"Yes, I did. And I'm using the text-to-speech function, so my correspondence with you is silent."

"Cameras?"

"I'm concealed by flowers."

"Pardon?"

"By—Agent Lehman, I'm fine. Please focus on your mission. My people are waiting for you. It's a long way from Homewood, Alabama to Hudson, Wisconsin."

"Yes, I'm on my way."

"I knew I could count on you, Agent Lehman."

"Thank you, Madam President." He wasn't sure how heartfelt he was. Part of him was over-the-moon with pride that his President trusted him above anyone else she could have called upon, but another part, possibly a larger part, of him was sickened at the thought of leaving his wife and job, and all of Birmingham for who knows how long. Would everything be the same when he returned? Would he be the same when he returned?

12

Lehman's first move was to assemble his team. On the top of the list was "The Beav", one of the former agents he knew whose security clearance had been revoked – the biggest scapegoat on the chopping block when the flushing of the agency began. Beav was spectacularly tangled up in the mess with Paul and the most obvious choice to sacrifice first. He had been present when an explosion took down two American presidents with one high-tech bomb that had been disguised as a bugging device. Beav, the team's technology expert, had failed to recognize the device as a bomb even after he'd hand-inspected it.

Of course Beav had no way of knowing that Paul was capable of that level of violence, nor should any reasonable person hold him responsible for anything that transpired, but anyone even remotely connected to that tragic and highly-avoidable national disaster was swiftly fired with no hope of working in government service again; and Beav was directly responsible for botching the inspection of the device. While Lehman had taken an early retirement with honors – having escaped the firing sweep because he wasn't anywhere near that fiasco—poor Beav, one of the best agents Lehman had ever known, was hung out to dry. Lehman's jaw clenched in memory of the witch hunt. The nation demanded that people be held accountable and naturally the easiest place to start was with the little people, the ones who put their lives on the line for everyone else. Lehman wasn't sure what washed up condition he would find Beav in. Would he even be fit to serve?

The Beav answered Lehman's call on the first ring. His voice was unnaturally chipper which was his typical state of being, especially if he had been up all night on a creative bender, sans alcohol or any other substance. He revved himself up on mania alone, the ideas churning inside his head, silenced only when his project was complete. Whether it was an underground library bedroom, a butterfly garden, or building a series of walls – Beav would not sleep until he hit a stopping point, which often drove him to the brink of insanity. It was in this crazed state of sleep-deprivation that Lehman found him.

"I just got back from a run, and I'm on my way to the gym," said Beav.

"Can you see yourself boarding a plane to Germany instead?"

"I'm in the middle of a project. Beating myself up at the gym to stay alert. Then I'm back at it."

"What project? Who are you working for?"

"Nobody. Me. I'm making a spiral staircase for my bedroom

library."

This was normal behavior, thriving even, for Beav. Yes, he had called the right man for the job. "Suspend the staircase plan for now. I need your help."

"Why Germany? Do they eat a lot of red meat there?"

Lehman ignored the meat question. The Beav's aversion to meat was well-known and not an issue he had time for. "The President believes that Serena Wilcox might be held there."

"Against her will?"

"Of course, against her will." Lehman wished he wasn't holed up in his car. He had a desperate need to walk off his frustration. "You need to go there, find her, and bring her back."

"Alive?"

"What? Of course we want her alive!"

"No, I mean: Do you think she is alive?"

"I hope so."

"Who has her? What do they want with her?" Beav piled dirty dishes into the sink to rinse them off. He spoke loudly over the running water.

"That's for you to find out. You'll meet with a guy, go from there."

"A guy? A contact? He's expecting me?"

"He's expecting the First Gentleman."

"Got it. Anything else I need to know?" Beav wiped down the countertop and took a quick inventory of the house.

"Nope, I sent everything else to your phone. Your flight leaves inside of two hours."

"Hey, bud, thanks for the gig."

"No problem. Beav? You know you can never be re-instated,

right?"

"Off the books."

"To your grave."

"Got it. I'll be in touch. Auf Wiedersehen!" Beav grabbed a leather backpack from his closet, already packed with essential clothing, supplies, and food to last for three days, five if he was conservative. He kept it at the ready for the call he had known would one day come. And that wasn't all he kept ready: all those days at the gym kept him pumped, primed, and more ready than he had been when he was still in.

To keep his mind sharp he of course had his impressive library of mainly nonfiction books, an eclectic assortment. And sure enough, his mission strategy was already forming in his brain, yes, easy-please-y, as if he'd never stopped working. He told himself that he would be in and out of there in time to tackle the spiral staircase by the following weekend.

He got himself on the plane with plenty of time to spare. He settled into his seat, placed his buckwheat travel pillow around the back of his neck, and allowed himself to sleep for the entire duration of the flight to Frankfurt. He barely stirred, even when his fellow passengers were restless and noisy. Upon arrival, Beav was well rested and primed. He grabbed his bags, joined the stream of unloading passengers, and made his way into the airport.

Travel to Germany was not much different than traveling anywhere else in the world but Beav remembered the old days, before the fall of the wall, when German airports were intimidating, especially if you were landing in Berlin. Armed guards with machine guns strolled the corridors. It was intimidating even for those who knew the language and carried a weapon of their own.

Germany today was such a far cry from those days of a divided nation, something that Beav saw happening right before his eyes in the United States: division before healing. Sort of. It was also vastly different, of course. Beav continued to muse and ponder the state of his nation, the state of Germany, the state of the world. He almost missed seeing the man who was following him, almost.

Beav took a mental snapshot of the man who was keeping pace with him on the other side of the walkway. He assumed he would turn up again, probably at his next destination: Geisfeld, a little village not far from Bamberg. It was quite a drive from Frankfurt to Bamberg, but Beav felt certain that his stalker would have no problem staying on his tail. Maybe he even had a team. Beav felt smug: he didn't need a team. More importantly, he preferred to work alone.

He drove the rental car to Geisfeld. He made few stops, but every time he did take a restroom break he saw a familiar Audi pull up shortly after him. He placed a bet with himself that the Audi would reappear in Geisfeld, and sure enough he was right. It turned up parked along a narrow cobblestoned street near the Edeka convenience mart. Beav assumed his stalker was now following him on foot so he headed to a public place, a nearby Gasthaus. He ordered only Pomfritz, fries being the only thing on the menu he was willing to ingest. He dug around in his bag for a can of tuna to eat from for his main entrée.

The German wait staff was already curious about this German-speaking man with an American accent and Romanian ethnicity sitting in their small village alone. What business did he have here? How did he know about this place? It wasn't listed in any tour guide that they were aware of. The Gasthaus was not only a restaurant serving typical German cuisine and pub style foods, but also served as a stable and arena for horses. Patrons of the restaurant could view the horses in their enclosed training arena via the glass windows that walled the dining space. Trainers led the beautiful animals into the arena to lightly exercise them and practice basic hurdles.

Was this mysterious American here for the horses, the food, or something else? Something else, the staff noted when another man joined the American at his table. The wait staff would have loved to have heard the conversation, but straining to keep up with English was difficult enough without competing with the din of the Fussball crowd who serendipitously entered the door at that moment. Besides, they had beer to pour – plenty of it!

The two men were satisfied that no one could listen in their conversation; there was no need to go to a more private location, and no desire. The Gasthaus was a good place to be on an evening that had taken on a wet chill. However, the two sat across the table from each other in silence. Beav held out for the other man to speak first. It was a long wait, but he won the battle of wills.

"I was expecting an American. I know it to be you," he said, with an accent Beav couldn't identify.

"You live around here?"

"No. I come for you."

"What do you want with me? Who do you think I am?" Beav spun his now-empty water glass like a toy top.

The stalker was briefly distracted by this. After a few seconds passed he said, "I know who you are. You are the one she sent instead of Mr. President. You take too many risks."

"I take risks?"

"America. America takes risks. I knew she wouldn't do what we asked." He fiddled with a coaster that had a beer logo imprinted on it.

"Then why ask it?" Beav was distracted by the perpetual motion of the coaster even though he himself had been spinning his empty glass only a minute before.

"We wanted her to send us a man she believes."

"She believes?" Beav stared pointedly at the coaster.

The man lay the coaster on the table. "Not believes. Trusts. We expected she would send more of you."

"No, I'm it."

"You will do. I must work now."

"Work?"

"It is the time for telling you the reason we asked for you to come here."

Beav focused on what he went to Germany for. "What about Serena Wilcox?"

"No, she's not here."

"Then where is she?" Beav studied the man's face but didn't see any hint of guile. Nor did he seem threatening in any way.

"She's in the States. There is a computer center there. She is there, working for us."

"For the Germans?"

The man laughed. "No, not the Germans."

"Then who?"

"We are Supporters."

"Of?"

"President Ann Kinji, United States President who sees beyond her own country."

Beav cut him off before the mysterious would-be kidnapper

launched into a political rant. "Why did you lie to her about Serena Wilcox?"

"She thinks Serena is here, that is good. We keep her thinking that."

"Because?"

"The corruption is deeper than she knows. We will work quietly, give her a wild duck chase."

"Goose."

"What?"

"Never mind."

"We keep her thinking Serena is in Germany. We get her to send a man to us, someone who can help us."

"I follow you so far. But who are the supporters exactly, and what do you need from me?" Beav didn't think he looked like the militia type, but what did he know about who was the militia type? He wasn't a profiler or even an agent anymore.

"We are an underground of patriots who met on the SM."

"The Social Media Channel?"

"Yes."

"I don't follow."

"We are mathematics. We are from Uni. Not all, but many."

"You are computer programmers?"

"Among other things. Researchers." The man's eyes darted back and forth.

"And?"

He leaned across the table and whispered, his breath heavy with medical spearmint from antacid tablets. "And we saw something we weren't supposed to see. There was an exposure."

"An exposure?"

"A crack."

"I don't understand."

"We could see in." The man's eyes opened wide, as if he were seeing everything all over again.

"I am still not getting it."

"We saw that they were there. You have a name you like to say. 'Big Brother'."

"The government?" Beav wondered if this man might be militia after all. He feigned dropping the coaster under the table so that he had an excuse to dart forward to pick it up. His sudden lunge didn't faze the man at all. He didn't seem like a soldier, not even of the home-grown variety.

"Yes, your government was inside. It started with the organ donor registry, it was before the SM Channel put all the social media together."

"Yes, I remember." Beav slid an elastic band off of his wrist and used it to pull his hair back. He hadn't cut his hair since he left the agency.

"Then they matched with birth certificates and blood types." The man had a smooth style of speaking even though English was obviously a second language for him.

"Yes, that's how it generally works."

"No, they matched in system. Database on every citizen has blood type."

"Creepy I guess, but I still don't understand." Beav's fries were gone and so was the tuna he brought with him. While he was no longer hungry, he considered ordering more food because he was restless.

"They track people on SM."

"Right, that's not new information."

"They track through digi pen, through phone, through everything all going to same place – the SM."

"Yes? And?" Beav grabbed a menu and skimmed through it.

"They track keywords."

"Like a terrorist watch list?" Beav dismissed the idea of ordering any of the rich meats.

"No. They track everything said."

"I still don't see a problem here."

The man reached across the table and removed the menu from Beav's hands. "They block things they don't want said."

"Are you saying that our government is censoring what people are saying on the Internet?"

"Yes. Censoring. They stop people from hearing things they don't want your people to know."

Beav waited until the server filled his water glass and walked away before continuing. "Are you trying to tell me that the United States government, without the knowledge of our own president, is controlling the Internet?"

"Yes."

"How is that possible? Of course the Feds have been after backdoor access and 'wiretapping' for years, and have succeeded in some cases, but the SM is an international cooperative. Getting access would require agreement with other nations. Are you saying that this is a global takeover of the Internet? If so, I find that hard to believe." Beav leaned sideways in his chair to see what the people in a neighboring table were eating.

"Some are working together with the United States."

"And their presidents don't know anything either?"

“I didn’t say that.”

13

Serena returned to the row of computers where Nicholas had been working. She expected to see him sitting exactly where he was when she left, but he wasn't there. Neither was her favorite hot-head Agent Estep.

"Where did everybody go?" asked Victor.

Serena studied Victor's expression. Was he calculating how quickly he could overpower her now that she was clearly alone? She would have reached for her back pocket to feign that she carried a gun, but she was wearing pocket-less loose-legging style comfort/yoga pants.

Out of habit her mind raced for an outwit-the-criminal Plan B, even though "physical response" was now a tool in her arsenal. How she was kicking herself for not reacting more quickly!

Because, between the last case and this one, she had finally wised up; for nearly two years now she had been training heavily, attending Aikido class three times a week. Funny how she had completely blanked. The sight of Victor's clown face could make anyone lose their head, she consoled herself.

Her evaluation and (intended) reaction time took only a few seconds, but as she had anticipated, it was enough time for Victor to make his move. He bolted. He ran like a girl, even screaming while he ran. He made it to the doors but no farther. Like the entry, the exits were also secured – probably to prevent visitors from stealing data. Serena was grateful that the security system trapped Victor inside the lab. She didn't like to run. She also recalled the risk of a severed arm if caught by the snapping jaws of the door. The brutality of that possibility was nauseating to imagine.

She waited for Victor to decide what to do. Surely he wouldn't attack her -- a realization that disappointed her a little. She had lost her window of opportunity to try her new Aikido skills in a real-life situation. She watched Victor as he searched for an exit. He looked like a giant guinea pig trapped in a cage.

"I can't get out."

Serena laughed. "I can see that. Nice try, though."

"I might as well help you."

"You might as well." She shrugged. "Can we get you started right now?"

"I want Henry."

"They took Henry. Will you settle for, what did you call the other one?"

"Who. Or whom."

Serena let that pass.

"Emily! Her name is Emily." He glanced around the computer stations for any sign of the mock iMac that Agent Estep's team had taken from his home. The system was already set up for him at a station he called his own without invitation. He marked his territory by pulling back the chair, plopping his butt onto the pleather seat cushion, and wheeling himself forward until his abdomen was pressed flush against the table. He booted up the computer, a process that took a surprisingly long time. While waiting for Emily to start up, Victor had a look on his face that reminded Serena of a dog in heat.

"I'll leave you two alone," she said.

"No, no, this will only take a minute. Pull up a seat." Victor made an air circle, an invitational gesture to have a threesome.

"I'm not into that sort of thing," she said.

"Huh?" Victor replied.

"Nothing. Go on." Serena shook off her revulsion. There was geek love, and then there was geek perversion. If ever a man had seriously fallen in love with a computer, it was Victor. If Serena could shudder on command she would have been shaking from head to toe to get all the willies off her.

"You won't believe the secrets Emily has inside her!"

"Oh, I don't need to know."

"What?" Victor spun around in his chair. His baffled expression made him look slightly less repugnant.

"Sorry, go on." Serena willed herself to focus.

"Emily has the facial recognition data for all of the FYD insiders. I can search via name, company title, role in project, anything, and watch this!" Victor typed in a name and the man's face popped up instantly.

"Who is that?"

"Oh that's nobody, an example."

"Can you pull up the data they wanted from you? What don't they want us to know?" Serena edged in closer while maintaining a big personal space bubble between her and Victor.

"I'm showing you. This, the facial recognition data, is one of the things they don't want you to know."

"But I don't get it. We can find that information through our own searches."

"No you can't."

"How so?"

"They hack their data, have been for as long as I've been involved."

"What do you mean? Have they assigned themselves a false identity?"

"Yes, using the IDs of dead people. It's old school identity theft, with a high tech way of doing it."

"How do you know this?"

Victor raised one enormous furry eyebrow. "Because I helped them do it. Who else would have the mad skills?"

Serena sensed she had offended him, but didn't have time to waste soothing his raw nerve. "Do you have record of this?"

Victor made a sputtering sound with his sucker-fish lips. "Surely you jest!" He punched in a few numbers and an impressive table appeared, complete with color coding. He had placed all the legal birth names on the X axis and the false identities, complete with photographs, on the Y axis. Several of his clients had over a dozen aliases. He scrolled down the first few pages.

"Stop! I recognize that couple." She pointed to the husband and wife duo on the screen. They were average looking, neither thin nor fat, neither ugly nor beautiful, neither light-skinned nor dark-skinned. They were forgettable and unremarkable in every way. She remembered seeing them in person, and even their height was average.

In Serena's mind, a dramatic outward appearance gave her a head's-up: this was a person to watch. Heavy or lean; tall or petite; hair in shades of raven, red, streaked, or blonde; tattoos and piercings, unusual facial features (a clown face for example, she thought as she looked at Victor), all of these were neon signs. Good or bad, such people were interesting and noticed. It was the average who blended into the fabric of society like a chameleon; it was the average she trusted least of all.

"They are Marci and Erik Chapman," said Victor.

"The names don't ring a bell, but I know I've met them. I'm having a hard time placing where."

"A fund raiser?"

"No, I'm not on the A list. I don't get invited to things like that."

"You are a personal friend of the President."

"Which hasn't boosted my status much."

"No, that's not what I meant."

"She doesn't expect me to join the political scene, it's not my world."

"Again, not what I meant."

"I could continue to try to guess what you meant, or you could just tell me." Serena had awareness that she was clenching her jaw; a habit that she knew from experience would bring on a stress headache unless she relaxed her jaw muscles.

"Regardless of your A-list snub, you probably met them."

"Where?"

Victor made a huffing sound of superiority. "They are on her staff. Do you watch the news? Follow SM Channel? Do you keep your eyes open when you walk the hallowed new-construction halls of the Cube?"

Serena ignored his jabs. "This makes no sense to me. These two are easily recognizable, by everyone but me apparently, even though neither of them looks anything but ordinary. So what good is changing their identities if people already know their faces?"

Victor apparently found her comment worthy of two hairy eyebrows because he raised them both and held them high on his pale forehead long enough that they began to quiver. "Think about it, you'll get there."

Serena nodded. "They change their faces."

Victor released his eyebrows. "Easy enough to do with latex. I programmed the template myself."

Serena sucked in a big gulp of air. "Got it now! You were jazzed about the facial ID data because you use it to create new faces!"

Victor made a trigger gesture with his hand, pulled the trigger and clacked his tongue, ending the routine with a slow wink of the eye. "No matter how much in the public eye, no matter how famous the celebrity or politician, everyone can go dark."

"And yet, with the right face, can still access secured areas. I can see where people would not want this information to see the light of day."

"Especially those who live a secret life of crime."

"And you know who these people are?" Serena prodded again.

"More than you realize." His clown-like grin hit a sinister level that was less Bozo and more IT.

"Care to explain?" Serena concealed a shudder.

"I told you, the FYD. They want my data."

"But why? What does Food Yield and Development want with this?"

"I'm not saying anything more in this place."

"Victor, you already mentioned FYD, you're already in deep. Tell me the rest of it."

"You're right. Cat's out of the bag now anyway. I said Marci and Erik's names aloud. I'm screwed."

"We are protecting you."

"You're joking, right? You can't protect me from them."

At that moment, the door to the lab opened. In walked an unlikely cast of characters, some of whom Serena recognized. At the front of the pack was Nicholas, who made a beeline for his computer. Bringing up the rear was a petulant Agent Estep. In the clutch was former Agent Lehman, the Beav, four other men Lehman chose for his team (unrecognized by Serena), and one last figure that astonished her.

Not much took Serena by surprise, but this blew her mind. What possible explanation could there be for Paul to be walking through the door in front of her? The answer would have to wait because Paul's grand entrance was interrupted by the sudden onset of gunfire.

14

Serena's ears felt like she had jammed cotton balls deep into her ear canals. For a few minutes she couldn't hear a thing. Her brain slowly processed what happened while the silence swallowed her. She stared in disbelief at the body slumped beside her. Then she screamed. It wasn't a prolonged girl-in-jeopardy kind of scream; it was more of a just-saw-a-rodent siren.

When she pulled herself together she said, "I should have known that his clown face wasn't real."

"It never occurred to me either," said Estep.

Serena pointed to her ears. "I can't hear you."

The two looked at the clown-faced man on the floor. His fat suit had slipped during his fall and was now twisted up around his hips. In the craziness Serena had somehow ended up with his latex face mask in her hand. She studied it, impressed with the quality and craftsmanship of the piece.

There was no need for any of them to hurry. Bound by his own disguise, Victor was not going anywhere. Of course they knew now that his name was not Victor. The man at their feet was easily recognizable as Erik Chapman, the very man that "Victor" had told them about. So many questions, so very many questions! But Serena's temporary deafness was too big of an obstacle. She stepped aside to let Estep sort out this bizarre situation.

Estep ushered everyone into the computer lab, guiding the group past Erik. He gave Nicholas a gentle push toward Serena, who caught on quickly that he was her charge. He led everyone else to the back of the room where a large conference table was the obvious destination. No one said a word as they obediently took a seat around the table. Estep orchestrated the entire transition without uttering a single word.

Once seated he broke the silence. "Pick him up and wheel him over here." He addressed no one in particular so at first no one moved. Realizing that no one was likely to volunteer, Estep leveled his gaze on the youngest man at the table who then bolted out of his chair and retrieved Erik. Everyone waited for Erik to be settled at the table, hands cuffed to the arms of the chair with two different sets of handcuffs.

Serena took the last remaining chair. "Nicholas' mother is coming to pick him up. We can muddle along without the child genius. He's seen enough action for one day."

"Agreed. Let's piece this together, shall we?" said Lehman. He surveyed the room in an exaggerated mime-like fashion: pausing as he examined each face. Estep was at the head of the table, with

Serena on the other end. Between them, clockwise from Estep, was Lehman himself, Beav, Paul, and the most academic member of Lehman's team Agent Hodgson. On the other side of the table, counter-clockwise from Estep, was Erik, bound to his chair, and the remaining three former agents on Lehman's team, two men and a woman, who had been mainly recruited for muscle.

Serena got the ball rolling. "I recognize most of you, but there are a few of you I don't know. More importantly, why are all of you here? This is an odd group. Why is Paul here? I assume you are in charge of this, Agent Lehman? Does that mean that Ann, President Kinji, has ordered this meeting?"

Estep snorted, "Are you done talking? I'd like to hear him talk." He jerked his head toward Lehman.

"I'm former-agent Lehman. I work for the private sector now. In fact, none of my team is currently in service, but all are all former agents. Yes, President Kinji asked for me to assemble a team. Why is Paul here? I have no idea. How we all managed to show up at the lab at the same time, I don't know that either. Your turn." He looked at Estep.

"Paul was picked up by my team. Serena, you should know, you asked for him," Estep scowled.

"I did not! I had nothing— oh. I may have mentioned to Nicholas that I could use Paul's help," Serena said.

"He took you at your word. He sent up a bat signal," said Estep.

"Do you need me or not? Why am I here?" asked Paul.

"Do you know how many strings I had to pull to get him out of prison? If you don't need him, I'll pull more strings to get you back in there with him," Estep threatened, no jest intended.

"No, no, I actually do need him. I didn't expect to have him here at my request, but yes, I do need his help," said Serena.

Lehman stood up to stretch his legs, which also put him in a position to command the table. "Before you get into that, which may or may not have anything to do with what I'm here for, I want the play-by-play on what went down. We have a man in a clown suit cuffed to a chair who happens to be a familiar face from Chicago. Why was he shooting at us?" Lehman looked across the conference table at Erik. "I'd ask you directly, but I'm fairly certain I wouldn't get an honest answer."

Beav was quick to respond, "Thank you for slamming him to the ground. Saved us from taking a hit, although he isn't much of a shot. I want answers too. This thing has fired up into a hot mess."

"What I want to know is how he got a gun in here," growled Estep at no one in particular. His team was still sitting in the sedans parked outside the lab. How they all missed a weapon, no matter how concealed, was a question Estep knew he would have to answer, and every word out of his mouth would be added to his permanent file. Unlike the others, Estep was still an active agent and he wanted to keep it that way. Everyone else could get sloppy or forget about protocol, but Estep had to watch himself or he too would end up on the team of rejects, or worse yet, assigned permanently to Serena Wilcox.

"Paul's presence is accounted for. Ditto for Agent Estep. The rest of you are all with former Agent Lehman – a team formed at President Kinji's request. You all showing up at the same time was a coincidence?" asked Serena.

"No, one of my agents phoned in that there were two unknown vehicles on route to the lab. We were already here, but I waited until Lehman's team pulled up to come inside," said Estep.

"And Nicholas? Why was he with you?" asked Serena. "He's gone now, by the way, I heard him leave."

"If you must know, I took him out for ice cream. He's fine," said Estep.

"You surprise me Estep. Sorry, it's hard to turn off the mother in me. Speaking of, when do I get to see my kids? President Kinji obviously already knows about me being here, so I'd like you to bring my family to me."

"She doesn't know you're here," said Lehman. "I didn't know myself until just now."

"I knew you weren't in Germany, I was just there," said Beav.

"Why were you in Germany?" asked Serena. "Looking for me? And why doesn't she know I'm here?"

"Yes, looking for you. Well, it's complicated," said Beav.

"All of this can wait, let's get into why Erik was shooting at us and why he was in a costume – what was he anyway, a clown?" asked Lehman.

Nine pairs of eyes zeroed in on Erik. But Erik said nothing. In fact, he didn't move at all. Not even his eyes. Slowly his mouth began to quiver as white foam bubbled up and spilled over his lips. His eyes rolled back into his head and his body convulsed violently. Everyone watched helplessly as their captive choked on his last breath.

"Great, now what!" said Serena. "Now we won't get anything more out of him."

"He wasn't going to talk to us anyway, that's why he did that to himself," said Lehman.

"Or maybe he didn't want to go to prison. It really doesn't matter why he did it. Either way, he's of no use to us now." Serena puffed her checks out and slowly exhaled.

"Search him," said Estep.

"I'm not touching him," said Beav. "And neither should anyone else. Trace amounts of whatever poison he took could transfer from him to us, through skin to skin contact. Honestly, I'm not jazzed about breathing the toxin either, especially since we have no idea what it is."

"How is it that none of us were watching him?" Serena complained to no one in particular.

Estep answered her anyway. "For starters, he jacked us around so much that I couldn't look at him without wanting to kill him myself, and I still want my job –no offense Beav. Secondly, why would any of us want to look at him?"

Everyone stared at the hideous creature still bound to the chair. Serena got up. "I'm going to roll him over by the door and call 911."

"For someone so smart, you are the ditziest woman I've ever met. You can't call 911. This is a covert operation," Estep said.

"Then call someone. None of us want to touch him," said Serena.

Lehman took out his digi pen to make the call.

"No, no! Don't turn that thing on!"

"Keefer, what aren't you telling me?" asked Lehman.

"Carla Keefer, as in the Agent Keefer in Lora's files?" asked Serena.

"Former agent. I was let go without explanation," said Keefer.

"She was my pick. I recommended her to Lehman," said Beav. "She came to me after she was terminated and my gut told me she was fired because she saw something she shouldn't have. Tell them what you told me."

Keefer began, "When Lora was investigated, for a supposed routine security check of flagged Town Hall messages, I was given the instruction to leave the room. I didn't think anything of it because I don't generally get an invite to the interrogation room. While I was waiting I ducked into the restroom, figuring I had plenty of time to return before they needed me. It was out of order and normally I would have turned around and left, but I, well, I really had to go, so I ignored the sign and walked in anyway. There were three people in there, and none of them female. They stopped talking when they saw me. I was fired before the end of the day."

"Did you know the men you saw in the restroom?" asked Serena.

"Oh yes, it was, well, the dearly departed Erik Chapman," said Keefer. She paused. Everyone looked at the dead man during an awkward moment of silence. "And the other two were not regular to The Cube, but I had seen them with Erik enough to know who they were."

"And they were?" asked Serena.

"Agent Browning and Victor something-or-other, a scientist I think. Agent Hodgson would know, she's the brain." Agent Keefer folded her arms across her chest, effectively concluding her presentation.

At this point everyone started talking at once, including those who hadn't chimed in before.

When the babble subsided, Serena asked, "Does the real Victor look like a clown?"

"Oh yes, because that's what's important to know," scoffed Estep.

"You mean like Erik does, er, did?" asked Keefer.

"Yes, does Victor look like that at all?" asked Serena.

"No, not really. Victor is an ordinary looking guy I guess. Wait, I know where to find a picture of him," said Keefer. She typed in a few words on her phone. "See? This is him. Don't worry, this is my photo archive, I'm not sending a traceable signal." She held the phone up for everyone to look at.

"How is it that you had no idea what Victor looked like?" Serena asked Estep. "This guy looks nothing like the parody of a man that Erik was passing off as Victor."

"And how is it that you didn't know he was in prison?" asked Paul.

"What do you mean?" asked Lehman.

Paul had everyone leaning toward him, bodies hovering over the table, ears straining for his voice, just like the old days when he was able to command a room. He savored the moment. Then he spoke. "He's a member of the Criminally Insane club, of which I am of course also a member. I know they fetched him from time to time, rumor was that he went to The Cube, but I didn't believe it. Apparently it was true. I didn't know his name, he answers to 'V'. He's brilliantly daft, always mumbling numbers and equations. As you can imagine it's not all that possible to socialize while in the booby hatch, but they do let us mingle on occasion. He stumbles about, drawing in the air with his finger like he's lecturing from a blackboard he sees in his head."

"No, that can't be right. The Victor I know looks and acts like a normal person," said Keefer.

"He can fake the funk when he has to. I've seen him snap right out of it, and act completely normal," said Paul.

"What is he in prison for?" asked Serena.

"That's easy to check," said Lehman.

There was a bit of commotion as everyone started to move at once, followed by the collective thought that, although they were in a computer lab with more than enough computers for each person, there was no need for all of them to look up the information. They settled on giving the task over to Lehman who had originated the suggestion.

"Why is it that none of us know anything about Victor? If he committed an unspeakable crime, wouldn't we all know about it?" asked Serena. "Surely you in government circles would know something, but even I would know. It would have been on the news, the SM Channel."

"I wouldn't be so sure about that," said Beav.

"What do you mean? What do you know that I don't? We have to compare notes on everything," said Serena.

Estep laughed. "Oh, you're leading this operation now?"

Beav was the next to stand up, deliberately creating a noisy ruckus with his chair as he did so. Quietly, and in a dramatically even tone, he said, "Someone has to."

Next, Estep was on his feet.

Lehman was the voice of reason. "Really? We're going to turn on each other? Isn't this display of testosterone cliché?" He remained standing, but gestured for the two men to sit back down.

Estep and Beav stared each other down, but they obediently took their seats without a fight. Serena, however, was the next to pop out of her chair. She was not imposing, in her under-five-two glory, but nonetheless she had their attention.

"I've been thinking about Erik. Why did he portray Victor in such grotesque fashion? I'm not talking about the clown suit, although that is bizarre of course, and it speaks to contempt, which is what I'm getting at. Erik invented an entire personality for Victor. You should have seen what Estep and I were dealing with! He carried on about naming his computers, he was lustful toward them."

"Lustful toward what, the computers?" asked Agent Hodgson, speaking for the first time.

"Yes, it was weird, like a fetish. He also went into a story about his pet turtle being flushed down the toilet."

"Wait, back up to the computer fetish," said Hodgson. She stared intently at Serena with her blue eyes.

Serena was surprised by the intensity of Hodgson's attention. "Are you saying that Victor is a freak? Erik was portraying him correctly?"

"No! Not at all. I'm saying the opposite. Victor is a reserved person, an introvert. He likely has Asperger's. He would never act in such a way that would give an impression of deviance. He's also not capable of anything remotely flamboyant or sexual. His body language is like that of a turtle, barely in motion," said Hodgson.

"Sounds like you respect him. Is he a colleague?" asked Lehman.

"Yes, sort of. I've admired his work and I've been fortunate enough to observe him while he was involved in a think tank. He's not anything like what you are describing."

"You mentioned a turtle. Remember that I mentioned Erik, while pretending to be Victor, cried over a flushed pet turtle? Did he have a turtle?" asked Serena.

"No, not that I'm aware of. But his nickname was Turtle, for the reason I said. He moved methodically, slowly. He showed little emotion. He did care only for his computers, but lust is not a word I can imagine in the same sentence with Victor," said Hodgson.

Serena smiled. "Then I think my theory is correct. Erik's portrayal of Victor was so over-the-top and nasty, that it screams anger. He wasn't content to use Victor's identity; he wanted to degrade him too. The turtle flushing really clinches it. And furthermore, Erik was arrested for doing something perverse while pretending to be Victor! So my question is, why? What did Victor do that would inspire such resentment?"

"I didn't realize you had a PhD in Psychology," said Estep.

"I don't," said Serena.

"My point exactly," said Estep. "This is going nowhere. Also, the real issue is that law enforcement relied on security scan to verify Erik's ID. If they'd checked him out, Erik would have been caught way back then."

Lehman stepped in. "What else would you have expected them to have done? Security scans are usually accurate."

"What was he working on?" Serena ignored the Estep-led tangent into a blame game that couldn't end well.

Hodgson was quick to respond. "He was working on the very issue that Beav talked about, the crack. He had a solution for sealing the crack and preventing it from being penetrated in the future. Of course at this time, I didn't know that we had this big of a problem, but everyone was aware of a few hackers here and there. Victor had the answers and was promising the patch by the end of the month."

The Beav leapt out of his seat. "Thereby shutting down Erik's access to the Dark Side!"

Estep was the next up on his feet, targeting his glower on Hodgson's pretty face. "And you didn't think that something like this would be important for us to know?"

"No, I didn't think of it. I suppose it should have occurred to me, but I didn't connect the dots. Well, not until Serena asked the right questions," said Agent Hodgson, a woman Serena appreciated so very much at that moment, especially when she thought she saw tears in Estep's eyes.

15

President Ann Kinji was busy with tasks worthy of presidential attention and even the real and present danger of a possible assassination attempt was not enough for her to abandon her post. After all, every day was a day when assassination was possible when one was sitting president of the United States of America! Fortunately nothing unusual was planned besides the typical ebb and flow of The Cube; meetings, conference calls, briefings, and documents demanding her signature.

One of the first things she did when she became the first elected president of the newly re-united post Big War States of America was establish a new style of governing. Ann Kinji would not be campaigning during her presidency. She would not be vacationing. The honor of the office was worthy of sacrificing her own ambitions and personal life for the years she was in office. Some argued that retreats are a mental health issue, with the loudest voices coming from Congress, in defense of their own frequent vacationing schedule, but that was what her garden was for – and yoga, eating well, and her alone time with God. She centered herself without abandoning her post, as many hard-working Americans must do. No, she told her staff, vacations are a luxury that the President of the United States should give up while in office.

She fully expected her precedent to be knocked down; probably as soon as the next administration, but she hoped that her example would inspire future American presidents to at least cut back on how long they stayed away from The Cube. Having come from humble beginnings, Ann was aware of what message luxury vacations sent to Americans who were struggling to pay the bills: Their president didn't care about their problems, but instead flaunted his/her wealth! Not during Ann's term! Ann was "for the people", a campaign now restricted to free publicity only.

Yes, Ann was idealistic. And incredibly, unbelievably popular. Some predicted she would be assassinated, and Ann surmised that those who held this opinion would feel validated when the truth about Covert Coffee eventually, and inevitably, leaked out. Others predicted she would be run over by her own party, by lobbyists, and by all the insiders to the Cube leftover from the pre-Big War days on the Hill. Yes, Ann would be blindsided they said.

Ann concluded that both schools of thought were correct, which was serendipitously verified by an urgent message from Agent Lehman:

<<MADAM PRESIDENT, I'M SORRY TO REPORT THAT YOUR SUSPICIONS WERE CORRECT. YOU NEED TO MEET

WITH ME, URGENT. THE LOCATION YOU SENT ME TO IS NO LONGER SECURE. PLEASE ADVISE.>>

No longer secure? How had that happened? The computer lab in Hudson, Wisconsin was top secret, hidden inside the walls of a luxury home near Willow Creek State Park. Experts insisted that the location would be secure for many years to come. How could it be compromised its first year in operation? This was a blunder to the tune of billions of dollars! First matter at hand was the immediate problem of where to meet with Lehman, and she realized that she couldn't meet with him herself. The cloak and dagger routine, as Beav had so boldly suggested, was ridiculous. She was President of the United States, not a member of Scooby-Doo and the Gang, although she did make a decent Velma with the right wig and glasses; her entry in a residence hall costume contest had won her a free pizza.

She called upon the only person left she could trust: the First Gentleman. Ted was the first man to ever hold that title and she was so proud of how he had defined the position. Ted didn't read stories to school children, even though he, of course, respected teachers and nurturers. He felt that his unique position in The Cube allowed him the opportunity to fill in the gaps. He wasn't a co-President, that would be a ridiculous exaggeration, but he was definitely a valuable asset to the presidency. He was with Ann most of the time, especially when the Vice President was required to be in a separate location from the President, as dictated by security or because the VP had a full agenda elsewhere.

Ann considered Ted to be her acting VP, her right hand man, something she knew her actual VP Morgan Canon was well aware of. Morgan was second chair and he was usually somewhere else.

She realized with a start that she didn't really keep track of where he was half the time. She relied on her staff to do that. She didn't need him, fetch him, or otherwise engage in anything to do with him unless forced to do so by the schedule. Truth be told she had wanted someone else, a young governor by the name of Carson Landon who had an excellent track record for keeping his campaign promises. Morgan Canon was not only not her pick, but she was opposed to him altogether; his flip-flopping on issues made him untrustworthy.

What exactly did Morgan do now that he was VP? Was he the source of the stink in the Cube? How could she have been so stupid? Uh oh, this is the moment when Velma knows who the man under the mask is but he's still out there, hovering about, lurking behind every corner!

Naturally her thoughts turned darker and more accusatory. Before meeting with Lehman, or rather asking Ted to do it, shouldn't she arrange for a private chat with Morgan Canon? Ann fact-checked her runaway thoughts: Was this the part in the horror movie when viewers shouted, "Don't go in there alone!" or was she paranoid?

She dismissed the thought that she could be in real physical danger if she met with Morgan alone. Secret service detail would be outside the room. She wouldn't eat or drink anything he offered her, so certain was she that Morgan was corrupt and, as crazy as it sounded, he might resort to trying to get rid of her. It was simply too obvious. He had to be the one! Who else had that much power? The list of people who had insider information and could work behind her back without her knowledge was short.

She set the wheels in motion to meet with Morgan within the

hour, face to face. And what a face that was! Morgan was not known for his good looks. He had a face like a ferret: narrow eyes set close together; a nose like a rodent's, long and sharpish; facial hair that lay short and fuzzy on his skin; coloring in browns and grays. Even his skin tone seemed gray.

Morgan was quick to agree to a meeting, so quick that she suspected he had been waiting for the call. He was in her office within ten minutes, a speed most impressive given that The Cube was a labyrinth of halls, rooms, and entire buildings. Like the Pentagon of glory days gone by, it was like a city within a city. How was it that Morgan was in the neighborhood when her staff called him?

And that was her first question. "How did you get here so fast, where were you?"

Morgan screwed up his eyes, now barely visible slits on a face even furrier than Ann remembered. "I was on my way to your office."

"You have something to discuss?" Ann let her skepticism show.

Morgan sniffed. "I see you won't be bothered to hide your doubt. Has our relationship sunk so low that we cast aside any attempt at social niceties?"

"Morgan, I never wanted you on my ticket, you know that. We've never been able to see eye to eye, and we haven't even seen each other period for weeks now. That's a bizarre President-VP relationship I must say."

"That's what I wanted to discuss with you. I have been advised of your upcoming schedule and I plan to be a part of it."

"Which part?"

"What do you mean?" Morgan was either truly baffled or a

mighty fine actor.

"The backstabbing part? The traitorous part? The serpentine part? Or how about the 'liar, liar, pants on fire' part?"

Morgan's mouth dropped open.

"I suggest you close your mouth before your forked tongue rolls out."

"How dare you!"

"How dare I what? Have an honest conversation?"

"What exactly are you accusing me of, Madam President?"

"This is you fishing around to see what I know. Well, you've caught yourself an old shoe."

Morgan blinked.

Ann clarified, "I'm not telling you what I know."

"I know what old shoe meant."

"But you'll tell me what you know, now."

Morgan crossed his arms and shifted his weight onto his heels. "You won't like what I have to say."

"We have about five minutes. We, our nation's president and vice president are currently in the same room together, doing nothing whatsoever to benefit mankind. I can't imagine that this is what the American people voted us into office for."

Morgan didn't hesitate. "It's Ted."

"Excuse me?"

"You heard me. Ted, the First Gentleman, your husband. Think about it, it makes sense. He is more of a VP than I am, don't you think I've noticed?"

"Then he already has what he wants. He has no motivation."

"No, he hasn't gotten what he wants."

"Which is?"

"Your job."

16

"Ah, the familiar smell of erasers with a hint of hotdog," said Serena. No one acknowledged that she'd said anything as the five of them (Estep, Lehman, Beav, Paul and Serena) walked the halls of Leesburg Elementary, a midsized public school in the Hoosier state.

Leesburg had been selected for a Presidential visit because Ann Kinji was from Warsaw, Indiana. Leesburg was one of several schools in the Warsaw community school district, and was not in any way connected to big money or politics. This school visit had been scheduled over a year in advance: a quick visit with school children followed by a Q&A session with the media to promote the new educational reforms that Kinji was pushing.

Local media was present and incredibly excited, each journalist hoping for their big break. National media was of course also in attendance, although the numbers were small compared to coverage for briefings on health care reform or the proposed tax reduction bill, but international journalists were sitting this one out altogether. Overall, it was a low-key event receiving little attention. All eyes were focused on events scheduled for later in the day; when Kinji was due to meet with the leaders of several oil-rich nations to discuss the GOB (Global Oil Bank) initiative. In addition, there was a professional sports press conference running at the same time as Kinji's grade school event. It was a no-brainer which one the public cared more about.

It was under this cloak of relative obscurity that Kinji arranged to meet Lehman and his cast of unlikely characters at Leesburg Elementary, right under the noses of the media and a community full of people who turned out for the event. After Kinji's Q&A session she did a mock good-bye drive past the parade of school children and their parents, and the reporters who were covering it all while impatient to head back to their respective stations. The children, now joined by the local junior high and high schools as well, waved flags at the presidential detail. They raised the flags higher when her limo passed by; accompanied by cheers, jumping around like popcorn, and screaming at volumes that could break glass. Then her driver pulled into an undisclosed location airstrip. From there they jumped through several hoops before doubling back to Leesburg Elementary where Lehman and crew were waiting for her in the school cafeteria.

The entire ruse was much more involved than one might expect, since far too many people knew of Kinji's plans. She couldn't pull off a clandestine meeting with former agents and Serena Wilcox without an elaborate plan. What the media, and even most of her security detail, didn't know was that there were two undisclosed locations. The real one was where Kinji got into a non-government issue vehicle, driven by her loyal friend Penny, who had been unofficially re-instated as her driver.

Penny circled back to Leesburg Elementary and drove so close to the building as to be parallel to the door on the passenger's side. Kinji quickly and easily exited the car and entered the school through the small maintenance door. No one was the wiser, although it took some sleight of hand to manage fooling her security detail up to that point.

Penny hand-picked a trustworthy driver on duty for the president's vehicle and hired a Kinji look-a-like to ride along at all times. The look-a-like stayed out of sight while the real president was in the vehicle, and then slid into Kinji's vacant seat when Kinji exited. A semi-truck driver was also in on the charade: he parked his truck strategically for enough seconds to allow Kinji to exit the vehicle unnoticed by her security detail. The whole exchange took place at a rest stop and couldn't have gone more smoothly. From there, they journeyed on to the decoy location where the President's jet was waiting.

The plan was for the look-a-like to fly back to The Cube in Kinji's place and quickly retire into Kinji's garden room, where she would enjoy her best acting job ever! Lounging in the presidential retreat, sipping wine and eating chocolate covered strawberries – oh how she pined to tell people! But sworn secrecy was the condition of her employment. There was hint of more work if she was trustworthy, and threats of being accused of traitorous acts if she wasn't.

The odds of a national emergency occurring during that two hour window when the presidency would be occupied by a B-movie actress were slim, but it was a frightening possibility nonetheless. Therefore, the escape plan, should the garden alarm sound, was for the look-a-like to activate an emergency signal and hide in the garden dressing room until Kinji arrived. It was a shaky plan, but one that might work if they were in a jam.

This whole nonsense is ridiculous, Ann told herself. I'm President of the United States and I'm sneaking around like a teenager climbing out a window.

Lehman and the rest of the group stood up when Ann entered the school cafeteria. They were speechless; an effect Ann was accustomed to, and bored with. Serena, seldom without something to say, was not under the Kinji spell. "As you can see, I'm not dead."

Ann hurried to give Serena a quick hug. "I'm so glad you are alive and well."

The four men silently observed the two women. Estep had an expression of horror on his face, which Serena noticed and addressed, "Don't look at me like that. I'm not the president's secret advisor, but it's nice to know that I inspire that much confidence in you."

Ann turned to face the group. "What is this motley crew I'm looking at? Paul out of prison? What's the story on that? Lehman, what kind of ragtag team did you put together? I only have a few minutes, and I have a bombshell of my own. Someone give me the condensed play-by-play."

"I'll do it," said Serena. "Special Agent Estep over here picked me up and enjoyed my sparkling conversation for the past couple of days." Estep growled, which delighted Serena. She continued,

"Seriously though, he did pick me up and he told me about Covert Coffee. They worked behind-the-scenes to protect you, so I guess you could call it Covert Coffee-in-Coffee."

Ann shifted her eyes dramatically away from Serena and locked eyes with Lehman.

"Serena, I'll take it from here," he said. He gestured toward an empty chair. Serena obediently sat, and for the second time during this operation the flush of humiliation brought warmth and color to her face.

Lehman began. "I did as you requested. Beav is one of my assembled team members, you recall he was terminated."

"Oh yes, I remember Beav," said Ann.

"These others are not my pick. Serena was already inside the lab when I arrived. Estep came at the same time I did, with Paul. He'll have to address that – I still don't know why Paul is here."

"You talk about me like I'm not in the room," said Paul.

"If you don't keep your mouth shut, you won't be in the room," said Estep.

Lehman continued, "I sent Beav to Germany to meet with your guy. It was enlightening to say the least. I have Beav's report right here." He handed Ann a document. "In a nutshell, the Social Media Channel is being controlled by several parties, some of them are our own government, some are leaders of other countries. We suspect that this is what is behind your traitorous situation in the Cube. Certain parties want to control what we see, for example, special interest groups. We have reason to believe that FYD might be one of those groups."

"What gives you reason to believe that? Is this something that came out of the Germany meeting?" asked Ann.

"No. It was something that Erik Chapman said before he died," Estep interjected.

Ann's face revealed her shock, "Erik's dead? What happened?"

"Madam President, he wasn't one of the good guys," said Beav.

"I see," Ann said quietly. "Go on."

"We can't vouch for Erik's credibility. There were some unusual circumstances," said Lehman. The five of them exchanged nervous glances. "But, we do know that he was privy to something, and we should start with FYD."

"Good work. This is certainly explosive enough to be the motivation behind the stink in the Cube. The conspiracy theorists will be happy: finally proof that the government wants to control information and brainwash them," said Ann.

"And not only our own government, but others as well," Beav reminded her.

"Yes, this is a problem bigger than the presidency, which leads me to my bombshell. Vice President Morgan Canon has pointed the finger at someone inside the Cube who is responsible for all of this," said Ann. She paused.

Serena couldn't stand the suspense. "Who?"

"Ted."

"Your husband Ted?" asked Serena.

"Madam President, I don't believe the First Gentleman would ever betray our country," said Lehman.

"Of course not! Morgan is stalling. I assume he thinks he's established doubt in my mind and I'll waste time investigating. I don't know what his thinking was really. But clearly he is involved. What's scary is that he was so cocky. What is he doing that he thinks will all turn out in his favor if he stalls me a little? He's not stupid. He knows I'll dig until I get the truth and that won't take long," said Ann.

"You forgot about me, didn't you?" said Paul.

"Yes, what about you? Why are you here?" asked Ann.

Serena stood up from her time-out chair. "I asked for him."

17

"Please end the suspense. Why did you ask for Paul?" asked Ann.

"When I was investigating Lora, you might remember that she wrote a Town Hall message?"

"Yes, I remember, go on," said Ann. She waved her hand impatiently, a trademark Kinji gesture that had been mimicked and made popular by a talented young Asian comedienne on the new-format Saturday Night Live.

Serena wondered why Ann was so snappish. Was it the pressure of the situation that was causing her to be so cross, or was it Serena herself who was the inspiration for the president's caustic tone? It wasn't a question she dared ask aloud. Instead, she brought herself back around to the matter at hand. "I was investigating Lora and found that her mother was in the same prison as Paul."

"The prison for the criminally insane."

"Yes. I don't know what I was fishing for, but on a hunch I got my hands on the visitors log. The records were on the system. Lora's mom got a lot of interesting visitors, but one in particular stood out. Although it's not quite the shock and awe it would have been if we didn't already know he was dirty."

"Who?"

"Erik Chapman. He visited Lora's mom in prison. I'm guessing he didn't expect anyone to ever look at the records, why would they?"

"It's odd, but what does this mean?" Ann looked reflective, as if she was puzzling it out, but in reality her mind was already multi-tasking through other items on the daily agenda. Even though her presidency had become absurdly bogged down with overlaying conspiracies, Americans still needed her to go through the motions of governing.

"I don't know, that's why I wanted to talk to Paul." Serena studied Ann's face for any sign that she approved.

"That's it? That's the only reason why Paul has been smuggled out of prison?

"Erik wasn't alone." Serena said mysteriously.

"Am I supposed to guess who was with him? Was it Morgan Canon by any chance?"

"Why yes, it was Morgan Canon, Vice President of the United States of America."

"Now that is certainly interesting enough to get Paul out of prison." Ann's tone warmed instantly. "Good work."

"I have to admit, she did get the job done," said Estep, who until now had stayed out of the conversation and far outside of Ann and Serena's personal space bubbles.

Serena studied his face but found no trace of sarcasm and no hint of a snide remark forming on his lips. "Thank you?" She dangled her question mark.

"Hey, whatever you think of me, I like you. I didn't like being assigned as your babysitter," said Estep in what was the closest thing to a peace offering Serena would receive. That, and the big smile he flashed her, a smile with the power to induce screaming and fainting in pubescent girls, a magic lost on Serena.

"The mission is exciting enough for you now I assume. Keep at it. I need to get back to the Cube before my look-alike is discovered," Ann said.

"What would you like us to do?" asked Serena.

"You aren't doing anything. You're coming with me. Ted is waiting for us on a private airstrip. Tom and the kids are with him. You do remember those people, right? Lehman, I need you—you're coming too," said Ann.

"But what about me? I didn't tell what I know yet," whined Paul.

Ann avoided any personal interaction with Paul but addressed the group as a whole. "Beav and Estep can get Paul's story and return him to prison. Tie up loose ends and report to Lehman. Anything else I need to know before I go?"

"There's something I'd like to say if I may, Madam President," said Beav.

Ann nodded.

"This is most unusual for a President to be so deeply involved in an investigation, and I admire you for it. I know you are trying to set things right. But President Kinji, if I should be so bold, you are putting yourself in a dangerous position, and thereby putting the nation as a whole in a vulnerable state. Please go back to being President and let us do what we do," said Beav.

"I appreciate you," said Ann. "And if I'm reading between the lines correctly, what you plan to do is something I will never hear about, and should never know about." She made eye contact with Beav to confirm his understanding, and communicate her consent.

On that note, President Ann Kinji left Leesburg Elementary with Lehman; who was more than willing to be in service to the President and First Gentleman again, but was already missing his wife; and Serena, who was so impatient to see her family that she had stopped listening to anything that was said.

When the three of them were on their way, Beav and Estep flanked Paul and herded him toward the government issue sedan parked in the empty back lot. Estep drove, Beav rode shotgun, and Paul had the backseat to himself, where he sat comfortably while sharing all that he knew, or most of what he knew.

"Let me begin with an overview of my life in prison," said Paul.

Estep and Beav exchanged a look. Neither said anything, not wanting to risk Paul taking even longer to tell his story. Estep concentrated on driving while Beav kept a sharp eye out for anyone following them.

"In regular prison there are big officers with equipment and a chip on their shoulders who step in if inmates are behaving badly; like if they are beating up a fellow prisoner, medical staff, or even the guards. But in the prisons for the mentally insane, or ill -- pick your terminology of preference-- there are only petite staff members to stop the madness if they are even around to help, and that's a big if.

I'm sure you noticed this scar I got on my cheek, what a handsome tat, don't you agree? I got it because most inmates walk around free, completely unshackled. And unlike inmates in a regular prison, the mentally insane are not under threat of going 'to the hole' if they misbehave, ditto for the fear of having a prison sentence extended – that tool is not in the toolbox. Take away the punishments, there's no incentive for inmates to cooperate.

A prison for the criminally insane is a fertile ground for crime. Of course one would assume that the fertile ground for crime implies the prison populace. Enter our good friends, Mr. VP himself Morgan Canon and one of his minions Erik Chapman. Isn't Erik an uptight and unlikely name for a minion?" Paul waited for a reaction. Receiving none, he continued.

"Serena already told you that Erik was a regular visitor to see Lora's mother, Vanessa. I so adored that woman, such a temptress. She had bad luck with men, liked the bad boys, and ran wild from the tender age of twelve until shortly after she turned twenty. That's when she was ready to settle down. She gave up on the bad-boy losers and went looking for a rich older man, much older. She was tired of men wiping out her bank account, squatting in her house, and using her body like a carnival ride.

With a sugar daddy, she figured two out of three aint bad. Plus if her future husband was old enough, her body wouldn't be in demand as often, or so she thought. She liked being taken care of, thought she had found the answer for her disastrous life. She'd been a runaway, and nearly a prostitute. She really had nothing left to lose, or so she thought, so she married the first one who asked."

Estep groaned, and then snapped. "Move on!"

Paul continued, "Long story short..."

"Not short enough!" Estep snapped.

"…the old codger abused Vanessa. He belittled her, he bullied her, and he babied her. He treated her like his princess, but also his possession. And when Vanessa ended up pregnant with Lora, he kept Vanessa in one wing of his mansion – I did mention he was disgustingly rich, right?

He kept her behind lock and key until she had the baby, right there in one of the rooms in her wing. He didn't even hire a midwife for her. She had the help of the untrained housekeeping staff, and that's it. They sure got more than they bargained for that day.

Lora was born healthy and fine, no problems, but she was not a boy. Vanessa's husband had no interest in a daughter – in fact he wanted to send Lora away, while keeping Vanessa as his wife and prisoner. Well, call it temporary insanity, postpartum depression, or a mental snap brought on by years of abuse: Vanessa went nuts. She bludgeoned the nasty old bugger to death. She hid his body, stayed on at the mansion and raised Lora there as if nothing had happened.

She didn't get caught until Lora was almost four years old. No one much liked her husband, and since he was frequently out of the country, no one had inquired after him. After all, he had no real job, being independently wealthy and retired. He wasn't a philanthropist, so he never attended any fundraisers. He wasn't a big part of the social scene and he was unpopular everywhere he went anyway, so people left the situation alone.

It was only after a neighbor's dog got into the estate gardens and began digging that Vanessa's crime was discovered. He brought bones back home with him. Even then, his owners didn't catch on until he brought them the matching skull."

"I remember this story now," said Beav. "Didn't they call her

The Grave Digger Widow? If she's the one, she was stunning. It was hard to believe she was a cold blooded killer – until she opened her mouth. She was a hard one."

"Yes, that would be Vanessa. But she's lost the hardness. She's so docile now, you wouldn't know she was the same girl. She's almost dotty, even without her meds. Like I said, I adored that woman."

"Why are you using past tense? Did something happen to her?" Beav's antennae were raised.

"I don't know. They came and got her one day, I never saw her again. By 'they' I mean FBI or whatever you guys are. They didn't introduce themselves and as you know, I'm America's favorite hero-slash-villain. I was a fly on the wall."

Beav turned around in his seat to look at Paul. "So far, you haven't told us anything useful. If you don't have anything productive to contribute, I vote we return you to prison before you warp our minds."

Estep snorted, a derivative of laughter; not to be confused with the contemptuous snort that he had perfected when assigned to Serena.

"I'm flattered, but my power to brainwash has dissipated." Paul looked wistfully out the window at the other drivers and passengers sharing the same stretch of road. How many of them had dinner waiting for them at home?

Estep knocked him out of his reverie. "You sound like an old guy when you talk. Prison has aged you, and made you even weirder. Seriously, you need to start saying something useful or else we're dropping your sorry deranged hide off at the boobyhatch."

"Okay then, I'll admit I do know what happened to Vanessa.

They made a deal of some sort with her and arranged an early release. She's at home, sipping tea and reading chick-lit. I never could turn her on to the classics. She writes me letters every now and then."

Beav longed for a few moments of silence, but he knew he had to get this over with. "This act of yours is tiresome. You know what we want to hear."

"You can't blame me for milking my hour of attention for all it's worth. You can't imagine what it's like to have no one to talk to for hours and hours, day after day, which brings me to what I know. I spent so much time on the Social Media Channel that I picked up on patterns. Solitude can do that, you know, make one's mind sharp and focused.

I was obsessed with the SM Channel. I never turned it off. I was tracking everyone I knew on there, and then I added hundreds I didn't know, across all the platforms. I was memorizing everything; user names, posts, tweets, statuses: everything that went out there. I even kept track of the global ticker tape of SM highlights. And when the data grew too large to keep in my head I put it all in a journal. Pages and pages of pointless information."

"This is pointless information," growled Estep.

"No, it's backstory. You need to know that I was in a zone, manic, scribbling in my journal. It's important because I have the journal. Not only that journal, but twenty-seven others just like it. You'll want to remember this because the journals are evidence."

"Evidence of what?" Beav was optimistic that Paul had finally started down a productive path.

"I was writing down the posts in real time, but tracking them afterward too. I don't know why, I was obsessed. It was an OCD thing, a way of coping with prison life. When people post something it scrolls off the screen a few seconds later, you get what I'm saying?"

"Yes, I know what you mean." Beav pushed the dialog forward. "And I think I know where you are going with this. People never bother to see if their posts are still there later. Are you saying they were deleted?"

"No, I'm saying they were edited."

Again Beav attempted to hurry the conversation along. "How so? Language or violent content removed? You mean censored?"

"No, worse than that. I mean that the posts were re-written. I need my journals. I could show you line by line, all easily verified if you subpoena the SM Channel."

"Think of some off the top of your head," Beav prodded. He avoided looking at Estep because the bulging vein at his temple pulsated in a most alarming manner.

"Many of the edits are to avoid bad PR, like a status that says 'I hate XYZ cars, they don't get the gas mileage they claim' would be altered to say 'I buy only XYZ cars, they live up to the gas mileage claim'."

Estep yanked the wheel, swerved across two lanes of traffic, and parked the car on the shoulder with a shriek of the brakes that reflected his mood. He glared at Paul, whose face was now ashen. "Stop jacking us around."

Paul was at a loss for words.

Beav also turned around in his seat for a stare-down with Paul. "Spammers are of trivial concern. Are you saying you have nothing more than this?"

"I'm not talking spammers. I'm talking hackers. You're not

hearing me. These are posts already on SM Channel, they are no longer 'live' in real time. They have scrolled off. Then they are altered. Big corporations are involved in this fraud; it's not your kid in the basement doing this. It's big money, fraudulent business practices."

"If the messages are gone, why would this benefit the corporations at all?" Beav didn't know if he wasn't following what Paul was saying or if Paul was spinning nonsense. Either scenario was equally plausible.

"I didn't say they were gone. I said they had scrolled off. Once they scroll off they are still forever searchable. Anyone looking for an XYZ car could call up hundreds, maybe thousands of favorable posts. The negative reviews are edited to the point of non-existence."

"What is the XYZ car you are talking about?" Beav made yet another attempt to find a point to grasp hold of.

Estep burrowed his head into his folded arms on the steering wheel. He let his right arm dangle, he grunted, and then he lifted his hand to turn off the ignition. He returned his arm to the steering wheel and held that position for several minutes.

"I know that I'm getting under your skin, but you are getting under my skin as well. The XYZ car isn't important. I made up the XYZ to indicate a random generic company. This isn't even of interest to you, this is still backstory. Bear with me. Let me try this again."

Estep made a wailing sound that was muffled by his arms.

"Hackers are altering posts, obviously getting paid by major corporations to paint their products or services in a positive light, scrubbing negative reviews, all to cover up their flaws, negative perceptions, bad customer service record, or even outright wrongdoing. But, that's not your deal, I know. What I'm leading up to is that corporations aren't the only ones doing this."

"You're saying that governments are doing this?" Beav's hopes rose that Paul had finally done it; he had finally gotten to something worth saying.

"Yes, there's—"

Beav interrupted. "A crack? Look, Paul, I hate to burst your bubble, but I already know this. Some foreign dude in Germany told me. But I'm curious about what you know about it."

"A German? Not foreign if you were in Germany," said Paul, pouting.

"No, he wasn't German. Not sure what he was. But anyway, he already told me about the crack in the SM Channel, and if you were eavesdropping back at the lab, and I'm sure you were, you knew this. Is that all you've got, a regurgitation of what you overhead us saying?"

"Did your German whistle blower offer you proof?" Paul made it clear from his tone that he expected Beav's answer to be no.

"Not German, and no. Are we back to your journals again?"

"I wrote down everything. You can verify it all. You'll especially find the references to the FYD interesting, and Erik, and the VP."

"Why didn't you lead with this?" Estep untangled himself from the steering wheel and started the engine.

"You needed the backstory," said Paul.

"No we didn't!" Estep peeled away from the shoulder and nearly hit a SUV driven by someone talking on the phone while also eating a sandwich.

Beav noticed the sandwich. "I'm hungry, let's stop for some grub."

Estep jabbed a thumb toward the backseat. "We can't go inside with him. I'll pull off at the next rest stop and park by the truckers. Get me whatever, as long as you don't forget a large coffee, black."

"I'll take a Reuben if they have it," said Paul.

Both agents immediately flipped Paul off in twin-like synchronization.

The two fell into silence so dark and hunger-driven that even Paul knew better than to open his mouth. When Estep pulled into the truck stop Beav popped out of the car, walked briskly inside, ordered the food, and waited on a bench until the order was ready. Estep slept in the driver's seat while Paul stared at his hands, brooding about his lot in life.

Beav waited for over twenty minutes for the order to be ready, but he didn't mind. He knew he would only pick at this nasty stuff anyway. He sat on the bench by the truck stop door and ate the tuna he brought with him. When the order was finally ready he emerged victoriously with two large white bags laden down with hot food. The grease was soaking through the bag and so was the aroma. He set the bags inside the car, took one look at Estep's granite face and marched back into the diner to fetch a large black coffee.

After Beav re-entered the car the three ate, each man concentrating on chewing. Paul knew better than to talk. Before prison, Paul had been a slick con artist, popular with the ladies, charming, playing his good looks to his best advantage. He hated seeing himself through Estep's eyes, and Beav's as well. Paul was pathetic and annoying, scrabbling for their attention like a puppy. Well, no more. He was getting a grip on himself. He would wait until they asked for him to speak, and then he would blow them away with what he knew.

"I need to get out and stretch," said Estep.

"What were you doing all this time?" Beav couldn't imagine Estep staying in the vehicle with Paul.

"He was sleeping," Paul volunteered, already breaking his code of silence.

Estep and Beav ignored him. Estep took a short walk around the parking lot and came back to the car. He got in quickly, belted up and headed back to the freeway.

"Tell us what you know. We're taking you back. We have officially run out of time. If you really do have something to say, do it now," said Beav.

Paul launched into his story without hesitation. "Erik and the VP Morgan Canon were there at the prison and I overheard them talking about FYD. What I couldn't hear directly I either got as a recap from Vanessa, or I could decipher by reading their lips."

"Lay it on me," said Beav.

"I need something first."

"Here we go," said Estep. "I was waiting for you to start in with that. This is why you've been stalling."

"What do you want?" asked Beav.

"I want to see Serena Wilcox. We didn't have time to talk."

Estep said, "That's your one wish? You do belong in the nut house."

"What do you want to see her for?" asked Beav.

"There's something I wanted to tell her, only her."

"Well, I can't arrange that. Serena is with the president back in Chicago, you know that. Why didn't you manage a conversation when you were with her?" Beav took over the conversation because Estep was too aggravated to speak.

"Someone was always around."

"Look, we're all you've got. Either give us your message or keep it to yourself. We are only five miles from the prison," said Beav.

Paul reflected upon that for a few seconds and then said, "Look into FYD."

"That's it? You aren't going to tell us anything else?" Beav could feel his blood pressure rising.

"Morgan wants her taken out," said Paul quietly.

"Who? Serena?" Estep was back in the conversation.

"He means President Kinji, don't you, Paul?" Beav congratulated himself at that moment for sticking with the interrogation no matter how tedious. This news was obviously way more than they thought Paul would deliver, and Beav shuddered to think what would have happened if they hadn't persevered. Would anyone have extracted this lead from Paul?

"Yes. That's what I meant. I didn't realize it until we were in the lab and I saw Erik's, uh, disguise. The strange clown thing, and how he was going around as Victor. It struck me why he was doing it."

By this time they were at the prison, parked and hanging on to Paul's every word. He finally had their undivided attention. Too bad his big moment was shattered by the blare of half a dozen sirens surrounding their vehicle. An officer stepped out and met Estep at his now-open window.

"You're late," he said.

"Sorry, got delayed," said Estep, with no hint of apology in his voice.

"Had to pull people off their shifts for this," he said.

Beav interjected before Estep could further antagonize the officer. "He's here now. You want to take him, or should we drive on through?"

The officer waved them through, then signaled for all but his own squad car to head on out. Once the windows were back up Paul started talking, as fast as he could get the words out:

"Victor had facial recognition ID for the highest levels of security at The Cube. That's got to be what Erik was up to. That's how they are going to get the president. Listen, I know you don't trust me, but deep down I'm a good guy, right? I'm not a face-chewer. I'm not your average insane criminal. I'm more of a vigilante, wouldn't you say? I like Ann Kinji. She never saw me as trash, always respected that I had something. When she was firm with me she was only doing her job. She actually believed I could be more. Her disgust in me was because I was, I suppose, a bad seed, but she never disrespected my potential. I'm telling you the truth. I know what I know. Take my journals, you'll see. Oh, and put that genius kid Nicholas on the crack in the SM Channel. There's a private conversation between Erik and the VP that you'll want to see. It's all in my journal, the purple one, volume 5."

Parked, doors open, and their passenger unloaded, Estep and Beav watched Paul as he was escorted into the building. He turned his head to look back one last time and mouthed a word they could clearly read off his lips, "Journals".

18

Vice President Morgan Canon blinked his rodent eyes rapidly. He was an eye-blinker when he was lying. “Everything’s under control,” he said.

“You forget I was married to you once, Morgan. Your pants are on fire.” Lita flexed her lips into an unnatural smile.

“What do you want me to say? That everything has hit the fan? You want the truth, how’s this for truth: Erik’s dead. He died in that stupid clown getup.”

“Only a matter of time before they figure out what that’s for.”

“Right. We have to move fast, and get Marci out of the way. She’s a loose cannon after IDing Erik at the morgue.”

“She’ll be back soon.”

“Marci?”

"No, Madam President."

"Back? I thought she was here." Morgan couldn't hide the startled look on his face from Lita, the woman who knew his every micro-expression. For the first time, he realized that he wasn't being kept in the loop.

"No, she slipped out. She left a body-double in her place, but that fooled no one."

"Where did she go?"

"Minneapolis."

"Minneapolis? Are you sure?" Morgan frowned. "This isn't good."

"They landed somewhere near there."

"Then drove somewhere else," he said with a flat tone of conviction and defeat.

"I take it that you know where that somewhere else is?"

"I have a fair idea. The lab is up north."

"The top secret Superman lab?"

"And we can guess what they were up to."

"I'm one step ahead of you. We have eyes on their investigation. They are closing in, Morgan. You'll have to take that Toto down."

"Toto?" Morgan never did enjoy Lita's sense of humor and he was gritting his teeth through it now.

"The witch threatens to take down Dorothy…" Lita mimicked Miss Gulch's voice, "…and her little dog too." She noted Morgan's expression of non-comprehension. She added, "Kinji's the dog."

"You must be the witch," he said, playing along. Rushing Lita through these things was never a wise idea. Without a clue in his head about what was going to happen to him in the next thirty seconds he asked, "Who's Dorothy?"

"You are."

Morgan's ex-wife leveled an adorably jeweled purse-sized handgun at the face she used to wake up to every morning, with the exception of those mornings when he was with his mistress: her very own dearly departed sister Lora. Funny how she held it against Lora until Lora died. Upon her sister's death Lita's rage transferred to Morgan, and intensified ten-fold.

Morgan's mouth made an O shape, his rat-like eyes large and round for the first, and last, time in his life. Even his nose seemed to morph into one big circle like a bull's eye. Her petite gun with bling and a white pearl handle looked like it should make a cute little popping sound. It didn't. It made a single ear-shredding crack. That was all it took to blow Morgan's head off at close range. Lita's years of target practice were overkill because, in the end, she shot him from only two feet away.

No one heard the shot that ended Morgan Canon's life, as it happened at his estate in a secluded area. Lita stood over his body for a few seconds, fixing her eyes upon his lifeless face. He doesn't look much different dead than alive, she thought. Then she made the call for a cleanup crew to take care of the situation. Because, while Lita had agreed to do it, she wasn't the person who had ordered the hit. Oh no, this was not a domestic situation but a well-planned execution. She had merely wanted to be the one to pull the trigger.

19

President Ann Kinji put word out that she needed to see the VP immediately. He wasn't answering any of her attempts to reach him, something she made clear to all of her staff that she was displeased about. Not for a minute did she suspect that he had come to a bad end. She assumed that he was still alive and well, plotting evil plans to overthrow her presidency, and avoiding her.

She was partly right: someone was plotting and hatching, but certainly not the man who lay cold and rigid on the custom marble flooring now accented by blood-spatter décor that really made the whole room pop. No, Morgan Canon was out of the picture. But, with no knowledge of his death, Ann's team was still actively looking for him, and investigating everything to do with him.

Fortunately their priority was with official contacts, not personal.

Had they known about Morgan's demise and Lita's involvement they would have been thrown off course. But because they had no idea what happened they were still plodding along toward answers. In this way, Lita did them a favor. Her quiet execution in Morgan's own home bought them all more time.

While Ann carried out her presidential routine as usual, allowing herself to be shuttled from one briefing to the next, Serena Wilcox was reunited with her family in The Cube's party room; enjoying karaoke, movies, snacks, and family entertainment. After a day or two of this impromptu reward vacation, Ann would send the five of them home. Serena was, after all, a private citizen.

Ann questioned her wisdom in even befriending Serena on a personal level, let alone using her as, what, a rouge agent? Was Ann so needy that she would glom on to a rather amateur former private detective for friendship? And then to go as far as to include Serena in a covert operation, one in which Ann had almost gotten her killed? She was a civilian! Did Serena even have much in the way of professional credentials? Of course her team had vetted her, but Ann hadn't even looked at the report.

No, this would be the last of their relationship. From this point on, Serena Wilcox would be one name of thousands on her automated Christmas card mailing. This being her frame of mind when Lehman appeared in her office with Serena in tow, Ann immediately stood up from her chair and stomped across the presidential seal to meet them.

"I know what you're thinking, but we need her," said Lehman.

"And why do we need her? She's a civilian. A fact I was reminding myself of right before you came in," said Ann.

"You were right to trust her, and right to maintain ties outside of

The Cube. Beyond that, she's also an asset. I don't know how she does it, she's like a savant. She can get into people's heads. My suggestion? Keep her on indefinitely, bring her in when you need her as you've always done," said Lehman.

"Thank you, Agent Lehman," said Serena.

"No, no, still former agent. In fact, Madam President, if you no longer need me, I'd like to go home to my wife," said Lehman.

"Any possibility that my family can help me with the investigation?" asked Serena.

Lehman and Ann looked at her, trying to decide if she was being facetious. Seeing no guile in her face, Lehman said, "To be clear, I wouldn't recommend an official relationship with Ms. Wilcox."

"Agreed," laughed Ann. To Serena she said, "I've been standing around here giving you," she looked at the holographic clock hovering near the wall, "five minutes of the nation's time. Conspiracy or no conspiracy, leak or no leak, I have work to do."

"I'll get right to it then," said Serena. "Agent Estep and Beav checked in. They have Paul's journals, but one of them is missing – the very one he most wanted them to retrieve. Not a big obstacle, Paul says the same information is in the security crack on the SM Channel, and Nicholas can easily find it."

"Get him on it immediately," said Ann.

"No, we can't use Nicholas anymore. He's the one who got the gun in the lab. No one ever searched him – it was in his backpack," said Lehman.

"What? Not our Nicholas! I met that boy, he is an amazing young man," said Ann.

"No, he had nothing to do with it. He didn't know someone put the gun in there," said Lehman. "It had to have been one of Erik's people, whoever they may be. We are no closer on that."

"What he's trying to say is that Covert Coffee has become too dangerous for him," said Serena.

"He is a child, what was I thinking? I agree with you," said Ann.

"And that's why you can't leave, former-agent Lehman. I'm not at Nicholas' level," said Serena.

"She's right. I'm sorry, but you're needed," said Ann.

Lehman nodded. "I'm not sure I can do it either. We need Victor. But I'll see what I can do, unless you have anything else to add."

"Thank you for keeping me grounded," said Ann. "I'll get you back to your wife as soon as possible."

Lehman smiled. "Anytime." He left Serena there, but not without eye contact with Ann to confirm he should do so. Ann waved him out the door.

"Serena, Lehman's right, I need you. Both your unusual investigative help and also your friendship. Olive branch?" asked Ann.

"Of course! I didn't even realize an olive branch was needed. Consider me on the job to the end," said Serena cheerfully.

"Glad to hear it. I need to resume whatever's left of this puppet show I call a presidency," said Ann. "I leave this mess in your hands."

20

Serena met Penny in a secret tunnel of The Cube parking garage. From there, she went to a residence hall on a heavily-populated college campus. One of the residence halls was temporarily closed due to the installation of a new sprinkler system and a few other minor renovations. Between the chaos of students fetching belongings from their premises and construction workers going in and out, the dormitory was an ideal location for hiding in plain sight. They set up a makeshift conference room in one of the common areas.

Beav kicked things off. “How much time can we possibly have left? This thing should have hit the fan before now. And is President Kinji an imminent target, as in within 24 hours?”

“I don’t know, but we should operate on that assumption,” said

Serena.

"You two might thrive on no sleep, but there isn't enough coffee in the world to keep me awake anymore," said Estep, too tired to growl. He stretched out on a well-worn and mysteriously-stained futon and within seconds was snoring at impressive decibels.

"Wow, how did he do that?" asked Serena.

"Ignore the buzz saw. Focus!" said Beav.

"Will do," Serena answered.

"I said that aloud? I was talking to myself."

The pair of them locked eyes and burst into a fit of giggles born out of sleep deprivation. Fifty-five hours without more than a few minutes of sleep here and there can do that. Serena steered them back on track. "First off, what do we know about what FYD is involved with?"

Beav launched into lecture mode, standing up and using a table as his lectern. "Biotechcrop is a big supporter of the FYD. They and others like them have been around for well over 20 years and haven't increased crop yields significantly in all that time. This lackluster result is despite an extensive effort by the industry to increase yields through GE, all of which is documented in Failure to Yield reports. Thousands of experimental field trials were carried out, involving GE – genetically engineered crops."

"Yes, I'm familiar with what GE means," said Serena.

"In all that time, and after so many experimental trials, only corn has increased yield. One likely reason is that new yield genes cause more genetic side-effects that often lead to undesirable agricultural properties. Irregardless—"

"Regardless."

"Regardless, even though GE crops haven't significantly

increased yields, many farmers adopted them for protection against insect pests and other reasons."

Beav helped himself to the wall-mounted dry erase board labeled "Campus Events" and made notes as he spoke. "Prior to the introduction of HT soybeans, conventional farmers often used three or four different herbicides applied several times a year. With HT soybeans, farmers could apply glyphosate herbicide only once or twice, instead of the several applications of before, plus they could apply directly onto the crop during the growing season."

"Your agricultural lesson is relevant because?" asked Serena.

"Because it didn't work. Weeds developed resistance to glyphosate: Several million acres of GE soybeans, and even cotton, are now infested with glyphosate-resistant and tolerant weeds. The number of glyphosate applications by farmers has risen considerably, and the amount of herbicide used on HT soybeans is considerably higher than it was prior to the introduction of this HT crop."

"Ah, gotta love food technology."

"Well, I wouldn't wave it away that easily. Food technology is not a new science; we can date it way back to 1810 with the canning process. And of course there was pasteurization and I could go on with a history lesson, but you get the idea. If we were only talking about food technology flops, there would be no conspiracy theory."

"The conspiracy lies with the money, like always."

"On the nose."

"So your theory is that the FYD stands to gain from GE technology so they are pushing it through even though it doesn't yield results, and are tampering with public reaction on the SM Channel chatter?"

"No, at least I don't think so. GE is an issue I tossed at you for an example of the type of issue FYD could possibly be protecting."

"Don't tell me you went through that whole lecture on GE foods only to tell me it's nothing more than an example!"

Beav averted his eyes sheepishly.

"You did! But why? You know we are short on time! The President could really be in danger. Unbelievable!" Serena said.

"We have to start somewhere. I think we should be looking for something like this, an issue that FYD wants to bury. And why not start with GE foods? Biotechcrop is one of FYD's biggest bankrollers. It makes sense to start with them and research what they do, which is GE foods."

Beav's lecture notes were sprawled all over the previously blank campus event board. Serena glanced over them dismissively. "You do that. Meanwhile, I'll call Lehman and see if he's arrived at the lab yet."

"No, he'll call when he has something. Let's get back to brainstorming. When he does call, something we say now could speed up the process later."

"OK then, I can think of another issue off the top of my head, one that actually turned up in our investigation. What about regulating private farms and home gardens?"

"As much as I agree it's a hot button issue, where's the big money interest in that?" Beav erased some of his notes, leaving the most important phrases behind.

Serena removed an obsolete tablet from her bag: it could still connect to the Internet in buildings that used old school connections. Campuses were notorious for lagging behind in technology, due to the cost to update entire buildings when budgets were already taxed.

Her hunch was correct. Serena connected to the web without any difficulty.

"Big money? Well, like you mentioned with GE, farm regulation is not a new issue. In 1942 a United States Supreme Court decision, Wickard v. Filburn, recognized the power of the federal government to regulate economic activity. I can read straight from Wikipedia as well as the next person. In fact, I'll do that now:

'A farmer, Roscoe Filburn, was growing wheat for on-farm consumption. The U.S. government had established limits on wheat production based on acreage owned by a farmer, in order to drive up wheat prices during the Great Depression, and Filburn was growing more than the limits permitted. Filburn was ordered to destroy his crops and pay a fine, even though he was producing the excess wheat for his own use and had no intention of selling it.'

The Supreme Court decided that 'Filburn's wheat growing activities reduced the amount of wheat he would buy for chicken feed on the open market, and because wheat was traded nationally, Filburn's production of more wheat than he was allotted was affecting interstate commerce. Thus, Filburn's production could be regulated by the federal government.'

If we bring this issue forward to more recent years, regulation included raiding family farms and even threatening moms with jail time if they didn't stop distributing food to their neighbors. President Kinji made a lot of government agencies unhappy with her reversal of many of the regulations imposed upon private farms by the past two administrations," said Serena, playing professor as smoothly as Beav had.

"I'm still not seeing the big money. With GE foods, I can see major government contracts ripped out from under fat cats. Motive.

Where's the fat cat in your issue?"

"I don't know, but my gut feeling is that we are looking at regulations of farms. The Town Hall messages I sifted through contained several e-mails about that issue, and I got a vibe that something was off."

"Off how?"

"The tone of the e-mail seemed inconsistent, like reading from a script. Well, technically writing from a script, which doesn't make sense. Copying from a script."

"I get it."

"I have a sixth sense for these things, it's how I roll," said Serena.

"You won't get an argument from me. I've never been a conventional person myself. I'm going to give equal weight to both of our theories, but let's keep it between us how you came to your contribution."

"Agreed. So we brainstorm some more?" Serena added the word "farms" and a "?" to the board. "Another thought comes to mind: what about the bioterrorism threat assessments? How do those relate to the FYD? Any fat cats threatened by the president's new bill?"

"Not that I can see."

"We really need something more to go on. We're sitting around guessing and spinning theories, based on stale intel and my gut. Where's Lehman with something new?" asked Serena.

As if on cue the incoming call light finally flickered. "I have something," said Lehman. He was on conference call with the pair of them.

"We're listening," said Serena.

"It's odd. Seems the FYD wants to cover up some experimental farming with genetically engineered foods that was secretly conducted on private family farms."

In unison, and barely above a whisper, Serena and Beav said, "We were both right."

"What?" said Lehman.

"Never mind. Has the real Victor been located yet?" asked Beav.

"No, but we're closing in on him," said Lehman. "I expect they'll have him any minute now."

"A big question is, will the real Victor confirm that FYD is involved at all? Erik is the one who told us about FYD. For all we know, it was all a lie to throw us off Erik and the VP's actual game plan," said Serena.

"No, there's no doubt. We were able to confirm FYD's involvement independently of Erik. Remember we have Victor's computers, and there was a lot we could learn without cracking anything."

"How do we know that this is Victor's data?" asked Serena.

"We don't know for sure, but we confirmed they are his machines, and the data bears out what Erik told us," said Lehman.

"Why did Erik tell us all of that though? It doesn't make sense," Serena said. "Why would he confess everything? Did he expect we would believe he was the real Victor even after strip-searching him at the prison door?"

"We did have his back against the wall. That's when most criminals start giving out information," said Beav.

"Besides, he told us only what we could easily learn for ourselves from Victor's computers," said Lehman.

"Next question: why was Erik at Victor's? To destroy the computers? Or was he looking for something?" asked Serena.

“I assume he was there to wipe the computers clean, but I have serious doubts he could do that. Victor would have had a back-up to the back-up, with encryptions I probably can’t crack,” said Lehman.

Beav said, “Whatever he was doing, he was already suited up, so to speak, for the security identification as Victor. He was off to The Cube next.”

“One thing I’m not clear on- if the Victor mask looks nothing like him, how does it get him through security?” Serena had been wondering about this for a while.

Lehman gave her a simplified explanation. “Erik only needed a few points of recognition to fool the scanner. The rest of the mask could look like anything he wanted. Why he chose something so hideous, that I can’t answer.”

“And why was he going to The Cube?” asked Serena.

“I don’t think you’ll find those answers in a computer,” said Beav.

“I say we talk to the vice president,” said Serena.

21

Ted found it easy to bail on his self-imposed duties as First Gentleman. After all, no one expected much from him. Today's agenda had an entire two-hour block dedicated to "fitness", which usually meant a light cardio workout, a jog inside The Cube's beautifully maintained park, cool-down stretches and a visit to the sauna and shower. Secret service lagged behind, giving him the privacy he requested.

He knew that when he didn't take a second lap around the park they would go looking for him, but he had plenty of time to slip away from the Cube and into a car that was waiting for him. The car, which was in most instances a government issue sedan, blended into the backdrop. The driver was again Penny, now the chauffeur of choice for all discrete travel, even road trips that President Kinji knew nothing about.

Penny drove directly to a cute suburban home in Arlington Heights, owned by Lora's grandmother. This was where Lora's mother Vanessa was currently living. She was expecting Ted. Penny waited in the car while Ted went inside. In his absence, Penny made a few calls to cover for his sudden disappearance. She blamed his absence, and her pick-up, on a sudden-onset gastrointestinal issue. She assured his detail that everything was under control. She did all of this partly out of patriotic duty (not to mention the generous off-the-books paycheck) and partly out of guilt.

After all, she was the one who had first alerted President Ann to the situation. If anything went wrong, she would always second guess her decision to come forward. If not for her, maybe this mess would have been the next administration's nightmare; dear Ann could have quietly retired into a much deserved uneventful life at the end of her presidency. Penny was going to do whatever she could to help, even if it meant lying to the president.

While Penny waited and kept a watchful eye out for any suspicious activity, Ted meanwhile was greeted, seated, and left alone with Vanessa. He cleared his throat, which prompted her to ask him if he wanted a glass of water. He declined.

"Mr. President's Husband, what do you want with me?" asked Vanessa. "Is President Ann as pretty in person as she is on TV?"

Ted decided to ignore the question; he had no time for fluffy conversation. "I need to know about your arrangement with FYD."

"My what? Honey, I have no idea what you are talking about. Are you sure you're talking to the right person?"

"You had visitors when you were in prison from the vice president and Erik Chapman."

"Oh, that's what all this is about! Sure, they came many times, but they weren't there to talk to me."

"No? The log shows that they were there to see you."

"Yes, I know. They saw me, but they said it was the only way to see Victor – that's who they really came to see, not me."

"Why didn't they see Victor directly?"

Vanessa looked surprised. "Oh, oops, I bet I wasn't supposed to talk to you. I thought you were in on it too."

"In on what? You might as well tell me the rest. I can find it out for myself."

Vanessa seemed to think it over for a few seconds, but she was eager to spill what she knew. "They didn't want anyone to know that they were interested in Victor, so they asked me to keep quiet."

"Do you know what they wanted with him?" Ted examined her face to judge her reaction.

"No." Vanessa's eyes slid down and to the left.

Ted had had enough psychology classes to know that this was a classic sign that Vanessa was lying. "The truth now please? It could help the president."

Vanessa fidgeted with the bangle on her wrist. "They did ask me to pass messages back and forth."

"Do you know what these messages were about?" Ted's focus on her face was unwavering.

Vanessa blushed. "I may have looked at them."

Ted softened his tone. "You aren't in any sort of trouble. Please tell me what the messages said." His soothing voice, his refined good looks, his caring eyes – he used them all to give her his charming best.

Vanessa met his eyes and nearly swooned. "I can do better than that. I copied them."

"You did? How did you manage that?" He exaggerated, by using a dramatic tone and even more dramatic facial expression, how impressed he was. He downplayed his eagerness to see those pages. He would keep this all about her, and flatter her as much as he could.

"I wrote them down, word for word. I have a friend in there. He keeps journals of everything important. He loaned me one of his journals." Vanessa touched her hair and began twirling it around her finger.

"This friend, would he be Paul Tracy by any chance?" Ted moved a little closer to her.

"Yes! How did you know that?" Vanessa batted her false eyelashes and leaned in closer to the handsome First Gentleman in the pin-striped shirt. She was so close that she could smell his cologne. Idly she wondered if President Ann had bought it for him.

"It doesn't matter. We already have his journals, but there is one missing." Ted stared meaningfully at her face. He had a hunch…

"That's because I have it. He told me to keep it in a safe place, and that one day someone would come looking for it." Vanessa looked pleased with herself. She knew that she had supplied the answer that Ted was hoping for.

"That day is today. I'm the someone who is looking for it."

"I'm not sure yet." Vanessa fidgeted with her bangle again, this time dropping it on the floor. She picked it up and slid it back onto her wrist.

"Not sure you should trust me?" Ted gestured at himself with both hands and tried to make light of her reservations, but his playfulness only intensified her bangle twisting.

“Paul said not to give the journal to anyone who doesn’t know the answer to a question.”

“What is the question?” Ted imagined a bangle on his own wrist; it was his turn to feel anxious. He hadn’t known there would be a riddle involved.

“It doesn’t make any sense.”

“Try me.”

“Who is Victor?”

“What do you mean? You know who Victor is.” Ted realized he had lost control over the conversation, and no amount of posturing was going to bring it back around in his favor.

“No, that’s the question Paul gave me. ‘Who is Victor?’”

Ted took a stab at it. “Victor is Erik?”

“No,” said Vanessa, shaking her head woefully. “That’s not it. I can’t help you.”

“Wait! I think I know. The answer is ‘a clown’.” Ted slapped his fist into his hand. That had to be it, he got it!

Vanessa stood up. “Yes! That’s the right answer! You are that someone. I’ll get it for you.” She left the room for a few minutes. Ted could hear the sounds of her rummaging through drawers. As the minutes began to drag on, he worried that she couldn’t find the journal, but she eventually emerged with a triumphant smile on her face. “I found it! It wasn’t where I left it, I swear.” She handed the journal to Ted.

Ted thumbed through it and frowned. “There are pages torn out of this one too.”

“Really? It wasn’t like that when Paul gave it to me.”

“Are you looking for these?” A woman’s voice came from behind them.

The hairs on the back of Ted's neck stood up. He knew who it was before turning around. "Marci? What are you doing here?"

Marci stood with her legs spread apart; a firmly rooted tree, her arms branches over her head. She rustled the torn pages like they were her leaves. Her face was stretched as if she had her hair pulled back too tightly. Her mouth was twisted. Her eyes were dilated.

"I'm sorry about your husband," said Ted. He took a few steps toward Marci while Vanessa froze.

"Don't come any closer! Erik told me all about you, and your grab for power. You are the one behind all of this. You are the one who hired my husband. You killed him!"

Ted showed the palms of his hands. "I'm not going to hurt you, clam down and let's discuss this."

"No, no! You stay right there!" Marci let the pages flitter to the floor as she scrabbled at the buttons of her oversized denim shirt to reveal a bra stuffed with something awkwardly bulky; an object Vanessa instantly recognized.

"Lora's gun! Where did you get that?"

A look of bewilderment passed over Marci's face, as if Vanessa's voice had confused her. She rebounded quickly and said, "I forgot you were Lita's mother."

"Lita wouldn't have given you her sister's gun, I know she wouldn't," said Vanessa.

"Of course she would, she did. A mother's love is always blind. Lita had her own axe to grind. Do you think she'd let Lora's memory go un-avenged?"

Vanessa gasped. "What did she do? Where is she?"

Marci removed the petite bejeweled gun from her bra and leveled it at Ted. "I don't know where Lita is. I have my own issue to deal with."

Ted adopted a soothing tone. "Marci, put the gun down. I'll do whatever you want. Just please, let's talk."

"What did Lita do? I have to know," Vanessa pleaded.

Ted walked a step closer to where Marci was standing.

"Don't move!" Marci shrieked. The gun wavered precariously at the end of her outstretched arm.

Ted let his arms fall passively until his fingertips rested upon his outer thighs. He stood without wavering, taking deep and controlled breaths. He waited.

Vanessa took her cue from Ted. She too struck a non-threatening pose and stood silently motionless. The minutes ticked by and it felt as if they had spent hours holding steady, casting their eyes submissively on the floor, trying not to think about the gun that Marci was holding in her trembling hand.

"Erik told me everything," Marci repeated. Her voice was flat now, her eyes dull and lifeless. "I know about your affair with Morgan's wife."

Vanessa forgot her code of silence and the threat of being shot. Her addiction to gossip overtook her. "The Vice President's wife? Oh poor President Ann!"

"Yes, can you believe it? They were together the entire time Kinji's been President, even before. Ted's no gentleman. He wants his wife out, himself in." Marci frowned. "But he couldn't do it without my Erik's help. And now Erik is dead." She held the light-weight gun with both hands to steady her aim.

"What is it that you want from me?" asked Ted.

"I want you dead!" Marci screeched.

"I can help you find the person who killed your husband." Ted made another attempt to move closer, his arms remaining limp at his sides, his gait slow.

"You killed him!" Marci was now racked with sobs, the gun shakier than ever.

"No, it wasn't me. You are right, I was pushing for the presidency. With the FDA lobbyists, and others, in my pocket, I could easily win an election."

"Where you planning to take the VP's wife too?" Vanessa's voice dripped with contempt, making it clear with one tone change that she had switched teams.

"No. She and Morgan were finished anyway, but no, we weren't staying together. She was a passing amusement," said Ted with nonchalance.

"A passing amusement!" Vanessa mocked.

"It was mutual. We were together for convenience, neither of us happy. She knew about Erik and Morgan working behind the scenes to get me lined up for my run at the office. In fact, I promised Erik to tap him for the cabinet position of his choice. Morgan would be my VP of course. He knew about his wife, didn't care."

"Erik didn't tell me any of that."

"He wouldn't have told you anything important." Ted shuffled a few inches closer to the ever-shaking bejeweled gun.

"He told me everything!" Marci blinked away her tears and visibly morphed from grief back to anger.

"I highly doubt that."

"Then how do I know so much?" She relaxed her stance for a few seconds, the gun no longer locked on Ted's face. "The lobbyists have taken over the SM Channel, for one."

"Everyone knows about the power of the lobbyists. Take the

food industry: Retailers, junk food manufacturers and the big Ag lobby are the USDA's customers. Nothing new there." Ted scooted his feet forward a few more inches, doing his best to keep his upper body seemingly unmoving. He kept talking. "We make no effort to track the money spent on food stamps. Where is the money going? Food lobbyists are going to do whatever they can to keep their power. Like I said, nothing new. You wouldn't need Erik to draw that conclusion. See? He didn't confide in you."

"Yes he did! He told me about the SM Channel secret mind control project. And I know it's not common knowledge because it's classified at the top levels of clearance, only scientists and top level brass know about it." Marci looked from Ted to Vanessa, who took eye contact as permission to speak.

"Is that what they wanted Victor for?" asked Vanessa. "Victor, Paul and I were friends. I saw him leave with the VP plenty of times and I know he was a scientist before he went crazy and killed all those people."

"Yes, that's right!" Marci nodded at the person she perceived as her new alliance. "They took him to make molds of his face. Victor had the security clearance they needed. No one had bothered to scrub it from the system when he left, so all they needed to do was use his identity."

"Erik came into The Cube as himself, put the latex mask on, and then sailed right through the areas beyond his security clearance," Ted added.

"See? You didn't think I knew all that, did you?" Marci narrowed her eyes smugly at Ted.

"What else did Erik tell you?" asked Ted.

"I proved he told me everything. I'm done talking." The finality in Marci's voice was unmistakable. She raised the gun, held it with both hands, and locked her arms out in front of her.

What happened next was a blur: Vanessa ducked behind the couch. Ted darted toward Marci. Serena, without anyone's knowledge, had entered the home from the back door that she had conveniently found unlocked. Unlike Goldilocks, she didn't find an empty house with bowls full of hot soup; she found a crazed woman holding a gun on the first gentleman. Having had learned her lesson from the incident with Eric-as-Victor, Serena didn't hesitate. She crouched down and ran, remaining hunched-over, to a position behind Marci. She hid herself by sitting down. What she did next shocked everyone, including Serena.

Aikido is a Japanese martial art designed to defend oneself while also protecting the attacker from injury. Unfortunately Serena's training was severely lacking. She had seen a demonstration of the "four-direction throw", shihōnage, in the situation of a standing attacker and seated defender, but she had never actually attempted it. The receiver of the throw should take a break-fall to safely reach the ground. Serena scooted into the proper position to perform this grappling maneuver from her seated position. At this same instant, Marci caught Serena's motion in her peripheral vision.

Serena grabbed Marci's arm to perform the throw. Marci sailed through the air – and simultaneously pulled the trigger. She landed on the floor with a hideous thud after hitting her head on the coffee table as she went down. The bullet zinged up and to the left, sailing through the drywall and lodging itself into the wall of the next room. The forensic team would find it easily when processing the crime scene later.

The clean-up crew heard the pop when Marci fired her weapon but they waited for orders before going in. The sudden appearance of squad cars and secret service agents was a game-changer. The crew drove away, wondering what went wrong in there and anxious about their vulnerability. Each man considered leaving the country before it all came down.

22

Ann listened to the entire recording. Then she said, “Do you think she went for it?”

“I certainly hope so,” said Ted. “She’ll talk to someone, especially if we let it happen. We might learn something.”

“Why did she think you were having an affair with Morgan’s wife?” asked Ann.

“I don’t know. I can’t figure out the logic behind that. I went with it, but wow was I nervous. I thought I would blab something that went against the story and she would know I was making things up,” said Ted.

“I think I know why she thought you were having an affair. When you sneaked out of the McDonald’s parking lot, did you happen to use Mrs. Canon’s driver? Or her car?” asked Serena.

"You know about this?" asked Ted.

"Sir, everyone knows about this," said Beav.

"Ted, you didn't pull it off, it was on the SM Channel within the hour," laughed Ann. "And yes, he did use one of the cars assigned to her detail. You're right, I'm sure they put two and two together and came up with a scandal."

"It was in the tabloids," said Beav.

"Ah, well, I don't read those," said Ann.

"Anyway, that's not much of a mystery. But if Erik told her that you were after the presidency, he was deliberately misleading Marci. Did Marci think she was on the good side of this? And if so, why? What was Erik really up to, that he didn't want his wife to know about?" asked Serena.

"Again, nothing new. We know that they were involved in something, but Erik is dead and Morgan is missing. I'm not sure either is a threat anymore, so if this doesn't go any further we might be looking at a cold case," said Beav.

"It would be easier if we could talk to Marci," said Serena.

"What are you talking about? She's in custody, isn't she?" asked Ann.

"She might not be able to talk for a while," said Ted.

"Why not? What happened?" asked Ann. A round of snickers, coughs and snorts made it difficult for Ann to hear Serena's accounting for how Marci became incapacitated.

"I performed Aikido on her and she had an accident," said Serena.

"You performed? Like a demonstration?" Ann's eyes registered disbelief. Laughter broke out.

"No, she flipped her like a ninja," said Beav, with a note of pride.

“Serena did this? When did you learn martial arts?” Ann struggled to keep a straight face.

“I’ve been at it a while. First time I’ve ever used it in a real life situation.” Serena’s earlier attempt at remorse was nullified by the gloating she was doing now.

“What accident?” asked Ann.

“I flipped her and she pitched into the table. She’s concussed and in the hospital. I didn’t mean to do that part, but at least she wasn’t able to shoot anybody,” said Serena.

“Madam President, we have people on guard at the hospital. Marci Chapman won’t be an issue,” said Estep.

“What was Ted doing in all of this in the first place? Why was he involved?” asked Ann.

“Sorry, he was the only person I could think of who could do some digging as a Cube insider. We had no idea Marci was there. The plan was to find out what Vanessa knew. The result was way better than expected.” Serena noticed the expression on Ann’s face. “Well, except for the First Gentleman almost getting killed.”

“And thanks to you, I’m fine,” said Ted.

“You were incredibly impressive. I can’t believe how well you could improv,” said Serena.

“I can’t believe what you did,” said Ted. “What are you, all of five two?”

“Ah, the mutual admiration club, may I join?” Ann smiled. “I would have loved to have seen Serena in action.”

“Oh you can! We had video surveillance. Estep and I have watched it more than a dozen times on the way over,” said Beav.

“Indulge me. Package it, put a bow on it, and make it my next

Christmas present." Ann quickly switched gears. While she enjoyed casual and light-hearted human moments, she was always aware that she was the President, although the title held little meaning at the moment, given that her cabinet, her staff, and even the vice president couldn't be trusted; world leaders of other nations were potential enemies, more so than usual that is, and worst of all, she was operating with a ragtag team of former agents and Serena Wilcox, who was in a class of her own. Nonetheless, she was still the acting president and she would fight to maintain some level of leadership.

She said, "While the rest of you wait for Lehman to report in with an update I need to get on with today's agenda. You'll have to excuse me while I peruse the latest Town Hall messages." Then she positioned herself in front of the screen on the back wall and turned her attention to what was on it. Everyone knew better than to join her; everyone except for Serena, who immediately stood up and walked to where Ann was already engaged in reading her inbox.

"I should read these with you," Serena said.

Ann nodded.

The two women read through the Town Hall messages while the rest of the group sat at the conference table silently waiting for Lehman to give them an update. While all were itching to get to work, they were also running on empty. Beav nodded off a few times, his arms folded upon the table as a pillow for his weary head. The minutes dragged with no activity except for the calls for Ann Kinji, all of which were routine. The President was not scheduled to be anywhere for another hour yet.

Lehman was in another wing of The Cube scouring video footage. He put everyone who was a new hire, no more than three weeks at The Cube, on alert to find what he was looking for: the image of a repulsive clown-like form of Erik-as-Victor entering and exiting the eighth floor on multiple occasions. He drafted every intern into the project, even though none of the newbies had clearances for a job that secure. They couldn't trust anyone who was working at The Cube when the first inklings of a rat started to surface. He also avoided using anyone who had connections or was over the age of twenty-two, but even with such narrow criteria to select from, he had fourteen pairs of eyes on the video feed.

Despite the unnaturally calm demeanor of President Kinji and her Covert Coffee team, time was of the essence. Ann and Serena wrapped up the Town Hall readings, finding nothing unusual. They (Beav, Estep, Penny, Serena, Ted and Ann) waited together without much conversation until Lehman reported in.

The six of them sat at a ridiculously long half-million dollar conferencing table in luxurious leather chairs. The digs weren't as exciting as the Superman lab, and the overstatement was vulgar, but the team was nonetheless relieved to be in the final stretch of the mission and sitting here instead of there. Sleep deprivation was still mostly unresolved, none of them had more than a few winks here and there when they could catch them. The offer of coffee was met with great enthusiasm by everyone but caffeine-avoider Beav.

"Finally a good cup of coffee! Covert Coffee made me crave coffee this whole time," said Serena.

There they sat, sipping coffee from red and green mugs, sugar and cream in most of them, reflecting upon the mission's journey. A good five minutes of quiet passed, a passage of time that felt long to a crew struggling to hold on to adrenaline while waiting for answers. They ran through the events of the past 48 hours.

"With Morgan's body discovered, and Erik's body already in the morgue, the bad guys are no longer a threat, wouldn't you say? We know where the leak was," said Estep. "No disrespect, Madam President, but I question why am I still needed, why any of us are still needed. At this point, the feds and locals can take care of it."

Beav agreed, "Marci was a loose end, but she is incapacitated thanks to Betty Boop over there, and besides that she was operating out of personal motivation, not conspiracy. Domestic situation of sorts."

"This is the part when the meddling kids explain who did it and why," said Ann.

"Scooby-Doo?" Serena guessed.

"Yes, it's been a running theme in my head all day. And that's how ridiculous all of this is. You're right, Agent Estep. This has gone on long enough. I'm down to only forty-five minutes before the GOB initiative," said Ann.

"Are we sure that Global Oil isn't involved in any of this?" asked Serena.

"We aren't sure of anything, but I need to carry on the business of the nation. You have five minutes more of my time, and then I'm off. In fact, Agent Estep, you can head on out now. I'd like you on my security detail today," said Ann.

Agent Estep needed no second invitation. He sprang out of his chair, gave them a two-fingered salute goodbye and bolted out the door before the president could change her mind.

After Estep had left the room Beav resumed dialog. "Madam President, I don't think you should stop turning over stones. The crack in the SM Channel isn't going to disappear simply because no one is fighting to keep it a secret. The mind control project is troubling as well."

"I'll keep you on until the end of the week, but after that I'll be reassigning Covert Coffee to agents who are still active," said Ann.

"The President is still in danger," said Serena.

"Is this fact or one of your hunches?" asked Ann.

Serena pointed at the door. "Fact."

Two masked figures entered the room. But it was the sight of the unmasked man between them that put fear into everyone's heart. Because, the man standing between them was Agent Lehman; bound, gagged, and strapped with explosives.

23

Before any of them could process what was happening, Agent Estep burst through the entryway. He had a dozen agents with him. At this point a chorus of “No, no, wait, wait!” and “It’s a bomb!” went up, but the alarm was only coming from four of them: President Kinji, Ted, Serena and Penny. Everyone else was quiet.

When the four caught on that Estep and his team were not backing down, and furthermore, Beav was on his feet gloating, they too fell silent. One of the masked figures, a woman, said, “What are you doing here? I thought you were fired.”

Beav smiled. “Just helping out.”

The figure swore, repeatedly.

“I’m confused. Why are we not worried about the bomb, is it fake?” asked Ann.

"No, it's very much real," said Beav. "But we aren't worried because it's one of mine."

"I'm in good hands," said Lehman. "He'll have this thing disarmed in seconds. You might not be aware that Beav is somewhat of a legend."

Estep jerked his head toward the two figures. His team cuffed them and dragged them out of the way. Beav ran to Lehman, grabbed the end of a small plastic strip located on the outer casing of the bomb and pulled, exposing a panel with ten digits on it. He punched in a code. The bomb beeped twice and powered down, lights out. "Voila! You're a free man, Lehman!"

"Well done, Beav!" said Ann.

Beav was speechless as he basked in his moment of personal redemption, making up for missing Paul Tracy's bomb. And wasn't President Ann the one most worth saving-- that is, if it were up to him? He stood looking at her; grinning, his eyes misting over.

Serena ended the moment. "This is the part when the gang takes the masks off the bad guys to reveal who they really are."

"Should we place bets?" asked Beav.

"You think you know who they are?" asked Ted.

"Nope, no clue," said Beav. "Serena?"

"If I had to guess, I'd say that this one is the real Victor and this one, being obviously female, is probably Lita," she said.

Estep gave President Kinji a quizzical look. Ann nodded. He signaled for his agents to remove the masks, revealing Victor and Lita, both of them red in the face from being overheated by wearing the masks.

Ann said, "How did you do that?"

"Well, you might remember that Vanessa kept asking what her

daughter did, and where she was. Marci alluded to Lita having something to avenge. I figured Lita was floating out there somewhere, somehow involved in whatever was going to go down, and I'm also suspecting that she killed Morgan, by the way. When one of them was female, I thought, 'oh Lita's turned up'. As for Victor, why hadn't anyone found him? He must have been trying to stay hidden. With our only other leads dead, he had to be Victor. Unless there was a surprise unknown candidate, which I thought was probably unlikely, so yeah, my money was on Victor. How much did I win?" Serena held her palm out.

"Does your bloodhound sense also point to where we can find evidence that will connect these two to more than what we saw for ourselves? Of course they'll never see the light of day after bringing a bomb into my office, but I want all the other rodents in the nest," said Ann.

"Yes, actually, I do know where to look. We have to get into the crack in the SM Channel. I also want those torn pages that Marci was throwing around. If I can get Paul to talk to me we might be able to get the information even faster. He obviously knows what's in those pages and for whatever reason didn't tell us," said Serena.

Lehman jumped in, "We've been working on two of those three things and are close. I'm not helping with Paul. We can do this without his help."

Serena turned to face Lita, who was standing directly behind her. "You have to know that there is absolutely no hope of you escaping prison. You might as well help us."

Lita's rage hit her with such intensity that she temporarily possessed supernatural strength. She bulldozed her way past the two agents who had been loosely restraining her. Not at all hampered by her hands cuffed behind her back, she bent her head down and charged at Serena like a bull.

Serena didn't need to remember her Aikido training; she simply had to move out of the way. Serena sprang backward with the speed and agility of a dancer. Without Serena's body to stop her, Lita was thrown off balance, sending her flying into the conference table. Her head slammed onto the tabletop and skidding into a landing just in front of Serena's green coffee cup, coffee that was now cold and completely unappetizing for other reasons. Lita's long hair spiraled across the table, blood flowing over and through it, pooling up around the coffee mug.

"She's done it again!" said Beav.

"Sorry, she won't be helpful to us now," said Serena.

"She wasn't going to tell you anything anyway," said Estep. He signaled for all of them to follow him into the blood-free adjoining room. Then he doubled-back to the scene of the newest drama. He made arrangements for three separate teams to come in and do their jobs; one of those jobs was to transport Lita to the Cube's ER wing via stretcher. Estep re-joined the others and caught up with a conversation already in progress.

"I'm going to be late for the GOB initiative if I don't leave right now," said Ann.

"I don't feel comfortable with you going. Give up on it and address the nation right now with the news of the vice president's passing. Explain that his sudden death requires your complete attention and sympathy. Back out now," said Ted.

"I agree. The plan to hold back on the news doesn't make sense anymore. Now we have these two and can piece the rest together with a little more digging. You won't be safe until we know the rest of the story," said Serena.

"I can postpone it until tomorrow, but no later. In the event of an emergency, tomorrow is the 'rain date'. I won't be consumed with the Morgan Canon situation enough to justify canceling the initiative altogether. Too many nations are involved – this has been in the works for two years," said Ann.

"Tomorrow's good. We can do that," said Lehman.

"I have a press conference to give," said Ann. "I'm leaving you to clean up this mess."

Serena said, "President Kinji?"

Ann raised her eyebrows.

"Don't say anything about what happened just now with Victor and Lita."

Ann nodded. Then she left with Penny and Ted in tow. Estep's team removed both Victor and the unconscious Lita from the room. Lehman, Estep, Beav and Serena were all that remained.

They all looked at the bloodied conference table. An investigation team would be in shortly to bag and tag, while keeping the investigation quiet of course. The sleuthing quartet needed a new room to work in; better yet, a lab fit for a super hero, complete with a young genius named Nicholas.

"How long would it take us to get back to Hudson?" asked Serena.

"You read my mind," said Lehman.

"I won't let anything happen to the kid," said Estep.

24

"It's good to be back," said Nicholas. "I'm sorry about the gun."

"That wasn't your fault," said Serena.

Lehman arranged for Nicholas' computer to be displayed on multiple monitors, including a large screen that Serena and Beav would be viewing from their location at the table. Lehman would be working alongside Nicholas. Their first order of business was to follow Victor's labyrinth until they found the crack in the SM Channel.

It wasn't difficult for either of them when they worked together. Lehman contributed what he and his team had put in and Nicholas had already stumbled on the crack by accident on a few occasions. He had used his own version of it when he connected with Paul in prison. The only real issue was finding the specific trail that Victor used so that they could retrieve his history.

Travel time shot up the rest of the work day; it was already past dinner hour and they were hungry. The good news was that the actual work to find Victor's trail took only fifteen minutes after their arrival at the lab. They sent Estep out for food while they dug into the secrets of the crack in the SM Channel. Who was talking there? And why?

The reading was juicy. They found all manner of illegal dealings and backdoor conversations. What was hilarious to them was that the conversations were treated the same as any data, and were searchable! Within seconds they found the exact conversation Paul had told them about, simply by typing in Erik Chapman and Morgan Canon. It was an audio file.

"I don't like using the Channel for this," said Morgan.

"It's safer than the phones. No tracing," said Erik.

"Victor can see it," Morgan sounded more irritated than alarmed.

"He's not looking."

"What?"

"I got him involved in a project that will keep him busy for a long time." Erik sounded smug.

"I'll be happier when he's out of the picture entirely."

"I have everything I need except for who's paying him."

Morgan was quiet for a few seconds. "Look, this has gotten out of hand. I want out."

"Too late now, you're all in."

"What are you saying?" At this point Morgan did sound alarmed.

"I have the ID. I am going through with it. You know about the plan. What do you think they will do to you if they find out you knew?"

"And how would they know if you don't tell them?"

"You're telling them right now. The crack has ears." Erik laughed. The audio file ended.

"We know why Morgan was murdered!" Beav said.

"But we're no closer to who killed him, besides Lita being the one who did the actual deed, which forensics will prove soon," said Serena.

"Victor turned out to be a most surprising villain. I wasn't getting an image of him as capable of being a criminal mastermind in this way," said Beav.

Serena thought about it. "Victor's profile would suggest that he is capable of doing anything, legal or illegal, if he believes it to be moral. When he killed those people, he did so accidentally. He was working on something that he believed would cure disease. Yes, he conducted experiments around the law, and those proved to be fatal. But you see what I'm saying?"

"We are looking for a cause," said Beav.

"Yes! Let's look into Victor's profile."

"Pulling it up now," said Lehman from his station a few feet away.

"What do you want me to do?" asked Nicholas.

"We need Victor's financial records, anything you can pull off his computers, anything you can find anywhere really," said Serena.

"You think that's what Erik was looking for?" asked Beav.

"I suspect Victor was hired by someone powerful, or someones powerful. If Erik could find out who that was, he wouldn't need Victor anymore," said Serena.

"Profile's up," called Lehman.

"I'm not seeing any— oh wait," said Beav. "He cited scientific misconduct as the reason why he worked outside of the system. He said that the system was corrupt, flawed, and too slow."

"OK then, so he doesn't trust the system. And he already knows that the vice president was in on the SM Channel security leak, spying, and whatever else they were doing with it. Isn't it possible that he assumed that President Kinji was also involved?" Serena stated this as a question but her voice indicated that she believed it as a fact.

Beav snapped his fingers. "So when he showed up in Kinji's office, he thought he was saving us all from… whatever it is that they are doing."

"Yes! I think so. I think he's actually trying to be heroic. Which means…he's on our side and if we can convince him of that, he'll help us," said Serena.

"Miss Serena? I found Victor's bank account. He has two of them," said Nicholas. "I'll put both up on the screen."

Serena clapped her hands together. "That was easy!"

Beav looked to see what she was so gleeful about and chuckled. There was only one form of income coming in, and the source was easy to identify: it was Uncle Sam.

"I think you're right about him. He's working for us, trying to seal that crack in the SM Channel, and he thinks we are the bad guys keeping it open," said Beav.

"I hate to burst your bubble, but why did Erik mention wanting to find who was paying him?" asked Lehman.

"Notice how Morgan got quiet and then uneasy. He wanted to get out at that point. He knew that Victor was on government payroll, and knew that Erik would eventually find out," said Serena.

"It's not quite adding up for me, but I think you are right: Victor will talk to us if he knows whose side we are on," said Beav.

"I think I know who can convince him," said Serena. "Nicholas, could you please send up another flare for Paul Tracy? I need his help again."

25

Paul Tracy knew that he'd hear from Serena Wilcox again, he was waiting for her call. He had been holding back on them – why shouldn't he? Nothing whatsoever had been offered to him, nothing at all, even though the crimes he was guilty of committing were acts that most Americans called him a hero for! Yet he had been thrown away to rot in prison with no concern for his welfare, and that was unacceptable. He stared at his digi watch, expecting that it would alert him of Serena's call any minute. When it finally did he took his sweet time in responding.

Nicholas warned Serena, "You better talk fast. When he answers I can only keep this line secure for five minutes, maybe ten."

Paul answered in a faux Southern drawl. "Hello? Is this by any chance my dear friend Serena Wilcox?"

"Paul, I need your help." Serena spoke quickly, in a vain attempt to minimize the effect that she knew the words 'I need your help' would have on Paul's ego.

"With?" If Serena could have seen him she would have seen that Paul wore a smile as wide as the Cheshire Cat's.

"I want to talk to Victor, but he doesn't trust us. If you talk to him, I think you can convince him to talk to me."

"Victor! Why Victor? It's me you want to talk to." Paul paced the cell, drawing attention from his fellow inmates on the block.

"Can you help us?" Serena dug deep within herself for patience.

"Yes and no."

"Yes and no?" She counted to ten.

"I can, but I won't until I get something in return."

"What do you want? You know we can't let you out of prison, that's not something I would even attempt to ask for." Serena glanced at Estep. If she was ready to snap, she knew he must be at his boiling point. She was surprised that he hadn't sparked off before now.

"I want privileges."

Estep interjected, "What kind of privileges?"

Here we go, thought Serena.

"I have certain requirements," he said.

"Dare I even ask what those are?" asked Serena.

"I want specific reading material."

"I don't want to hear more about his, will you help me or not?" Serena attempted to get the conversation back to a productive place.

"You don't even know what I want," said Paul.

"I don't want to hear about your tastes," said Serena.

"Why not? You probably like the same thing I do," said Paul.

"OK, that's enough!" snapped Estep.

"What did I say wrong? I want to read the classics, like Watership Down and Les Miserable. All I get here is contemporary drivel, unless I read digital books on the SM Channel. I want a real book in my hands, one that smells like library dust and mildew. I would have thought you to be a bird of a feather, Ms. Wilcox."

"Ah, yes, sure." Serena breathed a sigh of relief. "I'll get your books. Now please help me, we are wasting time." That was twice now that she had assumed that a criminal was talking about something perverse when they weren't. Not that she wanted to let her guard down, but she was relieved that her investigation hadn't taken that kind of a turn.

"I need more than the books."

"Quick, tell me everything you want." Serena put her hands together and squeezed them as hard as she could. She had a sudden urge to punch something.

"I want visits from Vanessa," he said.

"Eew, there it is! I won't help with that." She released the grip she had on her hands and shook them wildly, like a little girl might do upon seeing a spider.

"I don't mean conjugal visits! I just enjoy talking with her."

"We can do that," Lehman confirmed.

"And one more thing," Paul said mysteriously.

"What? Come on, Paul, we don't have much time!" Serena's voice took on a whiny quality that even her own ears didn't appreciate.

"Stay in touch. You need something, you call me. It's mind-blowing what I can find out from here," he said.

"We don't have time for this!" Estep bellowed.

"All right. I'll consider talking to Victor. But I'll do you one better. I'll tell you what I know. I was waiting until I could talk directly with you, Ms. Serena. Send everyone else out of there."

"This place, and actually yours as well I'm guessing, is wired. I can't give you privacy even if I wanted to," she said.

"OK then, at least I have your own ears listening to me directly."

Serena wasn't sure what he meant by this- her undivided attention maybe- but she didn't much care what he meant as long as he finally told her whatever it is he knew. "Yes, you do. Please, Paul, Nicholas is giving me the 2 minute warning."

"FYD is linked with big oil. They want Kinji taken down – out – they want her dead." Now that he finally had something important to say Paul was speaking quickly, so fast that Serena had to strain to catch what he was saying.

"Who does? What else do you know? When? Where?" Serena threw all the questions out of her mouth as fast as she could.

"It's going down at the Global Oil Initiative."

"Anything you know – tell me, please!" As Serena ended her plea she heard Estep start to add something of his own. She spun around to face him and put a finger to her lips. The last thing they needed was for him to interrupt.

"Multiple nations are involved. Kinji won't cooperate with their agenda, but they know someone who will. They want her out, and the VP in."

"Paul, that can't be right. You must have seen President Kinji's announcement today, addressing the nation about Morgan's death." Serena's shoulders slumped in resignation, another dead end.

Paul spoke rapidly, as if not taking any time out to breathe. "Exactly. They took him out. His ex-wife was simply a ready volunteer to pull the trigger, don't waste your time on her. Lita knows insider information, but her interest was personal. Her sister's death, her love triangle-gone-wrong, yadda yadda yadda. Wrong tree. You want to look at who is replacing Morgan."

Serena asked, "They planned to take Morgan out all along?"

"No, not all along, only when he got cold feet and became a liability."

"And his replacement?" Estep jumped in, despite Serena's reproachful eyes.

Nicholas interrupted. "Thirty seconds, that's all I can do!"

"Quick—anything else?" Serena squealed.

"They already bought the person they want as VP, but I don't know who it is. That's all I know, for real this time," said Paul.

"20 seconds!" Nicholas yelled.

"You'll talk to Victor?" asked Serena, trying to use her remaining seconds to nail down what she wanted in the first place.

"My books, Vanessa, and you, my dear?"

"Yes, yes, and maybe."

"Maybe doesn't get you Victor." Paul adopted a British accent for no apparent reason.

"10 seconds!" Nicholas made a frantic wrap-it-up hand gesture.

"Yes," Serena blurted out.

"You'll call?" Paul verified in his natural voice.

"Yes, yes! Victor?" Serena was down to the wire now.

"Will do," said Paul at the last possible second.

Nicholas disconnected the signal. "Whew, that was close."

Serena exhaled with a prolonged sigh. "Talking to him stomped on my every last nerve, but wow, did he give us an earful!"

Lehman shook his head. "I'm not convinced that there is any

validity to what Paul was saying. The office of vice-president won't be filled until President Kinji nominates a successor, and that person will only take office if approved by a majority vote in both houses of Congress."

"What if they already know who President Kinji would choose? Wouldn't that be something that insiders would know?" asked Serena.

"And they have paid off both the House and Senate? You're proposing a conspiracy that runs so deep and wide that it's taken over most of the United States government," said Beav. "Not that I'm saying it couldn't happen, just saying it's quite a tale. I'm afraid Lehman could be right. Paul gave us bupkis."

They sat in collective silence, each of them letting their eyes wander about the room. The Superman lab was a beauty, to the extent that machines could be beautiful. While they admired the gleaming technology, Lehman jumped as if zapped by static electricity. He walked to the nearest station and brought up one of his favorite database sites. He pointed a finger at Serena and gestured for her to come closer.

Serena looked over his shoulder to see the screen. "What am I looking at?"

"I spoke too soon. I did a quick search of a media line archive feed. And look at what's popped up; fifteen results." Lehman turned around to face everyone.

"Results for what?" asked Beav.

Lehman summarized what he found. "President Kinji was quoted regarding the office of the vice presidency. She has been fairly open in the past about her displeasure that Morgan Canon was pushed on her as a vice presidential candidate. When pressed for who she preferred to have as a vice president she gave an honest answer-- Carson Landon-- and this was as recently as two weeks ago."

Beav wasn't convinced. "Even so, nothing will be resolved by the time of the GOB initiative that has been rescheduled to meet in about fourteen hours from now."

Nicholas suddenly appeared at Lehman's side. His eyes were wide open, which was the most expressive emotion any of them had seen the mild-mannered Nicholas display. "I don't know how this happened, but someone is asking for you from Paul's connection, and it isn't Paul."

"Asking for who? Me?" asked Serena.

"Yes, she wants to talk to you." Nicholas scurried back to his station with everyone close at his heels.

Serena bent over the desk and spoke directly into the microphone source, even though the sensitivity of the technology made such a move unnecessary. "Hello?"

"It's me, Lita." Her text message flitted across the screen. The text-to-audio function was locked.

"Lita! How did you get this connection?" Serena continued to use the microphone, on speaker mode so that the team could jump in at any time.

"Paul and I have a mutual acquaintance on his cell block who has been eavesdropping on Paul's conversations. He gave me Paul's security codes."

"How did he get those? He wouldn't have gotten them from eavesdropping," Lehman asked.

"He heard the audio tones, memorized the code. He passed a message along through my mother that Paul had you in his digi watch and that this line is secure."

"Vanessa has been to see Paul already?" Serena was amazed. They had reached that deal only seconds ago.

"No, she was there to see our mutual friend. I promised him I wouldn't tell you who he is. Let's get off of this. I am contacting you because I know some things. I hated Morgan, that's no secret, and I have no regrets – I'd do the same all over again."

"But?" Serena prompted. She had absolutely no idea where this was going. The surprise turn in the case had her adrenaline pumping – oh how she loved a mystery!

"But I do regret that I helped them."

"Them?" Serena could hardly wait for the answer, and she thought she knew what it was: Paul was right about all of it; everything he said was the truth.

"Morgan wasn't their choice to be president and I got rid of him for them. President Kinji isn't their choice either. You get what I'm saying."

"Yes, I follow you," said Serena.

"They talked to me through the SM Channel. They said no one could see what we were saying, but we could find each other if we knew our handles. And I want you to have them. I only have two of them, but that's all you need to find them."

"Why are you helping us, Lita?" asked Serena.

"Because they killed my sister, and they'll get me next."

Beav entered the conversation for the first time. "We'll get them before they get you, or the president. Give us the handles."

"I can trust all of the people in the room with you? Never mind, I have no choice. This is what you need. 45671 and 23987."

"She's disconnected the call." Nicholas immediately pulled up a chair alongside Lehman. "Let me help you find them."

Lehman and Nicholas spent the next half hour sifting through the dozens of secret conversations found in the hidden world inside the SM Channel. Beav and Serena followed along on the big monitor. "Stop!" said Beav. "Right there! Look!"

And there it was, a conversation between the two handles 45671 and 23987, dialog that had been logged only twenty minutes before Paul Tracy spoke to them, a conversation he obviously saw with his own eyes because he quoted from it. These messages were in text form, audio files unavailable.

45671: "It's going down at the Global Oil Initiative."

23987: "I want assurances."

45671: "I can't do that. I've been told she'll name me as the VP selection at GOB. I can't verify it."

23987: "We need you in."

45671: "I know that."

23987: "We're down to a year. She won't be out of office before the agreement, she needs to be taken out."

45671: "I know, you've made yourself clear. I told you, I'm working on it."

23987: "The last guy we tapped got cold feet, and now his toes are tagged."

45671: "Don't threaten me."

23987: "I'm not. I'm telling you what will happen if you don't hold up your end of our arrangement."

45671: "I have no intention of backing out. I stand to benefit just as much as you do."

23987: "Good to know."

45671: "She contacted me right away. I don't think Morgan's body was even cold yet. No one will be surprised, she talked to the media about me a couple of weeks ago. All looks good."

23987: "Then what's the problem?"

45671: "I'm saying I can't guarantee it. She could change her mind last minute. I've done my part."

23987: "There's no one else she's even mentioned as a VP choice, no one but you."

45671: "Even so, I'm saying I can't guarantee it. I can only say that it looks like a done deal. She's announcing at the press conference at GOB."

23987: "That would be immediately following the initiative then."

45671: "I assume."

23987: "All interested parties will be at GOB."

45671: "I know that."

23987: "They expect to see you."

45671: "I'll be there."

23987: "In person meets are discouraged obviously, but they'll be watching you."

45671: "What are you telling me?"

23987: "Look sharp."

45671: "You contacted me. I told you all I know. What are you saying?"

23987: "Some don't trust you. Watch your back."

45671: "I told you that I'm on board. I've done all that you have asked. Are you telling me that they might kill me anyway?"

23987: "That's what I'm telling you."

45671: "I don't know what more I can do to gain their trust."

23987: "Turn up, be ready to give assurances."

45671: "I said I'd be there."

That was the last message transmitted. Serena said, "That leaves little doubt about what's going on."

"The good news is that it doesn't look like President Kinji is in immediate danger," said Lehman.

"The bad news is that multiple parties want her dead and we can't get to all of them. We're talking about entire nations declaring the assassination of our president," said Beav.

"We can start by making sure their guy doesn't make it to the office of the vice presidency," said Serena.

"We can flip him. He knows they might kill him, it would be easy." Estep's voice was difficult to hear because he was talking while moving around the room.

Lehman shot that idea down before it could take root. "Too risky, we can't trust him. He can't be allowed to work alongside President Kinji. We get him out, put someone we trust in. Keep President Kinji under heavy security at all times. That's the best we can do."

Serena nodded. "Agreed. After all, President Kinji lives with the threat of assassination every day. At least the GOB conspirators will suffer a setback when their puppet isn't selected."

"It will be satisfying to knock them off course for at least a little while." Estep wandered back to the station where the others were still gathered.

Serena raised her voice an octave and spoke in a teasing, sing-song rhythm that she used on her kids when she got them to do what she wanted. "If only we knew of someone to nominate for the office of the vice presidency, someone President Ann Kinji trusts with her most critical situations, trusts enough to pull out of retirement. Someone with a clean record free of scandal. Someone who is perhaps standing right in front of me."

Beav added, "Someone who is wearing a blue shirt."

"Oh no, no, no, no. Don't look at me," said Lehman. "She needs a governor or politician."

"That didn't work out so well, did it?" Serena reminded him. "She needs to look outside of the old boys' club."

"I'm going back to 'Bama." Lehman physically walked away, adding emphasis to his statement.

"Sure you are, to fetch your wife and pack your bags." Beav called out to Lehman's disappearing form, "Come on, you know you're going to do it!"

26

Lita was being held in a secured location near The Cube. Serena was thankful for the lapse in judgment that had allowed Lita to keep her digi pen. Thanks to this oversight, they now had the key information they needed. However, Serena knew that she would still benefit from talking to Victor, which is why she was headed for the prison for the criminally insane. Victor had already been returned there, deposited in his old cell.

There was no need for all of them to talk to Victor; Lehman and Estep stayed behind in the Superman lab. Lehman continued slugging though the SM Channel logs with Nicholas while Estep kept an eye out for anything suspicious, when he wasn't going on food runs or nodding off in a chair. Time was also moving sluggishly for Beav and Serena who were on a short flight on a private plane – car travel was too much of a time-waster this close to the GOB initiative. Beav slept during their flight while Serena used the time to reflect on everything that had happened over the past few days.

How they had managed to keep everything quiet she didn't know, but the bomb scare in The Cube would, against all odds, remain a heavily guarded secret until after the GOB initiative. After that, every second of that harrowing ordeal would be analyzed. Serena could already think of something off the top of her head that would be a huge issue during the investigation: why hadn't they cleared the room before Beav diffused the bomb? At the very least, President Kinji should have been whisked away. Ah, a problem for a different day, she thought.

In Serena's mind Operation Covert Coffee was wrapping up. Between whatever she would glean from Victor and whatever Lehman pulled off the computer (if anything), loose ends would be tied up within an hour or two. At that point, all that would remain would be the clean-up; explaining (some of, but never all of) what happened to the media and investigators, staying vigilant because the president's enemies were still too numerous to get rid of them all, keeping Carson Landon on their watch list and, while on the subject of vice presidential candidates, making sure that Lehman was the new VP.

Serena had helped find the biggest immediate threat to President Kinji, had flushed out several links in the conspiracy chain, and overall felt she had finished what she was hired, off record, to do. Soon all of the former agents and her own rouge self would be off payroll, and denied any further access to The Cube. Serena was more than ready! This was the longest she had ever been away from her kids. If she thought about that too long she knew that the tears would start flowing and she wouldn't be able to regain control of herself. Fortunately the plane touched down before her thoughts consumed her.

Serena learned that the FBI and Homeland Security had each had their go at Victor before their plane was even in the air, but Victor was talking to no one. She had a good feeling that she would be able to break his silence: Surely Paul had been effective in coaching Victor to trust her. She was banking on it.

Victor rose to greet Serena and Beav when they entered the room, causing three security guards to flinch. He sat back down. "We meet again," he said.

"Yes, under less stressful circumstances," said Serena. "I assume that Paul Tracy spoke to you on my behalf?"

"Yes he did."

"And you trust me?" asked Serena.

"I lack the ability to read social cues," he said.

Serena and Beav sat patiently, waiting for Victor to elaborate. Nearly sixty seconds dragged on before Serena gave up. "Are you willing to talk to me?"

"Yes, that's what I was implying. I failed to read social cues correctly and I erroneously aligned myself with the wrong side. My perception has 20/20 vision now due to the corrective lens gifted to me by Paul Tracy."

"You won't regret talking with me. I do have the best interests of this nation at heart," said Serena.

"I understand."

There was another awkward pause, in which Serena and Beav studied Victor. He was nothing like the garish portrayal that Erik's clown suit had given them, and yet, they could already understand why Erik was provoked to dish out such a mean-spirited parody. Anyone hoping to manipulate Victor into doing whatever they wanted would become frustrated. He had his own rigid set of rules that may or may not allow him to do whatever it was they wanted of him. Serena perceived that Erik had enjoyed the nasty impersonation of Victor because he had pushed his patience to the brink, and then over the edge. Talking with Paul Tracy was a delightful experience compared to the work required to get anything out of Victor. Serena was grateful that Agent Estep wasn't with them.

"What can you tell us about the work you were doing?" asked Serena.

"I can tell you everything." Victor sat across from them, arms hanging limply at his sides, his body slightly hunched over, his eyes cast downward. Eye contact was fleeting at best, at worst he studied the surface of the table in front of him as if he had forgotten that anyone else was in the room.

Serena and Beav waited. They looked at each other. Beav shrugged. They waited a few more seconds. Serena said, "Please tell us everything now."

"I agree to that. You will write everything down?" asked Victor.

"Everything you say is being recorded by the cameras in this room," said Beav.

"Technology can fail," said Victor simply.

"I will take notes," said Beav. He signaled to one of the guards who left the room briefly and returned with a notepad and a pencil that was as rounded as a preschooler's first writing instrument. No sharp instruments allowed, not even in the interrogation rooms.

"Shall we begin?" asked Serena.

"We shall," said Victor. "Do you want me to start at the beginning?"

"Yes, please do," said Serena. She willed herself to appear unhurried, completely patient, Zen-like. She hoped they got everything they could out of Victor before she lost it.

"We teamed up over mutual hatred, Lita and me, but that's not the beginning, that's the ending. The beginning is what you want."

"Yes, please continue." Serena smiled sweetly.

"In the beginning I was a scientist. I was doing a good job, and one day there was a problem. I knew that there was fraud. They were taking my findings and recording the data differently from the truth. I knew I had to stop them, and I did. Then I had to face trial for what I had done and I went here. I met Paul Tracy and Vanessa. They were my friends. Vanessa told the FYD that I would do what they wanted. She was helping me get out of here."

"That's when Morgan Canon and Erik Chapman were visiting her?" Serena wanted to clarify every point that cross-referenced testimony they already had.

"Yes. Morgan is dead."

"That's right. He was killed by Lita."

"That's what Lita wanted. I wanted it too."

"Why did you want Morgan dead?" Serena opened a door that she hoped would lead them toward something useful, but she risked falling down a rabbit hole. Fortunately Victor wasn't one to grandstand pointlessly as Paul was so fond of doing, so wherever he was taking them, he would get them there fast.

"I hated him because he lied to me. I created the crack in the SM Channel as he requested. He told me that the hidden room in the

Channel was for the purpose of discussing top secret research in the area of mind control, the very area he knew I had been assigned to before I was arrested and put on trial. He deceived me."

"What was the crack really used for?" asked Beav.

"It was a water cooler for liars and cheats. They spun their webs of deceit in the safe place I myself created for them, to make a mockery of science for their own gain. They were gathering data to manipulate it. What they couldn't alter they buried. Who they couldn't bribe, they threatened. They bought and bullied their way to the very top. They told me that they had President Ann Kinji on their side, but I understand now that they lied to me about that. President Kinji was never involved, and I see that now. Paul Tracy showed me how they are plotting against her. It went as high up as Morgan Canon, and now they want to replace him with another they can control."

"I think we can head that off, but we need as much information from you as possible. What can you tell me about who they are? What kind of research are they most interested in?" asked Serena.

"They have an interest in genetically engineered foods. The interest is of course financial, with a complete and utter disregard for science or ethics. I suppose you have an opinion about genetically engineered foods?"

Serena was caught off guard. She studied Victor's expression, which was difficult because his face was unnaturally blank. She tried to guess what a mind like his would want to hear. "I don't know what opinion I should have. I don't have the research to look at."

Victor appeared quite satisfied by her answer. He launched into a quote: " 'Science is built up of facts, as a house is built of stones;

but an accumulation of facts is no more science than a heap of stones a house.' Jules-Henri Poincare, who died in 1912, before you were born."

"Yes, before I was born. And you as well." Serena felt like she had fallen down a rabbit hole that had many more holes left inside it to fall through.

"The ingestion of genetically engineered food is not harmless, the genetically engineered materials are neither completely destroyed by stomach acids nor is this material prevented from reaching the bloodstream. Blood cells are also affected, as the body is incapable of preventing access. Toxins are in the food, toxins are then in the human body, including carcinogens. We cannot alter the foods without altering the human body. New proteins produced in genetically engineered foods are capable of acting as toxins or allergens in and of themselves, not to mention altering the nutritional value of the food through mutations. You mentioned research. Of course we don't have research, not of the long-term sort. Genetically engineered foods have flooded the market and continue to do so in great numbers, all without any hard data on its effect on humans. I am dumbing this down for you the best that I can."

"I appreciate that," said Serena.

"The GE projects dovetail the mind control projects. You see, when food is genetically altered and allowed to cause mutation in the human body, the concept of human DNA is now open to manipulation, interpretation, redefinition, recreation. Ethically, there are concerns, quite naturally, if one were to follow through with that line of thinking. 'Science without religion is lame, religion without science is blind.' Albert Einstein."

"You believe that genetically engineered foods are unethical and you voiced objection?" Serena ventured to guess. Usually she was quick to get into someone's head but Victor's mind was slippery.

"No, not at all. I haven't reached a conclusion yet. However, I object to motivation for advancement in research being greed. Large corporations stand to gain significantly, as do governments, both foreign and domestic. Gone is the scientist. Gone is the truth. Here is the false data. Here is the lottery ticket."

"I understand what you are saying. And at this point you said you wanted to stop helping them?" Serena tried to steer the conversation toward a resolution, if there was one.

"No. I was promised I would have access to my old research and I would even be given research privileges to continue with my work."

"Your work with the mind control project?"

"Yes. The two areas had become connected, and there were hungry parties bearing down on me to have my data. I knew this, and yet I believed that the end justified the means. My work in mind control was to be a contribution to science like no other. I was of the delusion that I could prevent nations, corporations and individuals from altering human DNA against one's will by getting my hands on the science first. One step ahead of evil, one step ahead of corruption. I am a protector of science and a preserver of that which is human. I have sworn an oath."

"An oath? Are you a part of an organization?" Beav asked.

Victor looked at him uncomprehendingly.

"Did you swear an oath literally?" Beav tried again.

"I swore an oath of my own."

"Like a superhero might do?" Serena was pleased with herself for intuiting at least a little bit about what made Victor tick.

"Yes! A person of science is held to a self-standard. 'You cannot hope to build a better world without improving the individuals. To that end each of us must work for his own improvement, and at the same time share a general responsibility for all humanity, our particular duty being to aid those to whom we think we can be most useful.'"

"Marie Curie!" Serena had a Marie Curie T-shirt, a side note she doubted would impress Victor.

"Well done. I hold myself accountable, being tasked with a mind that can delve into the mysterious unknown quicker and with greater grasp than this present generation. I am charged with a responsibility, a heavy weight, to protect and serve mankind." Victor's hair fell loosely about his forehead and was now dangling over his left eye. He didn't seem to notice.

"And you believe that by discovering the secrets you can then find a way to protect mankind from harm?" Serena was distracted by the hair over Victor's eye. Didn't that bother him? She resisted the temptation to reach over and push the hair away from his face, knowing that touching him would be a very bad idea.

"Yes, you understand me exactly."

"Please explain how your research led to the situation you find yourself in now," said Beav. He intended to let Serena lead, but this question was too pressing to keep to himself.

"Are you familiar with Synthia, the first so-called artificial life form created by Craig Venter, a billionaire entrepreneur? That was back when the field of 'synthetic biology' was in its infancy. NASA's researchers warned of hackers with the ability to engineer viruses or bacteria to control human minds, with genetic engineering the next frontier of computing. And indeed we are seeing the beginnings of such mayhem. To quote Hessel, 'I advocate that cells are living computers and DNA is a programming language.' He went so far as to say 'I want to see life programmed and used to solve global challenges so that humanity can achieve a sustainable relationship within the biosphere.' The danger of course is that 'viruses and bacteria send chemicals into human brains and could be used to influence, or even 'control' their host.' Fast forward a few short years, and we've arrived. We are already doing this, doing it as we speak."

Victor paused to take a sip of water which had been recently set before him via a plastic cup. Then he resumed, his pitch reflecting no emotion, but his eyes finally showing signs of life.

"Synthetic biology led to new forms of bioterrorism, already in the works as you probably heard about. A simple vaccine could do the trick, and there's our mind control, all ripe for bio-terrorism, a plot discovered only a week or so ago in fact—effectively prevented, but you see how narrow the escape was. As the technology advances, one day the hackers-of-the-mind will succeed. The body itself, our very own DNA, is not the next generation computer, but the computer of today, right now. Trust me, we are already there, and have been close for the past decade. Forget drones and global listening devices, we are getting literally inside people's heads. Let me make myself clear: we are already doing this."

"It's a lot to take in. And honestly, you're scaring me. I don't think I'll sleep for a week." Serena meant it. She wished she could take back the past few minutes of her life and not hear any of what he just said.

"Awareness is key."

"I'm not sure we need to know any more details about your research, only how it relates to the multiple conspiracies we are dealing with, and any information you can give us that can protect the president," said Beav, again attempting to zero in on what they needed to know.

"I laid down the foundation for that. You see, the mind control project is funded by the genetic engineering project and vice versa. The two are entwined and benefit much of the same people. The deal on the table with GOB is what they are protecting. Global Oil Bank has packaged a world-wide initiative to aid developing nations in the technologies to end world hunger and the conservation of resources. Naturally we look to big oil with this situation, as well as the nations who export the most oil. All fingers are in the pie. If you look to the lobbyists who have the most influence, you'll see that all of them have a stake in what's happening with GOB. Corn, food of any kind, it's all in line to profit. Food industry and oil industry have combined forces and are unbeatable. They have become so power hungry that they will take down the presidency to guarantee that they will get their initiative. And no one cares that their dabbling with genetics indirectly via our food supply will eventually render us into something not quite human, at least not composed of the human DNA we know today. Not to mention the ramifications of deliberately and directly altered DNA via vaccines or other vessels for the purpose of mind control or information retrieval."

"This sounds horrific and hopeless!" Serena wailed.

"No, not hopeless. Without much hope is more accurate. My appearance in President Kinji's office with a threat to detonate a bomb was my attempt to pre-empt the situation. I thought Kinji herself had been bought. I planned to disrupt the GOB and send the nation into chaos. I understand now that I was wrong about Kinji, and that my plan had no guarantee of serving as a large enough disruption to throw the GOB off track. However, I do have a better plan now that I know the truth."

"What plan is this?" asked Beav.

"Spy on the crack in the SM Channel. They don't know you can see in," said Victor. "With me out of the way, they will assume that they have use of it indefinitely."

"Already doing that, yes," said Serena.

"Good. Here is the heart of my plan. Promise me you will carry it through, deliver it to President Kinji."

"I can try." Serena nodded.

"It's critical for the future of mankind. Surely you can do better. While I was prepared to die for this cause, you can't be troubled to pass along a message?"

"I'll pass along your message. Please go on," said Serena.

"I have your word?"

"You have my word." Serena extended her hand for Victor to shake it, but he only looked at the hand. She let her arm drop.

"Listen carefully. Set up a body of ethical scientists as a watchdog over GOB. I know that there are pre-existing task forces and ethics-in-science organizations, but we need something new, something powerful, something now! Put the spotlight on GOB, expose them to the light! Get the media on it! Get everyone on it! Expose the crack in the SM Channel and let the entire world see their lie!" Victor suddenly showed emotion, and he almost moved his body. But this spark, this rare connection, was to be short lived.

"Excellent! I definitely agree. Do you have any names you can suggest? Any colleagues?" Serena asked.

"Why Albert of course, and Marie Curie. Females have brought a new voice to the field…"

"You do know that Albert Einstein and Marie Curie are long dead, right?" asked Serena, not sure she wanted to know the answer.

"Of course, of course," Victor muttered. He looked dazed for a few seconds and then he started writing numbers in the air with his index finger. He got up and shuffled about the room, mumbling to himself and writing in the air. The guards watched him closely but didn't interfere.

"We'll let ourselves out," said Serena.

Victor didn't acknowledge that she said anything.

"Wait, wait!" Serena doubled back to the table. "Victor, please focus! Do you hear me? Victor? Victor?"

Victor halted his steps but continued to mumble and draw numbers.

"Please, Victor. I thought of something. What do you know about The Supporters? They are a group of mathematicians. They seem to be on our side. What do you think of them? Victor?"

Victor seemed to snap back to reality as if he had never left it. He waltzed back to his chair, sat down and said, "Oh yes, I know them. The Supporters would make a fine watchdog group. They have been doing so on a volunteer basis without any real resources. They would appreciate a call, yes."

"Do you know how I can get in touch with them?" asked Serena.

"Use the word Supporters in any conversation in the crack in the SM Channel. Best to drop the name twice so they know you didn't mention them inadvertently."

"Then they'll tell us where to find them?"

"No. They'll find you."

27

"It's time to face the nation," said President Ann Kinji. "I have a lot of explaining to do, but I'll let my gifted people do all of that background. What I need to do is reassure America that I'm still effectively leading this country, all while also telling them that I've lost control of the presidency."

"Were you ever really in control of the presidency? Has anyone been?" asked Serena. "I'm not being facetious. You aren't Queen Kinji or Madam Dictator Kinji. Last I knew, this was still America and you are but one person in a body of government. Throughout history American presidents have had strained relationships with their government family. This is nothing new, and that's what you need to tell yourself."

"No American president has ever had this situation."

"I imagine the Civil War days were dicey. President Ann, I know it feels unprecedented, but is anything on this Earth ever really 'new'?"

"I hear what you are saying. So what did past presidents do?"

Serena strode swiftly across the room to her dear friend and President of the United States and gave her a strong bear hug; one squeeze and a quick release. "They gave American people hope for the future." Serena dug her digi pen out of her purse and began scribbling away.

"What are you doing?"

"I'm looking up a quote. And I found it already!" She selected speaker mode on the digi and a female voice said, "President Abraham Lincoln, July 28, 1862, 'I shall not do more than I can, and I shall do all I can to save the government, which is my sworn duty as well as my personal inclination. I shall do nothing in malice.' See? You aren't the only president to feel that government needed saving. And yet here we are, you and me, standing on top of the presidential seal."

"I don't suppose I can plagiarize what the American greats have said?"

"You'll figure it out. It wouldn't hurt to mention the name of God."

"Religion and politics don't mix."

"Religion and politics are always conjoined. Trying to separate the two gives us a fractured nation; one half without a heart and the other without a brain."

Ann laughed. "Well I certainly can't say that!"

"I look forward to hearing your speech. I'm so honored when you bounce things off of me, but you never need anyone's help as far as I can see."

"You don't follow politics and you haven't stayed current with government issues."

"Ouch."

"I like the fresh perspective. If I were to strip away the insular world of The Cube, what would the United States look like?" Ann opened her arms in sweeping gesture.

"I'm an independent and an idealist. Everyone has their bias."

"Independent thinking and idealism – we need more of that. You help me a great deal." President Kinji held the door open for Serena, the only cue that their conversation was over.

Serena squeezed her arm as she walked past the door. "God bless you."

Ann's expression softened and, to her own surprise, her eyes misted.

As Serena was escorted down the long corridor by two agents she called over her shoulder, "His name means something, doesn't it?"

Ann waved and closed her door. In two hours she would be addressing the nation. Her speech would make history books, one way or another. This was one of those rare open windows in time, in which one person's voice held the attention of the entire world. What would she do with that power, that awesome responsibility? Thoughts tumbled inside her mind, none of them productive or fruitful. She couldn't grasp hold of anything that felt right. She bit the tops off of three erasers before she was aware of what she was doing. Not knowing what to do, she found herself praying.

It wasn't a complicated prayer, just a general shout-out thought: "Please God, show me what to do." Then she immediately felt so sleepy that she could barely keep her eyes open. She lie down on the lounger near the mammoth SM Channel screen and instantly fell asleep. She woke only ten minutes later feeling refreshed and inspired. She spent the next fifteen minutes writing the speech of a lifetime. Ahead of schedule, she even had time to peel and eat an orange before her staff notified her that it was time to go.

At the podium, President Kinji commanded respect. Her eyes reflected unmistakable intelligence, her stance projected confidence. Her natural beauty and humor were the scale-tipping ingredients that won America's hearts. They hung on every word she said because she was a celebrity, but today they listened to her for reasons beyond her charisma and popular appeal; today they needed her to be their president.

"Dear Americans, what an earful you have had! I'm so sorry for the hand we've been dealt. The loss of a vice president is bad enough, but the conspiracy surrounding his death is a terrible blow. I'm pleased that my appointee has been warmly accepted, and I'd love to discuss him further, but today I have other things to talk about.

I need to talk to you about ideas that go beyond policy and governing. Before I get into that, let me bring you back to a time when policy and governing was the gut reaction to a dark time in not-so-distant American history when there was a spree of massacres. The horror of such events led lawmakers to create new legislation that would arm all active duty military personnel while off duty; they were, in fact required to take an oath similar to that of a medical doctor. If the public was threatened by violence, they must act.

The logic was that our military had the training to respond

quickly to violent situations in public places, much like the role of an air marshal on an airplane. It was also said that our military is to protect not only our interests abroad, but must protect us here at home as well. And this logic did indeed hold up. The incidence of massacre when down to, well, near zero. Even plans to commit such a horrific act of violence seemed to be statistically low. So the reaction was a success, no?

No. Unfortunately, you may recall that following the lull in violent acts there was an extreme uptick in murder-suicides in private homes, where of course no armed member of the armed forces was protecting citizens. The hatred, madness and despair simply diverted itself to places where no one could stop them. There was even a coordinated effort for multiple murder-suicides to transpire on the same date, effectively creating private mass murder events that rivaled the numbers of victims from all the previous public massacres combined!

It was only when churches stepped forward and offered free counseling, when schools addressed bullying and other related issues, and when American citizens banded together that the violence began to subside. I don't know how much credit to give the publishing and entertainment industry for policing themselves, and the American public for the reversal of the popularity of violent media, as well as other hard-to-quantify social factors. I know that the picture is complex, and that I would be naïve if I thought I could summarize this in a few moments of musing.

But my point is that policy didn't improve the bleak situation. Policy didn't prevent murderous hearts from festering, sated only after spilling the blood of their fellow citizens. While it's difficult to understand all the pieces of the puzzle, what we can clearly see is that it was the American people themselves who turned things around. Think of the many stories of heroism following the tragedies, think of the stories of strangers helping strangers for months – even years—after the tragedies, think of the kindness of ordinary citizens as they found one simple way they could make a difference.

We have a very recent example of American ingenuity and kindness coming together to make a difference. I was overwhelmed when you dedicated my beautiful garden sanctuary to me, the ribbon cutting ceremony will remain one of my most cherished memories. And best of all, when I challenged you to ride that momentum of generosity and apply it to Americans who need it, The New America Foundation was created. In addition, citizens acted independently to help and serve America's neediest towns and cities.

During those wonderful occasions our differences were set aside and we were truly as one nation, although simmering underneath we were still a polarized country. Never fully leaving our awareness was the unfortunate truth that we remain a divided nation. And yet, this is nothing new. A friend of mine reminded me of an American president who governed our nation way before my time. What nation could be more divided than a country actively engaged in Civil War?

Yes, I'm talking about Abraham Lincoln, a president quoted so often that it's become cliché. And yet, I feel a kinship with this icon, this man we know only through history books. Lincoln said something that I really took to heart. What I just mentioned earlier, about how the American people turned things around by their own initiative, was also a hint at something else the American people tapped into: Goodness. And that's where my Lincoln quotes come in.

Now keep in mind that I am using these quotes out of context to make my own point. I encourage you to do your own study of Lincoln if you wish for these quotations to remain in their original intent and context. However, having said that, I hope that I am correct in believing that Lincoln would give me his blessing to use his words today.

July 31, 1846: 'That I am not a member of any Christian Church, is true; but I have never denied the truth of the Scriptures; and I have never spoken with intentional disrespect of religion in general, or of any denomination of Christians in particular.'

January 2, 1863: 'But I must add that the U.S. government must not, as by this order, undertake to run the churches. When an individual, in a church or out of it, becomes dangerous to the public interest, he must be checked; but let the churches, as such take care of themselves.'

August 26, 1863: 'Let us diligently apply the means, never doubting that a just God, in his own good time, will give us the rightful result.'

And finally, on October 24, 1863: 'Nevertheless, amid the greatest difficulties of my Administration, when I could not see any other resort, I would place my whole reliance on God, knowing that all would go well, and that He would decide for the right.'

Abraham Lincoln's words give me assurance that my response to our current state of confusion and mistrust is on the right path. It is not my intention to disrespect any religion, belief, or freedom to reject religion. It is also not my intention to lead churches. However, like Lincoln, I too wish to defer to a Higher Power.

There are times of darkness that logic alone cannot address, when policy and governing have limitations. While I am at risk of offending you, may I suggest that you equate God with Love? What a beautiful world it would be if we were all in agreement that kindness makes a difference; that government can't fix all the things that are broken, things like the human heart. But you, my dear Americans, you have this power within you. If you are a praying person, please pray for our nation.

If you are offended by the very notion of prayer, please respect the freedom of others to pray, for prayer is a petition for help. Do not mix religion and politics. If I will agree to be a leader who stays out of church affairs, may I ask that you agree to stay out of the rights and freedoms of others to worship as they choose?

Stop fighting each other. Let statues stand, let people pray, let flags fly. Agree that Love is more important than settling who is right. When I close with my final words, may you hear them not with contempt or division in your heart, but with the goodness I wish for you; to be well, stay safe, fill your heart with hope, and love one another.

And these, my final words: God Bless America."

28

"Lehman, predictably, accepted President Kinji's Vice Presidential appointment, so we are on our own," said Beav.

"They'll never vote him in," said Estep.

Serena smirked. "Au Contraire! They've already agreed. Kinji mentioned that if anyone refused to sign off on the appointment, he or she would have to give her a plausible reason for why Lehman is not suited for the office-- or else she would explore their reason for bias; dig into their affiliations with lobbyists for example."

"Which means, like I said, we are on our own," said Beav.

Estep said, "I'm not in the loop. Isn't Operation Covert Coffee a completed mission? I've been reassigned to something else."

Serena filled him in. "We are wrapping things up, yes, but we need to get a few loose ends tied up. Obviously we can't hunt down every person who wants Kinji out of office, that would be a long list. Nor should we seal the crack. As you know, Operation Dumbo has begun." She noticed Estep's bewildered look. "Dumbo was the flying elephant with the big ears in the classic Disney film. Don't look at me, I didn't name it. Anyway, they have a team who is listening in on the crack in the SM Channel."

"Yes, I know. I wasn't assigned to the team because I was told I was still needed by you," said Estep, not without a dramatically resentful tone in his voice.

Serena ignored his theatrics. "We need to find the Supporters."

"Rather, we need to meet them. It seems they've seen our flare," said Beav. He pulled up the message for the three of them to examine together.

"It says for Serena to come alone, with no ears, not even a digi pen. I don't like it," said Estep.

"I have an idea," said Serena. "What if I wore a digi watch like Paul has? It's not common knowledge that prisoners have these, and they aren't available outside the prison population."

"That could work," said Beav.

"Unless they know someone in prison," said Estep.

"They'll scan me for bugs. The watch won't set anything off. If they don't know it's a digi I will pass their screen. You really think the odds are high that they know about the watch?" said Serena.

"No, I think it's a good risk. We can't send you in there with nothing," said Estep.

"Why won't they approve of me going with you? I already met with one of them once in Germany," said Beav.

"I don't know, but they said no and I think we should do what they want," said Serena. "They are on our side, remember? Beav said they are an organization of MENSA people, mathematicians mainly."

"Smart genius types have never been deranged and violent?" said Estep

"I don't think this group is something to fear," said Beav.

"Agreed, I have a good feeling about this," said Serena.

"We better get moving," said Estep. He signaled to his team via an old school radio cuff. "Bluebird is on the move."

"Bluebird?" asked Serena.

"You," said Estep. "You're my new assignment. Operation Bluebird."

Beav's laugh began as a snorting sound and developed into an all-out guffaw.

"Laugh it up. My bonus for protecting Ms. Bluebird is paying for new tires for my car," said Estep.

The three of them set out together, joined by Agent Bonifield and Agent Champlin. They drove in two separate sedans and maintained a mostly silent journey for the entire two hour trip from Chicago to a rural stretch of road in Indiana. Upon arrival they all got out to stretch their legs and breathe the Hoosier air. Row after row of corn went on as far as the eye could see, and since the farmland was entirely flat, with barely any discernible slope, the Supporters could easily be anywhere. They could be watching them right now from only a few feet away, completely camouflaged. The three agents, and one former agent, were well aware of this possibility. While each of them had served in war zones, and all had been in situations of high pressure, it was the corn that struck their hearts with terror.

Serena's digi watch lit up. "Estep, who knows this number?"

"No one." He grabbed her arm. The watch, too big for her wrist, slid down her hand and fell onto the ground. "Don't pick it up!"

"Shouldn't I answer it? What if it's them?"

Serena didn't know how to answer the call on the digi watch so after a few seconds of fumbling with it Beav grabbed the watch. He knew exactly what to do because, like most contemporary government projects, he had been involved in the design of it.

"Hello?" she said.

"We wanted you to come alone, and without communication."

"Sorry, I couldn't do that."

"We expected as much."

"Then why did you even ask it of me?"

"It cut back on how much we have to deal with. All you have is the watch, correct?"

"Yes. How did you know about it?"

"One of us was in prison. But don't worry, we aren't violent."

"How did you get the number?"

"They are all coded in a series. We tried several until one went through."

Serena racked her brain to think of more ways to stall, more hints about who they were, anything! "Where are you?" She looked around her, as if expecting them to pop out in front of her from behind the corn stalks.

"Leave the watch behind, no tracking devices. Enter the corn row immediately in front of you. Keep moving down the row until you see an arrow on the ground. Follow the arrow. No agents. If anyone is with you, we will leave without meeting with you."

"Maybe we should call off the meeting. If you were honestly trying to help you would have no issue with federal agents I can personally vouch for."

"No agents – those are our terms."

"I can't agree to that."

The line was disconnected.

At that moment they heard the sound of tires crunching over gravel. Everyone watched as a government issue sedan slowed and then stopped a few yards from where they were gathered. The back door opened and a man exited the vehicle, a man they all recognized instantly as Carson Landon. They all stood stock still with their jaws dropping as they watched him walk toward them. He was unhurried, taking care to protect his $700 loafers.

"Is that who I think it is?" Serena asked rhetorically.

Carson held his hand out to her. "Carson Landon."

Serena stumbled over what to say. "How? How did you find us and what are you doing here?" She looked around her at the faces of everyone on the team—all looked completely baffled by Governor Landon's sudden appearance. She reached out to accept his handshake, but found something already in his hand.

"That should explain what I'm doing here. The 'how I found you' part is easy: we've had a tracer on your car." Carson pointed to the car that had been assigned to Agent Estep. "I have to say, you ruined my undercover work. The agents who recruited me are not happy. If one government hand would talk to the other every now and then we'd avoid these things."

Serena examined the object in her hand: a single sheet of paper folded several times over. She unfolded it and saw Paul's familiar handwriting. "One of the missing pages from Paul's journal!"

"Yes, this is the page that they didn't want you to see. Paul sent me a message telling me where to find his journal. He suggested that I keep this page in case I needed it." Carson folded his arms across his chest and waited for Serena to read the journal entry.

She addressed the entire team. "You'll need to verify this of course, but I can tell that the page I'm holding is from Paul's journal. He writes, 'The governor is working undercover. This will probably cost him politically. I wouldn't be surprised if I have him as a cellmate one day, but he's the only one that could pull this off I suspect. Nice to know there are good guys left in politics after all, although Carson Landon should have been VP. They'll find out that Morgan Canon was a big mistake. By then, it could be too late. I'm doing my part to write everything down. I will ask to speak with Serena Wilcox when the time is right. Until then, I'll continue reporting what I see, and I'll let the Supporters know about the governor's involvement.' He signed it and dated it. This was from over a month ago."

Carson cut an attractive figure against the backdrop of the orange sunset sitting on the rural horizon, a view completely unobscured by buildings or even trees. As far as the eye could see there was nothing but farmland, corn, and blue sky that was beginning to darken. Carson stood tall in his crisp navy suit and slim coordinating silk tie. His hair blew in the gusts of wind that sporadically came and went, looking like a male model posing for a calendar cover. Carson, the assembled team, and the government sedans were all in disharmony with the farm scene.

Beav, never intimidated by powerful people, asserted himself. "What is your connection to the Supporters?"

Carson frowned. "I'm not affiliated with the Supporters, but I know who they are, and that's why I'm here. You need to stay away from them."

"Tell us about them," said Serena.

"They are vigilantes who don't believe that government can police itself. While we want the same things, we disagree about how to make those things happen. I work within the system…" Carson let his sentence dangle while he shrugged.

"And they don't. I see. You came all this way to warn us about them?" Serena fixated on the sinking sun behind him. Soon they would be standing amongst the corn in complete darkness, not a house around for miles.

Carson launched into a speech. "Morgan Canon is obviously out of the picture—I do know what happened, by the way, and I even know what almost happened. Beav, I know who you are, and what you did. Thank you for your service. I know you can't be reinstated, but I'd like to thank you on behalf of all Americans, and if there's anything I can do for you, let me know. As far as I'm concerned my role is done, and so is yours. President Kinji is well satisfied with what you did, and she specifically requested that none of you run this thing so far into the ground that you dig up new problems. You got lucky. None of you were hurt. But it could have gone either way."

Estep didn't know if he should refute the claim or let it slip away unchallenged. He settled for a response that was somewhere in the middle. "Are you saying that you were working for President Kinji all along?"

Carson nodded slowly, a gesture that irked Estep. Carson did his best to smooth the team's ruffled feathers. "Don't take it personally guys. President Kinji needed you and you were there for her. I was on a parallel team, the official one. You see, there needs to be some, shall we say 'discretion', in how details are recorded, reported and investigated. For example, as you probably already guessed, it is better for the president that former agents are ghosts. That was, after all, what you signed up for. Covert Coffee needs to go dark. And, actually, it's time for Covert Coffee to end---when the Supporters came up on my radar I came here to close the operation in person, before you peel a new layer of the onion."

Serena extended her hand to Carson; this time his hand was free of paper and he shook it. "Thank you for telling us this in person."

"Of course. Again, thank you on behalf of all Americans. While they may never learn what it is that you did to protect President Kinji and our nation, those of us who know what you did will certainly forever appreciate your service." Carson flashed them the smile of a man who might one day run for president and spun on heels the best he could on dry husks of corn. He strode to where his driver had been waiting, his shoes somehow managing to make a clicking sound, unless Serena imagined that sound.

As soon as the governor's car was out of sight and the team was preparing to head out themselves, the Supporters called. The voice on the line said, "Serena, take me off speaker. And hold the watch to your ear."

Serena looked at Estep and Beav. Neither objected. At this point, what would it hurt to hear him out the rest of the way? Besides, the longer they kept the line open the easier it would be for agents, the officially active ones, to catch them. Agent Bonifield and Agent Champlin indicated that they were paying attention.

Serena pressed the watch to her ear. "You're off speaker."

"Mommy!" An unmistakably familiar voice rang out, there were a few seconds of dead air, and then the call was disconnected.

A chill went through Serena's body and her fingers struggled to hold the watch. Her face froze. Her mind was a carnival of lights and sounds, but she willed herself into control. First, steady yourself. You can't let the team know that you heard the voice of your baby girl.

Serena gave the watch to Beav. Estep noted her expression and said, "What did he say to you?"

"I'm supposed to go in there, in the corn, to meet with them. I need to go alone."

Estep shook his head. "They said more than that to shake you up this much."

"The digi watch gave me a jolt when I had it next to my ear. Static electricity or something, still feeling it," said Serena.

Beav's eyebrows shot up in an unspoken question. Serena answered with a scowl. This exchange went unnoticed by the others who were already peering through the corn for any sign of the Supporters, but Beav understood her perfectly: don't say anything.

"I'm going in there now. Don't follow me; they won't talk to me if you do."

"I don't feel good about this," said Estep. "The governor made it clear that Covert Coffee is over, and the order to desist came down from President Kinji."

Beav jumped in, "The official team, as the governor called it, still wants the Supporters. She can at least get the ball rolling for them while we're here. If she doesn't come out in fifteen minutes we'll go after her."

"Five. Daylight's all but gone," said Estep.

"Split the difference—ten. Give me ten minutes before you go in." Serena didn't wait for an answer but disappeared into the corn.

Estep timed Serena's absence to precisely five minutes. "That's it, we're going in."

Beav grasped Estep by the arm and pulled him away from the team. "Unless you have any objections I'd like to lead."

"Beav, what's going on? Covert Coffee is over, you know that. You can't be reinstated. Let's get Serena and move on." Estep shined a light into the blackness of the corn, illuminating nothing but corn and mud.

"Covert Coffee has become Operation Bluebird Flown." Beav added his light to Estep's, doubling the glare on the cornfield.

"No need for a mission. I'll get her home in time to watch the late show if you stop holding me back."

"No, she's long gone," said Beav.

"What are you talking about?" Estep stopped dead in his tracks.

"He was lying. Check with President Ann. Carson Landon was in the crack in the SM Channel, I don't have to tell you that." Beav looked back at the row of government vehicles; all was quiet.

"He said he was working undercover." Estep said slowly, the words forming in his mouth as his brain ferreted out the truth. "But no one checked his story." Estep bolted into the corn.

Beav, a runner, was smaller and lighter than Estep. He navigated the corn rows easily. He snagged the back of Estep's shirt and yanked him to a stop. "Wait! Let me lead this. I can't be reinstated, my career is over anyway. You can walk away from this right now."

Estep turned to face Beav. "Why did you let her go in there? What else aren't you saying?"

"They have her family."

BOOK THREE

BLUEBIRD FLOWN

PROLOGUE

"We better get moving," said Estep. He signaled to his team via an old school radio cuff. "Bluebird is on the move."

"Bluebird?" asked Serena.

"You," said Estep. "You're my new assignment. Operation Bluebird."

Beav's laugh began as a snorting sound and developed into an all-out guffaw.

"Laugh it up. My bonus for protecting Ms. Bluebird is paying for new tires on my car," said Estep.

The three of them set out together, joined by Agent Bonifield and Agent Champlin. They drove in two separate sedans and maintained a mostly silent journey for the entire two hour trip from Chicago to a rural stretch of road in Indiana. Upon arrival they all got out to stretch their legs and breathe the Hoosier air. Row after row of corn went on as far as the eye could see, and since the farmland was entirely flat, with barely any discernible slope, the Supporters could easily be anywhere. They could be watching them right now from only a few feet away, completely camouflaged. The three agents, and one former agent, were well aware of this possibility. While each of them had served in war zones, and all had been in situations of high pressure, it was the corn that struck their hearts with terror.

Serena's digi watch lit up. "Estep, who knows this number?"

"No one." He grabbed her arm. The watch, too big for her wrist, slid down her hand and fell onto the ground. "Don't pick it up!"

"Shouldn't I answer it? What if it's them?"

Serena didn't know how to answer the call on the digi watch so after a few seconds of fumbling with it Beav grabbed the watch. He knew exactly what to do because, like most contemporary government projects, he had been involved in the design of it.

"Hello?" she said.

"We wanted you to come alone, and without communication."

"Sorry, I couldn't do that."

"We expected as much."

"Then why did you even ask it of me?"

"It cut back on how much we have to deal with. All you have is the watch, correct?"

"Yes. How did you know about it?"

"One of us was in prison. But don't worry, we aren't violent."

"How did you get the number?"

"They are all coded in a series. We tried several until one went through."

Serena racked her brain to think of more ways to stall, more hints about who they were, anything! “Where are you?” She looked around her, as if expecting them to pop out in front of her from behind the corn stalks.

“Leave the watch behind, no tracking devices. Enter the corn row immediately in front of you. Keep moving down the row until you see an arrow on the ground. Follow the arrow. No agents. If anyone is with you, we will leave without meeting with you.”

“Maybe we should call off the meeting. If you were honestly trying to help, you would have no issue with federal agents I can personally vouch for.”

“No agents – those are our terms.”

“I can’t agree to that.”

The line was disconnected.

At that moment they heard the sound of tires crunching over gravel. Everyone watched as a government issue sedan slowed and then stopped a few yards from where they were gathered. The back door opened and a man exited the vehicle, a man they all recognized instantly as Carson Landon. They all stood stock still with their jaws dropping as they watched him walk toward them. He was unhurried, taking care to protect his $700 loafers.

“Is that who I think it is?” Serena asked rhetorically.

Carson held his hand out to her. “Carson Landon.”

Serena stumbled over what to say. “How? How did you find us and what are you doing here?” She looked around her at the faces of everyone on the team—all looked completely baffled by Governor Landon’s sudden appearance. She reached out to accept his handshake, but found something already in his hand.

“That should explain what I’m doing here. The ‘how I found you’ part is easy: we’ve had a tracer on your car.” Carson pointed to the car that had been assigned to Agent Estep. "I have to say, you ruined my undercover work. The agents who recruited me are not happy. If one government hand would talk to the other every now and then we'd avoid these things."

Serena examined the object in her hand: a single sheet of paper folded several times over. She unfolded it and saw Paul's familiar handwriting. "One of the missing pages from Paul's journal!"

"Yes, this is the page that they didn't want you to see. Paul sent me a message telling me where to find his journal. He suggested that I keep this page in case I needed it." Carson folded his arms across his chest and waited for Serena to read the journal entry.

She addressed the entire team. "You'll need to verify this of course, but I can tell that the page I'm holding is from Paul's journal. He writes, 'The governor is working undercover. This will probably cost him politically. I wouldn't be surprised if I have him as a cellmate one day, but he's the only one that could pull this off I suspect. Nice to know there are good guys left in politics after all, although Carson Landon should have been VP. They'll find out that Morgan Canon was a big mistake. By then, it could be too late. I'm doing my part to write everything down. I will ask to speak with Serena Wilcox when the time is right. Until then, I'll continue reporting what I see, and I'll let the Supporters know about the governor's involvement.' He signed it and dated it. This was from over a month ago."

Carson cut an attractive figure against the backdrop of the orange sunset sitting on the rural horizon, a view completely unobscured by buildings or even trees. As far as the eye could see there was nothing but farmland, corn, and blue sky that was beginning to darken. Carson stood tall in his crisp navy suit and slim coordinating silk tie. His hair blew in the gusts of wind that sporadically came and went, looking like a male model posing for a calendar cover. Carson, the assembled team, and the government sedans were all in disharmony with the farm scene.

Beav, never intimidated by powerful people, asserted himself. "What is your connection to the Supporters?"

Carson frowned. "I'm not affiliated with the Supporters, but I know who they are, and that's why I'm here. You need to stay away from them."

"Tell us about them," said Serena.

"They are vigilantes who don't believe that government can police itself. While we want the same things, we disagree about how to make those things happen. I work within the system…" Carson let his sentence dangle while he shrugged.

"And they don't. I see. You came all this way to warn us about them?" Serena fixated on the sinking sun behind him. Soon they would be standing amongst the corn in complete darkness, not a house around for miles.

Carson launched into a speech. "Morgan Canon is obviously out of the picture—I do know what happened, by the way, and I even know what almost happened. Beav, I know who you are, and what you did. Thank you for your service. I know you can't be reinstated, but I'd like to thank you on behalf of all Americans, and if there's anything I can do for you, let me know. As far as I'm concerned my role is done, and so is yours. President Kinji is well satisfied with what you did, and she specifically requested that none of you run this thing so far into the ground that you dig up new problems. You got lucky. None of you were hurt. But it could have gone either way."

Estep didn't know if he should refute the claim or let it slip away unchallenged. He settled for a response that was somewhere in the middle. "Are you saying that you were working for President Kinji all along?"

Carson nodded slowly, a gesture that irked Estep. Carson did his best to smooth the team's ruffled feathers. "Don't take it personally guys. President Kinji needed you and you were there for her. I was on a parallel team, the official one. You see, there needs to be some, shall we say 'discretion', in how details are recorded, reported and investigated. For example, as you probably already guessed, it is better for the president that former agents are ghosts. That was, after all, what you signed up for. Covert Coffee needs to go dark. And, actually, it's time for Covert Coffee to end---when the Supporters came up on my radar I came here to close the operation in person, before you peel a new layer of the onion."

Serena extended her hand to Carson; this time his hand was free of paper and he shook it. "Thank you for telling us this in person."

"Of course. Again, thank you on behalf of all Americans. While they may never learn what it is that you did to protect President Kinji and our nation, those of us who know what you did will certainly forever appreciate your service." Carson flashed them the smile of a man who might one day run for president and spun on his heels the best he could on dry husks of corn. He strode to where his driver had been waiting, his shoes somehow managing to make a clicking sound, unless Serena imagined that sound.

As soon as the governor's car was out of sight and the team was preparing to head out themselves, the Supporters called. The voice on the line said, "Serena, take me off speaker. And hold the watch to your ear."

Serena looked at Estep and Beav. Neither objected. At this point, what would it hurt to hear him out the rest of the way? Besides, the longer they kept the line open the easier it would be for agents, the officially active ones, to catch them. Agent Bonifield and Agent Champlin indicated that they were paying attention.

Serena pressed the watch to her ear. "You're off speaker."

"Mommy!" An unmistakably familiar voice rang out, there were a few seconds of dead air, and then the call was disconnected.

A chill went through Serena's body and her fingers struggled to hold the watch. Her face froze. Her mind was a carnival of lights and sounds, but she willed herself into control. *First, steady yourself. You can't let the team know that you heard the voice of your baby girl.*

Serena gave the watch to Beav. Estep noted her expression and said, "What did he say to you?"

"I'm supposed to go in there, in the corn, to meet with them. I need to go alone."

Estep shook his head. "They said more than that to shake you up this much."

"The digi watch gave me a jolt when I had it next to my ear. Static electricity or something, still feeling it," said Serena.

Beav's eyebrows shot up in an unspoken question. Serena answered with a scowl. This exchange went unnoticed by the others who were already peering through the corn for any sign of the Supporters, but Beav understood her perfectly: *don't say anything.*

"I'm going in there now. Don't follow me; they won't talk to me if you do."

"I don't feel good about this," said Estep. "The governor made it clear that Covert Coffee is over, and the order to desist came down from President Kinji."

Beav jumped in, "The official team, as the governor called it, still wants the Supporters. She can at least get the ball rolling for them while we're here. If she doesn't come out in fifteen minutes we'll go after her."

"Five. Daylight's all but gone," said Estep.

"Split the difference—ten. Give me ten minutes before you go in." Serena didn't wait for an answer but disappeared into the corn.

Estep timed Serena's absence to precisely five minutes. "That's it, we're going in."

Beav grasped Estep by the arm and pulled him away from the team. "Unless you have any objections I'd like to lead."

"Beav, what's going on? Covert Coffee is over, you know that. You can't be reinstated. Let's get Serena and move on." Estep shined a light into the blackness of the corn, illuminating nothing but corn and mud.

"Covert Coffee has become Operation Bluebird Flown." Beav added his light to Estep's, doubling the glare on the cornfield.

"No need for a mission. I'll get her home in time to watch the late show if you stop holding me back."

"No, she's long gone," said Beav.

"What are you talking about?" Estep stopped dead in his tracks.

"He was lying. Check with President Ann. Carson Landon was in the crack in the SM Channel, I don't have to tell you that." Beav looked back at the row of government vehicles; all was quiet.

"He said he was working undercover." Estep said slowly, the words forming in his mouth as his brain ferreted out the truth. "But no one checked his story." Estep bolted into the corn.

Beav, a runner, was smaller and lighter than Estep. He navigated the corn rows easily. He snagged the back of Estep's shirt and yanked him to a stop. "Wait! Let me lead this. I can't be reinstated, my career is over anyway. You can walk away from this right now."

Estep turned to face Beav. "Why did you let her go in there? What else aren't you saying?"

"They have her family."

BOOK THREE

BLUEBIRD FLOWN

1

President Ann Kinji had requested a private meeting with Agent Estep. Yet when he arrived in her office, he was taken aback by how many people were crammed in what was usually a spacious room. He tried to do a quick head count and gave up. Thirty? Forty? Obviously this meeting was anything but private.

“Sit or stand, your choice.” Ann stared intently at the one empty chair at the table. Estep sat.

“We’re ready for you, Madam President,” said someone with a grating voice and oddly rectangular-shaped head. On his command the wall of screens behind President Ann Kinji illuminated the darkened room.

Estep recognized the information on the display as “the crack in the Social Media Channel”. The crack was a virtual hang-out for people who didn't want their conversations tracked. The highest levels of government were well aware of the crack, but were leaving it alone for now to spy on it. Hackers would likely detect Big Brother's presence within the week, and promptly clear out, but until then gathering intelligence was as easy as staring at a screen; watching a feature presentation in which every character incriminates himself. Estep half expected popcorn to be served.

President Ann stepped in front of the wall of screens, a movement that created a flurry of chain reaction as every person in the room leaned forward at rapt attention. She subconsciously tossed her famous Kinji-cut locks – a simple bob made glamorous by a sheen that was born out of a combination of genetics and healthy living.

Ann addressed everyone in the room with an intensity that dressed each person down individually and intimately. "I called you here today to get all of this out in the open. Some of you were involved with Operation Covert Coffee. In a nutshell, Covert Coffee exposed a conspiracy to assassinate the President, which would be me."

An audible collective gasp went up.

Ann waved her hand, a flick of the wrist that was another of her trademark gestures. "Oh don't insult my intelligence by pretending that you didn't know; move on from that quickly, ladies and gentlemen. I'll get right down to it: As President of the newly Re-united States of America, I am nothing more than a figurehead. Perhaps that's been true throughout all of American history, but clearly we have a problem."

Ann paused and peered into the full room at her captive audience. Nothing was heard except for the sounds coming from a heavy breather who was whistling through clogged sinuses with every breath. Heads turned toward the offending breather. Ann redirected their attention to the front of the room.

"It's time for a Show and Tell demonstration. Let me introduce all of the main players in our little game we call government. First, we have the presiding officer of the chamber, the Speaker of the House, who is third in the line of succession to the Presidency. Give us a wave, Joe."

Speaker of the House Joseph Smythe stood, waved, and grinned. He was received by a few snickers and a lone round of applause. He sat back down.

"Shall we begin with a history lesson? The Constitution doesn't require that the Speaker be an elected Member of Congress. Nonetheless, no non-member has ever been elected to the office until this administration. Naturally the norm is that members of the House vote for their own party's candidate, but apparently this time around there was opposition to electing the party's favorite – Joseph Smythe is not a Member. Several within the majority party refused to jump on board and therefore were penalized: they were stripped of seniority and all committee posts.

Make note of these issues I've highlighted for you. Mr. Speaker Joseph Smythe was elected as a non-member, his appointment was not well received by many members of his own party, and, most importantly, after the Vice President, Mr. Speaker is next in line for the office of the presidency.

Please stand, Mr. Speaker of the House, Joseph Smythe. In fact, do us a favor and step forward. Stand next to me. You'll be forming a line right here, boys." Ann's gesture looked like she was ground guiding a fork truck.

Smythe sauntered over to the exact spot Ann pointed out to him. If he resented being brought to the head of the class like a naughty schoolboy, it didn't show on his face or in his demeanor.

Smythe was a man of average height, but had the appearance of looking much taller due to his lanky frame. His boyish face was out of sync with the medium-brown hair that was graying at the temples. He wore a well-tailored suit that had been purchased off-the-rack, tweaked by a skilled tailor and carefully selected to bring out the blue in his eyes. His eyes dropped slightly at the corners, but turned up significantly when smiling. The creases on his face indicated that more smiles than frowns had aged him.

Ann stood much shorter next to Smythe, which gave Smythe a fatherly look. She faced the crowded room that was growing uncomfortably warmer with each passing minute.

"Continuing on, in both pre-'Big War' United States and now, the role of the speakership of the House is this: He actively works to set a party's legislative agenda; the office is endowed with considerable political power. Let me cite an example of a time in American history when the Speaker of the House was a controversial figure. Tip O'Neill comes to mind. O'Neill opposed the policies of President Ronald Reagan; challenging Reagan on defense expenditures, among other things. He was notorious for kicking up a fuss.

Smythe, like Tip O'Neill from days gone by, has actively opposed many of my policies. It is important to note that Joseph Smythe has an impressive amount of influence in the House and Senate, as well as the respect of the media. His rhetoric is more often quoted than any other political figure, barring yours truly."

Smythe stood and pantomimed tipping a hat at the crowd. Polite laughter briefly surfaced but was stopped cold when Ann pierced the mirth with one reproachful gaze.

"Let's move along from Mr. Speaker. I call Vice President Lehman to the front. I don't need to tell you that Lehman is next in line to the presidency. However, he is a new appointment, and my personal choice – we can dismiss Lehman as a threat for these and other reasons. I want him up here for a different reason. He is a stand-in for the VP that many of you seated right here in this very room wanted in this position instead of Lehman.

As you can see, Lehman is holding a sign with a familiar face on it. Surely you recognize that face?"

Lehman had made his way through the packed room and was now standing on the other side of Smythe. He held a poster print of Governor Carson Landon at chest-level. Carson's face flashed a campaign trail smile. In contrast to the Carson sign he displayed, Lehman kept his own face expressionless. He selected a focal point on the back wall and stared at it while Ann resumed her presentation.

"To be clear: forget Lehman. Focus on Carson, that's who is represented here in this line-up. We know that Carson was talking to someone from the Global Oil Initiative in the crack in the Social Media Channel. I have it on the screen right now. Let's read it together, shall we?"

Ann nodded to her IT right-hand man who promptly loaded the file that Ann had ordered shortly before the meeting. The file had been quickly converted from text-only to text-to-speech. It now scrolled across the wall of screens while audio narrated the dialog between Carson and an unknown person:

45671: "It's going down at the Global Oil Initiative."

23987: "I want assurances."

45671: "I can't do that. I've been told she'll name me as the VP selection at GOB. I can't verify it."

23987: "We need you in."

45671: "I know that."

23987: "We're down to a year. She won't be out of office before the agreement, she needs to be taken out."

45671: "I know, you've made yourself clear. I told you, I'm working on it."

23987: "The last guy we tapped got cold feet, and now his toes are tagged."

45671: "Don't threaten me."

23987: "I'm not. I'm telling you what will happen if you don't hold up your end of our arrangement."

45671: "I have no intention of backing out. I stand to benefit just as much as you do."

23987: "Good to know."

45671: "She contacted me right away. I don't think Morgan's body was even cold yet. No one will be surprised, she talked to the media about me a couple of weeks ago. All looks good."

23987: "Then what's the problem?"

45671: "I'm saying I can't guarantee it. She could change her mind last minute. I've done my part."

23987: "There's no one else she's even mentioned as a VP choice, no one but you."

45671: "Even so, I'm saying I can't guarantee it. I can only say that it looks like a done deal. She's announcing at the press conference at GOB."

23987: "That would be immediately following the initiative

then."

45671: "I assume."

23987: "All interested parties will be at GOB."

45671: "I know that."

23987: "They expect to see you."

45671: "I'll be there."

23987: "In person meets are discouraged obviously, but they'll be watching you."

45671: "What are you telling me?"

23987: "Look sharp."

45671: "You contacted me. I told you all I know. What are you saying?"

23987: "Some don't trust you. Watch your back."

45671: "I told you that I'm on board. I've done all that you have asked. Are you telling me that they might kill me anyway?"

23987: "That's what I'm telling you."

45671: "I don't know what more I can do to gain their trust."

23987: "Turn up, be ready to give assurances."

45671: "I said I'd be there."

"All of this was discovered in Operation Covert Coffee. The GOB initiative went off without a hitch, and Carson Landon was not present at the event. However, Carson is still out there, and I want to know what he's up to. His week-long retreat away from the Governor's mansion was scheduled months in advance, supplying him with a reason for his absence. But he's not there. No one has arrived at the vacation home on his itinerary.

Our last contact with him was when he turned up during the investigation I referred to earlier, Operation Covert Coffee. Classified at a security level that most of you here don't have-- and never will have-- clearance for, you shouldn't know anything about this, but I have a strong feeling that you do."

The sound of rustling feet and throat clearing confirmed her suspicions. She paused, narrowed her eyes in accusation, then resumed speaking.

"How did Carson know where to find my team? How did he get involved? And where is he now? I need answers."

Ann studied her fidgeting audience before resuming. "I notice a number of raised eyebrows on your faces – which has also been duly noted by my expert profilers, courtesy of the FBI." Ann indicated two people in suits, one male and one female, each positioned to view everyone in the room.

"Ah, surprised again, I see. All of you have been under observation from the moment you stepped into the room. Your reaction to my inquisition into the whereabouts of Governor Carson Landon might reflect your innocence, or it might not.

Yes, Carson was initially my own preference for VP, and even someone I thought of as a friend. I certainly can't blame anyone else for this predicament.

For those of you wondering about my true feelings about Carson's predecessor, Morgan Canon, what you heard from the media was dead on. Morgan was never my pick; I was vocal about that. I was right not to trust Morgan but wrong about placing my trust in Carson. I shouldn't have believed either of them.

I've always viewed myself as a person who possesses a gift for discernment, but I was way off the mark with Carson Landon. If not for the efforts of all the agents and investigators involved in Operation Covert Coffee, I would have played into your hand. I would have tapped Carson to replace Morgan, which is exactly what you expected me to do.

It turns out that both candidates were in the pockets of the mysterious powers that are operating independently of this office, so if Morgan failed them, they had Carson at the ready. It seems they had a backup to the backup and I fell for it - *both* vice presidential candidates had been purchased by unknown power players. Of course I want to know the name of every person involved.

The most logical place to start is with Carson Landon. Find him and learn the identity of the person he was talking to. Who is 23987?"

There was momentary confusion when several law enforcement heads questioned whether or not they should be popping out of their seats to assemble teams at this exact second, or if the president was not finished with them yet. The restlessness of the crowd created a comical stir.

Ann waited for the noise to settle before she began again. "I'm not finished yet. We need to add a couple more to the line-up.

Before moving on, let's review what any intern should already know: The Vice President of the United States serves as President of the Senate, casting the decisive vote in the event of a tie in the Senate. Wow, how convenient it would be to hand-pick the VP you want casting those precious decisive votes! No wonder our friends wanted to make sure they had a puppet in place.

I'll also remind you that the Senate has the sole power to confirm Presidential appointments that require consent and to ratify treaties, with a couple of exceptions, but you get the idea. The point is, the power the Senate has is considerable, perhaps formidable. And with term lengths six years long, with no term limits, some of our senators have had practically a life-time membership in the Old

Boys' Club.

It is with these thoughts in mind that I ask Senator William Casey and Senator Robert Lorry to come forward. Take your place in line, gentlemen."

Senators Casey and Lorry ambled to the front of the room. They obediently took their place in line, but unlike Smythe, who managed to maintain somewhat of an amused smirk on his face throughout this entire presentation, and Lehman, who remained stoic, both Casey and Lorry held pinched and petulant expressions. Although in all fairness, defensiveness and culpability may not have had anything to do with the reason behind these sour faces; they had looked this way for most of their lives.

"Senators Casey and Lorry, two long-time members representing both sides of the aisle, represent the heart of the Senate. I know that we've reformed and there's not supposed to be definitive party lines anymore, but no one is fooled by these redefinitions. The division in our nation is just as bitter as before the Big War, and new labels aren't going to make that go away. But I digress."

Ann strolled in front of the line of men, all of whom dwarfed her diminutive stature. Yet somehow she remained an intimidating force. She used a sweeping hand gesture to indicate all of them as a whole.

"Take a long look. Is it Colonel Mustard in the kitchen with a knife? Or Professor Plum in the billiard room with a revolver?

I'm calling upon our best people in every agency we currently have, and I'm creating new ones as well – agencies that my hand-picked crew will build from scratch. We have to clean house, and find all those who are working against us, all those with their own agenda, all those working outside of the system, and all those who are traitors to our country! I don't care how big the sweep is, I want every bad apple tossed out.

Agents: cancel all vacation plans and make your apologies now to your family members – you will be living here, and in the field, until our mission is accomplished. Consider this the game of Clue from hell. No one will be let out of the game until we reveal all the cards.

As we begin round one, study the gentlemen in this line-up and then cast an even longer look around this room. These are your suspects. Finally, hold up a mirror. One of you, more than one of you actually, wants me dead."

2

Beav was in the field and had gone dark – literally. He was mucking about in a corn field in the middle of the night; the moonlight bouncing off of his olive skin, his hairline damp with sweat, his nostrils clogged by gnats and his pulse racing. Serena Wilcox was long gone and Operation Bluebird Flown was well underway. Taking Carson's unintentional advice, Beav and Estep were working together, except that only Agent Estep's role would ever see the light of day. If all went well Beav would remain a ghost.

While Estep, on the official side of this operation, was digesting his thoughts about President Ann Kinji's show-and-tell presentation, Beav was unofficially searching for clues about Serena's disappearance. Using nothing more than a plastic flashlight, which was broken and held together by duct tape, he thought his mission was fruitless until his weak beam of light hit upon something. He recognized the object as Paul's journal page, the page that Serena was reading before she took off into the cornfield to meet the Supporters.

Beav picked up the page, which was now soggy from sitting on the moist ground. He examined the paper the best he could under the circumstances. The first thing he noticed was a black smudge on the back of the paper. He placed his dim flashlight close to the page.

It was a scan-read code, he was sure of it! He pulled his phone out of his pocket. Reading a backlit screen was much easier than reading a page by flashlight. He scanned the page, concerned that the quality of the ink and the dampness of the paper would interfere with reading the code. His fears were unfounded; the code scanned flawlessly.

Beav remained where he stood in the corn field, now oblivious to the unnerving aspects of being alone in the pitch black of rural Indiana (moonlight didn't count in his opinion). He heard and felt nothing as he read the short message from Paul Tracy. His thoughts did drift however to the idea that this discovery might be enough to turn his career around. *Could I be reinstated? Is it too much to hope for?*

The note was short but revealing: "If you found the code on my journal page it means that Carson Landon has gotten to you. The Supporters asked me to play along. They'll take care of it. If this is you Serena, sorry I couldn't give you a heads up. You'll find them at this address."

Boom- that's how it's done! Just like that I've found the big break in the case – in my team of one! Beav entered the address into his phone's GPS app. It popped up as only half a mile away from where he was standing in the corn field! He sprinted out of the field, leaping over mud clods and dodging corn stalks. He had only a ragtag support team at his disposal and none of them had arrived yet. Should he continue solo or wait? *Waiting could cost me the mission.*

His rigorous self-punishing extreme fitness routine had equipped him with an easy run to the farmhouse down the gravel road. He felt a whoosh over his head that may have been a bat in flight, but he didn't let that distraction get to him. It was only as he neared his destination that he slowed his steps, his spirit sinking. This house hadn't seen life in a long time.

Nonetheless, he rapped at the peeling door. A shrill bark jolted Beav into taking an involuntary leap backward, his 5'7 frame busting through a splintered stair rail, landing with a hard thud into the foliage below.

"Who's out there?" A man in his fifties held the door open and flicked the porch light on.

Beav shielded his eyes from the sudden glare. "I'm down here. I busted your railing, sorry about that. Gravity is a harsh mistress."

"What are you doing out here in the middle of the night?" He maintained a solid stance that was neither frightened nor angry.

Beav sized him up. He didn't look like a farmer, his skin was much too pale to have seen much of the sun. No, this was a man who worked indoors. So what was he doing out here if not farming? Beav knew this had to be the Supporters' safe house, or some sort of operations—Paul hadn't steered him wrong. Also, it was a safe bet that that this guy knew about Paul's message. Beav operated on that assumption when he said, "I found your address on Paul Tracy's journal page. Let me in so we can talk."

He nodded and walked back inside, leaving the door open for

Beav. Beav followed him into a living room area that was crammed with furniture – clearly Beav's initial impression that the house was abandoned couldn't have been further from the truth. The pet that had sent Beav hurling off the porch with his well-timed bark was a well-groomed toy poodle sitting innocently on a sofa pillow. Littered throughout the room were toys belonging to children and the dog. It was hard for Beav to distinguish the difference between the two.

"I'm Bob. Pull up a seat and start talking." He indicated the high-backed chair nearest to the door for Beav. Bob sank into the sofa, which was an invitation for the poodle to jump into his lap.

Beav sat in the chair offered to him, grateful for a rest. He had been in that corn field for six hours. He'd been near the end of his stamina and patience when he finally found the journal page, a page he now realized that Serena probably left behind for him to find, maybe even upon instruction from the Supporters. This obvious bread crumb didn't make the discovery any less his, a less dedicated field investigator would have missed it. No, he could rightfully claim this one. This single page from Paul's journal broke the case wide open, making his hours in the muddy field worth the fatigue, soiled jeans, chilled extremities, and sore muscles. Sweating while simultaneously freezing was a condition worthy of hazard pay in his opinion, and yet he would have done it all over again for that moment of glory when he found the page.

He couldn't wait to update Estep. Could Operation Bluebird be wrapped up before the end of the week? If so, it would be good news for Serena Wilcox, but bad news for him. He might need to line up a new freelance job sooner than he expected. Beav knew he'd be let go as soon as his services were no longer needed; let go, and never heard from again. He was torn between excitement about how fast this case was wrapping up and despair at the thought of his impending unemployment. *The money was good while it lasted.*

"I'm waiting. A name would be nice." Bob was staring at Beav, and had been for a couple of minutes or more.

Beav shook off his brain fog. "This was the address on the journal page."

"Yes, you said that. Who are you? Who do you work for?"

"People call me The Beav. I'm looking for Serena Wilcox."

"How do I know she wants to be found?"

"She's my friend."

Bob rubbed his chin, a motion that had less to do with deep thinking and more to do with soothing a raw skin patch due to a recent shave. "Give me more."

"I'm not going to hurt her. I think we are on the same side in this."

"That's what I'm trying to figure out but you aren't giving me much to go on." Bob rubbed the poodle's belly after the little dog flopped over, begging for attention.

"Ask me anything you want to know."

Bob told the dog to sit. When the poodle was settled he asked, "Who do you work for?"

"I can't fully answer that," Beav said without any hint of irony in his voice.

"What good is asking you questions if you aren't going to answer? How long are we going to be at this?"

Beav eyed him critically. "What do you do?"

"Not that I need to answer you, given that you aren't forthcoming with information yourself, but I don't see the harm. I'm a radio host."

"Internet radio?"

"No, old school radio broadcasting."

"People still do that?"

Bob mimicked Beav's tone. "Yes, 'people still do that'."

"Where do you operate out of?"

"Here."

"On this property?"

"Here in this house. I have a studio downstairs."

"You have a studio in the basement?"

"Yes."

"What for? Is there a market for this?"

Bob held up his index finger. "It's my turn. Why are you here, who are you working for, and why are you looking for Serena Wilcox? You have to give me something or I'm going to ask you leave."

"Serena was taken by the Supporters. This address is what I found when I was looking for her. That's all I know. I'm assuming you know how to find the Supporters, and Serena."

"I thought it might be something like that. Am I to assume you are working for the government – our home government?"

"As opposed to what? A foreign government?"

"So that's a yes."

"I really can't say." Beav had grown restless with the conversation. He roamed about the room, studying the pictures on the walls and piecing together the people who lived here. He shook his left leg which had fallen asleep and was now tingly.

"All right then, tell me what you know about Carson Landon."

"I know that he's a bad dude."

"You aren't working for Carson?"

"No." Beav saw so much evidence of Bob's life through the framed portraits on the walls that he didn't feel the need to investigate further. Bob wasn't a threat to anyone. From what Beav could see, he was a family man and even a pillar of the community, according to the awards and plaques filling up what little space remained after all of the family pictures. What Bob was doing with the Supporters was the question of the hour. Nothing about him screamed radical.

Unlike Beav, who had dismissed Bob as a person of interest, Bob's radar was on full alert. "Wait a minute, I recognize you. Weren't you involved with the infamous Paul Tracy bombing? Your face was all over the news. Is that your connection to Paul?"

Beav picked at the dried mud on his jeans. He made a note to self to alter his appearance. Who would have thought that he would be recognized? He hadn't really been "all over" the news; to the best of his knowledge his mug had only appeared once, for maybe a millisecond. "Hmm, you've got me. Yes, I'm that guy."

"They let you back in? I'm surprised you aren't in prison alongside Paul." Bob stroked his chin again.

"This should prove I'm on the right side."

"Not necessarily. Carson Landon has a lot of influence. He could get you a get-out-of-jail-free card."

"This has become tedious. Trust your gut. Which side do *you* think I'm on?" Beav didn't know how the tables had been turned on him, but he wouldn't be mentioning this part of his investigation in his report.

"You don't seem the type who would align himself with an entitled politician like Carson, but you don't look like you're active government either." Bob's eyes flitted to Beav's ponytail. "That's not a regulation haircut."

Beav touched the tip of his nose, charade-speak for "on the nose". With his hair pulled back he looked less agent and more gypsy, which suited him much more than the crew cut and suit ever had.

"You're not working for *any*one are you? You've gone rogue?" Bob glanced into the kitchen, wondering how close to the top of the silverware drawer his knives were.

"I'm not rogue. I am unofficial, for the protection of all involved. I'm one of the good guys. My back-up team will be here any minute. That should confirm what I'm saying."

Bob was at Beav's side in a flash, yanking him up on his feet by the arm. "Come with me." He dead-bolted the door, turned off all the lights, scooped up his little dog and led Beav to the stairs tucked into the back of the front entry closet. Hidden behind rows of coats, the stairs were effectively camouflaged.

Bob spoke quickly in a raspy whisper, "Keep quiet and I'll try to help you."

Noise wasn't an issue. The likelihood of being discovered after they were sequestered downstairs was practically nil. Besides, Beav knew his team wouldn't search that hard for him; if they found the house vacant, they'd do a cursory search, then call him, and then leave- regardless of whether he answered his phone or not. Bob had probably already thought of that himself. Beav's mind raced. Why *was* Bob here all alone in the middle of nowhere? Maybe Beav had dismissed him too soon. Where was the family in the pictures? Had Bob done something to them? Beav chided himself: he was sleep deprived. Nonetheless, he slipped his hand into his pocket and felt the reassurance of his favorite weapon – a humane gun; it shot tranquilizer darts that were effective on animals and humans alike.

In the bellows of the house, inside a windowless room with walls that had been modified with sound-proofing material, Beav felt silly. Besides the silence, nothing about Bob's basement studio screamed serial killer. Beav looked the equipment over and gave a low whistle. "You aren't playing around."

"This is my livelihood."

"And you do what? DJ?"

"Yes, and I host a talk show, I flip the switch on syndicated programming, I do everything else you might expect from radio." Bob slid behind his desk and sat down. He put his headset on.

"Why are you doing this from here?" Beav genuinely admired the equipment, and even fleetingly wondered if he might like to have a show of his own. Although much of the technology was now considered obsolete, he saw a few top of the line cutting-edge items in the mix. The cool toys alone made the gig appealing.

"I'm on a frequency no longer used." Bob spoke in a clipped hurried tone.

"Hiding from regulation?" Beav forced himself to focus on the investigation; he stopped eyeballing the toys.

"Now you understand." Bob flicked the on-air button.

"And this is how you talk to the Supporters?" Beav noted that Bob was fully suited up for broadcasting.

"This is how they talk to me, yes."

"Contact them now, tell them I found Paul's code."

"It doesn't work that way. They contact me. They phone in during my show, always from a different phone. They are careful. Don't bother trying to find them. They'll call."

"How long do we have to wait? I can't dodge my team forever. They'll send out the alarm if I don't check in within the hour."

"I thought you were operating on your own."

"No, not on my own. I said I'm operating 'unofficially'."

"What does that mean?"

"I have a team, I have people to report to. It's organized." Beav searched for a way out of the studio. The windows seen from outside the house were blocked by the sound proofing material.

"You're trying to take down Carson Landon?"

"Not me. My objective is to get Serena Wilcox back."

"That's going to be a problem," said an unknown voice that suddenly boomed at them from the surround sound system.

"You represent the Supporters?" Beav asked, to confirm what was obvious. Apparently Bob had been broadcasting their conversation.

"You know who we are. And you also know that we wouldn't hurt Serena." The man's voice wasn't digitally disguised. He sounded unhurried and in control.

"You took her child. She's with you now because you held her child as leverage." Beav's mind raced. He couldn't get a read on this guy.

"I regret that we needed to do that, but we didn't hurt her family. They understood that we needed her to believe that we might. Her little girl is quite an actress."

"You are telling me that Serena and her entire family are OK?" Beav was going off the play book: verify that Serena is still alive.

"Yes." The man's voice didn't reveal anything. He was either telling the truth or he was a sociopath.

"Why won't you put her on the phone?"

"She's occupied."

"With what?"

"Preventing the take-down of the United States." The man's tone held not a hint of sensationalism.

"Another attack?" Beav looked at Bob. Bob was somber and his body language looked like that of a person attending a funeral. What that meant was impossible to guess.

"No. A buy-out."

"A what?" Beav continued to monitor Bob's reaction, but Bob was giving nothing away, if he even knew anything at all.

"Foreign investors." The representative of the Supporters had a smooth speaking voice with excellent diction.

"I still don't understand." Beav admitted.

"I don't have time to explain this to you. Serena has agreed to help."

"Put her on the phone."

"I can't do that."

"Why not?"

"She isn't here."

"Where is she?" Beav didn't expect a direct answer, so what he heard next sent his head spinning:

"She's with Carson Landon."

3

Carson Landon was not happy to see her. Serena smiled at the thought of his displeasure. “Hello, Governor Landon,” she said.

“What are you doing here, Ms. Wilcox?”

“I could ask the same of you.”

“Is anyone with you?” Landon’s eyes darted from left to right and then back again. Given that he didn’t move his head, it was a futile attempt to survey the room.

“Oh, you’re wondering if I came alone. Don’t even think of whatever it is you’re thinking of doing. I have people, yes.”

Landon folded his arms across his chest in a classic defensive posture that made him look like a B-list actor playing the role of a dirty politician. His dialogue was equally uninspired. “I’m not going to tell you anything. I want you to leave.”

Serena laughed. “I’m not going anywhere. You have no power over me.” She meant it, he seemed like a cartoon to her now.

"This is private property."

"That's right. And it doesn't belong to you. I have permission to be on these premises. Can you say the same?"

Landon's eyes darted around the room again.

Serena enjoyed watching him squirm. "Don't bother looking for a way out. My people are waiting for you at every exit."

"What is it that you think I can do for you?"

"That's what we're going to do? Pretend that you don't know what I want?" Serena stood with her hands on her hips, her legs locked into a cowboy stance. She held her ground at not quite five two inches tall.

"Tell me what you want and I'll tell you if I can help you." Carson Landon slipped back into the golden tongue of a practiced diplomat.

Landon's bronzed skin had been fortified by artificial tanning, his hair had been recently styled by a professional who managed to charge five times more money to cut the locks of a governor than the hair of an average citizen, and something about his nose hinted that plastic surgery had created its mannequin-like symmetry and perfection. The total package that was Carson Landon had worked well for him over the years, but somehow his expensive grooming habits didn't do him any favors today. It was as if uncovering his deception had also unveiled the secrets to his empty good looks; revealing him to be the fool that he was.

"Governor, you were identified as one of the voices in the crack in the Social Media Channel, there's no doubt, and I think you know that. The jig is up. You were making plans to become the next Vice President, or should I say lining yourself up to be President? But the assassination attempt on President Kinji was aborted because your puppet masters knew that we were on to them. So now you are here, hiding. You should have played hide and seek more as a child."

"Why isn't anyone arresting me then? Why are *you* here? On that subject, what business do you have in anything at all?"

"I have many talents." Serena started to say more but she thought better of it. Why was she defending herself? Besides, there wasn't much to say. The main reason why President Kinji hired her was because Serena was a person she could trust. In Ann's world, where few people had anything real about them, transparency and honesty were more important than any credential or certification could ever be. But that sounded flimsy even to her own ears.

Serena moved on. "You're in a lot of trouble, and you wouldn't be hiding if you didn't think so yourself. So why don't you stop this nonsense and help yourself?"

"You're offering me a deal? How do I know you're in any position to do that? I'd want it in writing." Landon's expression was pinched, as if he was setting himself up to take the upper hand in a negotiation.

"Oh no, I'm not offering you a deal. That's never going to happen."

"What are you talking about then?" The mighty governor was indeed a B-list actor; he couldn't conceal his dismay.

"We can protect you from the people you sold out."

"I haven't sold anyone out." Landon's eyes darted. His face reminded Serena of a rabbit's.

"By running here, you all but signed a confession of guilt. It's only a matter of time before you tell us everything, and they know that."

Landon folded his arms across his chest again. He was cycling through his postures and movements like he had choreographed a routine. "They don't know that because it won't happen. I've told them I won't talk."

"And they believed you?"

Carson's face turned gray even under all that fake tan. "Leave me alone."

"I'd love to, but I think you'd prefer to have my help."

"Why would I trust you over them? You'll put me in prison."

Serena smiled until her green eyes sparkled like a cat who had gotten into the nip. "Definitely. You're going to prison whether you talk to me or not."

"Then put cuffs on me and be done with it." Landon held out his wrists.

"You could go to prison with protection or without it."

"Protection from?"

"From the people you've been working for. Come on, Carson, you can't be that stupid. You do know that they're going to kill you now, right? The sooner they get rid of you the better. They know that you'll talk eventually. Besides, you're no good to them now. You're better off dead." Serena fleetingly wondered if a funeral makeup artist would need to touch him up or if his fake tan would cross over into the afterlife.

"Witness relocation?"

"Never going to happen. You're a traitor."

"I'll take my chances on my own then. You haven't offered me anything." Landon crossed his arms and his eyes darted again in rabbit-like fashion; he had stepped up his routine to include a combo.

"So your plan is what? Carson, I'm not leaving. My people

aren't leaving. There's no escape for you. If you cooperate, you'll go to a special prison where cellmates are heavily protected. If you don't cooperate, your friends will have you killed as soon as you put on your orange jumpsuit, if not before. Do you want to die, or do you want to accept my offer of a VIP prison ticket?"

Carson put his head down in his hands and made a curious sound. Serena realized he was crying. He gasped and shook, sobbing until he was choked up and blowing his nose on a cloth napkin. Serena watched him cry, fascinated by how quickly his arrogance had become pitiful. He croaked out the words, "I want the VIP ticket."

"That can be arranged." Serena grinned. This was her first real interrogation and she had broken her suspect on the first try! Beginner's luck, or did she have the knack? Whichever it was, she took it as a serious win. "All we need from you is a list of names."

"Now?"

"Yes. And while you're at it, why Lehman's house? You knew it would be vacant, but wow, that's brazen. How did you even get in?"

"Celebrity has its privileges. I'm still Governor. I told the house sitter that I was invited here. She didn't bat an eye."

"Did you bat *your* eyes?" Serena knew the effect Carson had on women, but not from personal experience – she couldn't bear his type.

Carson's smile was almost a leer. There was no trace of his tears of ten seconds ago. "Something like that. How did you find me, have you been tracking me?"

"Something like that," she parroted back at him, with equal flippancy. "Give me the list of names."

"Those Supporters were tracking me, weren't they? You talked to them."

"Yes, and yes. The names please? Seriously, Carson, if you don't hurry, you'll be killed before I can help you."

As if on cue, they both heard what sounded like a round of firecrackers. Serena grabbed Carson's hand and pulled him behind the kitchen counter, but it was too late. Carson's eyes were round with the realization of his fate. A second later he was dead.

4

“That’s so cliché. He died before giving me the names!” Serena folded her arms across her chest. She dropped her arms the instant she realized that she was adopting the same posture that Carson Landon had repeatedly done just moments before his untimely demise.

Agent Estep raised an eyebrow but didn’t ask what her problem was. “You have a track record of informants dying on your watch.”

“I’d gotten him to accept the offer.”

“Does us no good now.”

Serena looked around Lehman’s kitchen. The Birmingham area house had a pending offer. She wondered if the blood spatter would complicate the closing. “I know, I know,” she said. “I really am sorry.”

“Why didn’t you call me sooner? I’m not your clean-up crew.” Estep maintained his grumpy old man demeanor even though he was almost twenty years her junior. Serena's ditzy personality, irreverent humor, and often insipid methods of investigation drove him to gnash his teeth.

"They asked me not to."

"What, you're working for the Supporters now?" Estep stared at her, his eyes reflecting a hard glint. He had come around to respect her unorthodox methods, and as long as they didn't have to spend too much time together they got along fine. He even enjoyed their repartee—exchanging barbs with Serena reminded him of the energy of his childhood family, his grandmother, his mother and a houseful of sisters; all of them strong and dynamic women. But this time Serena had pushed him too far: she hadn't contacted him since she went missing, not until now when there was a dead governor to take care of.

"*You're* working for the Supporters, since you're official government. They are American citizens, and last I knew, our government works for *us*."

Estep made a big show of expressing that he was dumbfounded. "Have you been sucked into their cult voodoo mind control? I don't work for vigilantes."

"Vigilantes? I wouldn't go that far. They aren't violent or anything like that. I don't even think they are crazy, well, at least not psychotic. There's a higher-than-average OCD vibe coming off those geniuses."

"You're saying that you trust them?" Estep's expression was hard to read but Serena thought she saw something that resembled human warmth. "Why didn't you contact me? We've been looking for you. Beav was in the field most of the night."

"Yes, I trust them. I left Beav a message, didn't he get it?"

"You mean the journal page? Yes, he got it. But you should have called me." Estep's voice trailed off because he was distracted. He was memorizing the crime scene while hashing this out with Serena. While he didn't think there was anything about the scene that would be of any use, he never left anything to chance.

Meanwhile, Serena had ruled out any importance to the crime scene details and had stopped expending energy on thinking about it. She wanted to ask Estep what he planned to do next, but she knew he wouldn't answer her. She had learned from experience that the best way to keep Estep's moods on even keel was to reign in her tendency to babble.

Thirty minutes later Estep finally released the scene at Lehman's house to the FBI investigation team and indicated for Serena to follow him to his vehicle. "Call them and arrange a meeting."

"By 'them' I assume you mean the Supporters?" Serena couldn't imagine who else he could be referring to, but she sought to confirm anything that could come back on her later if she got it wrong.

"You aren't working with them anymore without me there."

"You're worried about me!" Serena exclaimed. So that was the warmth she'd seen in his face!

Estep snorted, grunted, and looked ready to fly into convulsions. "I'll be there to make sure you don't screw this up."

The ride to the nearest fast food restaurant was long. Estep needed coffee, for both of their sakes. He pulled up to the drive-through window, ordered a large black coffee, and drove to the next window without asking if Serena wanted anything.

"Hey, I wanted to order a burger!" Serena yelped.

"You should have said something."

"Can I run in real quick and get one?"

"No."

"What good does it do to say something?"

"You asked too late. I'm already through."

"I can go in right now, won't take long."

Estep locked her door with his panel controls.

"Alrighty then." Serena glared out the window, looking more like a petulant child than a private detective for hire. Glaring was Estep's domain. Her attempts to dish it back out were ridiculous.

Estep paid for his coffee, grabbed the hot foam cup of joe and drank it without hesitation. Whether or not it scorched his throat was impossible to tell. Serena assumed he had built up so much scar tissue from this habit that he no longer felt the burn. Minutes later Estep mellowed out enough to initiate dialog.

"Before Carson kicked off, you had him dead to rights?"

"Definitely, and I recorded the whole thing, but you know that already. Besides, you know he was guilty. Why are you asking me this?"

"I have to be sure."

"There's no doubt." Serena made a crossing motion over her heart.

Estep nodded.

After a few seconds Serena asked, "Aren't you going to tell me what's going on?"

"No."

"What? Come on, I'm on this case too."

Estep pulled the car over gently, smoothly, and only after the flow of traffic allowed for the transition. He slowly set his coffee in the cup holder. He undid his seat belt and twisted his upper body toward Serena. "This is not a case. It is a high-level threat to the

President. You are not an agent."

"This is crazy! You know I was a big help with Covert Coffee."

"Random," Estep scoffed.

"Random? What do you mean by that? Come on, you know I was in the middle of that operation. If it wasn't for me…"

"If it wasn't for you, I wouldn't be sitting here right now!"

"What's going on? We were past all of this." Serena searched his face for clues. Again, she found a trace of humanity. "I was right, you are worried about me, aren't you?"

Estep buried his face into the steering wheel, his voice muffled. "You remind me of my grandmother."

"How old do you think I am? I'm barely old enough to have been your mother – maybe not even quite old enough for that. I'd have to do the math."

Estep continued to speak through the steering wheel, his forehead pressed hard against its leather cover. "She was spunky like you, short like you. She was funny and smart, and dead."

"I'm not sure why you felt the need to bring up the height issue, but I'm flattered by the rest. I'm assuming she didn't die of natural causes?"

"No. She got involved in something she shouldn't have messed in. Just like you."

"I'm an incredibly lucky person."

"Luck runs out."

"You can't pull me off this case. I already have authority to be on it."

"I can't be your bodyguard."

"Why not? Isn't that basically what President Ann asked you to do?"

"I can't because you won't follow protocol. You aren't dead right now because of dumb luck."

"Told you, I'm lucky."

Estep withdrew from his position at the wheel and looked her in the eye. "You don't respect chain of command, or me. You are, I repeat, not an agent."

"I do respect you, Estep. I'm sorry I've made you believe otherwise."

Estep made a murmuring sound that may have been forgiveness. "You'll do it again. There will be another dead body and next time it might be yours."

"I'll work on this with my own team if you aren't willing to help me."

Estep made an utterance that sounded like a strangled sigh, a cat in mid-yawn, or an expletive that Serena had never heard before. Then he snapped his seat belt back into place, turned the key in the ignition and steered the car back onto the freeway.

5

Three hours later, Agent Estep and Serena were at, of all places, the Medieval Times. Just outside Chicago, it offered them easy access from the freeway and a noisy chaotic environment – perfect for meeting with Beav, no one would overhear them here. While they waited for him to arrive they were barely able to hold a conversation over the din. Children ran to and fro, waving flashing wands and fighting with plastic swords. It was a relief when Beav approached them.

"Let's get on with it," said Estep.

They huddled in the midst of the packed lobby, between a souvenir stand and a line of people waiting in the beer line. It was an effective cloak of invisibility.

Beav began. "I spoke with the Supporters, someone named Bob and some other guy who didn't give me his name. They said that there is a financial take-over in the works, orchestrated at high levels of our own government as well as in a joint venture across the globe. We're talking about a buy-out on a scale we've never seen before, of the entire American government and our national business infrastructure. I don't know any details, nor would I likely understand it, but I believe them. Even if they're wrong, we can't ignore that they could be right." Beav had to shout over the sounds of war coming from three hyperactive boys running and jousting in and around their party of three. "And there was never really any threat to Serena's family."

Serena nodded. "Their threat was a carrot to get me to go to them, but Tom and the kids were waiting for me on the other side of the corn – not a scratch on them. All is well."

"Fine, good, I knew that." Estep gave one of the jousting boys his famous glare. The child's eyes flew open wide and he ran away with the other two at his heels.

Unlike Beav and Serena, Agent Estep didn't need to raise his voice; his deep baritone was always inescapably audible. "How did you end up with Governor Landon and why didn't you contact me?"

"What, this again? I left the journal page for Beav. I knew he'd find it and sure enough, he didn't let me down."

Beav mimed taking a stage bow.

Serena continued, "They asked me not to contact anyone until I spoke to Carson Landon myself. They were afraid he'd be tipped off otherwise, and now that he's dead, obviously they were right to be concerned."

Estep wouldn't let it go. "They got to him anyway. Going vigilante did nothing but botch the investigation."

Serena protested, "You don't know that you could have kept him alive any longer than I did. Which makes me question: how did they know I was meeting with Carson? Were they watching me?"

"We'll never know because I couldn't assign you a surveillance team."

Beav finally had enough. "Can we move on from this?"

Estep gave Serena one last dark stare and then complied. "Here's what I've got: President Kinji laid it all on the table. In a nutshell, she accused the whole room of wanting to kill her."

Serena leaned in closer. "Anyone look guilty?"

Estep shook his head. "Profilers didn't see anything, nothing much anyway. Suspects are Mr. Speaker of the House, Joseph Smythe, Governor Carson Landon, who is now dead and worthless to us…"

"I said I was sorry!"

Estep ignored her. "…Senator William Casey and Senator Robert Lorry. But like I said, President Kinji was accusing everybody. No one is above suspicion except for her emergency Vice Presidential appointee Agent Lehman, and yours truly."

"I wish I'd been there," Serena moped.

"President Kinji wants to do something historic and unprecedented." Estep relished knowing that he had witnessed something Serena would have given her eyeteeth for. He spent a few seconds people watching, letting Serena stew.

"Well, what? What is it?" Serena knew he was dragging out the suspense to get her goat, but she couldn't wait him out.

"She wants to invoke a UN loophole of some kind. She plans to take over the house and senate, temporarily having full authority: the executive branch would have full power to override the congress." Estep gloated- it was fun knowing something Serena didn't.

Beav whistled. "I didn't know she could do that."

Estep said, "It's never been done before. She has to get a UN resolution to pass. If she can manage it she'll be fully in control of the nation."

Serena questioned, more for her own ruminating than for conversational purposes, "What will she do with that power?"

Estep replied, "She'll replace long-time members of congress with newbies, none of them are career politicians. Then she's going to ask them to set term limits."

Beav asked, "Who? The new congress?"

Estep nodded. "Of course the new congress—the old regime would never vote themselves out, that's the point! She wants term limits to protect future generations from this happening all over again. To fix what's already been done, she's flushing congress of anyone who's been there longer than the past two years."

"Wow, I can't imagine they'll go away quietly," Serena worried.

Estep laughed. "If necessary she'll order the Department of Homeland Security to escort them out. All that stockpiling of weapons they put into the DHS back in 2012- bet they didn't expect it to be used against their own decrepit selves!"

"They're going in." Beav moved toward the doors.

Estep shook his head. "No, not yet. She doesn't even have the resolution yet."

Beav pointed at the double doors ahead. "No, I mean here, they're going in. What did you think we were waiting for all this time? That's where the dinner theater is."

"What? We aren't staying." Estep pulled him back.

"I'm starving. We're staying until we eat. I had to buy these tickets, and they weren't cheap. You're lucky they had anything available at the last minute." Beav donned his paper crown and merged with the crowd.

"Lucky." Estep snorted. Hunger weakened his stance. He followed Beav with Serena close at his heels.

Estep and Serena were prompted by the hostess to put their crowns on. Serena complied, Estep did not. They were led into the arena to their assigned seats, rooting for the yellow knight. Estep sat like a lump until the show began. Then, taking both Serena and Beav by surprise, he got into the whole affair. He was soon bellowing and booing above the rest. He appeared to be having fun, proving that anything is possible. As soon as the food was gone and the show ended, Estep's good humor was turned off like a switch.

"Time to hit the road." Estep glanced around the arena and was satisfied to find nothing unexpected. They hadn't been followed and they hadn't attracted any attention. Incredibly, the presidents' investigation trio, motley crew that they were, had slipped into The Medieval Times without notice. Slipping back out was just as easy. Of course Estep was the only one of them who looked like (and was) an agent.

"Are we riding together now?" asked Beav.

"What are you going to do with your car?" asked Serena.

"A friend dropped me off," said Beav.

"How did you intend to get back?" asked Serena.

Beav shrugged. "I find a way."

"Doesn't matter. He's coming with us." Estep settled into the driver's seat and waited for Serena and Beav to negotiate who was riding shotgun. Beav won, having longer legs and a better rapport with Estep than Serena had.

It was a relatively short drive to The Cube, but with traffic bumper to bumper the trip took over two hours. By the time they reached the secret entrance to the underground parking garage Estep was intolerant of any sound; radio, talking, even loud breathing. Even before the car came to a complete stop the three of them burst out of it like clowns in a circus act.

They hit the restroom, snack bar and conference room in that order. Armed with coffee and sandwiches, they were ready for a long session of whatever President Kinji had in store for them.

They didn't have long to wait. President Ann, as Americans affectionately called her, was always on time. The three of them stood up when she entered the room. Ann waved her hand dismissively. They sat. Ann cleared her throat and looked at them expectantly.

Serena got the ball rolling. "What we have so far: The Supporters claim that there is a financial takeover brewing; that's what Covert Coffee was about. Governor Carson Landon is dead, but he wasn't a big player anyway."

"It would have been nice to hear what he had to say." Ann scowled.

"I know, I'm sorry." Serena blushed.

Beav took over. "The Supporters gained my respect. I suggest that we assume that what they are saying is the truth until we disprove it."

Ann placed her elbows on the table, folded her hands without lacing her fingers, and rested her chin on her hands. "Who wants me dead and why? Why do I stand in their way?"

The three of them looked at each other, none of them prepared with an answer. After a few awkward seconds lapsed Agent Estep said, "We don't know. That's all we have. Should we talk to the politicians you brought to the front of the room in your briefing?"

Ann closed her eyes. She held that silent position for so long that the three investigators grew anxious. Then she inhaled deeply, exhaled slowly, opened her eyes, and lifted her face from her chin-on-hands pose. "I can't be involved in this."

"Of course not, you're the President," said Beav.

Ann shook her head. "No, I mean that I can't know what you are doing. It's beyond covert. There's literally no one left I can trust. And I was a fool to have thought that there was."

Serena reached across the table and gave Ann's hand a squeeze. "You are no worse off than you were before. You can trust Lehman, Estep, Beav, myself and child genius Nicholas from the Superman Lab. Tom and my kids are big fans, and your own husband has never given you any reason to doubt his devotion. I could keep going with this; Penny your former driver comes to mind. It's a big circle of trust –bigger than most people have actually, but you know that already. What's really going on?"

Ann locked eyes with Serena. "I'm not leading this country."

Estep stood up. When women started bleeding emotions his instinct was to bolt. President Ann Kinji may be his Commander-in-Chief, but at this moment she was acting like a woman. He knew the signs, having lived in a house full of sisters. "I don't think I'm needed here."

Transparent as he was, Kinji could read Estep like a large-print book. Ann stiffened her spine and gestured for him to sit back down. Then she stood up. "Make no mistake, I'm still leading *you*."

Estep was sufficiently chastised, another familiar scene from growing up with a strong-willed mother, grandmother and sisters. He slumped in his chair, knowing that he may as well be a fly on the wall.

With Estep muzzled, Ann launched into conversation. "To clarify, I've come to realize that the American government has, for longer than I care to think, been manipulated by the powerful few at the top – in congressional seats they've held fast to while presidents have come and gone. The reality is that the office of the presidency has been stripped of power a little at a time, year after year, until it has been diminished to this: I am nothing more than a puppet. I've been like Pinocchio, believing I'm real and then finally waking up to the realization that I've been dancing in a puppet show all along. Well no more! My eyes are wide open, painted wood though they may be."

"Surely it hasn't gotten that bad?" Serena volunteered. "And what about your overthrow of Congress? That had to have helped."

"Yes, it has. Nonetheless, cleaning house is going to be challenging to say the least." Ann stared out her bullet-proof office window, seeing nothing but sky due to being on one of the highest floors of the Cube.

Serena pressed forward. "Question for you: how does the new Congress help us in our efforts?"

Ann raised her eyebrows. "Help us? You mean investigation-wise?"

Serena nodded.

"It doesn't. Congress is to operate as normal. The old guard has been sequestered and the official independent investigation team is questioning them as we speak. Their investigation as well as yours will not further distract the nation from running as usual. Corruption from within has slowed me down throughout my entire presidency. I won't allow it to bog down the remainder of my term, and I won't leave this mess as a legacy for future administrations." Ann had worked herself up into a frenzy and was now pacing back and forth, moving so swiftly that it looked like Serena and Estep were watching a tennis match.

Serena frowned, fearing a tongue lashing. "I understand what you are saying. I'm doing my best to grasp what you want us to do. If we aren't needed to interrogate former members of Congress, or any of the prime suspects, what is it that we should be doing?"

Ann stopped short. "I expect you to figure that out. You three will have the lab at your disposal, a team, and anyone or anything you need. You can have a jet. Just say the word. It's a massive clean-up, and while I have everyone on it, our hands are tied by the law, and soon the media frenzy will slow us down significantly."

"I understand. We'll figure it out." Serena dared to make a promise that she had no idea how to keep.

"We'll start with your line-up then?" Estep asked. He recognized that the conversation had finally come back around to the investigation.

Ann shook her head with enough vigor that her bob shook.

"No?" Estep was baffled. There appeared to be no clear agenda and dragging one out of the president was seemingly impossible.

Beav took a stab at it. "You don't want us going over the same territory as the official investigation team."

Ann gave Beav the thumbs-up sign. "Exactly. My own team can handle the obvious, and following protocol will do. Beyond the obvious? Frankly, if I wanted by-the-book I wouldn't ask for you three: Loose Cannon, Loose Screw and, well, Serena." Ann paused. "Give me crazy. That's what we need."

"I can do crazy," said Serena.

Ann evaluated Serena Wilcox Bridges, former private detective, mother of three, and a person who had become a close friend, as close as anyone could get to Ann Kinji, a woman with an intimidating persona and emotional walls of steel. Serena's green eyes stared back at her, eyes incapable of anything but honesty; silly, raw, human honesty. Yes, Ann was confident she had made the right move.

The President of the United States left the table without another word or a look back. Because the corridor's motion sensors had been turned off for their meeting, Ann rapped on the door for her secret service detail to let her out, leaving the doors wide open behind her. The three remained seated, glancing at each other with raised eyebrows and shrugs.

"I'll take that as our cue to leave," Beav whispered.

Estep and Serena followed him out the door, down the corridor, and to another secret exit, one that Agent Estep never knew existed, but Serena and Beav had used many times in the past. It was the *secret* secret exit, the one for outsiders to the Cube, for people whose existence would be denied if necessary; for people whose existence would be terminated if necessary.

It was then that Estep understood what President Kinji had done. His career as he knew it was over. He had been cast out – he was dark! His heart sank as he realized that his only hope of ever acting as an official government agent again lay with Serena Wilcox.

6

Serena was back in the Superman computer lab, which had been previously compromised but had been relocated to a new top secret location. It was much closer to The Cube, just three hours' drive, near President Kinji's hometown of Warsaw, Indiana. The lab was in an underground location in the middle of nowhere. The nearest store was in Oswego, a tiny town with few shopping possibilities. Thankfully the lab was fully stocked with anything they could possibly need.

In newly re-united America, post Big War, everything that was D.C. based was now in Chicago. The new Wall Street was in Minneapolis. Because America's headquarters had relocated from the East coast to the Midwest, states beyond Illinois and Minnesota were becoming more important. For example, Indiana, with its state line so near Chicago, was now part of an even bigger sprawl – commuters were buying properties way beyond Gary, Indiana, often commuting three or more hours to work each way. Many employers offered sleeping rooms – commuters living at the workplace, coming home only on weekends or even less frequently, had become an acceptable modern day way of life.

The location of the Superman lab was considered to be relatively close, within commuting distance by today's standards. Yet according to yesterday's standards it would be considered a long drive out of state. Serena was just relieved that she didn't have to hop on a jet for Wisconsin this time around. Avoiding air travel felt like a big enough win in and of itself.

Serena surveyed the lab and noted that a few things had changed. The Superman theme was still intact, brought over from the old location as per Nicholas' specifications, but his favorite superhero was now forced to share the space . Newly added décor included Tardis replicas, Daleks, and Doctor Who posters. Styluses for all the graphic tablets were in the shape of The Doctor's sonic screwdriver.

It warmed Serena's heart to know that the powers that be still had a budget and a soft spot for catering to Nicholas' tastes. Then again, as much as the government used that child, they owed him so much more- a normal childhood for starters.

"Nicholas?" Serena didn't want to startle the boy wonder who was now almost sixteen years old. He was listening to music via microchip technology. The implant was a simple procedure, as routine to the younger generations as getting piercings or tattoos. The chip was easy to program and best of all, there was no longer any need to wear ear buds. The downside to the technology, besides questions about health side effects, was that it was difficult to tell when someone was listening to music. Teachers had been working to get the chips banned, but too many students already had them, and since removing the chips required surgery, the mandate against the chips was deemed unconstitutional.

Nicholas turned around slowly, not at all surprised to see her standing there. His microchip had alerted him that someone had entered the building. It was synched with the iris reader security so he even knew exactly who it was. Besides, he was kept in the loop about such things.

Serena greeted him with, "I suppose you wonder why I'm back?"

"No, I know why you're here." Nicholas turned off his music.

"Then can you fill me in?" Serena laughed, but she was entirely serious. They were taking a stab in the dark. She didn't have the slightest idea of who to investigate first. Everyone in our government? All of the international community as well? Every world leader? Every junior staffer – everywhere? Forget the haystack, it was like finding a needle embedded in thousands of other needles, and more than one of them was tainted.

"We need to rule out some suspects to start," said Nicholas simply. Perhaps to him it really was that simple. Maybe Serena could sit back and have a cup of joe, letting Nicholas do the work.

Beav and Estep had been clearing the area to make sure that they didn't have unexpected company. They were now hovering around Nicholas' computer..

"You can sit over there," he directed. He clacked at the keyboard, preferring the keyboard over most other methods of input, even though typing was considered nearly obsolete these days.

He cued up his latest creation; software designed to eliminate wild goose chases. He called it "The Golden Egg". The program opened with a holographic animated short film that awed the three adults. A line of cartoon figures ran between and around them, much like the young jousting boys had done at the Medieval Times. The first in the line was of course the goose from the fairy tale, the one that laid golden eggs. Next in the line were all the people who had touched it and had stuck fast. The hologram weaved around and around them to a merry tune that Nicholas had composed himself, a jazzy blend of blues harmonica, piano, and even some other instrument they couldn't quite identify.

When the cartoon segment ended the program launched without further entertainment or fanfare. However, the program itself was also holographic. Nicholas said, "I didn't have your measurements so I guessed at your eye level comfort. If you want to adjust data higher or lower, nudge it with your hand."

"Awesome!" Beav slid his hologram monitor around until he reached his reading-distance preference. Estep followed suit.

Serena couldn't resist playing with her hologram, adjusting it over and over until she realized that Estep's eyes were boring into her skin. She dropped her arms down to her sides and said, "Ready when you are."

Nicholas took what looked like an Irish tin whistle from a jeweled case. He whistled a jaunty little tune, causing files to open. He stopped. "I gave you some data to browse through. This is your basic criteria for setting wild goose chase perimeters. Make your selections by touching the files. You'll be able to figure it out as you try it."

"If you say so," said Estep dubiously.

"Um, actually, don't touch anything, sir. We only need one person messing with the files." Nicholas looked from Beav to Serena. "Out of the three of you, I pick Serena."

"I'll take that as a compliment," said Serena.

Nicholas had already turned back toward his computer. He turned his personal jukebox up so loudly that they could faintly hear music coming from the chip.

"Thanks, Nicholas." Serena said, even though she knew he probably didn't hear her.

Estep grumbled, "Let's get it done. I hate this place."

Beav clapped his hands a few inches from Estep's face. "Are you in there? This is the super-secret lab of the future! We are underground, protected by top-of-the-line iris-reading security, and at this moment we are interacting with holograms floating in front of us – brand new technology that no one else knows about. We'll be the first to use it!"

"I'll be the first, only I have permission to touch the files." Serena reminded him.

Beav laughed. "Only because he declared you the lesser idiot of the two of us. Estep wasn't even considered at all."

"To quote President Kinji, his choices were Loose Cannon, Loose Screw or me."

Estep scoffed. "I assume I'm Loose Cannon."

Beav said, "I wear Loose Screw with pride."

Serena pointed at the data in front of her. "Not that I don't enjoy your self-deprecating banter but I see something already."

Estep stared at the information and then let out a ridiculously long sigh. "How long do you think this is going to take? No one's out there doing surveillance."

"Did your team leave?" Serena asked.

"Besides them."

"Are you saying that you'd rather go sit out in the car?" Serena fed him the suggestion in case he hadn't already come up with it on his own.

"Let me know when you guys find something." Estep let himself out.

Serena turned her attention to Beav. "Look. Do you see the list in the blue folder?"

"Yes. I think we can get rid of all of that."

"All of it?"

"Why not? Postal employees, that's highly doubtful. Sanitation department. Natural resources. Parks and recreation. Libraries? Come on, Serena, we have to narrow this down and none of these agencies are likely suspects."

"Agreed." She closed the file shut by pinching it with her fingers. "What do I do now?"

"Try pressing it."

"Pressing it?"

"Tap on it." Beav demonstrated by tapping his finger on the palm of his other hand.

Serena tapped on the holographic folder and a menu popped out. She tapped on the option that said "Remove from search".

"It worked! What now?"

Beav shrugged. "I don't know."

Serena tapped on the folder again to bring up the menu she saw earlier. She tapped the option that said "Pinpoint". A flurry of hologram images burst out, scattering around the room, rotating and shuffling. The flurry was accompanied by musical chimes for every file. The sounds overlapped each other in such a jangle that it was like a porch full of wind chimes had gone off.

They waited for the files- labeled with every color in the

rainbow- to stop moving and for the noise of the chimes to die down. Serena looked at Nicholas but he was buried in his work.

"Reach out and grab one of the squares," Beav suggested.

Serena snagged the next square that floated in her direction. She read it aloud "Conservative". She let go of it and it stayed in front of her. She pulled a second square from its floating space. "Lobbyist". She let it go and it snapped on top of the first square, making a stack like a virtual deck of cards. She was catching on to this.

She grabbed another and another: Pro-life, Salary $1,000,000+, Unions, Environmentalist, In Favor of One World Government, Appointed by President Ann Kinji, Senator. The next pinpoint square that floated her way caused her to do a double take: The Supporters.

Serena made an "ahah!" sound. "I understand this now. All of these descriptors can help us narrow down our list of suspects. I can make a stack of words I don't think relate to our suspects and delete them in one fell swoop."

Serena and Beav collaborated over each of the keywords. They agreed to place The Supporters onto the top of the keep stack. They tossed out words they thought were irrelevant. Keepers included words relating to foreign governments, money, powerful positions, and controversial issues.

The sleuthing pair repeated the process through fifty folders, taking up the better part of the next four hours. Finally they decided to see where they stood, even though they didn't think that they had eliminated enough suspects for the computer to generate a manageably sized list. They were stunned when the results rang up only ten names.

So engrossed in their investigation, the two barely noticed that

Estep had come and gone, come and gone. Serena and Beav were still celebrating their list of ten names with whoops and high fives when Estep walked in with a tower of pizza boxes. He set the boxes on an empty work table, laid them all out and then grabbed a slice from the pie loaded with the most toppings.

Serena accepted a freshly-printed hardcopy of the list from Nicholas. "The first three on the list are the same crew that the Cube is investigating, so I suppose we leave them alone. That gives us seven remaining, four domestic and three foreign."

"Finally something concrete to work with," said Estep with his mouth full of pizza.

Serena folded the list and put it into her purse.

Beav made a *tsk, tsk* noise. "You're going to walk around with that paper on you? Did you never see a spy movie? Memorize the list and destroy it."

Serena grimaced. "My memory's not as sharp as it used to be. I'll have to make up a mnemonic trick for it. Let's see... Billy Bob and the Kangaroo went to the Bank to Cash a Check..."

"Give it to me." Estep snatched the paper from her hands, giving Serena a paper cut in the process. He looked at the list for no longer than three seconds before running it through a paper shredder. Then he headed out the door in his usual way – no good-bye. He doubled back for one last slice, his fifth, leaving the rest of the pizza behind.

Beav said, "Once again, our cue to leave is when someone walks out." He gave Nicholas a two-fingered salute off the imaginary brim of his nonexistent hat. He stacked two boxes of pizza and carried them out.

"Thank you for your help, Nicholas. You always come through for us." Serena extended her hand and gave Nicholas' a hearty shake. “The rest of that pizza is yours. Anything left over you can give to your family, or maybe heat up for yourself. It looks like you can get a lot of meals out of it. Your parents will pick you up soon? Should we be leaving you here by yourself?”

Nicholas laughed. “Ms. Wilcox, I do this all the time. Besides, I’m not alone. There are a couple security guards on duty at all times. What did you think of Golden Egg?”

“Fully awesome. You amaze me!”

Nicholas nodded and grinned. Then he stared wistfully at her purse.

“I saw that! You’re remembering that I gave you something the last time you helped us out. I haven’t forgotten.” Serena rummaged through her purse and pulled out something better than a pack of gum—a small retro Superman alarm clock.

Nicholas moved faster than she’d seen him move all day. He thanked her profusely and even gave her a hearty clap on the shoulder, a bit too hearty for Serena’s much shorter frame.

Beav and Estep came back inside to see what the hold-up was. Serena explained, “I was saying goodbye to my good buddy.”

Estep snorted. “If you gave me presents I’d be your buddy too.”

Nicholas protested. “Sir, that’s not why I like Ms. Wilcox.”

Beav gave Estep a shove toward the open door. “Leave the kid alone. He’s happy - something you wouldn’t know anything about.”

7

President Ann Kinji switched all incoming, and more importantly outgoing, communications to standby. She cranked up the ventilation system settings until its fans produced the obnoxiously loud mechanical whirring sound she expected. For good measure she spoke barely above a whisper. "Dr. Kendra Wellington, nice to meet you. I appreciate you flying out here on such short notice."

"Of course, Madam President. How can I be of help?" Kendra, a professor at a state university, was a young blonde married mother of a preschooler. She and her husband had tried to guess why the President of the United States requested to see her. There was nothing about Kendra that was political, except for having recently taught a 100-level political science course. The course had been dumped on her lap when the university couldn't find a substitute for a professor out on maternity leave.

Ann gestured for Kendra to come closer. She rasped, “I want to understand the authority of the UN.”

Kendra dropped her voice to match the president’s whisper. “What do you mean by ‘authority’?” Kendra realized that she had been right—President Kinji wanted Kendra for her expertise. Kendra hoped she knew the answers; she had taught at the general elective level, and she wasn’t sure how much of the curriculum she even remembered.

“Specifically, I want to know if I can make a direct appeal to the UN to give me the power to circumvent the House and the Senate. I am seeking a total bypass of the two governmental branches, making me temporarily Queen or, in a less kind but perhaps more accurate view, Dictator of the United States of America.”

Kendra’s eyes widened but she kept her composure. She hesitated for only a second or two before whispering, “To say that I’m speechless is an understatement. Please forgive me if it takes me a few minutes to formulate my response.”

Ann dropped the whispering, but still spoke quietly. “I understand.” She watched Kendra’s face as the young woman’s mind raced. When she saw that Kendra was visibly more relaxed she said, “Are you composed now?”

“I’m as composed as I’ll ever be.” Kendra said.

“Good. Before we begin I prefer, and even require, that my intentions be clear from the start. I’m recording our conversation and I ask you to pay close attention to every word that passes from my lips.”

Ann spoke directly into the microphone source. “My intention is to take over the United States government on a temporary basis not to exceed six months, in a temporary measure to gain control over rampant government corruption that is an immediate and direct threat to not only our nation, but to the world."

Kendra suppressed the urge to gasp. She formulated what she thought was a responsible question. "What will you do with your temporary circumvention of checks and balances?"

"Investigate every member of the House and Senate."

"I don't understand why you need the UN to give you sole authority for this purpose. You can investigate openly, you already have that authority." Kendra's eyes flitted about the room as if hoping that someone else would emerge who could take her place.

Ann shook her head with enough force that her signature onyx bob trembled. "No, I don't have authority to investigate as thoroughly as required. I want to restrict Internet access for all Americans and convince world leaders to limit Internet access abroad as well. That alone is a move that Congress will never agree to."

"That objective seems impossible. What basis do you have for believing you can accomplish Internet restriction?" As soon as the words left her lips Kendra regretted them. How could she be so bold as to challenge President Ann Kinji?

If Ann was offended she didn't show it. "I have access to people who know these things. They assure me that it's possible. Eventually hackers will find a way around the restrictions, but even a day or two of blocked communications will be of great help to us."

"Cell phones?"

"Now you are catching on. Yes, I want to block *all* communications. The powers behind the layers of conspiracy and treason are geographically spread out, of that I am certain. If we cut them off from each other, they will be forced to meet in person."

"Or wait it out? They may be patient."

"They know that I'm closing in on them. I predict that they will react by connecting with each other. However, it doesn't really matter which way they respond. If they think they can wait it out, I'll benefit from that as well."

"How so?"

"Whatever it is that they are planning, they will be thrown off course. It gives my team time to find them before they take another step. They have been blocking, tracking and censoring Internet communications for years. I feel strongly that shutting things down on their end is going to throw them for a loop. Regardless, that's only a small part of what I would do with full authority over Congress. Can it be done? Does the UN have the authority to grant me my emergency petition?"

The phrase 'emergency petition' jogged her memory; Kendra now understood why President Kinji had requested her. She had invited her political science students to join in class discussion online but the only person who visited the forum was a foreign exchange student who enjoyed debate. He and Kendra had a rather lengthy dialog about the history of the UN that was entirely public—how could she have forgotten this? Anyone searching for active scholarly discussions about the UN could easily find it. Yes, that had to be it.

Confident that she understood her purpose for being here, Kendra slipped into her comfortable role of teacher. "You might recall that the UN got a toehold into a one-world government of sorts when the child disability act was passed. That bill gave the UN the authority to regulate, or legislate, over our own laws. Since then, the UN has passed several similar acts, all of it leading to this situation. Yes, President Kinji, the UN most certainly can give you authority over the United States, superseding our own laws--assuming that you can convince them to grant it to you. You are proposing a temporary emergency measure, and it's possible they will be agreeable to it, but you'll have to make a strong case for its necessity. Do you have friends at the UN?"

"Friends, enemies, and frenemies."

"I don't like your chances, but yes, they have the power to give you what you want."

"Thank you for your time. That's all I needed to know."

"If you don't mind my asking, I'd like permission to stay on." Kendra couldn't believe she was daring to ask, but she'd never forgive herself if she didn't try.

"To stay on?"

"May I be an observer, a historian? I won't speak without your permission. My role is only that of a witness."

"I welcome your involvement. And you don't need to sit by in silence. Speak freely; I value your input."

Kendra took a deep breath. Should she dare say what's on her heart? "I do have a few thoughts I'd like to share with you right now, actually."

"Fire away."

"Obviously the UN had a major role in the rebuilding of the United States post Big War, otherwise known as World War 3 everywhere else but in our own country."

"We don't call it World War 3 because few nations other than our own were involved. It was a limited engagement, catastrophic as it was. We took care of it quickly, involving few."

"Ah, but that's far from the truth. The economic collapse affected everyone."

"The collapse was averted."

"That's my point. It was averted because the UN stepped in with the Global Initiative, the first of its kind. Of course the Global Initiative spidered into the Global Oil Initiative and several others, but the Global Initiative covers it all. Anyway, that's how all of this began, this corruption that you are addressing now. The desperation of the United States created a window of opportunity for the loan sharks of the world to jump through."

"Loan sharks? I haven't heard the global investors referred to that way before, yet I suppose I'd be hard pressed to find a more accurate description."

Kendra leaned forward and clasped her hand over the microphone sensor. She whispered as quietly as her voice could drop. "The sharks are calling in the loan."

Ann studied Kendra's face and after seeing fear in her eyes, she allowed her hand to remain over the microphone sensor. She followed suit and lowered her voice as well. "That's all out in the open. We all know that the United States is squeezed. We are loaning our military to all manner of global situations, all gratis, to pay down on our debts. We are also gifting food and other resources. We are making good on our word, on our agreement with the UN."

Kendra looked wildly about the room, this time worried that someone really would appear. "No, that's not what I'm talking about. The above-board loans are being paid as per the terms of the contracts signed by yourself and President John Williams. No one disputes that."

"What are you implying?"

Kendra hesitated. "I can't imagine that you aren't aware of the other loans."

Ann switched off the microphone. "Other loans?"

Kendra's arm ached from covering the microphone sensor for so long, funny how she hadn't felt the strain on her muscles until now. All of her sensations were off kilter. The confidence she felt a few minutes ago was gone. "The secret deals, the hand-shakes under the table."

President Ann was speechless. She was a statue, blinking at Kendra.

"You didn't know?" Kendra searched about the room, her longing to be replaced by someone else had intensified. And yet, she wanted to stay.

"Do you have any proof? How and what do you know about this?" Ann put Kendra on the spot even though she knew that her statements held an undeniable ring of truth.

"Well, I thought it was common knowledge. It's been rather out in the open. Don't you keep track of what's on the social media channel?" Kendra was proud of herself for not only staying in the room but for holding her own in the conversation as well.

"We track various keywords, yes. I don't understand how we could have missed something like this." Ann paced the length of the room, a large room the size of Kendra's entire modest floor space at her house, a home that felt far away from her at the moment.

Kendra rallied her thoughts and ventured, "They could have been cloaking themselves."

"Cloaking?" Ann was near Kendra's ear, rasping again.

Kendra again lowered her voice. "The Internet sources I'm talking about might have blocks on their content and their addresses so that you can't track them. But even so, why hasn't anyone brought it to your attention? Surely people have discovered it for themselves just by using the Internet on their own."

"I don't know how to answer that."

Kendra didn't know what to say either.

"Spies and patriots alike have been cloaking and blocking, censoring and hacking; both officially and unofficially. I don't see how we can control the anarchy that is the Internet. The only way to regain any sort of order is to shut it down." Ann threw her hands up in a flourish that sent her bob in motion, her turned-up locks swinging like a pendulum. She paced back and forth for several minutes, her head bent and her hands formed into fists. Finally she meandered back over to Kendra and looked at her expectantly.

Kendra had been digging into her purse for her phone while Ann was pacing. She held her phone out to her now. "Here, let me show you. It's easy to find layperson and expert forums about what I'm talking about."

"No, I'll do you one better. Wave your hand in front of the hologram."

Kendra's eyes lit up. "I've seen one of these before, but I've never used one. How do I do a search?"

"Talk to the hologram as if it was a real person. I call her Sally."

Kendra begged her mind to remember this moment always—she would be retelling this at dinner parties for the rest of her life. "Sally, please do a search for all articles relating to 'loan shark global deals'."

Forty-four results came up on the projection screen. As the two women browsed through the list, selected articles, and began to skim them, a red light flashed over the screen. It blinked without ceasing until Ann picked up her phone. The phone looked surprisingly vintage and appeared to be hardwired to the wall. "Nicholas, is this you?"

"Yes, it's me, President Kinji."

"If you are calling me on this line this can't be good."

"No, it isn't. I got a trigger."

"A trigger?"

"Your search kicked off a trigger. Someone was tracking your keywords, you know, like we do. Except this isn't one of ours. This trace is foreign."

"Foreign meaning not of our department?"

"No, foreign meaning not of our country."

"Which country?"

"I don't know. I'm working on it."

"Thank you Nicholas. Do you need more hands to sort this out?"

"I have the team you gave me. That's enough. But you better stop whatever it is that you are doing. Let me do it here."

"I already got what I need. If I need anything else, I'll let you know." Ann disconnected the contact with Nicholas and turned her attention back to Kendra. "All of these results are from fringe groups or extremists, not 'everywhere' as you've asserted."

Kendra blushed. "These are popular sources that have become mainstream. Like this one, The Supporters, they are especially good."

"The Supporters? That's one I'm familiar with. We're dealing with them right now."

"You should have been aware of this information. It's out there, in a big enough way that it's hard to imagine you not knowing about it. Who's in charge of the keyword traces you talked about? That person is either really bad at their job or deliberately hiding the information from you."

"The Cube is a vacuum. It's easy to be kept in the dark, even more so if someone wants it that way. Skip Sally, show me on your phone."

Kendra used a hotkey to call up a previous search. Nothing happened. She manually typed the search keywords into her phone. The search results were completely unrelated to her keywords. "I don't understand. How can this be? My presets are wiped clean and my searches are blocked. But my phone has never left my purse!"

Ann fumed, "Now we know why I didn't know about the so-called loan shark global deals- my entire office is hacked!"

8

"The president is in trouble," said Nicholas.

"Yes, I assumed that when the alarm sounded. I know I'm not a genius like you, but I'm further up the chain than a monkey," said Estep.

"Hey, easy. You're more snarly than your usual endearing self. Did your girlfriend dump you?" Beav stepped in.

Beav's girlfriend references and jabs were nothing more than barbs; Beav knew nothing of Estep's private life. Yet Estep visibly flinched as if slapped in the face.

"Oh, wow, hey man I'm sorry." Beav clapped him on the back. "Still no reason to take it out on the kid."

"Which girlfriend? Katalina?" Serena realized as soon as the words left her lips that she should have kept her nose out of it.

Serena didn't know much about Estep's private life either, but she overheard enough on-the-road phone conversations to know more than he would have liked for her to have.

But if Estep assumed that Serena enjoyed hearing about the gossipy details of other people's romantic encounters, he was wrong. Serena made a practice of avoiding such conversations. What could she do if she was stuck in the passenger's seat while Estep was having a loud personal conversation on the road?

"She said it's between her and the job."

"And you chose the job." Serena stated the obvious.

Estep stormed out of the room.

"That's your reaction to everything!"

Beav shut the door behind him. "Let him go. He's been fairly useless anyway."

The two contemplated how useless Estep was until Nicholas interrupted their thoughts. His voice sounded like he had been crying. "Please! I don't know what to do. I can't remove the blocks. I don't have their technology."

"Whose technology? What technology?" asked Beav.

Nicholas answered, "I don't know who is behind this. It's Japanese technology. People get paranoid about information being shared or sold, privacy violations, and all of that. This is worse. It's information *prevented* from being shared."

Beav said, "I'm not sure I follow."

Serena explained, "Our words are blocked, controlled, and denied free speech. Who knows how long this has been going on."

Nicholas' face was pale. "Ms. Wilcox, they have the Internet and there's nothing I can do to get it back. President Kinji's office is hacked. She can't use any device to connect to the Internet without hacker interference and spies tracking her every move."

"This isn't all on you." Beav ran his hands through his hair. "Crikey, this is too much for a kid to take on." His face reddened, not an easy feat given his olive skin tone.

"It's better than prison," said Nicholas.

"Prison? Why would you ever have to worry about prison?" Serena smiled. She assumed that Nicholas was being dramatic.

"That's where kids like me are going. It's called 'Proactive imprisonment'. They send us to the criminally insane youth house. That's what happened to some of the kids in my Mensa group. The only reason why I'm not on the list is because I work for the government. If I lose my job they'll put me on the list. I have to fix this!"

"Whoa, slow down. Tell us what's going on." Beav sat down and rolled his chair next to Nicholas.

Nicholas shrugged, a movement barely perceptible given his slumped shoulders. "People are afraid of kids like me after all that's happened. You know, with mass murder-suicides in schools, theaters, malls..."

Serena lunged forward and gave Nicholas a hug. "Just look at this computer lab with your favorite heroes all around you. They built this lab for you because you are one of the good guys. No one's putting you on a list."

Nicholas brightened up instantly, and even grinned. "But I can't trust your judgment, Ms. Wilcox. You *like* crazy people."

"You mean this guy here?" Serena jabbed her thumb toward Beav.

"No, I mean Paul Tracy and the others in the criminally insane ward. You're always asking me to get Paul online for you to talk to him."

"You're right, Nicholas. I like crazy. Not the criminal part, obviously, but this gives me an idea. The imprisoned haven't been cut off from talking to each other, correct? Last I knew, they had older technology, nothing but time on their hands, and still had freedom of information."

Nicholas agreed. "Right. There's no blocking software on their obsolete systems. Prisons, nursing homes, and even some schools haven't gotten the upgrade yet. They don't access the Internet the same way that private citizens or government employees do. But if you want to use their systems you have to go to where they are. I can't do it from here. What I can do is use their outdated software to make a patch to fix this blocking hack. Thanks for the idea Ms. Wilcox."

Serena shook her head. "No, no, I can't take credit for that. But before you get lost in that project, could you set something up for me? I don't want computer connections – I want people, real face-to-face communication. I want to assemble a think tank of people who have been in the loop on every conspiracy theory, every overheard half-baked half-truth and every resource for propaganda that every good extremist should know."

Beav laughed, "Those whack-jobs are *responsible* for most of those conspiracy theories!"

"Maybe so, but they get their ideas from things they've seen and heard. The best fiction begins with a kernel of truth. I want to sort the fact from the fiction and dig through the layers of paranoid delusion until I hit that kernel."

"And then?" Beav pressed.

"I'll trace it back to where it came from and voila! We'll have something to go on." Serena pulled an elastic ponytail holder from the outer pocket of her small travel purse and swept her long dark hair back away from her face.

"It's as easy as that?" Beav shook his head.

"Agent Estep's negativity is wearing off on you." Serena clucked her tongue.

"We can't let that happen – I must resist! Count me in." Beav pointed at Serena's ponytail. "I see you're ready for action."

Nicholas offered, "I can send for them so you don't have to go back to the prison."

Beav questioned, "Wouldn't that take a lot of red tape and time we don't have?"

"I have a fast-track. President Kinji gave me an emergency pass for anything you ask for. Well, I mean, anything official you ask for. I don't think it works on pizza delivery or something like that." Nicholas said all of this without any hint that he understood how powerful he was, this child who didn't even have a driver's license yet.

Serena clasped her hands together. "Wonderful! I want all the members of the criminally insane club: Paul, Victor, Lita and Vanessa. And I assume that their transport includes armed guards who will stay with them?"

"Yes." Nicholas hesitated and then added, "Can I ask you to add my friend? He's not insane and he didn't do anything wrong. He could help."

"You mentioned earlier that you and your friends are profiled and some are added to a list. I don't understand – enlighten me," Serena prodded.

Nicholas paused only a short while before filling them in.

"There's a watch list we aren't supposed to know about, and high IQ kids are on it. The government monitors our Internet usage and school records for any sign of fitting the profile for violence, like if we are taking any prescription drugs, or if we are bullied in school. And if any of us say things against the government, we get put on two lists that are cross referenced. My friend was on the potential mass murderer list and the terrorist watch list. When he got on the first list he was pulled in and questioned. After he was put on the second list he was arrested."

"How did he fit the profile for violence, besides his IQ?" asked Serena.

"He had few friends, he kept to himself, he was quiet, and he didn't join in – he was rated as an outsider and loner."

"Rated? What do you mean rated?" Serena asked.

"Oh, it's routine. They do the ratings at the end of fall term every year. There's a scale of 1-5 on criteria like 'joins in on social activities'. They rated him a 1. He didn't join in, but that's only because his friends don't go to his school. I'm one of his best friends and I'm homeschooled, so no one in his class ever saw me. Besides, the social activities were stupid. He didn't want to go. But he's not a loner, Ms. Wilcox. Another thing: he was bullied, so he got 5 points deducted from his score."

"Who's doing these ratings?" Serena struggled not to let her horror show.

"Classmates, teachers…" Nicholas said distractedly. He was typing in the forms to arrange for the criminally insane crew to be transported from the prison to the Superman lab.

Beav, who had been listening to the conversation and had been simmering on slow boil, could bear it no longer. Pounding his fist into his hand to punctuate his sentences, he jumped onto his soapbox.

"The *victim* of bullying is the one persecuted and prosecuted? Rather than resolving the bullying problems, they proactively arrest victims who might snap? Nice touch that Big Brother wraps it all under the terrorism umbrella. As of 2012, the American government has the authority to indefinitely retain anyone suspected of ties to terrorism. In recent years the definition for what acts can be considered acts of terrorism has broadened. I knew it, I knew it would lead to something insane. I see now it's come down to arresting people –kids! - before they even do anything wrong!"

Serena stood between Nicholas and Beav, putting one hand on each of their shoulders. "I know it's not likely that I'm the one to get us back on topic, seeing how it's me who got us off topic, but we need to plow through. Yes, Nicholas, bring your friend in too."

Nicholas spun around to face his computer. He hit the send button on the prison transport request form. "Done."

"I need a few others for the Think Tank," said Serena, just as the form went through.

"More prisoners?" asked Nicholas, despairing at the thought of entering another form.

"No. I want the Supporters brought in."

"The Supporters? I don't think I can do that. I can't hack them. They do things old school. I heard they even use carrier pigeons, but that's probably a hoax."

Serena laughed. "Relax. I don't know about the pigeons, but I do know how to get a hold of them."

"How?" asked Beav.

"Like this." Serena took her phone out of her purse and punched in a number. "It's Serena, can we meet?" She paused to listen. "Yes, at the lab." To Nicholas and Beav she said, "They'll be here within the hour."

"You weren't supposed to tell anyone about the lab!" Nicholas yelped.

"I didn't have to, they already know."

Beav gestured for Serena to follow him to the conference table area. "We need to talk. One day The Supporters are kidnapping you and your family and the next day you're old friends."

Serena stayed where she was, planted next to Nicholas' computer. "I'll catch you up to speed later. I need Nicholas to send out one more invitation first."

9

To say that Joseph Smythe found Serena's invitation unexpected was an understatement. What could it all mean? And a secret meeting at a secret government computer lab? He was truly living in a different world. No longer an ordinary politician, he was being drafted as a sidekick, assigned to either a superhero or a villain, and he had no idea which way the casting would go. It was a disappointment then when a perfectly drab government sedan was his transport.

"Is someone going to explain to me why I've been recruited for this Think Tank project?" Joseph Smythe asked the driver.

The driver was a personal friend of the President and the First Gentleman. Penny had been an official Cube driver for years, but had moved on when she graduated from law school. She was more than willing to get back behind the wheel upon special request for Operation Bluebird Flown. The sedan was not registered with The Cube, so even if someone looked into where the Speaker of the House was off to, there would be no record of it. Nothing but the video footage of the pick-up. To be sure that she wouldn't be identified, Penny had worn a disguise – she was made up to look like a man, which was why Smythe was calling her Kevin, the name on her uniform tag.

"Seriously, Kevin, as Speaker of the House I have clearance way beyond your pay grade. So tell me, where is this Superman lab?"

"Sorry, Mr. Speaker, I can't divulge that information," said Penny, knowing that the cat was out of the bag as soon as she spoke.

"You're a woman! I suppose I can stop calling you Kevin now. Tell me what the Sam Hill is going on!"

"You do know that President Kinji is investigating everyone."

"Yes, I'm aware. And she can do that right here. There's no need to send me off to Siberia."

"Calm down. The lab is not far. Depending on traffic flow, we could be there by dinner time."

"That eases my mind some. Tell me, Kevin, what's your real name?"

"Penny."

"And you're dressed like a man because you were tricking the surveillance cameras?"

"Correct."

"Is someone demanding a ransom for my safe return?"

"You haven't been kidnapped."

"A joke, a joke. I'm not upset. I rather like a good adventure."

Penny looked into the mirror to see Smythe's affable grin. "I'm glad you see it that way."

Smythe's nearly six foot frame was beginning to cramp up in his backseat position. His nickname "Beanpole" was apt, but the older he got the less flexible he was. Travel was a killer. "You say we'll be there soon?"

Penny had a lot of experience volunteering her time to youth activities. She used her best patient-adult voice when she said, "Mr. Speaker, why don't you listen to an audio book? There's a full library at your disposal."

Smythe got the point and left Penny alone for a good hour before he tried again. "You really won't tell me what to expect? Can you at least tell me if I'm on the winning team on this thing? This isn't an interrogation I've foolishly agreed to is it?" Smythe's love of adventure had its limits.

Penny turned onto a gravel road. "We're here, Mr. Speaker. You can ask them yourself."

10

Serena, Beav and Nicholas made party preparations for the Think Tank session. Nicholas showed them to a small lounge area, but that space was entirely too intimate. This group required a lot of personal space. The OCD guests would be quickly agitated if their personal space bubbles weren't respected.

The conference table area was the only viable option, but the table was too small to accommodate all of their guests. The three of them moved the table and set it in the back of the lab. They then wheeled dozens of computer chairs from the various stations, the conference table chairs, and even a few stacking chairs they found in a storage closet, and situated the chairs around the perimeter of the conference area. They closed their rectangular group "circle" in on one side at the back wall of the lab, in front of the table. The other side was closed in by cutting across the width of the lab, just before the computer stations. By using the entire conference area section they now had enough room for the Think Tank to sit with enough personal space for no touching.

Beav reflected on their work and remarked, “We’ll need to give them water.”

Nicholas remembered seeing a shockingly large surplus of foam coffee cups with plastic lids in the storage closet. No one had used them from the previous top-secret government labs over the years – disposable foam cups were no longer sold, after the EPA modernized the Toxic Substances Control Act, banning hundreds of products that were previously used daily by millions of people.

The banning of foam cups stemmed from a 2001 Department of Health and Human Services report that classified styrene, which is used in the manufacture of polystyrene, as “reasonably anticipated to be a human carcinogen.” Somehow the lab had acquired boxes and boxes of foam cups. Nicholas retrieved one of those boxes now and the three of them spent the next fifteen minutes filling twenty-five cups with water. They placed one cup of water on the floor beside every chair.

“I think we’re done here. We don’t need party favors.” Beav clapped his hands loudly, a sound that echoed in the nearly empty lab.

“Are you set up to record everything that goes on?” Serena directed the question to Nicholas.

“Everything that happens here is always recorded.” Nicholas pointed to the various cameras positioned so that not one inch of the lab wasn’t under constant steady surveillance.

“Beyond security camera footage – I need high resolution video with clear sound." Serena thought she was clarifying her point, but Nicholas was way ahead of her.

"Ms. Wilcox, all of the cameras in the lab are state of the art. In 'movie mode', which I already selected for you, the image quality is cinema grade."

"Ah, well, my apologies. I see you were already on it." Serena surveyed the room and found nothing else left to consider, nothing but how on Earth she was going to conduct a meeting comprised of criminally insane persons, a band of vigilantes and the Speaker of the House. She didn't have much time for musing. The first round of party guests entered the lab: The Supporters.

Nicholas had lost interest in the whole affair. He stayed at the lab in case he was needed, but he was released from duty and was already plugged into his ear chip sound station while simultaneously programming a high tech computer game he was creating in a joint project with other NASA I.N.S.P.I.R.E students. While Serena, always the mother, worried about Nicholas' exposure to potentially dangerous situations, she was reassured that he was checked out of the whole experience and was unlikely to hear a word they were saying.

Beav, however, was keenly interested and had no intention of missing a single second of the absurd Think Tank session about to commence. He could hardly wait to meet The Supporters and was completely thrown when he recognized not one, but two of the faces that came through the lab doors.

"We meet again," said Bob, the radio host Beav met in the rural Indiana farmhouse.

"Surprised to see you here, Bob, but not as surprised as I am to see *you.*" Beav bowed in an exaggerated gesture of respect.

Standing before him was mentalist Eric Dittelman, whose career began after becoming a semi-finalist on the 2011 season of the classic talent show "America's Got Talent", which had made household names out of hundreds of previously unknown talents. Dittelman had gone on to tour and fame of his own right. What was his connection to The Supporters? What could this be about? Beav peered behind Dittelman to Serena, hoping she would end his curiosity.

Serena shrugged.

Bob ended the suspense. "I see you know who Eric Dittelman is. He's not one of us, so you can stop looking at him like he's an alien from another planet, which do exist by the way, I have on good authority. Anyway, he came to us with a tip. He's a concerned citizen and a good guy – that's as far as it goes. He was kind enough to agree to come with us today to explain his observation in person."

"Wonderful! Thank you, Mr. Dittelman, honored to have you." Serena stepped into the gaggle of Supporters. Her not-quite-five-two frame was quickly swallowed up by the swarm. She extended her hand to shake Dittelman's.

Dittelman flashed his signature grin, a smile like that of a Yellow Lab – too friendly for guile, too honest for treachery. The instant trust established, Dittelman's words would carry a lot of weight. Serena hoped whatever he had to say was full of helpful details.

Bob, having been the only person to have met Beav, had taken it upon himself to introduce the others. "This is Joanna Murphy from Ireland…"

A beautiful woman with porcelain skin and carroty red tresses stepped forward. Her eyes were the same shade of green as Serena's.

Serena blurted, “My grandmother’s maiden name was Murphy.”

Joanna said, “Murphy is a common Irish surname, about 50,000 or so in Ireland alone. I doubt we’re cousins. Call me Jo, by the way.”

Serena complied. “Jo, why is someone from Ireland get involved with The Supporters?”

“I’m not presently living in Ireland. I’m a surgeon at the Mayo Clinic in Minnesota. Besides, America’s problems are world problems.”

Bob nodded. “Jo has been a huge asset to our group. The rest of our gang, as you can see, are all men. He pointed at each man as he said his name. “Devin, Craig, Dennis, Mahesh, Kobin, Garreth, Tristan, and Luke.” Bob addressed Beav. “Luke Halloway is who you were talking to over the airwaves in my studio.”

“You’re much younger than what I imagined,” said Beav.

Luke grimaced. “I haven’t heard that before.”

Serena ignored Luke’s dripping sarcasm. “So there are ten of you, plus your guest star Eric Dittelman? Or are there more of you at home?”

“Oh you have no idea how funny that is,” said Luke.

Jo added, “We wouldn’t fit in here if we all turned up, in fact, we could fill up an entire city. We have a massive Internet presence. But, if you want to count only those of us who meet in person, we have about 300 active members in our chapter, and there are over a dozen chapters across the nation. I’d say we have about 5,000 members who meet on a weekly basis. The rest are Internet-only, but the numbers are staggering and growing by the hour.”

“I’m afraid I’ll have a hard time remembering all of your names,” said Serena.

Jo dismissed her concern. "Oh, don't worry about that. Remember us three: Luke, Bob and me. Luke is the founder and head of all, Bob is our communications director and I'm a glorified secretary. If you need any archives, and we do record everything we do, come to me. If you need to get in touch with Luke, contact Bob. The rest of the group does the behind-the-scenes work. It takes five of them to handle the tech support for the Internet chapters."

Serena asked, "Luke, why do we have to contact you through Bob?"

Luke didn't respond.

Serena caught on that he was listening to music—he had an ear chip like Nicholas'. She tried again, louder. "Luke!"

Luke looked at her.

"Why do we have to contact you through Bob? Don't you have a way we can reach you directly?"

Luke said, "Few people have my contact information. I'm careful that way."

Beav said, "I'm confused. I thought Serena had already met your group – isn't that what that whole in-the-corn thing was about? Wasn't she with you?"

Serena explained, "I didn't meet anyone from the head organization. A committee from the Indiana chapter met me in the corn."

Their conversation came to an abrupt halt when they heard the lab doors open. Agent Estep, who had been kept in the loop, was not about to miss out on the Think Tank farce. If his career was going down the toilet, he had to at least give it a proper farewell. He entered the lab and strode directly to where Serena was standing.

Serena made generalized introductions and then led the group to the Think Tank rectangle. "Please sit together as a group. Our other guests will be accompanied by armed escorts."

Guffaws, murmurs and chuckles went up. All seemed game for whatever was about to happen. "Who else is coming? Criminals?"

The lab doors reopened and the Speaker of the House entered. "I wouldn't call myself a criminal."

The Supporters stood and a hush came over the room. Joseph Smythe, extended to his full lanky height, wearing a dapper wool blend brown herringbone fedora hat, a brown velvet sport coat blazer, slacks, a white dress shirt, a yellow tie, and brown loafers, looked like he walked right off the set of a classic Hollywood movie – before color film. His attire should have come off as outlandish, but he pulled it off with his boyish charm. Unlike Carson and his ilk, Smythe was genuine, with kind eyes. Or so the only two women in the room thought.

Serena, who had programmed her brain to never see another man as anything other than "somebody's son or brother" when she got married, was not smitten. However, Jo was practically swooning. Jo quickly collected herself enough to initiate conversation. She stepped forward with outstretched hand. "What brings you to Serena's Think Tank today, Mr. Speaker?"

"Call me Joe. And you are?"

Joanna blushed. "Also Jo."

Joe laughed. He looked expectant.

"Without the E, short for Joanna. Joanna Murphy."

"Oh! You really are named Jo. Good fun in that, Joe and Jo." He smiled broadly.

Jo's face revealed how much she liked the sound of that.

Spellbound by the awkwardness of spying on this magical

moment when dapper politician meets pretty Irish activist, everyone else stood frozen. Estep broke the spell by clearing his throat. He offered his own hand to shake and gestured for Mr. Speaker, or Joe as he had so casually renamed himself, to take a seat. There was a brief pause and a mournful expression that flitted over Joe's face as he realized that the seats on both sides of where Jo was sitting were already taken.

Joe settled in between Serena and Estep, which was a good idea since the pair of them were better off separated from each other.

"I'd like to wait until the others arrive before we get started. Oh, I think that's them now," said Serena.

There was a clatter of chairs as the newcomers seated themselves. The group was now situated in the rectangle and the twenty –five chairs were all occupied. Along the back wall area were the nine who came from the adult prison system: Paul, Victor, Lita and Vanessa, and their four armed escorts. They were seated with a guard between each of them. Along the opposite side, in the row of chairs that were in the middle of the room, where the flooring changed over from the commercial carpeting in the computer lab area to the tile under their feet in the conference area, were Eric Dittelman, Beav, Serena, Speaker of the House Joe, and Estep.

Along the sides of the rectangle was everyone else. The Supporters in key roles positioned themselves close to the middle of the room where Serena and company were seated. Luke and Jo were on the side nearest to Dittelman. Bob was on the side nearest to Estep. On Bob's left was Nicholas' friend and his youth prison escort. The remaining Supporters filled in the rest of the seats.

"Let me make a few introductions before we get started." Serena grabbed a notepad from her purse and referred to it as she spoke. "Beginning on my left, going down the row along the left hand wall, we have a young man named Marco…"

"Polo!" shouted several people.

Serena waited for the giggles to die down. She wasn't used to such a lively bunch. "Marco was arrested because he was on a terrorist watch list. We don't believe that he's done anything wrong, and his insights could be useful to us. Next to him is his armed escort. Along both sides of the room are members of The Supporters. Along the back wall are prisoners from the adult criminally insane facility who need no introduction since all are now infamous."

"In my own row here," Serena gestured toward herself and the others seated near her. She continued to gesture as she named each person. "We have celebrity Eric Dittelman who is here because he has something important to share, and on my immediate right is Beav, which is fitting because he's my right hand man in this investigation. Next to me on my left is, as you know, Mr. Speaker of the House Joseph Smythe – or Joe, as he has requested we call him. And on the other side of Joe is Agent Estep who is our official chain of command to President Kinji."

"If I still have a job," Estep said under his breath in a stage whisper that could be heard all the way across the room.

Serena was distracted by his grumbling for only a second. "Let's begin. What I want to hear is every conspiracy theory you know of, anything you've heard through the grapevine, anything you've come up with yourself, and most of all, anything you have proof of." The room immediately erupted in an impressive din of overlapping voices. "Wait, wait!"

Estep stood up and put his two fingers into his mouth. He whistled at a pitch that instantly silenced the room. He sat back down and threw his arms toward Serena in a "giving it back to you" gesture.

"Thank you, Agent Estep. Instead of a free-for-all, we have to do this one person at a time. Show of hands, who has actual proof to back up your theory?"

Serena, Beav and Estep gaped slack-jawed as every hand in the room was raised except for their own. The prisoners, the escorts, The Supporters, Eric Dittelman, and even Speaker of the House Joe – all had their hands raised.

11

Former Special Agent Lehman, recalled by President Kinji back into service, was now an emergency Vice Presidential appointment. His professional life after he left the civil service was fulfilling. He never once looked back. And yet, when the president called, he didn't even need to think it over – when his wife agreed he should go, he packed his bags. But things had gotten out of control. How did he go from enjoying GianMarco's Veal Osso Bucco to catching a cafeteria meal at The Cube? Sure, he could get anything he wanted ordered up, but somehow everything ended up tasting the same.

Meanwhile in his absence his wife had gotten a new job in Texas and that's where the two of them lived now – except that he wasn't living there. He was still here, living in a governmental suite on the outer perimeter of The Cube. What choice did he have really? Of course he would answer the call. He went to the hologram room to talk to his wife. She always got him refocused. He passed through the eye scan, recited his Texan address for the house he had only seen through pictures, and waited only a second or two before his wife appeared on the platform in front of him.

They talked about the learning curve at her new job and she asked him how he was coping with the stress of the investigation, that all of America knew about to some degree. He was about to say something when he felt someone's presence. His wife's face morphed into a mask of horror was the last thing Lehman saw before everything went dark.

When he came to, the first thing he saw was his wife's face peering at him from above. But how? How could the hologram image shift like that?

"Can you hear me?"

Lehman tried to answer but his tongue was too heavy in his mouth. Nothing came out but gibberish. It was enough.

"He's awake! He's awake!" Lehman's wife signaled for a nurse. Before long the entire ward filed into the room. It wasn't every day that the Vice President of the United States was their number one patient.

"You had a nasty hit to the head," said one of the doctors. Lehman tried to sort out what they were saying to him while his head was still too fuzzy to keep up. He motioned for all of them to stop talking. Then he fell asleep.

When he woke, he was started to see not his wife's face looking down at him but President Kinji's instead. "Good to see you are coming around," she said.

Lehman mumbled something incoherent. He groaned and tried

again. This time he managed to rasp out an intelligible sentence. “I’m sorry.”

“Sorry for what? You didn’t do anything wrong.” Ann’s eyes were soft and compassionate.

“I’m out of service,” he croaked.

“Only temporarily. You’re going to be just fine. But we need to find out who did this to you, and why? What purpose did it serve to knock you out like that?” Ann pondered the question and came up with nothing.

Lehman drifted in and out of sleep for the next ten minutes. Ann had planned to stay no more than fifteen minutes and was on her way out when he suddenly sat up in bed.

His heart racing and his mind clear, he reached out to grab Ann’s sleeve. She strained her ears to hear his whisper. “They took my eyes, they took my eyes.”

“Your eyes? What do you mean?” Ann hovered over the nurses’ station sensor. She paused to give him a chance to give her a reasonable explanation, hesitation that proved wise.

Lehman took a few sips of water before attempting to speak. “They carried me. I remember. Where did you find me?”

“In the Gallery.”

“Outside the Northwest wing?” Lehman attempted to clear his throat but his throat was so sore and raw that tears sprang to his eyes.

“Yes.”

“Top secret clearance to enter wing.” He was fading fast. He was losing his fight against the powerful sedatives coursing through his veins.

“Iris scanner!” It made sense to her now.

Before surrendering to a deep undisturbed sleep he said, “Yes. They needed my eyes.”

Ann squeezed Lehman’s hand, thanked his wife, and left the hospital with her security detail flanking her. She was on the phone with Nicholas as soon as she was in route to The Cube. “Hey, kiddo, we have another complication.”

“I’m sorry to hear that President Kinji. How can I help?”

“I can hear you. You don’t need to shout.”

“Oops, sorry, I had my ear chip on,” said Nicholas, his voice now at the correct volume.

“I need you to examine footage from The Cube. I need to know Vice President Lehman’s every move for the past 24 hours.”

“Hold on. It will only take a couple of minutes.” Nicholas’ fingers scurried across the keyboard like a vial of spiders on the loose. His keyboarding skills were not only self-taught, but he had somehow invented his own bizarre technique in the process. Both hands moved across the keyboard in sweeping patterns that resembled the movements of an accomplished pianist. If Ann was able to watch him she would have been mesmerized. “Got it.”

“What does that mean? You have the footage or you found something?” Ann was still in route, now at a stop-and-go choke point. She had some time, but not much. She wanted to finish their conversation before returning to The Cube, where the walls had ears.

“Yes.”

“Yes what? You found something or you have the footage?”

“Both.”

“Archive the footage…”

“Already did.”

"And tell me what you found."

"One guy hit Lehman from behind. Then two more guys came up and grabbed him under the arms. The guy who hit him got in front of him and there was another guy just sort of standing around. And two more guys in the back."

"You're losing me. There were six men?"

"Yes, six. They huddled around him in a pack so they could drag him off without anyone noticing." Nicholas hit a few keys. "I sent you a copy, password protected."

"No, no, it's not safe!" Ann squeaked.

"I know. I sent it to you in the mail."

"E-mail?"

"No, I would never do that! I put it on a chip and mailed it to you, United States Post Office. I sent it to your home address."

"Ah, smart boy."

"No problem." Nicholas' fingers scurried around the keyboard for a few seconds and then stopped cold. "President Kinji?"

"I'm still here." Ann held her breath. Whatever he was about to say, she was sure she wasn't going to like it.

"I did a scan on the men. The system could ID them."

"And?"

"Is anyone with you?"

"Just my security detail."

"It's your security detail."

"Right. No one else, just my security detail."

"No. I'm saying, it's your security detail. On the footage. It's your guys."

12

"Sorry to interrupt your meeting, Miss Serena, but something happened." Nicholas stood behind Serena's head, speaking to her in a low tone.

Serena stood from her chair and addressed the Think Tank. "Excuse me."

Beav gave her a questioning look which she answered by jerking her head in the direction of the Think Tank. Beav nodded. "I'll take over if you can't make it back in? Five? Ten?" Serena turned back in mid-stride and held up one hand, her fingers splayed. Beav called out, "Five minutes. We'll wait five minutes and then resume."

Serena pulled up a chair alongside Nicholas'. She looked at his screen. "President Ann's security detail. Why?"

"They dragged Lehman to use him to get past the iris scanner.

They got into the records room."

"This is disturbing. You told the President?"

"Yes."

"Good. Anything else?"

"She's still with them, with the security detail."

"Oh no! Well, that's not good."

"What do we do?" Nicholas grimaced.

"We tell Estep."

"On it." Estep had been behind her the entire time. One step ahead of her, he had already alerted his team.

"Do you need me or Beav?" Serena stood up and called to his disappearing back, a method of communication that had become routine.

"I don't see the point of that." Estep was out the door before she could reply.

Serena sank back into her chair with such force that the wheels shot backward and she almost took a dive. "Oh no, oh no, no, no."

Nicholas stared at her. "What?"

"The next in line to the President is the Vice President and Lehman is flat out on his back in the hospital. The next in line is the Speaker of the House, and he's… He's *here*."

Serena returned to the Think Tank. She didn't sit down. "There's a situation."

13

"Before we get dramatic, nothing has happened to the President," said Speaker of the House Joe Smythe.

"But shouldn't you be back at The Cube?" Serena had done it again. How her attempts to help always ended up convoluted and bungled, she didn't know. At least no one in the Think Tank had died, not yet anyway.

Joe looked at his phone and put it back in his pocket. "No. I should stay here. Unless I get a call, I'm better off participating in this history-making event you've set up. Let's do this."

Serena made eye contact with as many Think Tank members as possible. "Since we could be interrupted at any time, let's agree that everyone should get to the point quickly. When I move on to the next person, don't take it personally. We don't have the luxury of time. Let's start with Eric Dittelman. Why did you contact The Supporters?"

Dittelman pushed his glasses up his nose, being one of the few people left on the planet who still wore glasses. "I was invited to The Cube to entertain last week. It was for an appreciation day, for interns."

Beav interrupted. "An appreciation day during an national crisis?"

Dittelman continued, "President Kinji planned to meet with me but had to cancel. The Cube is a big place. Business as usual in one wing doesn't have anything to do with what happens in the President's wing."

"Go on," Serena encouraged. She frowned at Beav. "Let him finish his story, hold questions to the end."

Dittelman was visibly relieved to finally get his part over with. "Like I said before, President Kinji had to cancel her appearance at the preshow luncheon, but the First Gentleman attended. I noticed that he had a strange bruising around his right eye. I made a joke that President Kinji didn't like his politics. He said that he got the bruise from a faulty iris scanner. Later, I did my show and had a meet and greet photo op and signing afterward. I noticed that one of the interns had the same bruising on her right eye. It was a strange pattern, unmistakably the same as the First Gentleman's, and it couldn't have been random."

Dittelman said all of this at a hurried pace and then stopped. Serena waited for him to continue and when it was clear that he was finished she said, "I'm not sure I understand the situation."

Dittelman explained, "Interns don't have security clearance that requires the use of an iris scanner – at least not the one outside the

Gallery. I forgot to add that little detail."

"Oh! I think I get it now. What was the intern doing in the high-security wing for top government only? She was not assigned to anyone there?"

Joe raised his hand.

Serena laughed. "You don't have to raise your hand, Mr. Speaker. Go ahead."

"I can answer this one. Dittelman is right. Interns most certainly do not have security clearance to be in that wing so even if she was somehow included in something going on up there, which I highly doubt, she wouldn't have been using the scanner herself. Someone else would have let her in with a guest pass, hand-verified by the security guards. There's absolutely no scenario in which an intern would have used that particular scanner."

Beav, his mind always racing straight to the technical, asked, "Are we sure that it's the only iris scanner that has had issues? Is it possible that the same malfunction, and therefore same bruising pattern, could be happening with other scanners in The Cube?"

Luke jumped in. "We verified that there was only one malfunctioning iris scanner. Our group investigated Dittelman's story right away. That's what we do."

"Nicholas, are you hearing all of this?" Serena called toward the front of the lab where Nicholas was still sitting at his computer. Serena worried about that boy's physical health.

Nicholas answered, "Yes, I'm looking into it now."

Luke tipped the bill of his cap over his face at the sound of Nicholas' voice. He really *is* paranoid, thought Serena. She had to strain to hear what Luke was saying.

"He'll be able to confirm what I said. Maintenance records for government buildings are public record if you know where to look."

"I believe you, but before we run off accusing people we'll double check everything we say here." Serena smiled diplomatically at Luke. She didn't know if she liked that kid or not; his overconfidence rubbed her the wrong way. Serena leaned across Beav to reach Dittelman. She patted him on his arm. "Eric, thank you for coming forward with this, and for meeting with us here in person."

Beav added, "I wish we had time for you to do one of your mind-reading routines for us."

Serena added her ditto and moved the session along. "Mr. Speaker, please go next."

Joe stood up as if delivering a political speech. His full height was ordinarily on the taller side of average, but when he was standing while everyone else was seated, he towered over them like a beanpole giant. "I want to confess that I've been running my own private investigation. In part, I've been doing this to clear my own name, since it was obvious that I was on the list of suspects from day one. But also, I caught on quickly, shortly after I became Speaker, that I had stepped into something funky. People didn't look me in the eye, people stopped talking when I entered a room. Records went missing. People avoided answering my questions. I didn't want to come off as paranoid, so I kept my thoughts to myself and hired two separate private investigation firms that specialize in high-level cases. I got my money's worth, both were discreet and got the job done."

Luke raised his index finger. "Not as discreet as you might think."

Joe faced Luke. "What do you mean? What do you know about

this?"

"One of your guys went straight to me, straight to The Supporters anyway. In fact, he's the source of most of our information," said Luke.

Serena said, "You two can tag-team this story, fill in each other's gaps."

Both men looked at Serena dismissively before Joe resumed speaking. "The investigators didn't uncover much, but it was enough for me to have a good idea of what was going on. Senator William Casey and Senator Robert Lorry – the two senators that President Kinji called out – those two are definitely involved. Each of them has a mutiny in the works, recruiting more crew members every day. These ties can be traced back to the top, to Governor Carson, and beyond."

Joe stopped talking and sat back down.

Serena followed up with, "And you say you have evidence that connects these men?"

Joe replied, "It's all there in Carson's phone and Internet records. It should have been brought to your attention already."

Luke cleared his throat. "Actually, these records have been covered up. They never made it past the federal agencies who recovered them."

Joe's face registered genuine surprise. "Then how?"

Luke advised, "Mr. Speaker, you can neither confirm nor deny that you know anything about those records. Mahesh and Kobin can shed a little light on this."

There was a second or two of awkwardness as Mahesh and Kobin worked out who would speak. Kobin won the mental rock, paper, scissors. He quickly explained in layman's terms how they retrieved the information. "We hacked into the FBI. Or, rather, we hacked into one of their agents' server accounts."

Luke took back the reigns. "The records never made it past the FBI and other agencies involved. If you look into the evidence locker you won't find any of Governor Carson's electronics."

Joe stroked his chin. "The plot thickens. I must say that I find it rather disturbing that you were able to hack into classified FBI communications. I hope the end justifies the means—but I can't promise you that I won't look into this. Well, that's basically all I've got. I thought I had something to offer but it sounds like this group was already onto it."

Luke said, "I wouldn't have told you anything if you could catch us. All you have is a story, which I will recant."

Jo spoke up for the first time since the meeting started. "Mr. Speaker..."

"Joe." His voice dropped into a lower register that was intimately masculine.

"Joe." Jo repeated. Her face flushed; her fair skin gave her away every time.

Serena and the rest of the Think Tank watched the flirting play out, all of them wondering if they should avert their eyes, but none of them willing to turn away. Serena prompted, trying to divert the runaway train back onto the right track, "Jo? You had something to add?"

Both Joe and Jo looked at her as if they had forgotten she was there.

Serena made a "heh" sound and clarified. "Joanna, do you have something to add?"

"I know that Luke can be a little hard to take, but in his defense, when a government buries information only extreme measures will uncover it. And yes, the end justifies the means. What I wanted to say though is that the reason why we looked into Governor Carson Landon's records is because we got a ping from Mr.—uh, Joe's—investigator. Joe, if you hadn't initiated an investigation, we wouldn't have gotten the tip."

"I'm relieved that I was able to contribute." Joe smiled.

Joe was about to say something more to Jo but Serena cut him off before the train could derail again. "Moving along to The Supporters. Luke, do you have anything more for us?"

Taking a cue from Joe, Luke stood up for his turn to speak, but when he heard Nicholas sneeze he abruptly sat down. "I have a filing cabinet full of evidence. We have traced communications, we have transcripts, we have documents. What's funny is that most of this is public record. They are hiding in plain sight."

Serena said, "If they are so blatant, why? Do they think they'll get their agenda in place before we catch up to them? Or are they so arrogant that they think we can't possibly catch on?"

Luke said, "Probably both. We have enough to bury them, and enough to know that an assassination plot is in the works. We also have a few international names to add to the list of domestic traitors. What we don't know are the details of the plot."

Paul, who had been uncharacteristically silent since the moment he shuffled into the room, said, "I do."

14

Before Paul could say anything more, the Think Tank was shut down by the return of Agent Estep. Estep burst into the rectangle, taking center stage. His posture was that of a knight who had valiantly slayed a dragon. "President Kinji is safe. She is in an undisclosed location and will remain there for the time being. Mr. Speaker, please come with me."

There was an exit of controlled chaos as Estep and Joe hurried out of the lab. Quick-thinking Beav arranged for two members of Estep's team to escort Eric Dittelman home, with instructions to provide Dittelman 24 hour surveillance for his protection. Eavesdropping on that arrangement created panic in most of the Think Tank members as they realized for the first time that all of them were potentially in danger.

Serena gasped. “Nicholas!”

Nicholas responded. “Yes, I was able to verify everything said so far.”

Serena held up her index finger to indicate that the group should wait for her. She walked over to where Nicholas was. “No, that’s not what I meant. Nicholas, this has gotten out of hand. Once again, I’ve put your life in danger. It’s time for me to call your parents.”

“I’ve done things like this before,” Nicholas protested. “Can I hear what Marco has to say first?”

Serena had forgotten about poor Marco. “I’ll ask him to speak right away so that you can go immediately afterward. Better yet, I’ll dismiss him too—neither one of you should be here.”

Serena returned to the Think Tank with Nicholas, who sat next to Beav in Dittelman’s vacant seat. She addressed Marco. “I’m sorry you’ve been waiting all this time. You had raised your hand earlier, indicating that you have evidence to share.”

Marco’s left leg bobbed up and down in a tic-like fashion. He spoke in restricted prosody, a classic characteristic of someone diagnosed with Asperger’s syndrome. “I was watching videos and the ones I wanted didn’t stream. I had to get to the server myself to retrieve the ones I wanted.”

Beav’s ears perked up. “You hacked into the prison server?”

“No. I hacked into the Cloud.”

Beav whistled in admiration. “How did you get past the prison firewall?”

“I’m not in an adult prison. The youth facility has a weak firewall. It was easy.”

Serena noted that Marco seemed more relaxed now that he was talking about computers. “Marco, what did you find?”

Marco didn't make eye contact but he launched smoothly into the rest of his story. "I saw other videos. They didn't run right. Video files overlapped. I wanted to know why so I looked at the code. I saw another video file embedded in the one that was displayed. The overlap was hiding something else. I copied the code and…"

"Marco, you can tell Beav how you did it later, but for now, please tell us what you saw." Serena gently prodded.

"I saw them giving instructions."

"What kind of instructions?" Serena had a sinking feeling that she knew what he was going to say.

"Instructions on how to kill President Ann Kinji, and how they would get their money."

"Oh my. Thank you for telling us about this Marco. Did they discuss details about when this is supposed to happen or where?" Serena kept her voice calm despite the alarm bells ringing in her head.

"No. That's all I saw. Can I go home now?"

Serena felt tears stinging her eyes. She blinked them away and took a breath. "I'm sorry, Marco, I can't do that for you today. But I promise that we'll help you, even if I have to go to the President."

"If they don't kill her," said Marco simply.

"Yes, if they don't kill her." Serena knew that it wasn't the right time to wallow in this child's situation. She wrapped things up. "Thank you for being brave enough to share what you know. Now it's time for both you and Nicholas to go. You've both served your country well today. I'm proud of you."

Bob initiated a standing ovation. Every remaining member of the Think Tank stood up as the two boys- as well as Marco's prison guard escort, Nicholas' father, and three of Estep's agents on loan for Nicholas' family- headed toward the exit. The applause carried on until they were all out the door.

While the group was still distracted Serena used the time to sneak in a quick text message. "I love you" was instantly sent to her husband and to all three of her kids' accounts.

When she noticed that everyone had settled down Serena resumed leadership of the ever-shrinking Think Tank. "Let's come back to you now, Paul. What details were you talking about?"

Paul glanced around the room as if he were evaluating their trustworthiness. He let a dramatic pause hang before he dropped his bombshell, relishing in the spotlight. "The assassination is set to go down in 48 hours and counting." He made a show of looking at his watch. "Make that 42 hours."

Beav said, "If you knew this, why didn't you contact us right away? Why are you just now telling us this?"

Paul replied, "I've been blocked for months now, cut off from the world. It doesn't matter, I knew you'd be in touch."

Serena shivered. While she had good naturedly taken her relationship with con-artist sociopath killer-of-two-presidents Paul in stride, over the past year he had developed a stalker-like fixation on her. Nonetheless, he was a valuable resource and she knew it. Unfortunately, so did he. In fact, Serena suspected that Paul worked tirelessly and obsessively to be an asset not out of patriotic duty but for the express purpose of gaining access to her.

Paul had nothing else to share but he was loath to admit it. He shot daggers at Victor when Victor volunteered to speak next.

Serena hesitated, thrown off balance by the disturbing possessiveness Paul was displaying so Beav stepped in to keep things rolling along. "Go ahead, Victor."

Victor, who had earned his criminally insane title when he torched his old chemistry lab with his co-workers still inside it, was quite the specimen. He spoke now in such a personable and rational way that it was hard to imagine that he was capable of such a monstrosity. "We can still access the crack in the Social Media Channel. The prison system hasn't been upgraded. We can still see their messages."

"What did you see?" asked Beav.

"I didn't see anything, but Lita did." Victor pointed to Lita, even though Beav and Serena knew who she was, as they had been uncomfortably close to dying by her hand.

Lita tossed her long hair, hair that hadn't seen shears in months. She didn't care about split ends in prison. "It's nice to be a part of this. I hardly get a chance to talk to anyone in the outside world."

Serena grimaced. It was harder than she thought it would be to interact with the criminally insane club. "Tell your story, Lita."

Lita cackled and said nothing.

Tristan spoke up. "Perhaps I can be of help."

Serena sighed. "Please."

Tristan grabbed one of the five chairs that were unoccupied and moved it directly in front of Lita. He positioned himself so that the two of them were face-to-face. "Lita, focus. What do you know?"

Lita looked into his eyes and began thrashing her head around. Her hair was a tangled blur. It was like watching the Tasmanian Devil in a Looney Toons cartoon.

Tristan placed both of his warm hands on Lita's knees. His hair fell over one of his eyes as he bent forward. With steady deliberation he placed his face precariously close to the whirling madness of head tossing and teeth gnashing. Lita's armed escort popped up beside them, ready to restrain her if necessary.

Lita responded to Tristan's touch by freezing in mid-motion. Her hair drifted slowly onto her back and shoulders. She blinked at him a few times before her face twisted into a seductive leer that went unnoticed by Tristan. He was too busy addressing his audience, "See now? She's like a wild animal in need of a little taming."

Beav crooked his finger in a frantic aerial point-point-point motion. "Uh, buddy, you might want to…"

It was too late. Lita kissed Tristan full on the lips and then head-butted him. The whole thing happened too fast for the guard to stop her. Tristan was knocked out cold.

"Oh no, I thought we'd make it through without any casualties," said Serena.

"You thought wrong," said a new voice they hadn't yet heard.

Serena, Beav, Luke and several others leapt to their feet. Three of the armed prison guard escorts also rose. There was momentary confusion when the group thought that the guards were standing to protect them. The guards' intentions became clear when they leveled their guns at Serena.

Serena Wilcox Bridges, the petite dark haired green-eyed private detective wife to Tom, mother to Carrie, Sam and Rebecca, personal friend and contract hire of the President of the United States, was reflecting on the possibility that she would die today. As time stood still, something primal kicked in for Serena.

She was blinded by the vision of her children's faces. *You will not break the hearts of my babies!* Her battle cry was a scream not unlike the sound of a helium balloon that had been stretched to maximize a slow ear-splitting release. She charged forward with her weapon-less arms thrust out in front of her, the element of surprise her only real offense.

Shots rang out by the dozens. When the noise stopped, Serena surveyed the resulting carnage and said in an unnaturally bright tone, "Why this got a little more violent than anticipated. I'm glad I had the foresight to send the boys out."

The guards were laying on the floor, writhing around in agony. One of them managed to maintain his grip on his gun. Luke darted toward him and for a second the guard looked confused. The guard's eyes then re-focused and zeroed in on his target. He aimed the gun directly at the man on the other side of the room and fired.

Paul Tracy never saw it coming. His eyes had been on Serena. He had been rehearsing what new juicy information he would share when his heart felt strangely hot. Paul put his hand on his chest and slowly pulled it away—it was covered in his own blood. He knew he was going to die and he thought about his brother Clyde. *Was this what Clyde felt?* He looked at Serena, the woman he would never have. All the plans he had made for the future were fading along with his heart. He opened his mouth to speak but no words escaped.

15

President Ann Kinji was brought up to speed with what happened in what was already known as The Kneecap Massacre. As the miserable would-be assassins found out the hard way, one should never bring a gun into a meeting full of vigilantes. No fewer than six shooters (all from The Supporters) obliterated the kneecaps of the prison guards from the adult criminally insane facility, thus ending the first and last assembly of Serena's Think Tank with a fanfare. There was but one fatality, the guards' true target: Paul Tracy. It seemed that Paul knew even more about the assassination than what he had already shared. Typical Paul, he was holding back to milk the attention. Now he would never have his final bask in Serena's spotlight.

"I don't want to be briefed in detail. This is your operation. Leave me out of it," said Ann.

Her private de-brief meeting with Agent Estep was held at her safe house. Estep had broken protocol, had jumped through hoops, and had taken a buzz saw to the red tape between himself and the president's undisclosed location. He refused to accept that he had done all of this only to be dismissed without being heard.

Agent Estep began his rebuttal. "I made the decision to read you in because this situation shortens our time window for flying under the radar. The prison guards were due back at the facility. We stalled off notice by putting our own people in their place. But someone will notice that the prison guards have been replaced by our people, and of course Paul Tracy didn't make it back. It's only a matter of time before the jig is up."

"You can't read the prison administration in? I don't see why you are involving me." Ann reached for her sandwich, the first bite of food she'd had in over twenty-four hours.

Estep explained, "We suspect that the corruption at the prison goes higher than the prison guards. Someone will report this to whoever they work for, and we still don't know who that is. Reading them in will give them more information faster."

"I'm already in an undisclosed location, sitting on the sidelines of the presidency." Ann tossed her barely-touched sandwich on the table in front of her.

"This is going to get much worse. We've poked a stick in the hornet's nest. I think we should admit defeat on this one, Madam President." Agent Estep glowered at his feet. If his career wasn't already toast, surely it was dead now.

"Stop the cryptic gibberish and come out with it."

"You need to give up on the idea that your friends can play detective. Serena Wilcox investigating high-level government corruption? She almost died today. Her idea of defending herself was to scream like a banshee and run directly at her attackers."

Ann grabbed a pencil and chewed on the eraser. "She's a survivor."

"Even cats have only nine lives... Madam President, I strongly suggest that you pull her out."

"I hear you, but let me ask you this, did Serena's Think Tank end in a bloody mess?"

"You know that it did." Estep couldn't follow the president's train of thought in the slightest but he did see enough of the track ahead to know that wherever this was going he wasn't likely to have a job at the end of the tunnel.

"Then Operation Bluebird Flown is working. She's drawing them out of the sewers. She's like a Pied Piper to the rats. Stay on Serena – let her do what she does."

Estep felt uneasy, but why? He rolled President Kinji's words over and over in his mind until he was aware of why he felt a twinge on his conscience. "I don't feel comfortable using Serena as bait. She's a civilian."

Ann raised her eyebrows. When she recovered from Estep's unexpected protest she said, "Exactly. Until we know more about who is committing treason and who isn't, we can't trust anybody in the government." Ann bit the entire eraser off the pencil and then spit the eraser into the trash.

Estep pretended not to notice. He was, however, too distracted by the eraser spew to formulate a thought.

Ann leaned across the table until her face was inches away from his. "How much power do you think I have as President?"

Stunned by the question, Estep was again at a loss for words.

"I'll answer that question for you: I'm powerless. My administration has been infiltrated, if it was ever mine in the first place. I've been blocked and bugged. I've been kept in the dark. I need information and Serena's the one to get it to me. Do you really think I'd use Serena as bait? I call upon her because she has an uncanny knack for finding the right people – she's a natural at bringing unlikely people together who somehow complete an overall human puzzle. When we were at the brink of apocalypse, only government insiders and powerful people had an inkling of what was to come, yet Serena just happened to have a friend who heard from a friend in Iraq. Serena got herself and her family to safety. She then managed to bumble about until she connected with none other than Paul Tracy. I don't understand how she attracts the right, or the so-wrong-they-are-right, people, but she does. What did she do with the Think Tank – who was there?"

Estep stared at her blankly. "I thought you didn't want details."

Ann sighed. "I need another pencil."

"President Kinji, I'm having a hard time keeping up with you."

"Ah, Estep. You're right, sorry for giving you whiplash. As much as I'd love to know what bizarre conglomeration of assorted oddball characters Serena assembled, I can't delve into this right now. I know that the Speaker of the House was included in that motley crew and I'm burning with curiosity on how that all went down. But you are right. I can't know the details. This is far from over. When the dust clears, there will still be an American government left standing in the rubble; and at the heart of the ruin will be the office of the President of the United States. The more bits and pieces I know, the more of this absurdity taints the office and I owe it to future administrations to leave the office a better place. When I'm a private citizen again I can call upon Serena for a cup of coffee and a long chat about who was involved in the Think Tank. I can satisfy my curiosity then. For now, you are right to remind me that I don't want details."

Estep gave up. "So you are insisting that Serena stay on."

"Let me tell you something. Serena wanted you specifically. Because of her, you're heading up the most important operation in possibly all of history. Think about that the next time you have the urge to tell me that Serena doesn't know what she's doing."

"Understood." Estep stared at his feet.

"While you're here, I want to give you a heads-up. I'm about ready to do something about that presidential impotence I was talking about. And when I do, I need your best profilers and snipers on hand. Consider this a hostage situation because it will be."

"Have you received threats? I mean beyond all of this? Has someone given you a direct threat?"

"No."

"I'm sorry, I can't for the life of me follow you and I've been trying." Estep scratched his head like a confused cartoon character might do.

"I'm the one making threats."

"Threats to?"

"Congress. But never mind that. Be there with your team in case they don't go away quietly."

Estep groaned. "I thought you'd call upon DHS to handle it."

"Is there a problem, Agent Estep?"

"No, no problem."

Ann stood up, slipped a piece of paper into Estep's hand, and opened the door for him to exit. "And Estep?"

"Yes?"

"With or without Serena. Your call."

"But you said..."

"Never mind what I said."

16

Serena's teenage son changed his favorite T-shirt, breaking a 72 hour wear-a-thon. Her daughters cleaned the guest bathroom. Serena and Tom cleared clutter and shut bedroom doors. The family ate a quick lunch of leftover taco meat on tortillas before the kids retreated into the family room downstairs. The trace of onions was still heavy in the air when Agent Estep rang the doorbell.

The first thing Estep noticed when he entered the house was an upright piano topped with picture frames and candles. He wondered who played the piano. *Surely not Serena?* He couldn't imagine her having the patience to study music. As for himself, he had been forced to take piano lessons alongside his sisters. He was tempted to sit on the bench and tickle the ivories; he hadn't played in years.

"Would you like something to eat? A cookie?" Serena held out a plate of oatmeal chocolate chip cookies.

Estep laughed.

"I'll take that as a no." Serena started to pull the plate away but Estep's hand shot out, snagging two cookies.

"It's hard to take you seriously when you're in all-out mom mode, offering me cookies."

Estep took a large chewy bite.

Tom returned from his workshop in the garage and shook Estep's hand. "The president wants her back?"

The thought of leaving home again was already twisting Serena's stomach into knots. She had been under the impression that she was off the case.

"No, this time it's me," said Estep.

Serena and Tom exchanged a puzzled look. Serena said, "What do you mean, it's you?"

Estep sank into the couch without an invitation to sit. "I mean, she gave me the option to include you or not."

Tom said, "And you chose to include her?" His voice held an incredulous note.

"Against my better judgment maybe, but President Kinji is right. Serena has a way of bringing the right people together, people I'd never think could be useful. It's like she can read their minds." Estep looked wistfully at the kids' empty milk glasses on the side tables.

"You want milk with those cookies?" Serena asked.

Estep nodded.

"It was easy to get inside your head just now, Estep. Deep down we all want a Mom. Even Moms want a Mom. Get inside people's heads and you'll be able to guess what motivates them, what drives them, and what makes them want to kill." Serena said all of this while pouring a glass of milk in the kitchen, her voice barely heard from where Estep was sitting in the living room.

Estep groaned. "I could respect you easier if you wouldn't talk so much."

Tom walked into the kitchen, took the glass of milk from Serena's hand and said, "I've got this." Even though Estep was a tall and broad shouldered young man in his twenties, he suddenly seemed like a sullen teenager in his low-seated position on the family couch.

Serena returned to the room. Both she and Tom remained standing. They watched Estep drink his milk. "The mission is dangerous," he said.

Tom grabbed Serena's arm. "You don't have to do this."

Serena nodded. "I know." She folded her arms across her chest. She asked Estep, "Why do you need me?"

"I want you to do whatever it is that you do to make all the crazy happen. My plan is to do exactly as I'm trained to do. I'll get the snipers in place, I'll put the profilers in the room, I'll bug the place, I'll do it all by the book. What you do is…"

"Magical?" Serena offered.

Estep sighed noisily, dramatically. "I don't know what you do. Can you just do it? This has to happen tonight."

Serena looked at Tom. Tom said, "Take me with you."

"No-can-do sir. Not a good idea." Estep rose from the couch and handed Serena his drained milk glass.

Serena took the glass from him without saying a word. Her heart was in her throat– while she had been watching bad guys get their knees blown to bits she had missed her youngest daughter's last visit from the Tooth Fairy. She put Estep's empty milk glass in the kitchen and viewed the clutter of the room.

This was *her* kitchen, but she hadn't spent any real time in it for so long that the room didn't feel like her space anymore. Used freezer bags on the counter tops told the story of how her family had been living off of the casseroles she had baked ahead for them. The pile-up of pizza boxes told the tale of what her family did when they were weary of eating frozen casseroles. Dinner with her family was one of her favorite times of the day and she had given that up for over two months. As she felt a tear slide down her cheek she promised herself that this would be her last operation.

The kitchen seemed to wave goodbye to her. Its cheerful lighting, its red and yellow décor, its cooktop stove with its baked-on mess, and its new additions of a lingering smell of onions and a platter littered with cookie crumbs all cried out for her to stay.

But staying wasn't an option when she was so certain that she should see this through. She really did have a gift and she believed she had a moral obligation to use that gift, especially when lives depended on it. She told herself that she could catch up on family time when the job was done.

Once in the car she had second thoughts. She prayed silently for validation that she was doing the right thing. Estep respected her time of reflection simply because he was relieved that Serena wasn't talking. Serena looked out the passenger side window and felt her spirit sinking further and further as each familiar milestone slid out of view. Then she did a double-take. She saw a moving billboard that alternated between two randomly selected ads. One was a recruitment slogan for a local university. It said, "The world needs people like you." The other was an advertisement for a real estate agency. The image depicted a happy family, two parents and three kids, in a kitchen with yellow and red décor. The slogan read, "Because at the end of the day, they're waiting for you at home."

Serena giggled.

Estep glanced at her. "What's so funny?"

"God works in mysterious ways. I asked for a sign and I literally got not just one sign but two. And by literally I mean that these are actual signs."

Estep raised an eyebrow. "Am I supposed to ask what this is all about?"

Serena noticed a look of annoyance creeping into Estep's expression. She sighed. "No, I'm good. Tell me about the mission. Is this still a part of Operation Bluebird Flown?"

"Yes, it was never closed. It's all a mess though. I'm not sure Covert Coffee ever ended. It doesn't matter what we call it."

Serena, having been given her sign, was ready to give her 110%, which she expressed by jumping back into the game with both feet. "Fill me in."

"President Kinji is getting UN backing to temporarily gain full authority over the nation, superseding Congress."

"Oh my, she got what she wanted! That's a drastic measure for sure. She'll make a lot of new enemies."

"And will provoke the enemies she already has."

"You're needed for security then, and in anticipation of investigating whatever happens, you'll be proactive in recording the event, surveillance, and the usual."

"Correct."

"What you need from me is a covert team that the official covert team doesn't know anything about, in other words, my usual."

"Yes."

"First you have to get Beav. We need him on the B team. B stands for Badass by the way."

Estep's voice was flat. "No."

"But Beav is our best guy."

"I mean, no, don't ever say 'badass'."

"You're getting Beav?"

"Yes."

"Good. I also want The Supporters."

"So far you've been highly predictable. Maybe I didn't need you after all."

"Oh really? Well I bet you'll be surprised by my last three picks."

"Speaker of the House?"

"Why would I want him?" Serena scoffed.

"Why did you want him last time?"

"I was trying to rule him in or out as a suspect. I had a gut feeling he was one of the good guys but I had to be sure. He's solid. I wouldn't want to put him in harm's way or bring down his reputation by attaching this operation to him any more than we already have."

"The nutters from the criminally insane netherworld?"

"No, no. We got what we wanted from them, which wasn't much this time."

"All right, I give up. Who?"

17

Serena waited for Beav to get in the car before revealing who else she wanted on her team. Beav had been waiting for them outside a movie theater where he had been working concessions. Why he was working there, they didn't know. They had learned that with Beav there was never a simple explanation; unless there was time for storytelling, it was best not to inquire.

"I want the intern," said Serena. "The one that Eric Dittelman told us about, with the iris scanner bruising on her face."

"Ah-hah!" Beav clapped his hands together. "I've been working on that."

Estep admitted, "I'd forgotten all about her."

"What did you learn?" asked Serena.

Beav grinned. He had worked a shift at the theater after a

grueling workout. He was now in overdrive. "I bet you are wondering why I was at that particular cinematic location?"

"Not particularly," said Estep.

"She works there," Beav gloated.

"Then why are we still driving away from the theater? Let's go back and get her!" Serena said.

"No, we don't need her," said Beav. "I got all the relevant intel, easy-peasey. Sharing a ride with her would be annoying, trust me."

"Fill us in," said Serena.

"Typical story—she was having an affair with a politician. He asked her to retrieve something from the room, a bug. She did it, end of her involvement."

"You're sure of that?" asked Estep.

"Oh yeah, I'm sure. I went to great lengths to vet her. The things I had to do…" Beav grimaced.

"Oh no, you didn't?" Serena gulped.

Beav threw his head back and laughed. "No, of course not! I had to listen to her gum-smacking jaw-jabbering barely coherent confessional. Excruciating! Women shouldn't enter this world until they're at least 30."

Serena wasn't sure whether to agree or disagree. "That's an odd tangent, even for you. Moving along, what did she say?"

"That was it. I've skipped all the pointless minutia. Her boyfriend dumped her after she was done spying for him. I had to hear all about that. She did mention that she got access to the iris scanner through temporary top security clearance. Sometimes a temporary clearance is granted for the purpose of entering an area for a final interview process before an inner-departmental hire. Because she was already working at The Cube, her information was already on file. Someone only needed to upload it into the iris scanning software for that reader. So, what we're looking for is a person who had access to the scanning software. The official team at The Cube can handle that small detail."

"Aren't you going to tell us who the politician boyfriend is?" asked Serena.

"Silly me, that's the fun part. Senator Robert Lorry." Beav flashed a triumphant smile.

"Lorry, I knew it. One of the prime suspects is confirmed," said Estep.

"I'm glad I could do that, but President Kinji wanted us to look beyond the obvious. I was disappointed when she said his name. I was hoping for a new lead," said Beav.

Estep said, "Nice job though. It means we don't have to pick her up, whoever she is. You didn't even tell us her name."

Serena spoke up. "I think I know her name."

Beav said, "Really? Go for it."

"Breyana."

Beav yelped. "What? How did you get that?"

"Breyana is President Kinji's assistant. When you were talking about the boyfriend motive for spying I thought of all the young female interns that would have had the best access to Ann's office in the past year. Breyana isn't an intern, but she looks young enough to be mistaken for one. She genuinely admires Ann, which is why we never considered her as a suspect. We were short-sighted; some girls will betray their best friends for love, and Breyana has the most access to Ann's office, and to Ann herself. I put two and two together."

"I wish I'd remembered that Breyana was President Kinji's

assistant. I vaguely recall having seen her before now that I think about it, but she must have been quiet when I saw her. Believe me, if she had opened her mouth I would have remembered that voice. Still, I'm mad at myself for screwing this up!" Beav pounded his fist into his hand.

Serena laughed. "I never noticed anything wrong with her voice."

Beav grumbled, "You would have if you'd had to listen to her until your ears bled."

Estep started to turn the sedan around. "We're going back for her then?"

"No, keep going. Phone it in and let law enforcement pick her up. They can take it from here," said Serena.

Estep straightened the wheel. "Are you sure? I thought you wanted her on your team."

"Not anymore. She was used to spy on Ann and that's probably the extent of what she knows. Senator Lorry dumped her which means she's nothing to the inner circle. She's not worth our time."

Estep said, "Then tell me where I'm going."

"I was getting to that. Do you remember that President Kinji had someone with her when she called Nicholas, that day at the lab when we were there? Her name is Dr. Kendra Wellington."

Beav jumped in. "I remember. What do you think she can do for us?"

Serena pondered that for a moment. "I don't know, maybe nothing."

Estep scoffed. "Then why include her?"

Serena explained, "Because Ann trusts her."

Estep was impressed. "That actually makes sense. Who else?"

"One of the prison guards who had his knees blown off."

"What? No, I don't want somebody getting blood and pus all over the seats." Estep drummed his fingers on the steering wheel. "What do you want him for anyway?"

"Only one of them lawyered up right away. That's the one I want," said Serena.

Beav asked, "What's your thinking on that?"

Serena answered, "He's the one who's in contact with the bigger fish. He'll want a deal and I think we can get more out of him outside of an official investigation."

"He's still in the hospital, I assume?" asked Estep.

"He's about to be released," said Serena.

"When will this happen?" asked Estep.

Serena said, "When we release him of course! I think it's worth it to get him. Call it a hunch."

"Everything's a hunch with you," said Estep.

"He's as cheery as ever I see," said Beav.

"He chose me for this mission. His bite has no venom, " said Serena.

"Still, Estep, dude, you need to lighten up. I bet you have high blood pressure already. What are you, twenty-five or something? You need to find a new girl, or get yourself a good loyal dog," said Beav.

"Yes, that's what he needs—a dog!" Serena clasped her hands together, her eyes sparkling with the joy of her plans.

Estep snapped. "I'm not getting a dog!"

Serena turned around in her seat to face Beav. She whispered, "We're getting him a dog."

18

Ann's meeting was to be held deeply underground, in a large open space inside a cave – a hole so deep that spy satellites couldn't see it. Ann's people were the only ones who could record the event, thus protecting the misuse and doctoring of footage. And, although it was not her plan to do so, Ann herself needed to cover up a few truths should anything go wrong.

Veiled Abyss cave, discovered only within the past decade, was a popular tourist attraction. However, as of four hours ago, it was eerily empty. All of the attraction's employees had been sent home, the entire area had been cleared out, and all of the inroads had been blocked off. A special ops team had swept the area and had set up shop in the largest space of the cave, an open area about a quarter of a mile from the cave entrance.

The gift store was located in the open area, which also served as a lobby where patrons could wait for their turn in the cave tour queue. President Kinji's set-up crew had removed all of the gift store's vendor equipment, product inventory, and everything else that wasn't nailed down. In its place they installed conference seating, two hundred chairs wedged in tightly.

Leg space was nearly non-existent, but comfort wasn't Ann's concern. Two hundred carefully selected guests would soon face the designated back cave wall, where a small podium had been erected and two rows of additional chairs on each side of the podium had been reserved. Counting herself, and all of her team who would remain standing, Ann was expecting two hundred and forty-nine people to gather inside Veiled Abyss, concealed and sheltered in what could well become a mass coffin.

Ann heard a noise and jumped. "Oh it's you!"

"I'm here. I have my inhaler with me, so I should be good." Serena took a deep breath that she instantly regretted. There was a funky odor in the cave that she couldn't quite place. *Bat guano? Mold? Snails? Do snails have a smell?* Serena studied the space, her eyes wide with claustrophobic terror.

"I see you've assembled another Serena special team," said Ann. She gestured to the three people who had separated themselves from the others. "I recognize the prison guard, the crutches gave him away. You'll have to explain to me later why you brought him here. And of course I know Kendra. I intended to invite her here myself. She had volunteered to attend significant events as a historical witness. How did you know about that? Or did you invite her here for some other reason? Well, you can fill me in later. She's a good choice. The only one I don't know is him – why did you bring a child with you?"

"He's Marco, a friend of Nicholas. He is profoundly gifted and has been unfairly imprisoned under the Proactive Imprisonment Act that allows the government to place youth at high risk for mass violence events into corrective mental facilities."

"Oh dear. You know that I opposed the Proactive Imprisonment Act. Just another example of how I have absolutely no real power in this country. But why did you bring Marco here? I can't guarantee his safety."

"It can't be any worse than what he's going through in the youth facility. He has an amazing gift of heightened perception. He's possibly our best asset."

"I'll allow it – but give me your digi pen."

Serena handed it over.

"I uploaded my signature seal. Marco is to be released immediately from his so-called corrective mental health facility. As soon as you are done with his involvement here, send him home."

Serena's face lit up. "Absolutely!"

"I have a few opening statements to make. Afterwards, you'll have time to prep your team. Good luck to you and your people. Thank you for your service."

"Ann, let yourself be a real person for a minute. You need a hug." Serena rushed at her with open arms before Ann had a chance to respond. She gave Ann a quick squeeze and said, "I'll pray for you."

"Appreciated." Ann's eyes misted over. She abruptly turned away from Serena before her emotions got the better of her.

Five minutes later Ann was fully engaged in the task at hand, with her brief lapse into humanity already behind her. After all, lest she forget, she was President Ann Kinji; the first female President, the first Japanese-American President, and the first President ever to take control of Congress.

President Ann took the podium. "Please be seated."

Serena and her team obediently sat in the first row. "I thought you didn't want the Speaker in on this?" Beav whispered across Estep to Serena.

Serena said, "I didn't. Ann must have asked Joe to come."

All heads had turned when Joseph Smythe entered the meeting space, but only one of them had Joe's attention in return. Joe maneuvered his way through the aisle, his lanky frame unable to handle the narrow space. He made a jumble of the chair alignment as he quipped "Sorry" and "Excuse me" while tripping over himself and everyone else on his way to the center of the room. After the noise from clanging chairs and clomping feet finally ceased Joe had settled upon a chair next to Jo, the curly-haired Supporter from Ireland.

However, that chair was already occupied by Bob, the affable radio show personality Beav first met after his late-night run from the cornfield in Indiana. Bob gave up his seat and moved to another chair further down the row. Joe embarked into the chair beside Jo in the most ungainly way imaginable.

Ann chastised, "Mr. Speaker, none of the other one hundred or so empty chairs appealed to you?" As she anticipated, a soft collective chuckle went up, and so did the red pigment on Jo's face.

She waited for complete silence before resuming. "I asked the Speaker of the House to come here today because I have confided in him my plans. He is completely on board with helping us with this mission."

She detected the collective exasperation rising from the peanut gallery. “I know, you have no idea what the mission is. I’m getting to that. First off, I want to express to each of you how grateful and appreciative I am that you are here today. The next few hours may be dangerous. If anyone has second thoughts, it is not too late to change your mind. However, you must leave now. Once I brief you, you cannot leave until the mission has ended.” She amended her statement. “With the exception of young Marco, who will be escorted out when his role is completed.”

Ann surveyed their faces and saw not a trace of regret on any of them. What she did see was curiosity and impatience, in all but Joe and Jo. The two of them were swooning over each other in their confined space in the dank and chill of the Veiled Abyss cave, moments before a briefing about the biggest covert operation of their lives, lives that were threatened to be cut short. Ann could think of worse first dates.

She moved on. “This mission is part of Operation Bluebird Flown, which originated as an operation to find and protect Serena Wilcox. While that situation was quickly resolved, Serena’s involvement in helping me peel back the layers of government conspiracy has been ongoing. Therefore, Operation Bluebird Flown was never closed, but instead has evolved into today’s events involving all of you.”

She paused for a sip of water. “Serena has an uncanny knack for bringing the right people together, people who would normally never speak to each other, let alone work cooperatively on a joint venture. I trusted her to bring the right people here and I believe that she did. What I’m asking you, Serena’s Dream Team is this: solve the investigation on the spot, live, while I’m speaking.”

She noticed puzzled expressions on several of their faces. She attempted to explain. “As in, imagine me up here as I am now. Except, imagine that this is the real deal and I’m addressing my hand-selected people of interest, delivering the most important speech I will ever deliver. Before I reach the end of my speech, I want to see your hands in the air. I will call you up to the podium and you will reveal what you know. I want all the secrets out in the open before anyone leaves this place tonight.”

Serena raised her hand.

“Yes?”

Serena got up from her chair and walked directly to the podium. “Just like this? Is this what you want us to do?”

“Yes. Come up here when you know who the remaining suspects are and tell me before it’s too late. Your job is to watch what happens. Keep an eye on everyone and everything. I know that I’m asking a lot of you. You don’t have your computers or the luxury of time. I’m asking for you to rely on your intuition and powers of observation. We can flesh out all the evidence later. What I want to know is who we need to detain for further questioning. I don’t want any of the rats to slink out of here. If any of the guilty parties are let loose, her or she will head straight to the airport and there won’t be any way to stop them. Because after I make my announcement, the culpable will know that the game is over. If you let them out the door, they’re gone.”

Serena asked what several of the others were wondering. “Why come to you at the podium? Why not tell Agent Estep and let his security detail take care of it?”

“I want all of you to see all the developments as they unfold, live. Think of it as mystery theater and you’re the leading actors.”

Ann smiled. "I know that this is unorthodox, but I've learned from Serena to think outside of the box. I'm confident that this method of putting everything out on the table will generate the results I'm anticipating. By surrounding ourselves with solid witnesses to protect the integrity of how this event will be reported, portrayed, recorded, and presented in court we will even up the David verses Goliath odds. It's going to take all of us working together to fire the sling that will bring down this giant."

"We can do this," Serena assured her. When she looked out at the front row, she saw that Estep was aghast but everyone else looked agreeable.

Ann applied her wrapping-things-up tone of voice. "I want everyone in the room to know how fast we are circling the wagons. I also want our investigation to be out in the open where my journalist guests can see it for themselves. Everything must be recorded and everything must be above-board. When all the pieces come together live, for all to actively experience, we will have enough witnesses to validate what happens here tonight. While false accounts and conspiracy theories will develop despite our best efforts, we will have ample documentation to convince reasonable citizens that our version of the truth *is* the truth."

"And when will this happen?" Luke asked.

Ann waved him off. "Serena will conduct a briefing now. I'll turn it over to her. Before I do, I want to wish all of you a safe journey through this dangerous expedition. God have mercy on us all."

19

President Kinji left them to their own devices, presumably to collect her thoughts before the big event. Behind the counter in the cave's tourist information bay was a small office. Ann slipped into that office, alone, and shut the door. How she prepared herself was a mystery, but whatever it was, it always worked.

Serena clasped her hands together. "I have some ideas."

Estep put his head in his hands. Because he was a large guy in the front row, it was a distraction that Serena had to ignore. Fortunately she had had plenty of practice with ignoring Estep's drama. "I know that this is a lot to take in and you probably feel like this will never work, but with some planning we can do this brilliantly."

Serena felt silly standing behind the podium. Standing at not-quite five two, all that could be seen above the podium was her face and neck. She imagined herself as a talking floating head. “Let’s make a circle.”

Estep muttered, “Again with the circle.” Yet all of them, including Estep, popped up at once to comply. The din of clanking and clattering chairs echoed in the cave for what felt like an interminable period of time.

Once seated in a circle, they could now see each other’s faces, which was the purpose of the exercise. Serena began. “We don’t have much time so I’ll dig right in. Marco, I have some happy news for you. When you are done working with us today, you can go home to your mom and dad. President Kinji has ordered that you be released. You’re going home today, Marco!”

Marco’s expression didn’t change much. “The cat will be there.”

“Yes, the cat too. I’m glad you are going home, Marco. May I ask for your help now?”

“My mother says that I have a gift for focusing.”

“Yes, you do. Marco, Paul Tracy was killed during the Think Tank session after you left. He knew information that powerful people do not want us to know about. I think you know what that information is.”

“I do know what that information is.”

“Will you please share that with us, Marco?” Serena held her breath, hoping that whatever he said next would be the break in the case they needed.

Marco spoke slowly and deliberately, at a volume that was difficult to hear. Everyone in the circle leaned forward. “Paul Tracy knew about RDAD. The assassination of President Ann Marie Kinji will occur in 1.32 hours.”

Several in the group gasped. Serena whirled around at the offenders and held a finger to her lips. "Go on, Marco. Take your time. Please tell me what RDAD is."

"Re-Direct And Distract. It is an acronym."

When Marco didn't say anything more, Serena prompted him. "What does the acronym mean?"

"RDAD was developed in 1993. It is a strategy to redirect and distract the American people from the business of the government. The populace focuses on the decoy issue. The government focuses on the actual issue. I play chess. Do you play chess?"

Serena assumed that the correct response Marco was going for was yes. "Yes," she lied.

"The populace are pawns."

"I understand." Serena was relieved that his chess analogy was so basic. "Is there anything else you can tell me about RDAD?"

Marco didn't respond. He already looked fatigued. Serena moved on. "How does RDAD relate to President Kinji?"

"President Ann Marie Kinji is a pawn too."

Serena worked hard to grasp what he was saying. "But if she is a pawn, isn't she doing what the government wants? Why do they want her taken out?"

Marco's energy was renewed now that he was engaged in educating Serena about chess. His voice remained flat and unhurried, but he was much more talkative. "A pawn that advances all the way to the other side of the chessboard is typically queened, the pawn is promoted and has more power to win the game. President Ann Marie Kinji has been in office long enough that she will soon reach the end of the board. She will be queened."

Serena blinked her eyes slowly. "I'm trying to understand. Can you please explain your chess analogy to me?"

Marco looked down at his hands.

"Let me help," said Mahesh, one of the members of The Supporters.

Serena gestured for him to go for it.

Mahesh brought his chair close to Marco, until he was face to face with him; a move that made several of the former Think Tank members squirm and cringe, remembering how unfortunate the result was when Tristan did that to Lita. They breathed a sigh of relief when nothing happened.

Mahesh said, "Marco, I want to suggest something to you. Please tell me if I am correct or incorrect. When you refer to President Kinji as being queened, you are saying that she will have the same abilities as more powerful chessmen, correct?"

"You are correct," Marco confirmed.

"President Kinji will soon learn about RDAD and she will not go along with it, am I correct?"

"You are correct." Marco confirmed.

Mahesh continued slowly, careful not to shut Marco down. "Because she will not go along with it, the people who use RDAD will be forced to stop using it, correct?"

"You are correct," he said again.

Mahesh kept going. "Because they don't want to stop using RDAD, they want President Kinji out of office. Correct?"

"You are correct."

Mahesh nodded. "Thank you, Marco. Ms. Wilcox may have some additional questions for you. If it's okay with you, I'd like to stay here next to you."

Marco said, "It is."

Serena mouthed "thank you" to Mahesh. "Marco, how will President Kinji learn about RDAD?"

Marco looked tired again. "The United States has allies. The allies will tell her about RDAD at the next meeting of the Global Initiative."

Serena followed up, "Did you learn about this from hacking into the security crack in the Social Media Channel?"

"Yes, I did. Members of the Global Initiative had secret meetings in the security hole on the Social Media Channel. I could see them talking."

Serena hoped that Marco had enough juice left in him to address the most important matter. "Marco, please tell me everything you know about the plan to assassinate President Kinji."

"They want the assassination to happen before the next summit. Economic issues and world issues will be undermined if an American president interferes with the Global Initiative agenda." Marco stopped talking and looked meaningfully toward the cave tunnel.

"Wow, that's a lot of information, Marco! Thank you for sharing all of that. I'll let you go home to your parents soon. Please hold on for just a couple more minutes. Can you tell us anything that could help us stop the assassination from happening?"

"Yes." Marco stared straight ahead and said nothing more.

Serena prodded. "Please tell us."

"Men were hired to kill her but she is here in this cave. They won't find her when they wait for her outside of the scheduled press conference today. They will move to Plan B. They will kill her in here, in 1.13 hours."

Serena held her voice steady, speaking to Marco as calmly as if she were reading him a story. "What is Plan B, Marco?"

Marco pointed past Mahesh to the man directly across from him.

Chairs suddenly crashed to the cave floor, creating confusion, and a cloud of dust. People moved in all different directions while a few remained frozen in their seats. Someone, who later was identified as Beav, shouted, "The President!"

Ann heard the commotion coming from outside the tourist bay. She knew better than to poke her head out there. Her team would be safer if she didn't make herself more vulnerable by presenting herself as an easy target. She crawled under the only large piece of furniture in the room, a short metal desk.

She waited for what felt like an immeasurable period of time. Her life flashed before her, as she'd always heard can happen to those who recognize that this may be the end. She saw herself as a child, growing up in Warsaw, Indiana, about three hours' drive from The Cube in Chicago. She saw herself during happier times with her parents. She saw highlights of her entire married life with Ted through images that burst through her mind in a rapid-fire slideshow.

Funny how she didn't see her many accomplishments, not even the day that she was sworn in as President. No, all she saw were the people she loved, and the people who loved her.

She heard the sound of something hitting the wall separating the tourist bay office from the rest of the cave reception area. She heard two more thuds against the wall before the fourth airborne object burst through. She heard a hissing sound and then smelled something funky that she couldn't identify. She felt herself drifting away, looking over her prone body, curled up in a fetal position. As she hovered there, in that twilight between life and death, she mourned for the children she would never have.

20

The door flew open, slamming into the adjoining wall with such force that the plaster shattered as agents Meril and Banert from Agent Estep's team barreled into the office. Banert pulled Ann out from under the desk. "Come this way, Madam President."

He stopped short. "She's not breathing!"

Meril cried out, "What do we do?"

Estep appeared out of nowhere, barking, "Pull it together! Do what you're trained to do!"

Banert and Meril stared at him, unable to move.

"Get out of the way!" Estep gently lifted the president in his arms and carried her into the open cave reception area. Beav ran to meet him, the on-hand emergency medical staff at his heels.

Beav spoke rapidly, but enunciated every word he said so that nothing would be misunderstood. “This is Cajan Powder. I know what this is, trust me. Do as I say. She has angioedema. You have to open her airway. Now.”

No one questioned Beav’s authority, but the approach to open her airway required a fast judgment call by an experienced surgeon. The most senior staff medic ruled out intubation, going straight to the last resort: a cricothyrotomy. He skillfully made a vertical incision on the skin of the neck of the President of the United States of America, something he would talk about for the rest of his life. He then stepped aside to give room for two of his medics to insert a tracheostomy tube and supply the president with a bag-valve device to administer oxygen.

“She’ll be okay?” Serena asked the medic who had performed the emergency procedure.

“She needs to be hospitalized immediately, but she’ll pull through, barring any complications.”

Serena got out of the way and let the medical team pass. She and dozens of others parted into two lines of solemn observers as President Ann Kinji, her body small and still, was carried out on a stretcher. It was the first time any of them had seen her as anything but a tigress. Her fragility shocked them into collective silence; the only sounds were the clicking of swaying medical equipment, the steady dripping inside the cave, and the footsteps of the medics as they shuffled their way into the cave tunnel.

Even when medics were long gone no one moved. No one spoke. No one wanted to be the one who broke the silence. And yet, someone had to do it. Speaker of the House, Mr. Joseph Smythe, in his first opportunity to lead when it really mattered, stepped up.

He said, "We have to get back on task. President Kinji will survive this and when she comes to, I want to tell her that we did our jobs. Let's get these demons and throw them back into the pit where they belong."

Serena signaled for everyone to return to the circle of chairs that now had four missing seats. She took a deep breath and again regretted it. The dank of the cave was getting to her. She focused her thoughts: *I need to shake off this feeling of Think Tank déjà vu. I can do this, I'm good under pressure.*

She began, "Let's begin with a debrief about what happened. President Kinji benefited from immediate medical care. Her top medical team used a surgical airway kit- not a straw, a ball point pen, or anything like that. She'll have an uneventful recovery and she will be released from the hospital in six days, if they can keep her there. She'll want to leave the hospital as soon as she is able to move."

Beav took over. "Allow me to cover the next issue, involving what occurred. The timeline we've established indicates that the device was assembled on site right under our noses. They carried the pieces in separately, sat next to each other, handed the pieces over to an assembler who then put the device together. This manner of smuggling parts of a weapon to assemble on site is typical; what's atypical is the brazenness and the arrogance of those involved. They did all of this while we were sitting together in the front row, while the President of the United States was speaking just a few feet away from them. They caught a few breaks that made this an easy task. For example, when we were distracted by Mr. Speaker tripping all over himself to sit next to Miss Irish Red- sorry, I'm blanking on your name- they would have had the cover they needed to assemble the noisier or more tedious parts of the weapon."

Both Joe and Jo blushed.

Beav carried on. "So the answer to 'how did they get that in here' is that they did it in pieces, none of which triggered an alarm when scanned separately. But I haven't figured out how they got the powder in. The powder would have had to have been encased in plastic. Agent Estep assures us that all of you were patted down thoroughly before entering the cave. How did we miss the Cajan Powder itself?"

Marco raised his hand.

Serena grimaced. She had forgotten that the child had witnessed the entire event. She pointed to him.

He said, "He didn't search everyone."

Agent Estep shook his head. "I assure you that everyone was searched."

Marco disagreed. "You didn't search her." He looked at Serena Wilcox Bridges, mother of three, the last person anyone would suspect of smuggling poison to kill the president, who had also become her dear personal friend.

Beav stood up, his chair falling backwards from the abrupt motion. He lunged toward Serena, who defensively shielded her face with her hands. He snatched her purse from her lap. "Your inhaler!"

He rummaged through her purse until he found the plastic instrument used to administer Serena's asthma medication. The plastic casing had no prescription label on it. "They switched it out before you went into the cave. That's how they got it in."

Serena's eyes were wild and big with terror. "You mean that I'm in a cave with no inhaler?"

Estep snapped, “The medics have oxygen, you’re fine.”

Beav accentuated the positive. “At least you didn’t try to use it when it was still full of toxin. When did you leave your purse unattended?”

Serena retraced her steps in her memory. Recognition washed over her face. “I left it in the car when we were standing around waiting to get in. They could have gotten it then.”

Beav nodded. “Definitely. It wouldn’t have taken them more than a few seconds to switch out the inhalers. I wouldn’t use that one by the way.”

Estep snorted.

Serena ignored the pair of them. “I’m horrified that I brought the toxin in here, but I can’t let my emotions slow us down. Moving on to the next question: Luke, how is it that no one in your group suspected your own members of being spies? I don’t understand how they got past such a naturally paranoid group of people. Isn’t your whole mojo about being suspicious of anyone and everyone?”

Luke said, “Obviously.”

“What’s done is done,” Joe said. “What we need to do now is move on quickly from this and prepare for the meeting. Ms. Wilcox will to have to fill in for President Kinji.”

Beav leaned over and said in a low voice, “Can you do that?”

Serena assured him. “She left her notes on the podium. I know Ann—what she calls ‘notes’ is essentially an entire speech, word for word.”

Bob voiced the concern that was on all of their minds. “When you’re doing that, what are we supposed to do?”

Joe said, “Do what we originally planned. Come up to the podium when you discover anything suspicious.”

Estep scoffed. "The odds of that far-fetched plan working were slim to none in the first place. We need to shut this thing down."

Beav's eyes narrowed. He stood up, so although he was the smaller man of the two, he seemed at that moment like the larger. "We'll carry out her plan, that's what she would have wanted us to do."

Estep stood. He dwarfed Beav. "She'd want us to do what needs to be done. We have to get everyone out of here."

Joseph Smythe stood. He dwarfed both of them. "Sit down."

All three men sat.

Serena said, "Thank you, Joe. We need to hurry to get this back on track before we run out of time. Here's what I want you to do: infiltrate into the crowd. The people in your immediate vicinity are your responsibility. I don't know what President Kinji's speech is, and I don't have time to look it over before we begin. I'm guessing that she wrote a few shock and awe points to deliberately provoke people into expressing guilt through their reaction to whatever bombshells she planned to drop. Remember, the guest list was chosen based on other suspicious behavior, so your observations are only one of the criteria that will earn them a seat on the detainment bus. Don't be afraid to point fingers based on little more than a hunch: President Kinji is counting on us to help her round these people up. Pay attention!"

Marco raised his hand.

By now everyone knew to listen to this kid when he spoke. All were straining to hear what he had to say. "I know what she wants."

Serena encouraged him to continue.

"She wants to know which members of the Global Initiative are traitors. Those are the people she can't track with our resources."

Serena agreed. “Yes, but since she didn’t specify that, I think she wants us to watch literally every single person in the room. There may be surprises, like the one we just had. We vetted all the Supporters. I don’t know what happened.”

Luke offered up his theory. “Craig’s wife has cancer and the medical bills were piling up. He could have been bought after he was cleared. Everyone has a price.”

Serena waved them off, already mimicking something President Kinji would have done had she been there. “I’m not blaming you. We missed it too. I’m merely saying that we can’t trust anyone, and President Kinji knew that better than we did. Marco, you’re right, the Global Initiative is our number one concern, but probably not our only concern. Keep your eyes everywhere, all the time.”

The group fell silent as they looked around the cave lobby, all of them imagining the area packed with suspects. Their team seemed too few in number to watch them all.

Serena addressed Marco. “Do you know anything else that could help us?”

Marco shook his head slowly. “I told you everything I know. I’ll have to observe to learn more.”

Serena said, “No, Marco, you need to go home now. You’ve already seen more than a child should ever see.” She gestured at Estep. Estep snapped his fingers and an agent appeared to escort Marco out of the cave.

Serena reached out to hug Marco before he left, but he shrank from her touch. She extended her hand to him instead. He reluctantly shook it. Because his facial expression was blank it was difficult to tell if Marco was relieved or disappointed to be leaving them.

Serena resumed. "Let's run down what we know."

Beav volunteered. "We are down by three Supporters: "Dennis, Craig, and Garreth. We still have Bob, Jo, Devin, Mahesh, Kobin, Garreth, Tristan, and Luke. Marco is now on his way home, so we are down to ten of us: the eight remaining members of The Supporters, plus Mr. Speaker and myself. Serena will be up at the podium and Estep will be managing security – his team needs to be focused on security as well, so it's up to us ten to observe and profile. Ten of us inside the body of about two hundred is indeed a David and Goliath situation."

"A group is coming in right now." Serena pointed toward the narrow channel that led into the open space of the cave. "Places everyone. It's show time!"

They broke up the circle of chairs and placed them back where they belonged. Next, they strategized their seating plan. Mr. Speaker was in the direct center in row one. In row two, Bob was between the left end and the center. In row three, Luke was between the right end and the center. In row four, Beav was in the direct center. The pattern was repeated to the end of the rows.

As people filed in, Serena Wilcox Bridges gripped the podium with both hands and shifted her weight from one foot to the other. The last thing she needed was to have a fainting spell induced by standing still for too long during a stressful social situation. To distract herself from obsessing about vertigo she thought about her best friend and husband, Tom. She imagined him sitting there, smiling at her, and encouraging her to go on. She tried not to think about her missing asthma medicine.

Serena observed every person when they filtered in and when they took a seat in their designated area. President Kinji had arranged their assigned seating herself to ensure that key members of Congress were seated next to each other so that she could watch them from the podium (especially the oldest and boldest senators–the thirteen who hadn't been ruled out as suspects). Now this task was left to Serena, who didn't keep up with politics and had no idea who most of the senators were. Without any insight into their personalities or their records as lawmakers she would have to rely on her skills as a profiler. Fortunately profiling had always been one of her strengths as a private investigator.

Members of Congress who had already been cleared of traitorous activity were not invited to the Veiled Abyss party, but were watching everything via a delayed stream; the cave's environment had proved to be too challenging for streaming live feed. To transmit the stream, agents needed to route the data in relay-race fashion, by hand-delivering the data to tech agents positioned nearest to the cave exit; the only spot where they could find a signal.

Even though the tech team knew that their signal would most certainly be hacked, they weren't concerned. They had assured President Kinji that by the time anyone caught wind of what was going on it would be too late for outsiders to mobilize. The meeting would have a dedicated and secure transmission for the duration of the reading of President Kinji's speech. Everything was all set; the stream was live and running, all parties were seated (except for those who would remain standing for security purposes), and all eyes were on Serena.

21

"Let me begin by saying that I know you were all expecting to see the wise and beautiful President Ann Kinji at this podium instead of me, someone most of you have never seen before. President Kinji is recovering from an unfortunate incident that you will all be briefed on later. She will be absolutely fine and there is no cause for alarm. However, she is unable to deliver her presentation and rather than reschedule this for a later date, it is best that I deliver her speech on her behalf."

Serena held the president's speech in front of her, her hands trembling so hard that the paper made a crinkly sound amplified by the microphone. She said a silent prayer and steadied herself. No one objected to her announcement that she would fill in for President Kinji.

"Again, I'll remind you that these are President Kinji's words, not my own. I'll begin.

'Welcome to the Veiled Abyss Cave, the best gathering place for what I have in store for you. The word *Veiled* means hidden; we are at this moment hidden from the prying eyes of artificial intelligence as per my intention. The word Abyss means deep hole, and that's what we've found ourselves in.

I am'—

I'll stop here and remind you that this is President Kinji talking, not me, Serena Wilcox Bridges. I'll continue reading now.—

'issuing an Executive Order beyond anything history has ever seen.

How does an Executive Order apply to the crisis we are dealing with today? First I'll address the purpose of an Executive Order, and then I'll describe the status of what I referred to as a crisis. Finally, I will explain how my Executive Order meets our needs to resolve our national crisis.

Executive orders aid officers and agencies of the executive branch in managing operations within the federal government. Executive orders have the full force of law, and as President of the United States I have discretionary power as well as power granted directly to the Executive by the Constitution. Throughout United States history, challenges to the legal validity or justification for an Executive order have resulted in lawsuits.

I'm aware that if you do not agree that my order is a legal application of the power constitutionally granted to me you may bring forth a lawsuit, as is your legal right to do so and I wouldn't expect anything less from you. However, I'm more than willing to move forward as I am confident that the American people will find my actions to be justified, imperative, and ultimately appreciated. I am not the first American president to use an executive order to create big change.

Huge history-changing reform and large-scale policy changes have been created by executive order. Dwight D. Eisenhower used one to mandate the desegregation of public schools. Harry Truman used an Executive Order for the integration of the armed forces.

Of course not all usages of Executive Order have been full of greatness. Franklin D. Roosevelt delegated military authority to remove people from military zones, and then targeted Japanese Americans and German Americans, paving the way for Japanese-Americans to be sent to internment camps during World War II. You may well want to pay attention to what I just said about the use of military authority, as it is a hint about what is to come.

The crises I've been referring to cannot be resolved without the cooperation of Congress. Until the House and the Senate can compromise and work together we can't move forward as a nation. How many more years must we languish before we admit defeat? We have let Congress deteriorate to the point that we are now at risk of an irreversible breakdown of our entire system of government.

We need a swift response to avoid a complete and irreparable economic collapse that will devastate not only our own country, but the world markets as well. Because Congress has proven to be incapable of doing the work that they were elected by the American people to do, I must act immediately to replace them with individuals who can and *will* do the work that is urgently needed. Desperate times call for desperate measures: we are in a state of national emergency!

Therefore, I am delegating military authority to remove people from Congress. Any and all persons suspected of treason and traitorous acts will be imprisoned while awaiting trial. I will emphasize that all those arrested will receive a fair trial. I will also be clear on the following: There will be no arraignment hearing. No legal tactics that might delay or evade detainment will be tolerated. Senators, I'm giving you a Go-to-Jail card that should have been played a long time ago.'"

An audible gasp went up in the crowd- it was impressively loud, given how many collective gasps were simultaneously sputtered. Serena found this reaction to be quite satisfying. She wished Ann could have experienced it herself. Serena took a sip of water, then continued.

"I'll resume reading now. 'With the full backing of the UN, I will have temporary authority over both the House and the Senate, therefore bypassing Congress entirely. How is this possible, you might ask?

You might recall that before the Big War, we, the United States of America, freely gave up our power to the UN. We granted the United Nations power to create laws that supersede our own laws! Many Americans, including myself actually' *and by 'myself' I remind you that we are still talking about President Kinji and not me, Serena.*"

Serena paused before continuing. "'Many Americans, including myself actually, cried out that our freedom was in jeopardy. Today I am ironically using the power that we gave to the UN, to take back our power; to give authority back where it belongs, to the people. We are the people.

Congress is supposed to represent us, not rule over us. Their tyranny over the office of the presidency has rendered the Executive

Branch powerless. I can't govern without a functioning Congress. American government has been deadlocked, inefficient, and unfit for so many years now that we are not only straining from the weight of tremendous debt, but we are also fast becoming morally bankrupt.

Without further ado, I will conduct the business that this gathering was created for. Members of my War Cabinet are here today, and I give them immediate authority to carry out my order, Executive Order number 03262785476. The first task at hand is to flush out those who have been involved in…' *At this point I ask that you give me, um, Serena, a second.*"

Serena sped-read through the next paragraph. Ann addressed the plot to kill her, explaining that she knew about the assassination attempt. Because the assassination had already been attempted, (unsuccessfully, thank God) shouldn't Serena skip this part? Ann also went on to question the motivation behind the attack, which was also now known, thanks to Marco's information about RDAD and the Global Initiative. Serena couldn't deliver this section of the speech as written.

Serena considered herself to be a fairly decent writer, surely she could go off script? Should she dare? She had to do something to fix this, and she had to do it now. Everyone was waiting. If the seconds dragged into minutes, the element of surprise would be long gone. Members of Congress were already chewing on the news about their impending arrest – she couldn't give them time to digest, regroup and mobilize!

It is with this logic that Serena, former private detective and mother of three, delivered a historic improvisational speech that would be truncated to sound-bites and often repeated.

"Before continuing with President Kinji's speech, I have some information of my own to deliver. President Ann Kinji knew of the assassination plot. She knew that some of you people in this very room, or rather in this cave, wanted to kill her, or more accurately were planning to have her killed, which was unsuccessful..."

Serena noticed Beav was giving her a funny look. She made a bigger effort to focus her thoughts before speaking.

"President Kinji also had an awareness that this was supposed to go down at the Global Initiative. She was on to you, so you had to step up your timetable. You tried to kill her today, but you were not successful. President Kinji will be fine. She is resting comfortably now, under the best of medical care."

Serena surveyed the shocked faces, realizing that her vantage point was the optimal position from which to observe facial reactions. Unfortunately all of them looked shocked. Were they genuinely blown away? Were some merely following the crowd; mimicking the reaction they saw in everyone else? How many of them feared Ann's Go-to-Jail card? Serena identified four people she would watch closely for the duration of her speech, four that she thought were exhibiting a fear of an impending life in prison.

"President Kinji, as I said, will recover, but the point is, the assassination attempt was real, and it did occur. We also know why it happened. We know about the RDAD agenda. An acronym for Redirect and Distract, RDAD was used to, well, redirect and distract the American people from the true agenda of the United States government."

Serena noticed a stirring in the crowd. Some of them had actually flinched at the mention of RDAD. She kept her eyes on the most agitated responders, three of whom were the same people she already had her eyes on. She let them rev up for a few seconds, then continued with her improvisational speech when their babble died down.

"For example, any issue that created polarization was a contender for RDAD. Any issue that threatened freedom was especially popular, drawing fire from both sides of the aisle, keeping the American people and Congress divided, distracted and impotent.

Issues such as gun control, abortion, marriage equality, increased government regulation over both public and private institutions; businesses, farms, schools– the list goes on—have kept Americans distracted for decades. While some, or even all, of these issues are socially and morally important, and many are human rights issues, statistics don't offer up any good case for prioritizing these issues over the larger issues that have been threatening to destroy us.

For example, let's look at the failed economy. If the economy hits a state of total collapse it affects 100% of Americans directly and all of the world population indirectly, which eventually becomes direct. What I'm trying to say is that no other issue, none of the issues pushed on us through RDAD, effects 100% of our population. While we were distracted by issues that don't carry a total-population impact, and many times not even close to that, our government kept on doing whatever it is that they were doing, which is unclear to me. My point is that we didn't demand reform because we were too busy fighting with *ourselves* about other causes.

Any time you threaten an American's freedom to make private choices, an American's freedom to defend home and family, an American's freedom to make lifestyle decisions based on religion, ethics, or personal safety, well you certainly achieve what RDAD is all about. Americans have been stepping over each other to fight for freedoms that have been denied or threatened. RDAD worked as intended.

I get it now, that RDAD was what former president John Williams must have been involved in, something he colluded about with the president before him who probably colluded with the president before *him* as well. RDAD didn't die when they did, it got stronger.

Except, RDAD lost its executive branch. You didn't trust this new President to go along with RDAD, and you are right about that. I know Ann—President Kinji—wouldn't have had any part of a program designed to deliberately mislead the American people. I know she would never subscribe to a program whose sole agenda is to create division and disharmony, to disrespect the values and beliefs of the American people by manipulating them into fighting against each other.

Anyway, you were right. She'd never go for RDAD. So you wanted to get rid of her. I know that some of you have a huge financial stake in corporations that benefit from legislation you are either preventing or pushing. I struggle to guess your motivations when you don't have financial stake in…"

Serena noticed that Beav was shaking his head and flapping his arms like a duck flying against the wind. She ignored him and kept going.

"You probably hoped that she would go away after her temporary emergency appointment post Big War, but when we elected her for an official term, in the biggest landside in history I should add, you had a problem. The American people were starting to listen to President Ann, their popular Princess. We were coming together more, and there was a glimmer of hope on the horizon that we could bridge some of the distance between the extreme left and the extreme right.

And that's exactly what you feared! The extremes are where you *want* us to be. When we are incapable of unifying, we are powerless. We spin our wheels year after year while you achieve your sneaky slimy agenda. Which is what exactly? I think I have some ideas.

The American dollar has depreciated so much that it's barely worth the paper it's printed on. We're beyond going broke, and if there's no money, there's no country. Other countries own too many of our institutions. So what happens if they call in all these debts? Foreign nations could take us over without a single shot fired. They can simply evict us. Our own government will be replaced, except maybe you snakes who are working with the foreign leaders, all members of the Global…"

Serena stopped short, noticing Beav standing and waving his arms. He gestured a director's "wrap it up" sign, a "cut" sign and some other gesture Serena had never seen before.

"Sorry, I got more off-script than I intended. My point in all of that is that we know some of you are guilty of treason. It has been established through the actions of today, of less than two hours ago. The rest of that was my own conjecture, but I stand by it. I know the evidence will bear out everything I said."

Beav vigorously shook his head. Serena made eye contact with him and shrugged. She scanned Ann's speech until she was past the section about the assassination attempt.

"Anyway, at this point I will return to President Kinji's speech."

Serena removed a few pages from the stack and set them on the podium before reading the rest of Ann's speech. The crowd shuffled their feet and shifted their weight in the chairs that had grown intensely uncomfortable during their odyssey with Serena at the microphone.

"*Remember this is President Kinji talking now, not me.* 'How can I whip Congress into shape? How can I find the world leaders who have created alliances and have conspired with members of our own government to work outside the knowledge and interests of the American people?

While I was initially selected as an emergency appointment after the Big War, I stand in front of you today as your officially elected president whose first term is almost at its end.'"

Serena hesitated. *Should I be reading this part? It's too late now, I'll have to read the rest.*

She continued, "I have been your president for three years, and during all of that time, I have struggled to see through the dense fog of subterfuge and conspiracies. I ultimately became depressed, nearly despondent. I had all but given up until I understood this simple truth: I am the one person who can do something about this. I have not only the power of an Executive Order, or rather a series of several separate orders, but I also have a new power source at my disposal: the UN. And, apparently I have more friends at the UN than I thought I did because they are backing my actions unconditionally.

You see, I thought I was powerless to go up against Congress, but I was wrong. I am the one person who can make a difference. The health of the United States effects the global population. Therefore, with the full backing of the UN behind me, I have temporary emergency authority over all branches of government. With this authority I am ordering the following, effective immediately:

I hereby order, forcibly if need be, the removal of members of Congress who are known traitors.

Secondly, I order the disbandment and dissolution of the Global Oil Initiative and its parent organization, the Global Initiative.

The only way to clean house is to start over. Senators who committed treason will be immediately replaced by emergency appointees, all of whom are private citizens of upstanding character who have never had a formal association or affiliation with any political party or office.

I strongly suggest that the new Congress' first order of business be to set the term limits that have been bandied about for years. Any member of Congress whose term limits have exceeded the new regulations will be immediately placed into mandatory retirement.

The American people will later hold elections to fill the vacated congressional seats. At which time, the emergency appointees will have the option to run for office if they desire, or step down if they choose not to run. To be clear, my appointees are only temporary: the American people will elect all members of Congress as soon as we can reasonably make that happen.

Meanwhile, however, Congress will be stripped of at least three-fourths of its career politicians, due to ejection by arrest or through the new term limits regulation that I believe will pass. The majority of Congress will be flushed out and given a clean slate. There will be a period of at least thirteen months in which most of Congress will be composed of American citizens who have never held a political office. This is our best chance to have a Congress that is willing to put the needs of the American people ahead of their own.

This is the freshest start I can give you, and to create the upmost clarity in my intentions, it is imperative that I do not run for re-election."

Serena wasn't expecting Ann's speech to make such an announcement. She looked up and noticed the stunned expressions on everyone, especially those close to Ann. The transformation from surprise to sorrow was already showing on some of their faces.

She hurried to read the rest. "How can I clear Congress of its most senior politicians, stack things in my favor by appointing novices, and then run for a second term?

No, no, I will step aside for the good of the nation. It is with this in mind that I do offer you a recommendation for my replacement, someone I believe would…'"

Serena looked up from the papers she was holding with a death grip. Should she continue reading? Wasn't she over-stepping? This part could wait until President Kinji herself could deliver her speech. She had already said too much, having announced Ann's plans not to run for re-election. Why hadn't Ann warned her about what was in her speech? Serena hesitated for long enough that the crowd began to talk amongst themselves.

Serena was about to wrap things up when she detected a flurry of movement. Luke and Bob were making a beeline toward the podium.

Luke took the microphone and calmly stated, "President Kinji asked us to identify those who should be detained. I speak on behalf of my colleagues when I say that I feel certain that these persons of interest will receive a fair trial. Therefore my conscience is clear when I, and others, recite the names of those who will now be immediately arrested and escorted out of the cave, to a nearby detainment facility for interrogation and briefing."

Luke added, "We now instruct the members of Agent Estep's team, as well as members of the armed forces who are positioned just outside these cave tunnels, to arrest the following people we suspect of committing treason."

What happened next was so quiet and orderly it was dreamlike, so much so that Serena felt like everyone was in a collective trance. Bob and Luke recited four names each. As they named names, each person obediently stood up, walked down the narrow no-leg-room aisle of their seating area, and followed an agent or officer out through the cave tunnel exit.

There was not a sound beyond the soft shuffling of feet, the steady drip of the cave's ceiling over their heads, and the solemn recital of names. Each person stepped up to the microphone for their turn except for Joe. As Speaker of the House he had a conflict of interest and was advised by Dr. Kendra to refrain from comment.

Serena was next to take the podium, adding the four people she had kept an eye on during her speech; she had to point them out because she didn't know their names. Beav was next, adding seven more. The remaining Supporters named seventeen among them. When it was all said and done, thirty-six people were arrested.

All thirteen of President Kinji's congressional suspects were confirmed as suspects. The other twenty-three persons of interest included two United States governors and members of the Global Initiative, of which ten were foreign and eleven were domestic.

But all Serena cared about at that moment was how fast she could get out of that cave, back to the surface of Planet Earth, something she could never again take for granted. The first thing she would do when she got out was take a big deep breath – minus dank, mold, bat guano, and slug. Even better than her dream of a lung-full of fresh air was seeing Tom waiting for her at the cave exit. She raced toward him until the look on his face stopped her cold.

22

Tom whisked Serena away from the mouth of the cave and led her to a waiting vehicle. An agent held the door open for them. They stepped inside and barely had time to get fully seated before the driver took off.

"You're scaring me Tom. What's going on?"

Tom cleared his throat several times, a nervous habit that alarmed Serena even more. "President Kinji took a turn for the worse after a second attempt on her life while at the hospital."

"What? Oh no! How did that happen? She was under high-levels of security!"

"They gassed the entire wing. Her security detail died trying to protect her." Tom reached across Serena's lap to hold her hand.

"Oh no, this is horrible. I can't believe it."

"They think she will pull through with no setbacks or damage."

"So you aren't saying that she's dying?"

"No." Tom looked away.

"Then what is it that you aren't telling me?"

"You didn't get news coverage while in the cave. But we got yours-- I saw you on TV and so did everyone else."

Serena tried to process what he was saying. "What do you mean?"

"The whole world knows that President Kinji has taken over the government. The reaction has been violent."

Dread settled like a ball of lead in Serena's stomach. "How violent? What's happened?"

"The kids are fine."

"What do you mean 'the kids are fine'? Why wouldn't they be fine?" Serena's panic registered in her voice. Her hand subconsciously scrabbled at the door latch, even though they were still on the road, and nowhere close to her children.

"They didn't just gas the hospital. They gassed our house too."

Serena's tongue felt like cotton in her mouth. "Our house? And you were home?"

"We were home."

Serena could hear herself ask the next question as if she was listening to her own voice from outside of her body. "Where are they?"

Tom gave her hand a squeeze. "They're at the CDC. We're headed there now."

Serena pulled her hand away. "They're fine? What do you mean fine? They are *going* to be fine, or they *are* fine? What's the level of fine?"

"They're fine. They are under observation. Do you think I'd leave them if they weren't okay? They're watching movies and eating pizza."

"You scared me. You really, really scared me. I shouldn't have put them in danger. My work for the president is over as of now."

"Hey, I said that they're okay. You'll see for yourself soon. You did good today. I watched the whole thing."

"Until you got gassed."

"Right." Tom said nothing for a few seconds before adding, "I saw most of it. You were impressive."

Serena smiled. "I could be President."

"You were."

"Yes, for a little while there I was, wasn't I?" Serena thought about that.

Tom's phone buzzed. He glanced at the number. "It's for you."

Estep's voice was so loud and abrasive that Tom could overhear everything he was saying, including the tone he was saying it in. "Where are you?"

"On my way to the CDC. My kids were…"

"I know about that. That's under control. You should be here."

"Where? The hospital?"

"The Cube. We're interrogating suspects."

"Can't it wait?"

"Gee, I don't know. Why don't we let riots build until civil war breaks out?"

"I want to see my kids first."

"I'm sending Beav. He'll brief you on the way."

"Estep, I'm not leaving until I spend some time with my kids."

Estep disconnected the call.

Serena stayed with her family through the rest of the movie. They had saved her a slice of pizza. She didn't realize how hungry she was until she smelled the food. It felt good to eat with Tom and the kids, even though they had already eaten and all they could offer her was cold leftover fast food.

She hugged each of them multiple times when Beav turned up at the door. Tom assured her that he could hold down the fort, but Serena had already vowed that her investigative work was over. As she walked the halls of the newly built Center for Disease Control, located within a few miles of The Cube, she better understood why Ann hated The Cube. It *did* suck people in. Well, no more. Let this be a wake-up call; she would see this thing out and then she would go home – to stay.

Serena didn't think she could take any more of Estep without more food in her first. That one slice of pizza only served as an appetizer. She hadn't eaten anything else since early that morning. She could also do with some coffee. Her hunger and fatigue must have shown on her face because Beav suggested that they stop along the way.

"Estep is in a hurry for me to get there. He's in a mood."

"We need to get him a dog."

Serena agreed. "But that idea won't help us get through tonight."

"I know a friend who can make that happen."

"Beav, you always know a friend."

"She runs an animal shelter. She'll open for us."

"You mean now? We're getting him a dog now?"

"Why not? Today could have been the end, but it wasn't. We're alive. You just saw your family. And I, well, I have me. What does he have?"

They left the discussion hanging while the two of them rested in the diner that Beav had referred to as a hidden treasure. They ate together in companionable silence. When they were finished eating every crumb off their plates, which took only a matter of minutes due to their state of hunger and their hurry, he calculated a modest tip and paid the tab.

Then he took up where he left off. "Estep is never going to get out of his funk if we don't help things along. He needs a dog."

When Serena didn't come back with another rebuttal, Beav placed a call to his friend Christine. Within a half hour they were at the animal shelter. Christine greeted Beav warmly, Beav thanked her for opening the doors after-hours for him, and a quick introduction of Serena was made.

Christine then showed Serena and Beav the kennels, which were all full to maximum capacity, and beyond. A few animals were in plastic crates along the floor. Serena suspected that this practice was bending regulations. Word had apparently gotten out that the shelter had a soft spot for taking in any stray, even reptiles and—*surely that wasn't a goldfish?*

Christine led them directly to a dog that was barking for their attention. "This friendly guy is part Welsh Corgi with a mix of something else. Look how loveable he is. It breaks my heart that we haven't found a home for him yet."

Beav opened the enclosure and knelt down on the concrete slab kennel floor. The dog bounded over to him and tried to jump into his lap. Beav sat on the floor to accommodate the dog's wish. He was a big dog, taking up more than Beav's available lap space.

Serena laughed. "He sure is friendly, you're right about that."

"Aww, how can you turn this guy down? I don't think I can

leave him here." Beav stood up and tried to avoid the dog's pleading eyes.

Christine moved down the row, past the cages containing kittens, cats, and an obese rabbit.

"Ooh, what a beautiful dog!" Serena stopped in front of a kennel that Christine had passed by.

"Roxy is a Jack Russell. I'm watching him for my friend Marie. She'd be upset with me if I gave her dog away! But I offer you this handsome German Shepherd."

"A Shepherd does sound like a good fit for Agent Estep."

Christine said, "We're so fond of Finn. I'd keep him myself if I didn't already have too many animals. He was a service dog."

Serena clasped her hands together, a gesture which made both dogs' ears perk up. "Yes! He's perfect. Estep needs a highly trained, highly disciplined dog."

Beav couldn't let go. "How is a highly trained dog better than this loveable mutt I have right here?"

Serena groaned. "Because Estep will be a tough sell. The service training issue will help."

They both looked at the German Shepherd. Finn certainly did have a noble quality. He tilted his head and looked at them with his kind soulful eyes. Oh yes, Estep would most definitely fall in love with this dog. They had nothing to worry about.

"We'll take him," said Serena.

Beav dragged his feet. "And him too." He pointed at the friendly mutt with the wild eyes and the tongue hanging out of a big toothy grin.

Christine's face lit up. "You want both dogs?"

Beav had made up his mind. "I can't leave him here. He's

coming home with me. You like that, don't you, Toby?" The dog barked happily as if on cue.

Serena asked Christine, "Do you name all the animals as they come in?"

Beav laughed. "I named him when he jumped into my lap."

The animal shelter visit took less than ten minutes and created a rift between them and their unsuspecting driver. And when those minutes were added to the time they spent at the diner, and the extra drive time spent getting on and off the freeway twice, they were almost an hour behind schedule.

With no time to figure out a better plan they put both dogs in the backseat together. Serena was worried that the dogs wouldn't react well to that situation, but Beav was confident that the two fellows would get along splendidly. Beav was right. By the end of the trip, Toby had fallen asleep with his head on good-natured Finn's back. Finn, awake and alert for the entire trip, seemed to watch over Toby.

"Aww, look at that," said Beav.

Serena was quick to say, "You can't keep both dogs!"

"I know, I know. Let's get Finn to Estep before I lose my willpower. I'm having doubts that he will be good to this dog."

"Oh come on, you know he will be. It won't take him long and he'll be asking me to knit sweaters for Finn."

Beav was astonished. "You knit?"

"Theoretically he might ask me to knit a doggie sweater. And if I knew how to knit I would do it."

"HA! I didn't think that sounded right."

The two chatted about nothing important while the driver grudgingly took them where they wanted to go. Their next stop was to drop Toby off at Beav's friends' house. The Sharot family was available at this hour to take Toby, and they did live nearby, but this pit stop added even more delay to their already tardy arrival. Serena had grown anxious and had already checked in several times for updates about what was going on with the investigation.

Finally they arrived at The Cube. They brought Finn with them, with no plan for how to smuggle him in. Serena regretted the impulsive decision to get Estep a dog; but because Finn was a German Shepherd, no one even asked why they had a dog with them. It was shockingly easy to sneak an unauthorized dog into The Cube.

Of course security was lax because they had access to the private back entrance. If they had tried the standard employee corridor, or worse yet the public access entrance, they wouldn't have gotten Finn past the first checkpoint.

However, being on the super-secret covert team had its perks, and this was one of them. They trotted Finn all the way to the conference room where Estep was already in a mood – this dog was absolutely necessary. Their plan could go either way, but looking again into Finn's beautiful eyes, Serena couldn't imagine how it could go wrong.

When Estep saw Finn he stopped dead in his tracks. Whatever he was in the middle of saying would remain forever unsaid. He was slack-jawed and speechless, for about two seconds. "That thing better not have anything to do with me."

"That *thing* is a dog, *your* dog," said Beav.

"I don't have a dog. I *won't* have a dog."

Serena threw something directly at Estep's feet.

Estep flinched and yelled, "What the--!"

Finn shot over to Estep in a flash. He scooped up the object and obediently sat directly in front of Estep as if waiting for a command. Estep studied him. He said, "Drop."

Finn released the object.

Estep picked it up – a sticky peanut-buttery ball, a canine treat that Christine had given Serena for Finn. Finn watched Estep take the treat away. Estep muttered to himself and threw the treat. Finn retrieved it and returned to where Estep was standing. Estep tried the command a second time. "Drop."

Finn obeyed.

Estep patted Finn's head. "Good boy."

Finn tilted his head.

"It's yours."

Finn picked up the treat, lay down, and settled in for a good chew.

Estep turned toward Beav and Serena. He ignored their self-righteous expressions and said, "You're late."

Serena said, "His name is Finn."

Estep admired his new best friend. He was so impressed with Finn that his hostile obsession with his ex-girlfriend felt far behind him. He didn't even care that Serena and Beav were acting superior. In fact, he could even admit that he was grateful that they had pushed this dog on him.

Best of all, Finn was already generating impressive results as an anger management therapy dog for Estep. When Estep brought Serena back to the interrogation room he made no further mention of the fact that she was over an hour late. Incredibly he didn't utter a single snarky remark during the entire two minute walk through the maze of corridors.

The Cube had never been a holding place for criminals.

However, government insiders arrested for treason were a different breed of criminal and due to the extreme situation at hand, and the sheer number of individuals involved, the judgment call was made to conduct the interrogation just a few doors down from President Kinji's office.

An entire wing of The Cube watched the proceedings from the peanut gallery in the conference room. With no two-way mirror in their makeshift interrogation room, they watched the interrogation via a live feed on multiple screens. Serena, Estep and Beav observed the interrogation from a separate room with a few other investigators and profilers. They too watched from a live feed. None of the signal problems existed in The Cube that had challenged the tech support team at the cave earlier that same day, but with all personnel tapped out and sleep deprived even a routine job was taxing.

The late hour, now pressing toward midnight, did nothing to deter the media from camping out on The Cube's lawn. The media circus was definitely in full swing, and the American people had also begun to gather. By morning Chicago would be a powder keg for riots and all manner of chaos. Chicago's finest had already stepped up their patrols and had assembled their best teams. Security teams that normally scheduled high-profile events at least a year in advance were forced to coordinate full-scale security of the nation's new capital with merely a few minutes' notice.

Serena addressed Estep. "I'm still not clear on why the interrogations are being held here instead of at the agency or at the prison. This is crazy!"

Estep nodded. "I can't believe I'm saying this, but I agree with you. President Kinji insists that there is no place more secure than

The Cube. More importantly, she wants every word witnessed by as many in government as possible, and the best way to do that, she says, is to bring the traitors directly to the government. By the way, if any of those witnesses want to go into the interrogation room itself we are to escort them in. Can you imagine? So far no one has asked. Then again, I didn't tell them that they have the option. I figure I had leeway to make a judgment call."

Serena asked, "How is President Ann doing?"

Estep snorted. "She's fit to be tied that they won't let her out of bed yet. She was online with me as soon as she came to."

Serena laughed. "That sounds like her. What a relief, huh? This has been a harrowing journey."

"Yes." Estep answered in one syllable.

With a break in the interrogation, and nothing to watch on the feed, there was no reason why their conversation couldn't continue. Serena prattled on. "I can't imagine keeping that woman down under normal circumstances. The nation is a circus and she's stuck in a hospital. She must be going out of her mind. I bet she's giving Ted a hard time."

Estep raised his eyebrows. The conversation was becoming too chatty; he wasn't Serena's gal pal. He was about to make a snarky remark when his eyes rested upon Finn's silhouette. *What a fine dog.* Estep forgot what he was planning to say.

Serena followed his gaze. "Ah, yes, Finn. I almost forgot about him. He's been so quiet."

"Hey, what's that he's got?" Estep moved in closer.

"That's my inhaler! I see my name on the label – look!" Serena bounced up and down like a child on Christmas morning. "Get it from him! That's our missing link!"

Estep instructed, “Finn, Drop!”

Finn walked directly to Estep and dropped the inhaler at his feet.

Estep took a cloth from his pocket and used it to pick up the inhaler. He turned it over to read the label. “It’s yours. What do you mean by missing link?”

Serena explained. “We know who attempted the Plan B attack on President Kinji in the cave. It was obvious because it happened right in front of us. But who else was behind it? I can’t imagine that all of the members of the conspiracy, the many layers of it, are all accounted for. We need the link to the others, especially the ones still here in The Cube. And this is it. When we find out where Finn got that from we’ll have our missing link.”

Finn’s movement had caught Beav’s attention. He ambled over to where Estep and Serena were standing quietly, staring at the dog. Beav said, “The question is, how do we get Finn to tell us where he found the inhaler?”

Serena shrugged. “I don’t think we can do that, but we can figure it out ourselves. Find his treat and you’ll know where he’s been.”

Estep didn’t find the treat itself but an askew grate caught his eye. He moved the grate, a heater cover with missing screws, with his foot. Finn’s treat was resting on the heating duct. “How much you want to bet that Finn dropped his treat in there, and found the inhaler when he tried to retrieve it?”

Serena solved the mystery aloud. “The inhaler switch was made outside of the cave, when my purse was briefly left unattended in the car. We can assume that someone went back to this room after the switch was made. That doesn’t make sense. Why not toss my inhaler into a Dumpster? Hiding it here is absurd. So we can surmise that this hiding place wasn’t intentional. He or she removed the grate screws and dropped it in the heating duct because there was no opportunity to get rid of it elsewhere."

Serena pondered that for a second before saying, "Where are the screws?"

Beav noticed the feed was back up. "They're starting back up again."

Serena shook her head. "This is more pressing. You go watch. Agent Estep and I should focus on this. Buzz me if I miss anything important."

Beav gave her a thumbs up and re-joined the group gathered in front of the feed screens. Estep and Serena searched every desk drawer, every trash bin, and every pencil holder they could find. They searched under desks, chairs and tables. They searched under seat cushions. "If he shoved the screws into his pocket, they won't be in this room," said Estep.

"We're assuming that this is a man? That's my gut feeling too I suppose. If he was antsy to get the inhaler off of his person, why would he then keep the screws? No, they are here. We have to keep looking," Serena insisted.

Estep examined the ceiling tiles for any sign that one of the tiles had been moved. He looked at the light fixtures and the beams.

Serena was a bit too short to easily reach the window sills, but she slid her hand along the sills over her head. She found nothing but dust on the first two window sills she tried. When she hit the third window sill, the one nearest to the grate, she was rewarded with a tell-tale sound of metallic clinking when the screws hit a metal desk near the window.

"Now what? This doesn't tell us anything." Estep said.

"It confirms that someone deliberately removed the screws to hide the inhaler in there. We were right about where Finn found the inhaler. That being confirmed, if the person who hid the inhaler didn't wear gloves, we should be able to get an ID from the screws or the inhaler."

Estep pointed out, "The inhaler has dog slobber on it. We might not be able to pull anything usable off of that."

"But the screws don't. We have lab tech on emergency call."

Estep scowled at her. "Yes, I know, I set that up." Finn sat at attention when Estep's tone of voice changed. Estep noticed this and when he spoke again it was without the abrasive tone that Finn had reacted to. "Finding the screws is a good lead, good job."

Serena glanced at Finn and smiled. She whispered, "Thanks, buddy."

Estep called the lab team. They arrived in under two minutes, beating their personal best drill response time. They tested the screws and Serena's inhaler. They confirmed that the inhaler at the cave had been used to transport the powder. The powder residue proved beyond a shadow of a doubt that this was the plastic casing used to carry the toxin into the cave. If they could lift prints from Serena's inhaler or the screws, they would have the connection they needed – the evidence to link the two inhalers, the assassination attempt to someone at The Cube, and probably additional people after following known associations to the person they were hopefully about to catch red-handed.

The worrisome part of this is that the person who hid the inhaler must have been present at the cave. There hadn't been an opportunity for a known suspect to hide the inhaler because all suspects were immediately detained. There was no other explanation; someone who should have been marked for detainment had slipped through the cracks and had then gone straight to The Cube. Serena picked her brain for anything that she may have forgotten about. *How could she have missed this? Who was it?*

The interrogation had hit another lull and Beav had wandered back to where Serena and Estep were. He had watched the lab crew with great interest. “Don’t worry. If the prints are there, we’ve got him so jammed he’s ready for toast. The lab team used a scanning Kelvin probe fingerprinting technique. It makes no physical contact with the print and there’s no use of developers. Fingerprints are recorded while leaving intact material we’ll put through DNA analysis later to confirm the results.”

Serena stared at him, “What are you talking about?”

Beav clarified, “Rest assured, if the prints are there, we can make a solid irrefutable identification from them. We’ll have a tentative ID right away. I give them all of fifteen minutes and they’ll be back here with a name. Because whoever it is, they are obviously in the system.”

“I don’t care who it is anymore. I’m too tired to think. I want to go home.”

Beav clamped a hand on Serena’s shoulder. “Sometimes it’s better not to think aloud.”

23

Mr. Speaker Joseph Smythe was not in The Cube. He was discouraged from attending due to President Kinji's hospitalization. While Vice President Lehman had everything under control and was technically the acting President of the United States, it was Joe who they relied upon to keep America running while Ann was recuperating. The inner workings of the government didn't stop because a sensational situation was ablaze at The Cube. No, someone needed to be at the wheel of the old grind. Between he and Lehman, the nation would run as usual in most areas of government. Regardless of what was going on at The Cube tonight, a mundane yet grueling schedule was on his plate for tomorrow. There was nothing to be gained from watching the play-by-play on social media at 1:00AM.

Joe had drifted off to sleep when his intercom system buzzed. "Who could it be at this hour?" His stomach tightened, knowing that the answer couldn't possibly bring good news.

Joe was not a good fighter. He intimated people with his confident persona, but the truth was, if he was ever pressed into action he wasn't of much use defending himself or others. Because of this, he brought the nearest thing to a weapon that he saw; a rubber mallet he had recently used to pound a wooden leg back into a kitchen stool that had fallen apart.

"Yes?" he said through the intercom.

"It's me, Jo." Her voice was garbled but still recognizable.

"Irish Jo?"

"You know a lot of Jo's do you?"

"No, only you."

"Will you let me in now please?"

"Oh of course," he said into the intercom, realizing too late that yet another word via the intercom was ridiculous when he could have simply opened the door. He was still holding the rubber mallet when Jo walked over the threshold.

She smirked.

Joe followed her gaze to the rubber mallet in his hand and gave himself a mental head slap. "I didn't know who would be at the door at this hour."

"Clearly. I could have been a mole."

"Please don't even joke about being a spy."

"I wasn't. I meant as in 'Whack-a-mole'." She gestured at the mallet.

"Oh, ha. Yeah, funny." Joe tossed the mallet on the sofa, barely missing hitting the lamp on the side table. "What brings you here in the middle of the night?"

Not that he minded. He admired her red hair, and the way it curled down her back. When she moved her locks bounced off her body. He contemplated this for much longer than he realized. Joe ran his hands over his face and analyzed his intentions. *What am I doing? How could flirting be appropriate during a time of national crisis? I'm the Speaker of the House, not your average Joe – Get a grip, Joe, get a grip!* Hadn't he disgraced himself enough with the show he put on in the Veiled Abyss?

The story of Joe bumbling through a row of chairs, inadvertently giving terrorists the diversion that they needed to assemble a weapon, had hit the Social Media Channel news just before midnight. The media lifted an image from video feed that they had somehow obtained from the tech team – Joe made a mental note to find out how that happened. The chair incident occurred before the public broadcast, yet the media had gotten hold of it and was looping Joe's bumbling-chair buffoonery.

"Tell me why you're here," he tried again. This time he kept his eyes above her neckline, which was cut distractingly low.

"I'm here because I think I know something. It occurs to me that I don't believe Luke."

Joe struggled to remember who Luke was. Of course, he headed up The Supporters. Yes, he knew Luke; Luke was the one who Joe had, in his private thoughts, renamed as 'the punk kid'. "They vetted all of you, so I've been told. How could they get it so wrong? Are you sure?"

"No, I don't mean that Luke is a traitor. But I do think that he is covering for someone else. Luke's behavior hasn't always added up." Jo twirled a curl with her finger, a nervous habit that was driving Joe wild.

"This won't wait until morning because...?" Joe couldn't stay on the straight and narrow for long. She needed to get to the point fast.

"Because if I'm right, you guys missed a suspect. He's probably at The Cube right now. The conspirators are losing, and time is running out. They have nothing left to lose – that's a dangerous situation for anyone who is in the vicinity when they pull their next stunt."

"I understand, but President Kinji is still hospitalized. They did attempt to kill her there, as you are probably aware of, and while they did take out her security detail, they didn't cause her any real harm. She's under even more security now. Point is, she's not at The Cube, so what are you suggesting?"

"I don't know. I think the plan might be terrorism in general, not necessarily with President Kinji as their target. If The Cube were destroyed, or at least partially destroyed, all while the president is also hospitalized, wouldn't it be enough to tip the scales into chaos? The nation is already on the brink. Don't they keep you informed? Haven't you at least been watching the news? Americans are ready to do themselves in with violent and lunatic mayhem. A country can only take so much disruption before all hell breaks loose."

"Hold on, I've only been home for about forty-five minutes at the most. Yeah, they keep me informed." Joe laughed. *Flirting again, stop it!* "Yes, you could be right about terrorism. I'm taking you seriously. I don't know what I can do though. Unless you know who to look for specifically, there's nothing new to report. They're already on high alert at The Cube. Honestly, I don't know why you felt the need to come here. This could have kept until morning."

"I know who to look for."

Joe blinked, startled. "Then stop playing around and tell me." He was ashamed of himself for flirting and delaying her message.

"They need to take a long look at Kevin Port."

"Kevin Port? I've never heard of him."

"He worked with Governor Carson Landon. He was a friend of Luke's. I'm realizing now that he was probably spying for The Supporters. But can anyone trust him? Kevin's probably been playing both sides all along!"

"Do you have any proof?"

"I remember something that Luke had let slip when Carson died. He said 'I hope Carson didn't tell them anything.' He was worried that before Carson did himself in, he may have talked. About what?"

"I don't know. I can ask that the team look into Kevin Porch."

"Port. It's Kevin Port."

"Isn't that what I said?"

"No, you said Kevin Porch." The name Kevin Porch struck her funny bone. Maybe it was the lack of sleep, but she was struggling not to break into hysterics. Yes, she must be hitting delirium, she thought. *Kevin Porch won't seem funny after I get some sleep.*

"I'll call right now. Stay here and listen." Joe made the call, and he was careful to get the name right: Kevin Port.

"I feel better now, thank you." Jo looked up at Joe, and wondered how urgent her message really was. Had she somehow invented the crisis as an excuse to come over? Was she really that much of a basket case? Yes, maybe she was. The thought of going back to her empty apartment after everything that happened in the cave was hard to stomach.

The more she thought about it, the more Jo wondered if there was nothing to this sudden insight into a suspect, nothing but her imagination inventing a reason to see Joe. She twirled her hair with her pinky finger and brooded. She didn't realize that she was staring up at him for so long that he mistook her preoccupation with his face as a signal, as permission.

He held her face with both of his hands and leaned in to kiss her. His lips lightly brushed hers before she reacted to his touch by jumping backwards as if she was bitten by a snake, kissed by a toad, or something equally hideous. Joe responded by saying the first thing that popped into his head. "No offense."

Jo's face flushed a brilliant magenta. "No offense? You should be offended, Joe. I'm so sorry. I didn't mean to—you startled me. I didn't expect—oh come here!" Jo pulled him close to her by tugging on the collar of his shirt, the pale yellow dress shirt he hadn't bothered to change out of. When his face was close to hers, she looked into his eyes. She hesitated only slightly.

Joe didn't need any more encouragement than this. He kissed her again, and this time she received his kiss, for a long time. Minutes passed. Neither of them knew how many. When they finally stopped for a breather they suddenly felt as if they needed to know everything there was to know about each other right now, all at once. Joe moved the rubber mallet off the couch and they sat there, gazing into each other's eyes and chatting all night long.

They were still sitting there together as dawn approached and Joe's phone buzzed. Jo heard his side of the conversation:

"Yes, I see."

"No, Kevin Porch was only a possibility."

"Yes, that's who I meant, Kevin Port."

"I know, I said 'Porch'. I did mean Port."

"I understand. I was following a tip."

"No, I don't want to pursue it further. I understand what you meant by 'he had an alibi'."

"No, I don't want to place a formal inquiry since you already informed me that he is not a viable suspect."

"Yes, actually I do have another concern. It's not about Kevin Por-"

Jo whispered "Port."

"It's not about Kevin Port. It's about footage airing on the Social Media Channel."

"Yes, I'm talking about the chair footage." Joe snapped.

Jo giggled.

"Yes, that's the one. How did they get it?"

"Oh, I see. I didn't know that those were released."

"I want to know if you can zoom in on the part where I'm, um, not tripping on the chairs."

"Yes, the background."

"Right. Can you do it?"

"You're looking for anyone who isn't watching me tripping on the chairs."

"Very funny, everyone was watching, right. Whoever wasn't watching was assembling a weapon."

"Yes, you idiot, *that* weapon."

24

"Nicholas, what are you doing here?" Serena rushed over to him, her arms outstretched.

"Ms. Wilcox, you do a lot of hugging," he said, while allowing himself to be squeezed. The zipper pull on Serena's leather jacket scratched his check when he pulled away.

Estep answered, "The lab tech guys are wearing down. They're calling everyone in."

"Maybe you'll help us solve the case. We have them working on lifting prints," said Serena.

"No, I don't think so. They put me on database duty." Nicholas was taken aback by something he saw out of the corner of his eye. "Hey, what's he doing here?"

Serena looked around her, startled. No one else was around. "Who?"

"That guy who just left. I know him from Clyde's computer lab. We worked on the Angels Mark technology together."

Serena raised her eyebrows. "Oh? Is he an old friend of yours?"

Nicholas scowled. "He's a liar and a thief."

The hair on Serena's arms rose—goose bumps. "What was he stealing?"

"He was selling my work. Clyde caught him and kicked him out of the program."

"Your work on Angels Mark?"

"Yes."

"What could it do? Besides the way Paul wanted to use it, could it do more?"

Nicholas nodded. "It could do a lot more! It could track the Internet history of hundreds of users simultaneously. It could block searches too."

"Who did he sell it to?" Serena saw that Estep and Beav were starting to pay attention to their conversation. She held her finger to her lips. They kept a respectful distance, allowing Serena to question Nicholas without interruption.

"Paul Tracy said that he was selling to someone who works for the president. Not President Kinji, the dead one."

"President John Williams?" Serena's pulse raced. *Could it be that pieces of the puzzle that had been missing for years were finally starting to come together?*

"Yes."

"Nicholas, remember how frustrated you were when President Kinji's office was hacked? I think you were fighting against your own genius. That was Angels Mark technology, I'd bet on it."

Nicholas tugged at his Superman shirt, cracked his knuckles, and ran his hand through his hair. "I think you're right. I was fighting against myself."

"Bizarro, huh?"

"Yeah, I guess so. I know how to remove the hack now. Thank you, Ms. Wilcox."

"Your friend…" Serena made eye contact with Estep. She tapped her wrist where a watch would have been had she been wearing one. Estep nodded and signaled an alert to his team.

"He's not my friend."

"This guy you worked with, do you know his name?"

"Luke Halloway."

Commotion erupted as Estep took off running down the corridor. His team was strategically placed throughout the entire wing of The Cube so that there was no way that Luke could slip past them. Serena wanted to see the take-down for herself. Apparently so did Beav because he sprinted after Estep, soon overtaking him.

Serena never ran anywhere unless she was being chased by something, so she didn't venture any further out than the next room over. As fate would have it, the next room over was where Luke was. Serena saw him before he saw her. She whispered to Nicholas, "Go back!" Then she added, "And call Estep."

Serena made sure that Nicholas left before she crept deeper into the room, hiding behind bookcases. The space was a dedicated study and library area, for browsing records or for leisure reading. What Luke was doing there was a mystery that soon became clear. He was leaving a message for someone by putting a piece of paper into a book and then returning it to the shelf where he got it from.

When he turned around, Serena was standing there, a few inches from his face.

"You're taller," he said.

"I'm wearing boots."

"I suppose those gorillas in the hall are looking for me."

"I suppose so." Serena knew that Luke couldn't have gotten past security with a weapon, and she was fairly confident that if put to the test she could take him. Someone needed to give this kid a hamburger—and let him outside more often.

Luke apparently thought more of his own physical strength and abilities than Serena did because he leaned into Serena's personal space and gave her a shove.

"You pushed me!" Serena grabbed Luke by the collar of his hoodie and pulled him close to her. "I have to warn you that I'm a hugger." She snatched him up and managed to turn him around. Holding him with his back against her chest, and grateful for the leather jacket barrier between the two of them, she locked her arms into a physical hold.

Luke thrashed around, swore, and flung his legs back to kick her in the shins.

Before now, she was physical with Luke only to restrain him, but the pain sparked her temper. The sharp pain of his shoe on her leg caused her to lash out and slap his face. Serena's slap left a handprint.

Estep and Beav rushed into the reading room at that instant. Upon seeing the handprint on Luke's face, both men burst out laughing. Luke glowered and jerked his body around as he was dragged off in handcuffs while being serenaded by laughter. It was only after Estep was crying and Beav had the hiccups that the two men finally composed themselves.

Meanwhile, Serena hadn't left the reading room. She removed the book she had seen Luke put the message in: there it was! The paper was incriminating indeed. It said, "Dead man can't talk. Paul's gone. I want my money."

She ran down the corridor, realizing that she was willing to run for a good cause. "Wait, wait!"

The two agents who held Luke's cuffed arms stopped.

Serena triumphantly raised the note above her head. "Recognize this? We have you for treason and murder. Anything you want to say to help yourself?"

Luke said nothing.

Serena tried again. "Who hired you? Who is the message for? You have nothing left to lose. You're under twenty-one. The judge may be able to award you protective custody in prison, if he's feeling charitable."

Everyone in the corridor held their breath waiting for Luke to speak. Beav had the presence of mind to initiate the video function on his phone to record Luke's confession. Estep quickly read Luke his rights, even though that routine was likely unnecessary given that Luke was a terrorist. Even so, there was no room for error in this investigation. With their I's dotted and their T's crossed, they were ready to listen to what Luke had to say.

"I worked for President William's administration. When he died, nothing really changed. I kept on giving them what they wanted. They didn't have Williams anymore, but they still had control of the Global Initiative. I've told you everything. Give me an offer for protection—in writing."

Serena put her finger over her mouth and maintained a thinking pose before saying, "I'll talk to the judge for you. I'll tell him how your actions put some of my favorite people in danger, including myself. And I'll tell him that when you were cornered by a weapon-less five-foot-two middle aged woman you kicked her in the shin."

25

Lehman shielded his eyes to see past the glare of the stage lights. "Is that you, Serena?"

"Yes, I'm here with Agent Estep."

Lehman hopped down from the stage and invited Serena and Estep to sit. They were alone in the convention hall, an audience of three facing an empty stage. Within the hour the room would be filled to capacity to hear Lehman's address.

"Does it seem funny to have me on the other side of this?" Lehman asked.

Serena thought about it. "No, not really. You've always had a leadership quality about you. Do you plan to run for office?"

Lehman shook his head. "My wife and I bought a house in Texas. As thrilling as it is to temporarily act as President, I don't want to be in this role, or in the role of Vice President either. When President Kinji is back on her feet I'll ask her to find a replacement for me. I'm going home."

"I wish you all the best. I've enjoyed working with you sir," said Agent Estep.

Lehman nodded. "I don't have much time to talk before things get busy. I want to run down what we know. Please stop me if I get something wrong. The people behind this were part of the Global Initiative, and that's the connection to foreign interests. The financial take-over had been in the works for over twenty years, even further back than that for some key properties. It's fairly obvious what the motivation was regarding other countries wanting to take us down, buy us out, and take us over. It's the usual subjects as far as foreign terror is concerned – no surprises."

Serena confirmed, "Yes, you've got it right so far."

Lehman asked, "The other handle communicating with Carson Landon through the crack in the media channel- was it foreign or domestic?"

Serena leaned her head back and let herself sink into the chair. She closed her eyes. "Foreign. None of that seems important now. We can easily bust that up, especially with the help of the UN. The UN will give President Kinji whatever she wants, for as long as the health of the United States economy is in dire straits."

Lehman continued, "There's no single enemy here. There's no one person to blame. Covert Coffee has led us to multiple persons and groups who wanted to sabotage President Kinji's administration and even wanted her taken out of office entirely by way of assassination, of which there were multiple plots and two actual attempts that resulted in serious injury to the President."

When Lehman paused, Estep said, “Correct.”

Lehman went on, “No one will be surprised that foreign nations were involved, and their identities will be of no surprise either, as they are the typical suspects. It’s no shocker that Congress was working against President Kinji, but I am blown away by how deep the traitorous activity went and how far-flung it was. I can accept that we won’t have one villain to pin everything on. Few things in life have tidy resolutions. I do need to offer somebody up though. Americans are going to want a name and a face.”

Serena sat up straight. “Give them the person who was directly responsible for assembling the weapon that nearly killed President Kinji.”

Lehman flipped through his notecards. He chose to use actual paper cards because he felt more in control over his public speaking experience when holding his words in his hands. There was something about reading from a screen that made him feel anxious. He couldn’t find any reference to what Serena was talking about in his notes. “Have they released that name yet?”

Serena said, “I don’t know, have they?”

Agent Estep answered, “I don’t think so, but it’s solid. We have him in custody.”

Serena explained, “You can offer up the three men from The Supporters who were involved in the assassination attempt in the cave: Dennis, Craig, and Garreth. Those three were caught in the act with too many witnesses for them to stand any chance of getting away with it. They were arrested immediately and removed from the cave. We went on the best that we could. We identified many other suspects but one of The Supporters involved in the assassination attempt slipped through the cracks.”

Estep added, "Serena's inhaler was used to bring the toxin into the cave. The man who masterminded the attack walked right back out of the cave with it. It was only after we found the inhaler at The Cube that we were able to identify the subject."

Lehman addressed his comment to Estep, "I heard that it was your dog Finn who found the evidence. People love animal hero stories, that's good for me to put into my address."

Serena continued, "After the identification came through we were able to cross reference it with video footage from the video stream the tech team had at the cave. When the Speaker of the House…"

"Tripped over the chairs?" Lehman guessed.

Serena nodded. "When he tripped over the stairs The Supporters used that distraction to assemble the weapon. So, between the inhaler found at The Cube and the video footage we have absolute proof of his involvement."

"Who's involvement?" asked Lehman, his pen ready.

"Luke." Serena looked down at her feet.

"The leader of The Supporters?" Lehman asked.

Serena confirmed, "Yes, he was a double agent. He fooled everyone. Bob is in charge of The Supporters now. It really is a good group of citizen watchdogs—they aren't a militia or even vigilantes in the true sense of the word. Ninety-nine percent of them are law-abiding citizens who only want to protect America from corrupt government through knowledge; not through violence, hacking, spying or anything else that is illegal or treasonous. Unfortunately a lot of people were betrayed by Luke and have left The Supporters. Jo was so humiliated by this experience that she went back to Ireland."

"Joe's Jo?" asked Lehman.

"Sadly, yes."

Lehman patted Serena's shoulder. "Hey, you have nothing to be ashamed of. You and everyone else did a beautiful job. The layers of conspiracy were from the world's biggest onion. Don't worry, I'm not going to paint an ugly picture of The Supporters. To help repair their image, I'll invite Bob to participate in the press conference following the address. He can handle any questions about the group."

Serena brightened. "That's an excellent idea!"

Lehman asked, "Is there anything else I should know about?"

Serena mulled it over. "You might want to talk about what happened when President Kinji shut the Internet down for five hours."

Lehman laughed, "Oh they'll bring it up during the press conference, no doubt. I won't help them get to it sooner. That was an awful mess, wasn't it? It was effective in cutting communications to bring down the Global Initiative, but President Kinji had no idea how badly Americans would react to having no Internet or wireless service for just a few short hours. She was also apparently unaware how much of a snarl it would cause in the economy."

Estep said, "They're calling it Dark Tuesday."

Lehman agreed, "I've heard that too. Yes, it was a horrible day. It achieved its objective though; the nation was headed for ruin and the Global Initiative had to be shut down. Best to take the bull by the horns, which is what I'll say in defense of the decision to block communications for a few hours. The damage was horrific though. The Red Cross is still helping people recover from disasters that could have been prevented if people had had use of cell towers. I guess it wasn't such a brilliant idea for most of the country to get rid of private landlines and public pay phones."

Serena stood up and Estep followed suit. Lehman also rose. Serena said, "Good luck, Lehman. If I were you I'd spend as much time as possible talking about Finn."

26

Ann had requested a quick meeting with Serena in the VIP box before delivering her final speech to the nation. "I can't thank you enough for everything you've done."

"Of course." She saw Ann not as President, but as a friend in need of a hug. She offered her a hug now and Ann readily accepted.

When Ann broke away she wiped a tear from her eye. "It's been a long journey."

"Yes, it has. And we almost lost you."

"We almost lost *you*. You used up a few of your nine lives."

Serena shrugged. "I came away without a scratch. You're the one who was hospitalized on and off for six weeks."

"Lehman and Joe did an amazing job holding down the fort while I was down for the count. And I can't be happier with how the new Congress has been faring with so many private citizens taking on congressional seats. They did vote for term limits, did you hear?"

"Yes, I did. I'm pleased that you appointed Bob from The Supporters."

"Oh, he's been brilliant. And he has the gift of gab, being a career radio host."

"From Indiana, right? That's where Beav met him."

"No, he's from Wisconsin. He was only in Indiana for a short term assignment."

Serena laughed. "I'm remembering how Beav told me that he trusted Bob because he studied his home environment, his family pictures, and even his little dog."

"None of those things were his, no." Ann laughed too. "I'm going to miss this."

Serena shook her head. "No you won't. You're ready to move on."

"I suppose you're right."

"To be honest with you, I hate politics."

"Then why have you been a part of this for so long? You've been with me from the beginning."

"The nation has been obsessed and negative for so long that our media, our entertainment industry, our music, our social interactions, and even our cartoons are steeped in it. When people share a common misery there's no escaping it. Everyone's talking about it, everywhere. Since I can't get away from it I may as well try to help."

Ann ignored Serena's rant. She asked, "Do you remember something you told me about religion and politics?"

Serena drew a blank.

Ann refreshed her memory. "I said, 'Religion and politics don't mix.' And you came back with 'Religion and politics are always conjoined. Trying to separate the two gives us a fractured nation; one half without a heart and the other without a brain'."

"I said that? That seems wiser than my usual rantings."

"You also said that you are 'an independent and an idealist'. Do you still feel that way?"

Serena nodded. "Oh I'll never align myself with the left or the right. I avoid extremes."

"No, I mean, do you still see yourself as an idealist."

Serena noted that Ann was watching her intently. "What's this about?"

"I have a job proposal for you."

"What kind of job proposal?"

"Listen to my speech."

Serena started to say, "Of course I will," but Ann had already left for the stage.

At the podium, President Kinji commanded respect. Her eyes reflected unmistakable intelligence, her stance projected confidence. Her natural beauty and humor were the scale-tipping ingredients that won America's hearts. They hung on every word she said because she was a celebrity, but today they listened to her for reasons beyond her charisma and popular appeal; today they needed her to be their president.

"Dear Americans, I know you are saddened by the news that I will not be running for re-election. I know that many of you believe that I've only scratched the surface of the work that needs to be done. And I agree. But I am recommending an amazing leader to take my place. You'll find that Speaker of the House Joseph Smythe is a warm and wonderful human being, with quick wit, an engaging sense of humor, and an incredible work ethic. Most importantly, given all that we've gone through, the Speaker is honest. Joe has become one of my dearest friends; I trust him wholeheartedly and I can't say enough good things about him. If anyone can move our nation forward in the right direction, it's Joe.

He will lead you into better days, times of prosperity and freedom, days that will remind you of the old America that your great-grandparents remember. I ask that you trust me and vote Joe into office. I will sleep better at night if I leave you in his hands.

And of course, I can't leave you without giving you my final thoughts, which are substantial. I dearly hope that you are listening, and that you take what I say to heart. It is my wish that my words be my legacy to this nation, and to you.

Please don't allow the bitterness and division of the past to creep back in. Don't allow government to hold that power over you, to distract you from your own ability to reason for yourself. There are big issues that have never been resolved, and will never be resolved.

When issues become more important than people, more important than truth, and more important than love – how can we justify the fight? Without mutual respect, and even support, the two will negate each other. And all that will remain is a dark void that quickly fills with anger, resentment and a house so divided that it collapses in on itself.

If you want change, you must stop doing what's always been done. Shouting to be heard above the noise merely creates more noise. You cannot win this battle: you cannot change your neighbor's point of view. You cannot legislate peace. As surely as one side wins a ruling, the other side will work to get the ruling overturned. The fight will go on and on and on.

Both sides have stated their case, loudly, redundantly, and ineffectively. Channel the energy you expend on fruitless debate into creating real change.

For example, one issue that was used against us, to deliberately divide and distract us, was women's rights. It's simple: Work together to respect and love all women. Pregnancy is a woman's right; it is personal, it is sacred, and many believe it is from God. Respect a woman's right to believe that babies are human beings from conception onward, even if you yourself don't agree. And on the flip side, if you support the pro-life moment, don't attempt to shame people into conversion, but instead extend your love to women in difficult situations.

Notice that I mentioned what *you* can do, not what your government can do. Remember, neonaticide and other atrocities weren't sanctioned by the government, but were criminal acts. Laws alone cannot protect women or babies. *You* need to step up! Clothe, feed, heal. Love women, work together. Divided you accomplish nothing but malice.

Now apply this same logic to *all* of the issues that divide us. Government can't resolve the issues that the American people have been fighting about for decades. Women's rights is only one example of hundreds of hot-button issues that we can't find resolution for. Our habit of expecting 'the system' to settle our disputes has created a backlog of unresolved issues that have divided our nation.

The more we expect government to fix our problems – to

regulate or reverse regulation – the longer we ride the merry-go-round of division and malice. No, we don't need more government. We need more tolerance. *We need to stop hating our own people*.

I'll give you an example of what I mean. In pre-Big War America, after 911, persons of Islamic faith were feared to be terrorists simply because they were Muslim. I see a similar situation happening today with Christians– are all Christians bigoted, highly political and full of hate? Of course not! The actions of some have led to the fear and mistrust of all.

I'm telling you right now, and I hope you are all listening to me. If you don't get it that you must put your differences aside and love each other, you will be right back to where you started from. Can't you see that we are destroying ourselves? The fall of America isn't coming from outside, it's coming from within. We are doing this to our*selves*!

How can we avoid making the same mistakes we've made over the last three decades? For starters, don't mix religion and science with politics. The moment you ask government to regulate your values, you give up your freedom. You open the door for the horrors of misdirection that was RDAD. Solve your own problems!

Get off the Internet, get off the couch and *do* something about the things that you're riled up about. When you blast your views without respect for anyone else, you contribute to the hate that gave us a broken nation. Let's accept our differences instead of attempting—in vain—to convert others to our views. We can apply that energy into actually doing something to prevent tragedy from happening, into doing something to help those who have already fallen, and most of all to hold the hands of all who are currently struggling.

I know I'm beating a dead horse, but that horse has been rotting and stinking for a long time and yet we step right over it. Anger doesn't work. We must agree to disagree. We must respect each other even when we do not agree. I don't know how to say this more plainly, and I am flabbergasted that my final presidential address sounds like a 'welcome to kindergarten' lecture.

Incessant debate is a carping, a dripping, a persistent nagging. How patronizing of me that as your President I feel the most important thing to say to the American people is: Shut up.

And on that note, this is the last of my long-winded speeches: I am going to practice what I preach. I will shut up and do something!

One of the reasons why I am not running for re-election is because I can do great work as a private citizen. When I leave this office, I will step into my role as owner and CEO of a new independent investigation company, the likes of which you've never seen before. I am assembling a team of incredible people ready to tackle America's worst nightmares.

As President I've heard whispers of governmental experiments, advancements, and technological discovery that have made the hairs on my arms stand on end. Government has done a pathetic job of policing itself. Science is too big for us.

Remember what I said earlier? Science and religion shouldn't be regulated by government. These truths are *our* responsibility – we are all responsible for what we do to this planet, what we do to ourselves, and what we leave behind for future generations.

While I'm fighting the good fight against corruption and horrific futuristic technology, I ask that you too stand up and fight for something. Government grew big and became corrupt because we allowed it to happen – we didn't want to do our part. We wanted to live our lives in a bubble. It's not too late; it's never too late.

Volunteer at your local food bank. Donate your time to help children learn to read. Visit a nursing home. Post your progress on the Social Media Channel for all to see and be encouraged by. Think of the power we have if we all do our part. Together we can make a difference, I sincerely believe that. Don't fight with your words, as a coward, a thug or a fool. Fight with your good deeds; as a pacifist, as an activist, as a hero. Lay aside your bickering and get to work! There's a big world to save, beginning right here at home."

Ann paused to take a long draught of water. The rest of her speech made her "Play nicely together" opener seem like the spoonful of sugar to make the medicine go down. The truth, as Ann saw it, was that Americans were much more comfortable fighting about moral issues than facing up to economical ones. Ann knew that while the rest of her historic speech could impact generations to come, it could just as easily fall on deaf ears.

27

Ann prayed silently before launching into the meat of her speech. She coached herself with these thoughts: *This is the final stretch, you're almost done.* She looked directly into Camera One and spoke without looking at the teleprompter.

"But of course fixing what is broken in American government is not as simple as begging all of you to be kinder to one another. As we continue to reel from the complicated terrorist plot to financially take over our nation, we have to take a good look at ourselves. How did we get to such an insolvent state? How did we become so vulnerable? Well, I have a few thoughts that I'd like to share with you, and once again we find hate at the root of our problems.

In the days of Old America, in the dear idealistic past, Americans felt the romance of commercialism. Americans were great dreamers; anything could happen in America, and American ingenuity was rewarded financially. Living the good life was a worthy dream, even wholesome and honorable.

But somewhere along the way, we fell down. Greed and corruption changed us to the point that we began to equate wealth with evil, and wealthy Americans with people to fear, despise, and blame for all of our own shortcomings. Suddenly it was the rich who should pay for our nation's ills, and money itself was despicable in many aspects. Media portrayed the pursuit of wealth in the form of sharks, mobs, and corporate scum. Like a child whose parents believed the worst in him, our nation grew more and more corrupt – living up to our poor expectations. We have stopped seeing money as a blessing, and have focused on money as the root of all evil. As soon as we equated money with evil, money became evil.

I know I'm talking in metaphors and fuzzy grey emotional language, but I'm making my best attempt to inspire you to reach back into the past and draw from it the American spirit. You see, you have to decide how you want government to serve you while going forward, moving out of insolvency and into something new. Are you a capitalist nation? Are you a democracy? You can't hate money if you wish to rebuild this nation based on American dreams. You can't despise the wealthy or hate the poor. You must come together and desire the good in people.

Don't bite the hand that feeds, but instead encourage loyalty; loyalty to the nation and loyalty to you. How can you foster feelings of good will, cooperation and charity? Surely you are still an innovative people! Look to the old programs that have worked in the past. When did people pull together for the common good? When was it fashionable to be selfless and patriotic? I'm afraid that if you want to move forward, you must go backward, or risk losing forever what America once was.

We are battling a new kind of war, a financial one. You as a people have the power within you to raise the funds that can save your government and protect it from further attack. My best minds in finance have put together a number of packages that I hope you will be receptive to. However, much of that work will fall to the new administration. I can't even begin to address all of those issues today. I can only give you my best attempt to encourage you to fight for the American dream, and to work together during this crisis.

We were not always a nation of ugliness and division. We were once a people that other nations wanted to be: when the Americans came, others were happy to see us – we were kind, we were selfless, we were pure joy. Not without exception, of course, but we have been a nation that has birthed many heroes and heroines. May this be true of us again.

You're going to need American ingenuity to save yourselves. You're going to need to spend money—out of your own pocket, not government money. At this point you might be tuning me out, if I hadn't already lost you early on. This should get your attention: America is broke. Our government can't fix our problems.

Our government was bribed and sold to the highest bidder time and time again. Our food supply was tainted by greed; we poisoned our own people. Horrific acts of violence were committed; we disarmed our own people. When mass domestic violence continued unchecked, we pressed forward with increased gun control legislation, which as you know led to riots. Tensions escalated from protests about bill of rights violations, to what would become the worst massacre in American history—as over a dozen American cities rose up against armed government officials in our streets. Now let me say this again: The government can't fix our problems. Let's observe a moment of silence while you let that sink in."

Ann bowed her head and said nothing for sixty seconds of dead air that she counted inside her head. The videographers didn't know what to do. Camera One remained focused on the president for a full minute of complete inactivity. She then lifted her head and resumed her speech.

"Who can help us then? We can look beyond the government, to the church. Research by political scientists Putnam and Campbell attests that religiously observant Americans are more generous with their time and money. In this way, churches provide a necessary function in our nation outside of politics, transcending government for the good of all people.

Don't worry, I'm not advocating a national religion. I'm a firm believer of the separation of church and state, which I will repeat later on in my speech. However, is it the role of government to rally citizens to be charitable? I have tried to rally you, yet I fear that my words have fallen on deaf ears. The church is uniquely suited for this role, this necessary role, in a healthy society.

The church should open its arms to citizens in any sort of need, with complete disregard to politics. When the focus of the church is on healing its people, supporting its people, and fortifying its people to take care of each other, many shortcomings of politics and government can be overcome through acts of love rather than through force, malice, hatred and division. Dark days are coming—prepare now! When the soup lines are long, the church will be pressed upon to open its doors to feed the hungry.

We were once a religious nation, a solace for the persecuted. We can be again. Yet we continue to suffer from the great division between the extreme right and the extreme left, leaving citizens in the middle out in the cold; and of course all of our people suffer when the nation is in a perpetual state of disharmony.

Therefore I propose that we bring together the best minds; our scholars, our psychologists, our scientists, our religious leaders, our political analysts – you get the idea – bring them all together under one roof for a series of talks. I've already spoken to several dozen people from all walks of life, representing many faiths and ideologies, with the one common goal of reaching peaceful resolutions that will heal and unify our nation. If we are on board and fired up we can make changes, it is well within our power.

Before you all get your backs up let me be clear: I'm not talking about converting anyone or watering down the religious beliefs of all Americans until what we are left with is a generic national religion that can be expressed on a bumper sticker! No, I am saying the polar opposite of those two extremes: I'm saying that we go back to respecting the *individual* religious freedoms of all Americans, that we honor the reason why our country was founded in the first place. Respect our differences, don't fight to make us all the same!

I am calling upon all of you to join us in these talks in your own communities, churches and homes. We can change the face of America, it is not too late. It is never too late. We were once a nation grateful for religious freedom. We can be that nation once again; we merely need to open our hearts to a new definition of what this means, and how we can work together to respect the faiths of all people. We can't do this alone—don't let your personal baggage cause you to reject sources of help!

Removing God from our nation is not the answer. Removing *self* is the answer. Becoming *selfless* is the answer, and it is the way to self-reliance: let's forget church and state for the moment. We have been so distracted by religion and government that we neglected the power we all have, as private citizens, to create change. When did it become fashionable to rely upon institutions to fix us?

While legislating fair wages, protecting vulnerable persons, and passing laws that protect us from all manner of criminal and heinous activity is a noble effort, and of course must be attempted, legislation is not nearly enough! Once our government has done all that it was established to do, continuing in that vein will strip the American people of the freedom we require to self-govern. We, the people, wear the ruby red slippers: we have had the power all along. We can work harder, do more, give more and love more.

I'm not saying that all of the talking we've done hasn't been beneficial; education and information are the first steps in creating change. But isn't it time for less talk and more action? Let's drop our extremism in favor of balance—don't be so quick to reject what you are afraid of.

When we are not grounded in our beliefs we are like boats adrift without an anchor; it's far too easy for us to go off course when the winds change or when larger boats toss us around in their wake. If we had been a stronger people perhaps we wouldn't have been so easily manipulated by the global campaign to distract us from the real problems we were facing, perhaps we would have seen the truth before so much destruction had already been done. I know we are hurting, but giving up is not the answer.

Our strength lies in our freedom, our faith, and in each other: draw upon those things now and fight! Preserve the separation of church and state: it is this separation that gives Americans religious freedom. And while keeping the two entities fully separate, utilize both! We will never agree with each other about what we should believe, but we must agree to protect our individual rights to believe it.

If you only take away one thing from my speech let it be this: Keep an open mind and contribute. I am asking this of you in my final request during what has been a remarkable term and a monumental chapter in American history. However, I would be doing you a grave disservice if I left you with only these motivational sound bites. I'm afraid that I need your attention for a while longer."

President Ann Kinji opened the orange cloth-bound book titled "Democracy in America Volume 1" by Aexis de Tocqueville at the page she had bookmarked.

"'Democracy in America', published in 1961, has been quoted often these days. I'd like to highlight this section in particular. I know this is a tedious passage but please bear with me.

'... it is almost always by the abuse of its force, and the misemployment of its resources, that a democratic government fails. Anarchy is almost always produced by its tyranny or its mistakes, but not by its want of strength...

If ever the free institutions of America are destroyed, that event may be attributed to the unlimited authority of the majority, which may at some future time urge the minorities to desperation, and oblige them to have recourse to physical force. Anarchy will then be the result, but it will have been brought about by despotism.'"

Ann held her place in the book with her finger and spoke to Camera Two, causing a flurry of commotion for the videographers.

"Despotism isn't a word we use every day, so I'll define this term for you before continuing. Despotism is a form of government in which a single entity rules with absolute power; the implication is that despotism involves tyranny of some sort, in which the government, in this case the majority rule, suppresses the rights and freedoms of the citizens."

Ann opened the book and resumed reading from it. 'Mr. Hamilton expresses the same opinion in the Federalist, No. 51 when he states that it is of great importance in a republic not only to guard the society against the oppression of its rules, but to guard one part of society against the injustice of the other part. ... In a society, under the forms of which the stronger faction can readily unite and oppress the weaker, anarchy may as truly be said to reign as in a state of nature, where the weaker individual is not secured against the violence of the stronger.'"

The crinkly sound of pages being turned was picked up loudly by Ann's microphone. The tech team scrambled to balance the sound.

"I'll end with a Jefferson quote from later in this same section: 'The tyranny of the legislature is really the danger most to be feared, and will continue to be so for many years to come.'

I know this is dry, and that I've lost some of you. You may be wondering what this has to do with anything. My dear Americans, I'm afraid that what Aexis de Tocqueville wrote in 1961 is sadly something I need to warn you about.

We are ripe for a civil war. Yes, I know, first I told you that America is bankrupt, and now I am telling you that we are at the point of collapse. RDAD may have distracted us from the truth but it didn't change what the truth is. While some aspects of our national economy have improved, we are overall a sinking ship. The leaks created by corruption and bad management have put us in dire straits. As we point fingers and attempt to legislate solutions to our problems, we meanwhile continue to suffer.

We have been bitterly divided for so long that we have allowed our democracy to become oppressive, and the legislature has become a bully. If my desperate plea for you to come together as a nation, to love each other, to respect each other, and to resolve your differences goes unheeded, I must warn you that our country is just one spark away from setting off a powder keg of resentment that will result in a civil war. As each side blames the other for the woes of our nation, the economy being the most bitter pill for most people, we have set the stage for the minority to rise up against the majority rule. Popular and electoral vote will mean nothing as citizens wish to overthrow the tyranny of the majority rule.

I'm sorry to deliver such a dramatic and dire warning, but I must reiterate: if we stay on this course, we are headed for civil war in the not so distant future. Since there is no suitable transition from this bleak warning I'll simply say that I am finally drawing this speech to a close. Let me remind you that I gave you a clean slate in Congress. When I leave this office, the pre-Big War regime will be officially over—no more 'old boys' club. This is a second chance for America! What will you do with it? Will you trust government to take care of you, and when that fails will you attempt to use religion to legislate? Or will you give unto Caesar that which is Caesar's and worship freely separately from the government, rising up with courage to work hard as individuals; as innovators, healers, inventors, philanthropists, creators, teachers, leaders, parents, students—*citizens*?

Will you put decency ahead of profit? Will you be generous instead of holding back on what you have to offer? Will you push yourself harder when life deals you a difficult hand? Will you dare to dream—and will your dreams benefit others? I meant what I said: if you continue on your current path you will destroy each other. I love you, the American people, and I wish that no harm come to you. Thank you for allowing me the podium for such an extended period of time.

My dear Americans, it has been my greatest pleasure to serve you as your president. Beyond the presidency, you have taken me into your homes and into your hearts, as you have been in mine. I've thought long and hard about what I want to say to you in my last formal speech before the nation. In closing, I have decided to repeat, verbatim, the same closing paragraphs of the speech I delivered to you early on in my presidency:

Stop fighting each other. Let statues stand, let people pray, let flags fly. Agree that Love is more important than settling who is right. When I close with my final words, may you hear them not with contempt or division in your heart, but with the goodness I wish for you; to be well, stay safe, fill your heart with hope, and love one another.

And these, my final words: God Bless America."

28

"Agent Estep, I'd love to have you on my team. How does the private sector sound to you?" asked President Kinji.

"No disrespect to you, Madam President, but I want to stay on at the agency. In fact, I'm on my way now to receive my next field assignment, my first one in years sans Serena Waldo."

"Serena Wilcox," Ann corrected.

Serena explained, " He means Waldo, as in 'Where's Waldo?' because he spent so much time looking for me."

Estep reiterated, "Madam President, I do appreciate your offer, however the answer is a definite no."

Ann smiled sweetly. "Well, if you change your mind, I'll be here for a while longer."

When Estep was out of earshot Serena challenged Ann. "What did you do?"

Ann held up her hand. “He’s just around the corner. He’ll be back in three, two…”

Estep stormed past them. He then spun on his heels and walked back to where President Kinji was waiting for him. “He won’t give me my assignment. They’re giving me a desk job!”

Ann patted Estep lightly on the arm. “When you join my team you’ll take lead in all field investigations.”

Estep prepared to walk away.

Ann waved a carrot in front of his nose. “I’m sure I can arrange that you stay on with the agency, and work for us only on loan. Give it six months or so and I’m sure they’ll let you back in the field.”

“I’ll still be on payroll here? It won’t affect my standing with the agency?” Estep was listening.

Ann coaxed, “I’m sure of it. Consider it done.”

Estep nodded, mumbled a thank you, shook her hand and left, but not without a parting withering look at Serena.

Serena watched Estep’s back disappear out the door. She squinted her eyes at Ann. “*You* told them to give him desk duty, didn’t you?”

Ann winked.

Serena laughed. “Well played. But when we are working together, promise me that you won’t manipulate *me* like that.”

“Oh I never make a promise I can’t keep.”

Serena decided to be honest about her feelings. “I do need to talk to you about something.”

Ann nodded.

Serena took that as a green light. “I’ve been a stay at home mom for my kids’ whole lives. These Covert Coffee and Bluebird adventures have been torture.”

Ann looked genuinely puzzled. “All of your kids are older, right? Teenagers at least?”

“They’re fine. It was temporary. But I won’t leave them like this again. If I’m going to partner with you I’ll need to work from home.”

“I see.” Ann appeared to be studying the ceiling tiles. “Let’s continue this at Laurey’s.”

Serena agreed. The two dark-haired petite women attracted attention from Cube employees as they walked the quarter mile of corridors and went up two flights of escalators to get to the food court. Laurey’s sit-down restaurant sat in the outer ring, beyond the burger and taco stands.

Once seated at Laurey’s they ordered drinks and an appetizer, and chatted about their personal lives for a while. Then Ann resumed their conversation. “First of all, you have misunderstood the situation. You won’t be partnering with me, you’ll be working for me. Consider me your President. Except instead of governing over the smallness of the United States I’ll be dealing with the fate of the entire planet, and beyond.”

Serena stared at Ann. She could see that she wasn’t playing around. “What do you mean?”

“You’ll find out.”

“No, I don’t think that I will. I’ve already explained that I won’t be accepting your offer unless I can work from home.”

“You can do the research aspects from home. The field work will obviously need to be done in the field.”

“I’m afraid I’m going to have to turn this opportunity down then.” Serena took a bite of chicken from the appetizer platter. She figured she might as well enjoy this one last perk.

"Take time to think it over."

"I'm sorry, Ann, but I have sacrificed my career before and I'm definitely willing to do it again, no matter how great the opportunity you are offering me, I value my family life more."

"Even if it means passing up the opportunity to time travel?"

"What? Did you just say 'time travel'?"

Ann smiled.

"You're serious? What do you mean time travel?"

"You'll have to join my team if you want to find out. It's 'need to know'."

"I-I don't think I can pass this up. I don't know what to do. Time travel." Serena breathed deeply and counted to ten. Her mind was full of colors and sounds.

Ann folded her hands and made a steeple with her index fingers. "Your kids are well behaved, surely. And maybe they can be an asset? They could assist you?"

"Are you saying that I should bring my kids with me in the field; to be shot, abducted, or bludgeoned? I can't imagine Tom agreeing to this."

"Bring him along, he can protect the kids. And when have you been concerned about being bludgeoned?"

"You're saying my whole family should come with me into the field? You're messing with me now."

"No, I'm saying that I don't care what you do. The field work is not considered dangerous. You can bring the whole family if you want to. I'm only saying that you can't do the work from home."

"Time travel. I'd be a time traveler? How is that possible? Would I travel in a time machine like the T.A.R.D.I.S? What happens exactly?"

"Ah, well, 'need to know'. Trust me. Time travel is possible and it has been for at least a decade."

"What would be the purpose of me doing this? What exactly would I be investigating?"

"I can't tell you that. What I can say is that time travel technology has been abused from the start, from even before it began actually. I'm afraid you won't be on a pleasure trip. You'll be doing what you do best: solving crimes."

"Ah, the truth comes out. I don't see how I can bring my family into this. We're back to me saying that I can't accept your offer."

"The bad guys are long gone- they are locked up or dead. You'll only be figuring out what they did and why so that we can stop some of the damage from happening. You'll report what you find, that's all. No face-time with criminals. Consider it a genealogical project: Perfectly safe."

"I'll talk it over with Tom."

"Yes, do that."

Serena frowned, biting her lower lip. She hated making heavy decisions. If only there was an obvious factor that would tip the scales toward going one way or the other. She turned to leave.

"Oh Serena?"

Serena stopped.

"You might want to show this figure to Tom. This is my proposal." Ann handed her a slip of paper.

Serena gasped. "Wow, that's a lot of zeros. I have to admit that it would be good to have an annual salary. This is more than I've ever made from contract work."

"Who said anything about annual? That's your *monthly* take-home."

Serena blurted, “I’m in.” Then she nearly ran out of the restaurant. Once outside the doors she sang, “I’m traveling, I’m traveling!”

EPILOGUE

Serena Wilcox takes on a new adventure as a time travel investigator in Project Scarecrow while working for former United States President Ann Kinji; President, Founder, and CEO of GSI (Gödel Solution Institute).

Scientists have discovered that inside every human brain are memory impressions of the past, present and future; a complete record of one's life from birth to death. While most of us can only access the present and part of the past, people with brain anomalies can access all past memory impressions and/or have what was previously thought of as psychic ability.

Through blood and spinal fluid samples from centenarians and newborns, scientist gained access to memory impressions of 100+ years into the past, and potentially as many years into the future.

Digitized memory impressions, combined with quantum physics and teleportation, made possible time travel. Naturally, in Serena's world, time travel technology was immediately abused. In Project Scarecrow, criminal investigation takes Serena to the past, present and future.

The Serena Wilcox Mysteries Time Travel Trilogy will take you backwards and forwards with favorite returning characters and suspense that will keep you turning pages to the end.

Look for Serena Wilcox Mystery #7,
Book #1 in the Time Travel Trilogy

Project Scarecrow

The Serena Wilcox Mysteries
By Natalie Buske Thomas
Gene Play
Virtual Memories
Camp Conviction
Angels Mark
Covert Coffee
Bluebird Flown
Project Scarecrow

Stay in the loop!
www.nataliebuskethomas.com

Author Notes

As the Serena Wilcox Dystopian Trilogy comes to an end I realize that I've been holding my breath. *Angels Mark* took me about three years to write. I was dabbling and unfocused, partly because my three children were young at the time, but also because I was nervous about re-entering the writing scene after ten years of absence.

About a quarter of the way through *Angels Mark* I experienced multiple losses that led to spiritual and personal growth (the death of my mother being one of those). During that time, *Angels Mark* seemed to write itself. Writing a heavy-hitting political thriller with controversial themes was never my intention. I simply wanted to write a good mystery that showed improvement from my previous work.

My mystery became more of a thriller and eventually the word "dystopian" was added to it as well. The Angels Mark project had evolved into something quite different from what it was in the beginning.

Within a few months after my return to writing and publishing, *Angels Mark* hit Amazon's bestselling list. The ride on the bestselling list was brief, but over thirty thousand people downloaded my book and I enjoyed the best paycheck I'd ever received for my artistic endeavors. I had arrived!

Unfortunately people cut me down almost faster than I rose. I knew that some readers would find fault, but the venom in which they found fault took me aback—few attacks had anything to do with my writing or the story; most were personal, irrelevant or religious/political (or all three of these). I even feared for my family's safety if I were to continue writing these books.

My daughter said that I must be doing it right if both the extreme left and the extreme right are unhappy with me. There was nothing fun about being hated: I wanted to get off this ride.

That was my state of being while I was writing *Bluebird Flown.* My attitude comes across in ways both subtle and obvious, mainly through the character of Serena Wilcox. I identified with Serena the most when nearing the end of *Bluebird Flown.*

Like Serena, I just wanted to "go home". I wanted to return to the life I had before *Angels Mark* was released. I wanted this experience to end. But then again, like Serena, I can't resist the allure of a time travel adventure. Some of my favorite books when I was a kid were: *Danny Dunn, Time Traveler*; *Charlie and the Great Glass Elevator*; *A Wrinkle in Time*, all of the Frank Baum *Oz* books; and of course *The Chronicles of Narnia*. I'm thrilled to have time-traveling sci-fi adventures as a grownup too: my son is a devoted Doctor Who fan; he insisted that the whole family watch it with him and now I'm hooked!

The time-travel sci-fi genre is also where my early writing experiences came from. My first published story was an alternate time, space and dimension sci-fi adventure called *The Personalities**. I won my high school writing contest for that story, ten dollars! It was the first time I made money as an author. Later on down the road, when I was in my twenties, I wrote the second book of the Serena Wilcox Mysteries, *Virtual Memories*, featuring sci-fi alternate reality. It's been a long time since I've thrown myself into that genre. Oh how I look forward to escaping into the Serena Wilcox Time Travel Trilogy!

I'm prepared to put myself into this with both feet with research and back-story like I did with the dystopian trilogy. My reward for this effort will be the fun I'll have writing as Serena, Estep, Beav, Lehman, Ann Kinji and the new characters Jo and Joe. And of course I'll enjoy inventing revolting villains and outrageous situations, plot twists, cliffhangers (moohoohaha!) and everything else that makes the Serena Wilcox series what it is. The series is bigger than me now, it's taken on a life of its own and it now belongs to all of us.

There's a sparkling future waiting for me, should I choose to accept the challenge of writing the Serena Wilcox Time Travel Trilogy. Yes, there may be danger—if there's no risk involved, are we truly living? I'm in. And there's a new adventure waiting for you too. Are you in? Sing with me:

We're traveling, we're traveling!

**The Personalities* story is available to read (free) online: www.NatalieBuskeThomas.com

ABOUT THE AUTHOR

Natalie Buske Thomas is an author, artist and entertainer. She is working on her first music single and is currently traveling with her new Serena Wilcox Time Travel Trilogy.

PROJECT SCARECROW:
Serena investigates horrific crimes of science and technology; traveling through time and space to repair the damage and save the world before it's too late. Meanwhile Speaker of the House Joseph Smythe becomes the next American president, but does he get the girl? Ann Kinji, Estep, Lehman, and the Beav welcome Jo from Ireland to the team. New adventures await – are you in?

Twitter: @writernbt
Pinterest: @writernbt
Facebook: Natalie Buske Thomas
Easy "follow" buttons are on the authors' website; as well as free games, news about Natalie's books, oil paintings, comics and more:

www.nataliebuskethomas.com

www.ingramcontent.com/pod-product-compliance
Lightning Source LLC
Chambersburg PA
CBHW030823310726
48980CB00006B/614/J
9780966691955